WITHDRAWN

# Don't Turn Out the Lights

Also by Bernard Minier

*The Frozen Dead*
*The Circle*

BERNARD MINIER

# Don't Turn
Out the Lights

*Translated by Alison Anderson*

Minotaur Books
New York

DON'T TURN OUT THE LIGHTS. Copyright © 2014 by XO Éditions. Translation copyright © 2016 by Alison Anderson. All rights reserved. Printed in the United States of America. For information, address St. Martin's Press, 175 Fifth Avenue, New York, N.Y. 10010.

www.minotaurbooks.com

Library of Congress Cataloging-in-Publication Data

Names: Minier, Bernard, author. | Anderson, Alison, translator.
Title: Don't turn out the lights / Bernard Minier ; translated by Alison Anderson.
Other titles: N'eteins pas la lumière. English | Do not turn out the lights
Description: First U.S. Edition. | New York : Minotaur Books, 2016. | "First published in France under the title N'eteins pas la lumière, by XO Éditions"— Title page verso.
Identifiers: LCCN 2016027888| ISBN 9781250106056 (hardcover) | ISBN 9781250106063 (e-book)
Subjects: LCSH: Suicide—Fiction. | BISAC: FICTION / Mystery & Detective / Police Procedural. | GSAFD: Mystery fiction. | Suspense fiction.
Classification: LCC PQ2713.I54 N4813 2016 | DDC 843/.92—dc23
LC record available at https://lccn.loc.gov/2016027888

Our books may be purchased in bulk for promotional, educational, or business use. Please contact your local bookseller or the Macmillan Corporate and Premium Sales Department at 1-800-221-7945, extension 5442, or by e-mail at MacmillanSpecialMarkets@macmillan.com.

First published in France under the title N'eteins pas la Lumière by XO Éditions

Previously published in Great Britain by Mulholland Books, an imprint of Hodder & Stoughton, an Hachette UK company

First U.S. Edition: December 2016

10  9  8  7  6  5  4  3  2  1

# Don't Turn Out the Lights

# Overture

*Bialowieza forest, on the border between Poland and Belarus*

He was walking deep in the forest, through the blizzard and snow. It was so cold his teeth were chattering. Ice crystals clung to his eyebrows and lashes; his down ski jacket and the damp wool of his cap were crusted with snow, and even Rex was having trouble making headway through the thick snowy blanket, sinking up to his withers with every leap. The dog barked at regular intervals, no doubt to convey his disapproval, and the sound echoed all around them. From time to time he stopped to shake himself as if he were emerging from water, sending a cloud of soft snow and sharp icicles flying from his fawn and black coat. His muscular paws made deep tracks in the white shroud, and his belly left a curved imprint along the surface, like that of a plastic sledge.

Night was beginning to fall. The wind had risen. *Where was it?* Where was the hut? He stopped and caught his breath. He was puffing hoarsely, his back soaked in sweat beneath his clothes. The forest was a living organism – the rustling of branches heavy with snow, swaying in the wind; the sharp snapping of tree bark cracking in the biting cold, the whispering of the bitter wind that, from time to time, seemed to swell immeasurably in his ears, the crystal-clear babbling of a nearby stream that had not yet frozen over. And then the smooth crunching of his steps, the rhythm of his progress, as he lifted up his knees, making an ever greater effort to extract himself from the grip of snow. Good God it was cold! He had never been so cold in his entire life.

Through the grey twilight and the snowflakes stinging his eyes he thought he saw something in the snow up ahead. Glinting like metal, two jagged hoops ... *A trap* ... A dark shape caught in its metal jaws.

For a few seconds he succumbed to an indefinable malaise: whatever was in that trap no longer resembled any living creature. *It* had been devoured, ripped apart. Sticky blood mixed with fur stained the snow around the trap. There were also little bones and pinkish viscera covered over with a fine layer of frost.

He was still gazing at the trap when he heard the scream, and it went through him like a rusty blade. He could not recall ever having heard such a cry – so filled with terror and pain, an almost inhuman suffering. No human being, anyway, could have made such a sound. It was coming from the heart of the forest, straight ahead of him. *Not far from here.* His blood ran cold when the scream again broke the evening air, and every hair on his body stood up straight at the same time. Then the cry faded into the twilight, borne away on the polar wind.

The silence seemed to return for a moment. Then other screams echoed the first one, more modulated, further away: to the left, to the right, *everywhere* – emanating from a forest overcome by darkness. *Wolves.* A long shiver went down his spine. He began walking again, lifting his knees even more vigorously, with a desperate energy, towards the place where the cry had come from. And he saw it. The hut. Its dark, huddled form at the end of a sort of natural avenue formed by trees. He covered the last few frozen metres practically at a run. Rex seemed to have sensed something, because he bounded forward with a bark.

'Rex, wait! Come here, Rex! *Rex!*'

But the German shepherd had already slipped through the half-open door, wedged in that position by a high drift of snow. An unusual calm reigned in the clearing. Then a howl, louder than the others, suddenly rose from the depths of the forest, and a concert of yapping came in reply: guttural calls echoing each other. Getting closer. He climbed clumsily over the snowdrift and entered the hut. He was met by a light as warm as melted butter from the storm lamp illuminating the interior. He turned his head. Stood stock still. A needle of ice pierced his brain.

He closed his eyes. Opened them again.

*Impossible. This can't be real. I'm dreaming. It can only be a dream.* What he saw was Marianne. She was lying naked on a table in the middle of the hut. Her body was still warm, literally steaming in the icy air. It occurred to him that Hirtmann must be close by. For a moment he was tempted to go after him. He realised that all his limbs had begun to tremble, that he was on the edge of a black abyss, about to pass out or go mad. He took a step. Then another. He forced himself to look. Marianne's torso had been split open from the little hollow at the base of her neck down to her groin – and clearly she had been alive at the time, because there was a great deal of blood. Her executioner had then pulled apart her skin and thorax. Her organs seemed intact; only one was missing: *her heart*. Hirtmann had delicately placed it on Marianne's groin before he left. The heart was even warmer than all the rest: Servaz could see the white steam rising in the icy air of the hut. He was surprised he did not feel any nausea or disgust. There was something wrong. He should have been puking his guts out at such a sight. He should have been sobbing. Screaming. He had succumbed to a strange stupor. And just then Rex growled and bared his fangs. He turned towards the dog. His fur was standing on end and he was looking out of the half-open door. Threatening and terrified.

Servaz felt a wave of cold go through him.

He went over to the door and glanced outside.

They were there. In the clearing. Surrounding the hut. He counted eight in all. Eight wolves.

Thin, and famished.

*Marianne* . . .

He had to get her back to the car. He thought about his weapon, forgotten in the glove box. Rex was still growling. He could imagine his dog's fear, his stress, and he stroked him gently on the top of his head. He could feel Rex's muscles trembling under his coat.

'Good dog,' he said, with a lump in his throat, as he crouched down and put his arms around him.

The dog's eyes, as he turned to him, were such a gentle golden colour, so affectionate, that he felt tears welling. Servaz knew he had only one chance to make it out of there. And it was the saddest, most difficult thing he had ever had to do.

He went over to the table, took the heart and put it back in Marianne's chest. He gulped, closed his eyes and lifted the naked, bleeding body in his arms. It was not as heavy as he would have thought.

'Let's go, Rex!' he said firmly, heading to the door.

The dog let out a yelp of protest, but he followed his master, growling again, his hindquarters low to the ground, his tail between his legs and his ears flat.

The wolves were waiting in a semicircle.

Their yellow eyes seemed incandescent. Rex's fur bristled. Again he bared his fangs. The wolves replied with even louder growls – their mouths gaping, snarling, showing their terrifying teeth.

'Go, Rex!' he said. 'Go on! Attack!'

The tears were pouring down his cheeks, his lower lip was trembling, and his mind was screaming, *No, don't do it! Don't listen to me!* The dog barked several times without budging an inch. He had been trained to obey orders, but this one went too far against his survival instinct.

'Attack, Rex! Attack!'

But this was his master giving the order, the master he adored, and for whom no human being would ever feel as much love, loyalty and respect as he did.

'Attack, for Christ's sake!'

Now the dog could hear the anger in his master's voice. And something else beneath it. He wanted to help him. To prove his attachment and his loyalty. However frightened he might be.

He attacked.

At first he almost seemed to have the advantage: one of the wolves – no doubt the leader of the pack – rushed towards him and Rex dodged skilfully and grabbed him by the neck. The wolf howled in pain. The others cautiously took a step back. Then the two animals were wrapped around each other. Rex himself seemed to have become a ferocious, bloodthirsty beast.

Servaz couldn't wait any longer.

He turned away and started walking. The wolves were no longer paying any attention to him. For the time being. He went up the natural avenue between the trees, with Marianne in his arms, his down jacket soaked with blood and his face soaked with tears. Behind him he could hear his dog's first cries of pain, and the renewed growling of the pack. His blood froze. Rex let out another cry. A shrill cry full of pain and terror. *Rex was calling to him for help.* He clenched his teeth and walked faster. Another 300 yards . . .

A last cry in the windy night.

Rex was dead – he could tell from the silence that followed. He wondered if the wolves would be content with this victory or whether they would come after him. He had his answer soon enough. He could hear the yapping coming closer. Some of the wolves, at any rate, had resumed the hunt. And this time, he was their prey.

*The car.*

It was parked on the path not a hundred metres away. A layer of snow had begun to cover it. He tried to walk even faster, crazy with fear, his lungs burning. He could hear the growling just behind his back. He spun around. The wolves had caught up with him. Four of the eight. Their yellow, faded eyes, like amber, staring at him, gauging him. He would never make it to the car. It was too far. Marianne's body was growing heavier and heavier in his arms.

*She's dead. There's nothing more you can do for her. But you can still make it out alive.*

No! His brain refused to accept the thought of it. He had already sacrificed his dog. She was still warm. He could feel her blood seeping into his jacket. He looked up at the sky. Snowflakes were falling down on him like stars, as if the sky were coming loose, as if the entire universe were hurrying to bury him. He screamed with rage and despair. But it did not seem to impress the wild beasts. The skeletal wolves had waited long enough, they sensed there was no reason to be afraid of this solitary target. They could smell his fear – and above all the blood oozing from another prey. Two feasts for the price of one. They were too famished. Too excited. They moved closer.

*Get out of here! Get the hell away! Bastards, go!* He wondered if he had really screamed – or whether it was just his mind screaming.

*Move it! Now! There's nothing more you can do for her. Save yourself!*

This time he listened to his inner voice. He let go of Marianne's legs and her feet landed in the snow. He plunged his hand into her chest. His gloved fingers grasped the heart, firm and elastic. He pulled it out of the gaping wound and slipped it under his jacket right against his chest, right against his own heart. Then he dropped her body into the snow and it sank pale and naked into the white shroud with a muted hiss. He took three steps backwards. Slowly.

The wolves immediately leapt on her. He spun on his heels and hurried away to the car. It was unlocked, but for a moment he thought the cold had frozen the door. He pulled on the handle with all the strength in his blood-soaked fingers. He almost fell over backwards when the door opened suddenly with a groan. He collapsed onto the driver's seat. His hand was trembling violently as he pulled out the key, and he almost dropped it between the seats. He glanced in the rearview mirror. And realised that there was someone sitting in the back seat. He knew he was going mad. *It couldn't be!* And yet she opened her mouth.

'Martin,' she implored.

'Martin! Martin!'

He shuddered. Opened his eyes.

He was slumped in the battered old leather armchair; Rex was licking his right palm where it lay on the armrest.

'Scram,' said the voice. 'Go pester someone else! Martin, are you all right?'

Rex moved off, wagging his tail. Looking for someone else to play with. He would find someone quickly. Rex belonged to everyone and to no one; he was the true host of the place. Servaz was alone in the lounge, apart from Élise. He realised he had fallen asleep in front of the television, overcome by the building's heat on that endless, torpid winter afternoon. He looked over at the picture window, where all morning the sun had been shining on the white landscape. For these few, ideal hours, with the smell of coffee drifting down the corridors, the laughter of the employees, the tall fir tree with its decorations and the dazzling whiteness outside, he had found some traces of his childhood soul.

Then not long after lunch in the common room, the sun had gone behind the clouds, a cold wind had risen, and the bare branches had begun to sway beyond the window while the outdoor thermometer plummeted from five to minus one. Feeling sluggish, he had slumped in an armchair in front of the television with the sound off, before dozing off into a sleep filled with nightmares.

'You had a bad dream,' said Élise. 'You cried out.'

He looked at her, still dazed. He shivered. Again he saw the vast snowy forest, the hut, the wolves . . . *and Marianne.* The nightmare that was not a nightmare. What hope did he still have? The answer: none.

'Are you sure you're all right?'

In her forties, plump, with laughing eyes, even when she tried to seem concerned, Élise was the only employee at the centre that he

6

liked. And probably the only one who could stand *him*. The others were former cops who had come for treatment before taking up their positions as the bosses of the place: they were known as health-care and social welfare police assistants. They treated the boarders with a mixture of openness, fraternity and compassion, which made Servaz think of something slimy. And they did not like him much at all. He refused to play along. To fraternise. To feel sorry for himself. To *collaborate*. Unlike them, Élise expected nothing from him.

'Your daughter rang.'

Servaz looked at her, raising an eyebrow.

'Since you were asleep, she didn't want to disturb you,' she added. 'But she said she would come by again soon.'

He switched off the television with the remote and got to his feet. He glanced at his worn jumper, which was beginning to fray at the elbows and cuffs. He remembered that the next day was Christmas.

'You might want to have a shave,' she suggested defiantly.

He was silent for a moment.

'And if I don't?'

'Then you will merely confirm what most people round here think of you.'

He raised his eyebrow again, almost to the middle of his brow.

'Which is?'

'That you're uncouth. No one wants to mix with you.'

'And is that what you think, too?'

She shrugged. 'It depends on the day.'

He laughed, and she echoed his laughter as she walked away. But the moment she was out of sight Servaz's laugh stuck in his throat. It was not that he cared what others thought, but he didn't want Margot to see him in this state. The last time she had come to visit him here was over three months ago: he had not forgotten the sad, embarrassed look in her eyes.

He walked across the entrance hall and up the stairs. His room was all the way up under the eaves. Hardly more than nine metres square, his bed as narrow as Ulysses' when he returned in secret to Ithaca, with a cupboard, a desk, a few shelves with books: Plautus, Cicero, Livy, Ovid, Seneca. A Spartan décor. But the view onto the fields and the woods was beautiful, even in winter.

He pulled off his old jumper and the T-shirt beneath it, and put on a clean shirt and jumper, his down ski jacket, a scarf and gloves, then went down the stairs again to the back door, the one that opened out onto the immaculate expanse.

He walked silently across the white plain to the little woods, breathing in the cold, damp air. There were no footsteps in the snow. No one had come this way.

He happened upon a stone bench under the trees, brushed off the snow with his gloved hand and sat down. He felt the damp and cold beneath his buttocks.

Crows were keeping watch in the sky, which was almost the same colour as the rest of the landscape.

As for his thoughts, they wore the same dark plumage as the crows. He leaned his head back and took a deep breath, while *her* smile came once again to his memory. Like something printed permanently on his retinas. He had stopped taking the antidepressants the previous month without consulting the doctor, and he was suddenly afraid that the darkness might swallow him up again.

Maybe he was going too quickly.

He knew the illness he was suffering from could kill him; that he was merely struggling to survive. Six months earlier UPS had delivered a package to his home. The sender was a certain Mr Osoba, residing in Przewloka, a village in eastern Poland in the middle of the forest near the border with Belarus. The cardboard box contained a second package – insulated this time – and Servaz had felt his pulse begin to beat faster when he broke the wax seal with a kitchen knife. He no longer remembered what he'd expected – no doubt that he would find a severed finger, or even a hand, given the size of the parcel. But what he had found was far worse. It was red, the fine shiny colour of fresh meat, in the shape of a large pear. *A heart.* Quite clearly human. The note accompanying it was not in Polish but in French:

*She broke yours, Martin. I thought you would feel free after this. Of course you will suffer in the beginning. But you won't have to keep looking for her or hoping. Think about it.*
*Warm wishes,*
*J.H.*

One last hope. Tenuous, flickering.

The hope that it might be a bad joke, a terrible joke: someone else's heart. Police forensics had run a parental DNA test using DNA from Hugo, Marianne's son. Science had handed down its verdict, and Servaz had felt his reason falter. The address was that of an isolated house at the heart of the vast Bialowieza forest. DNA samples confirmed that Hirtmann had stayed there. So had several women who had disappeared from various countries in Europe over recent years. Including Marianne. Servaz had also found out that the name *Osoba* means 'person' in Polish: Hirtmann had read his Homer, too.

Of course, after that the trail ran cold.

Servaz had been sent on sick leave one month later to this centre for depressive cops, where they obliged him to do two hours of sport a day and to perform various everyday tasks such as sweeping up dead leaves. He did his chores without complaining; he refused, on the other hand, to attend the group counselling sessions. Just as he avoided the company of the other boarders: whether it had something to do with what they had been through or some atavistic inclination, they were nearly all alcoholics when they arrived. Cops who, after years spent up close to the most sordid aspects of life, had eventually cracked. Who couldn't stand being called rozzers and pigs and bastards and scum all day long, and seeing their kids get bullied in the playground simply because their fathers were policemen, or watching their wives leave them because they were fed up, or spending their entire life being despised while the real scum were lolling about at outdoor cafés or in their beds. Most of the cops who were there had already, at least once, put the barrel of their service gun in their mouth.

Among its other effects, depression left you incapable of performing even the most minor tasks. Stehlin, Servaz's boss, had quickly seen that Servaz was no longer in a fit state to perform his job properly. Something Servaz himself could have confirmed if they had simply asked him: he couldn't give a toss now about murderers, rapists or all those other bastards. He cared as little about that as about anything else: the taste of food, the news, the state of the world – even his beloved Latin authors.

And Mahler's music.

This last symptom was the greatest cause for concern. Was he on the road to recovery? He wasn't sure. But for a while now, as if there were a slow thaw, little buds were beginning to sprout in the dreary, desolate landscape his life had become, and the blood seemed to be flowing in his arteries again. Recently, too, he had begun to notice an itchy feeling whenever he talked about a certain file that was waiting on his desk. He had even asked Espérandieu about it – his assistant and only true friend. The young man's face had lit up: 'Well, well!' and Servaz too had smiled. For all that Vincent listened to indie rock and read manga and felt passionately about things as soul-sustaining as video games, clothes and high-tech gadgets, he was someone whom Servaz listened to and respected. Espérandieu had filled him in on the latest developments in two particularly sensitive cases they had been working on together and which were still not solved, and his smile had spread like that of a kid who has just played a clever joke on someone, when he saw the little spark of longing in his boss's eye.

'At the mid-point of the path through life, I found myself lost in a wood so dark, the way ahead was blotted out.'

'Huh?' said Espérandieu, frowning.

'Dante,' said Servaz.

'Hmm . . . Did you hear, Asselin has left.'

Commissaire Asselin. He had been head of the Criminal Affairs Division.

'What is the new bloke like?'

Espérandieu made a face. Servaz saw a sunlit forest in springtime. The ground was still frozen. He was lost in the woods, cold to the bone in spite of the feeble rays of sun between the branches. He banished the vision. A simple dream. In the not too distant future he would get out of the forest. And not just in his dreams.

# ACT I

In everlasting torment
May your wicked soul perish.

*Madame Butterfly*

# I

# Curtain Raiser

*I am writing these words. The last ones. And as I write them, I know it's over: this time there won't be any going back.*

*You'll be angry with me for doing this to you on Christmas Eve. I know it is the worst possible insult to your bloody sense of propriety. You and your fucking manners. To think I believed your lies and your promises. The more words there are, the less truth there is: that's the way of the world nowadays.*

*I really am going to do it, you know. That at least is not hot air. Is your hand trembling a little now? Have you broken out in a sweat?*

*Or maybe, instead, you are smiling as you read these words. Are you behind all this? Or is it your slut? Are you the ones who sent me all these operas? And the rest: was that you, too? It hardly matters. There was a time I would have given anything to know who could hate me so much, a time when I was desperately trying to find out how I could have caused so much hatred. Because it must have been my fault, obviously – that's what I thought. But not any longer.*

*I think I'm going mad. Completely and utterly mad. Unless it's the medication. And anyway, this time, I don't have the strength. This time, it's over. I'm stopping. Whoever it is has won. I can't do it any more. I can't sleep any more. Stop.*

*I'll never get married. I'll never have children: I read that somewhere in a novel. Shit. Now I understand what it means. There are things I will miss, of course. Life can be really lovely sometimes, no doubt to hurt us all the more later on. You and I might have ended up making a go of things, over time. Or maybe not . . . it doesn't matter. I know you will forget me soon enough, you will file me away in the drawer of unpleasant memories, the ones you don't like to bring up. You will tell your slut, with a penitent look in your eyes: 'She was crazy, depressed; I hadn't realised how much.' And besides, you will move on quickly to something else. You will laugh and you will fuck. I don't care: you can die. In the meantime, I will.*

*Have a happy Christmas all the same.*

Christine looked at the back of the envelope: no sender. No stamp, either. *Not even her name, Christine Steinmeyer.* Someone had left it directly in her mailbox. It must be a mistake. It had to be a mistake: the letter had nothing to do with her. She looked at the rows of mailboxes along the wall, names handwritten on the labels; whoever had slipped the envelope through the slot had picked the wrong box, that was all.

*The letter was meant for someone else . . . someone else in the building.*

Then a thought went through her mind that almost took her breath away: *is it really what it seems to be?* Oh, dear Lord. The only tangible sensation she noticed was a momentary loss of balance. She looked again at the tightly folded piece of paper: *and if it is, then someone must be notified.* Yes, but who? Christine thought about the person who had written the letter – the state she must be in, what she might be doing at that very moment – and she clutched her stomach, her fingers icy. She read the penultimate line again, slowly, analysing every word: *You can die. In the meantime, I will.* There could be no doubt: this letter was from someone who intended to put an end to her life.

Shit . . .

On Christmas Eve, someone in this town, or not far away, was preparing to kill herself – or perhaps she had already done it – and Christine was the only one who knew. And there was no way around it, because the person who was supposed to read the letter (and the letter was, quite clearly, a call for help) was not going to read it.

*A hoax. It had to be a hoax.*

If only there were a first name, something, she could have gone around knocking on every door, asking, 'Do you know so-and-so?'

The automatic timer went off, plunging the hall into darkness, a darkness broken only by the light from the street that came through the double glass and wrought-iron door. She gave a start and looked towards the door, as if whoever had put the envelope in her mailbox might reappear at any moment. On the pavement across the street, the artisan boulangerie had decorated their window, and through the snowflakes she could see Santa Claus's sleigh. She shivered, and not just because of the letter: the danger of darkness, to her, was as terrifying as a razor's edge.

Just then her mobile began to vibrate in her pocket.

'What the hell are you doing?'

She slammed the heavy door behind her. Out on the pavement a cold wind tugged at her scarf. Her cheeks were wet with the snow that had begun falling again; a fine layer was already covering the tarmac. She looked up and down the street until Gérald flashed his headlights at her.

There was a blast of Nick Cave singing 'Jubilee Street', a pleasant smell of leather, new plastic and male aftershave when she opened the passenger door. She collapsed onto the seat of the bulky white SUV, but left the door slightly open. Gérald turned to her with a special Christmas smile on his lips, and when he leaned over to kiss her, a soft grey silk scarf tickled her chin. She felt the warmth radiating from his body and smelled the pleasant scent wafting from his clothes. Like a shot of heroin: she felt the addiction biting, the jab of need deep in her guts.

'Are you ready to face Monsieur Things-Were-Better-in-the-Past and Madame Why-Aren't-You-Eating-My-Dear?' he asked, leaning over to her with his phone. He opened the photo app.

'What are you doing?'

'Look, I'm taking your picture.'

His voice warmed her like a smooth sip of Irish coffee, but she was finding it hard to smile sincerely.

'Take a look at this first.'

She switched on the overhead light and handed him the letter and the envelope.

'Christine, we're late already.'

His voice was like a caress, but firm: a mixture of gentleness and authority. This was what had struck her when they met, much more than his looks.

'Take a look all the same.'

'Where on earth did you get this?'

His tone was almost disapproving, as if he held her responsible for having found the message.

'In my mailbox.'

In spite of the dim light, she could read the intense surprise behind his glasses. And the annoyance: Gérald did not like the unexpected.

'Well?' she urged. 'What do you think?'

He shrugged. 'It's got to be a hoax. What else could it be?'

'I don't think so. It sounds real.'

He sighed, pushed his glasses higher up his nose, and in the pale glow from the overhead light looked again at the sheet of paper in his gloved fingers.

'Then in that case, it's a mistake,' he concluded. 'The letter was meant for someone else.'

'Precisely.'

He looked at her again. 'Right, listen, we'll get to the bottom of it later. My parents are already waiting for us.'

*Yes, yes, of course: your parents. Christmas. Who cares if a woman tries to commit suicide tonight?*

'Gérald, do you realise what this letter means?'

He took his hands away from the steering wheel and placed them in his lap.

'I think so, yes,' he said solemnly, but a trace half-heartedly. 'What – what do you think we should do?'

'I don't know. Don't you have any ideas? We can't just sit here and do nothing.'

'Listen.' Again that disapproving tone, which seemed to say, *No one but you would go stirring up such a hornets' nest, Christine.* 'We're expected at my parents', darling: this is your first meeting with them and we're already nearly an hour late. This letter may be real, or it may not. We'll deal with it once we get there, I promise you, but now we really have to get going.'

He had spoken calmly, in a reasonable voice. Too reasonable: it was the tone he used when she was getting on his nerves, which seemed to be more and more frequently lately. The tone of someone saying, *Have you noticed how incredibly patient I am?* She shook her head.

'There are only two possibilities: either it's a call for help which won't be heard because the person who was meant to read the letter won't read it, or someone really is going to commit suicide this evening – and in either case, I am the only one who knows.'

'So . . . what?'

'We have to inform the police.'

He rolled his eyes.

'But the letter isn't even signed! And there's no address! Even if we go to the police, what do you want them to do? And can you imagine how long it will take? It's going to completely screw up our Christmas Eve!'

'Our *Christmas Eve*? We're talking about a matter of life or death!'

She could sense him stiffening with exasperation. He let out a sigh, like a punctured tyre.

'What the fuck, what the hell do you want us to do?' he shouted. 'We have no way of knowing who it is, Christine! No way at all! And besides, there's every chance the person is bluffing: you don't go putting a letter in a mailbox when you're at the end of your tether, you leave a note where it can be found! It's probably just some delusional woman who's alone on Christmas Eve and this was the only thing she could think of to attract attention. She's calling for help, but it doesn't mean she'll go through with it.'

'So you want us to go and celebrate as if nothing had happened?'

'For Christ's sake, Christine, what the hell do I know! This will be the first time you've ever met my parents. Can you imagine the impression it will make if we get there three hours late!'

'You make me think of those morons who say, "Couldn't he go and commit suicide somewhere else?" when their train gets delayed.'

'Are you calling me a moron?'

His voice had gone down an octave. She stole a glance at him. He was pale: even his lips had drained of colour.

*Shit, she'd gone too far.* She raised her hand in the hope of a truce.

'No, not at all. Of course not. Forgive me. Listen, I'm sorry. But we can't just pretend nothing happened, can we?'

He sighed, furious. And thought about it. His hands in their leather gloves gripped the steering wheel again. The strange thought suddenly occurred to her that there was far too much leather in his car.

He sighed once again.

'How many flats are there in your building?'

'Ten. Two on each floor.'

'Here's what I suggest. We'll knock on every door, show them your letter and ask the tenants if they have any idea who might have written it.'

She looked at him carefully.

'Are you sure?'

'Yes. Anyway, I'll bet you that half of them will have left to celebrate Christmas elsewhere, so it won't take that long.'

'And what about your parents?'

'I'll ring them and explain what's going on and that we'll be late. They'll understand. And we can limit our search even further: the letter is obviously addressed to a man. How many men are there who live alone in the building, do you know?'

She did know. It was an old building, and for the most part had been divided up into studios and one-bed flats by the previous owner, eager to make as much money as possible off his investment. There were only two big family flats, on the floors below her own.

'Two,' she replied.

'In that case, it will only take us a few minutes. Even supposing they're in.'

She realised he was right. She should have thought of this sooner.

'And we'll ring at the other doors too, just in case,' he added. 'It shouldn't take too long. And after that we'll go straight to my parents'.'

'But what if we don't find anything?'

He shot her a look that said, *Don't push your luck.*

'Then I'll call the cops from my parents', and ask them what we should do. Christine, there's nothing more we can do. And I'm not going to ruin Christmas because of something that's probably a hoax.'

'Thank you,' she said.

He shrugged, and glanced into the rearview mirror before opening his door and stepping out into the cold night, leaving behind a ghost of male warmth and scent.

Nine twenty-one p.m., 24 December. For once it was snowing hard in Toulouse. The night sky was full of clouds, and the crowd hurried by in a whirlwind of shapes and glimmering light while the Christmas decorations gleamed on ever-whiter pavements. She had changed the station on the car radio. Her colleagues from Radio Five seemed as excited as if they had announced the end of the world or World War III. All around them cars were blowing their horns, people were shouting, the place was buzzing with an electric mixture of general impatience and overexcitement. Gérald himself was fuming, but silently: they were over two hours late.

She thought about the letter again. The person who had written it.

Of course they hadn't found out a thing. All the single people had gone out for Christmas Eve, and so had the couples. Only the two families in the building were at home, one of which had four kids who were as overexcited as the rest of the population, shouting so loudly that Gérald had to raise his voice as he brandished the letter in their parents' faces. At first neither the husband nor the wife seemed to get what he was saying. Then when understanding finally dawned, Christine thought she saw a gleam of suspicion in the woman's eyes as she looked at her husband. But his cluelessness and stupefaction seemed sincere.

The second family was a young couple with a child. They seemed very close, very together, and for a moment she wondered whether she and Gérald would look like that someday. They had seemed sincerely shocked by the letter: 'My God, what a horrible story!' cried the young woman, who was very visibly pregnant – and for a moment Christine thought she might burst into tears. After that, she and Gérald went back downstairs in silence.

She stole a glance at him. He was clenching his jaw as he drove. He hadn't said a word since they'd set out. And on his forehead was that almost painful line which she was sometimes surprised to see there.

'We did what we had to do,' she declared.

He didn't answer, not even to nod. For a moment she was angry at him for trying to make her feel guilty. Because that's what he was trying to do, wasn't it? Shouldn't they have felt guilty, rather, for the sake of that person they wouldn't manage to save? She wondered whether it was just her imagination, or whether the more serious things got between them, the more he told her off and contradicted her. Then he erased everything with a smile and a kind word, but still: his behaviour had changed lately. She knew when it had started. When the word *marriage* had first been uttered.

*Christmas. Shit. Our first Christmas Eve. His parents tonight and mine tomorrow. Will they like him? Is he going to like them? You shouldn't get so worked up: everyone likes Gérald. His colleagues, his students, his friends, his mechanic, even your dog. That's what you thought the first time, wasn't it, at the reception at the Capitole? Remember? There were prettier women there, with better figures, slimmer and even, I'm sure, more intelligent – but you're the one he went up to; even when you gave him the brush-off, he returned for another shot. And then he said, 'Your voice sounds familiar . . . where have I heard it before?' Even when you went on about your job at Radio Five a bit too long, he listened. Really listened. You wanted to be funny, witty, but in the end you weren't, not all that much. Except where he was concerned: he seemed to think everything you said was ever so amusing and entertaining.*

Maybe everyone liked Gérald – but her parents were not everybody. Her parents were Guy and Claire Dorian. *The Dorians who used to be on TV . . .* Who knows what it would take to get yourself liked by people who had interviewed, among others, Arthur Rubinstein, Chagall, Sartre, Tino Rossi, Serge Gainsbourg and Jane Birkin . . .

*That's the thing*, added the little voice she had learned to hate and obey at the same time, as the years went by. *Papa will neither love him nor hate him: he won't care. Quite simply, my father is only interested in one thing: himself. It's not easy to have been one of television's pioneers – a guy who spent all his time on the small screen – then to become anonymous all over again. My father is constantly marinating in nostalgia and memories, and drowns his ennui in alcohol and doesn't even try to hide it. And besides – so what? He's free to destroy the final days of his existence if he feels like it: I'm not going to let him destroy mine.*

'Are you all right?' asked Gérald.

In his voice there was a faint hint of contrition. She nodded.

'You know, I understand you felt bad because of that letter.'

She looked at him. Nodded 'okay'. And thought, *Of course you don't, you don't understand.* They had slowed down; she looked at a huge poster inside a bus shelter: an ad for Dolce & Gabbana. Five strong young men surrounding a woman lying on the ground. Their bodies were muscular, oiled, gleaming. Handsome. Hypersexual. The men were bare-chested and one of them was pinning the woman to the ground. *A cheap come-on for zombie consumers*, she thought. Poster-women, trophy-women: public space was saturated with women's bodies. Christine had invited the director of an association for victims of domestic violence onto her programme. Seven days a week she received calls from battered wives, wives who were not allowed to speak to their neighbours, let alone any men other than their husbands, wives who were terrified that the dinner might be overcooked or too salty, wives whose bones bore the traces of fractures and blows, wives who had no access to either a bank account or a doctor, wives who – when they found the courage to go to the association – had an empty, desperate look in their eyes.

*One day, when she was still just a child, she herself had witnessed a scene . . .* That was why she felt the need to invite strong, exemplary women onto her programme, women who were bosses, activists, artists, politicians – and that was also why she would never let a man tell her how to behave.

*Are you absolutely sure?*

Gérald was no longer paying any attention to her. Staring straight ahead, he was lost in his thoughts, and she had no idea what they might be. Who was the author of the letter? She had to find out.

# 2

# Score

She dreamed about the woman. It wasn't a pleasant dream. The woman was standing in the moonlight in the middle of a lane lined with dark yew trees, not unlike the entrance to the cemetery: further along there was a gate with two tall stone pillars, one on either side. It had snowed and the night was very cold, but the woman was wearing a light nightgown with only two thin straps over her bare shoulders. Christine wanted to continue to the cemetery, but the woman was blocking the way. 'You did nothing,' she said. 'You let me down.'

'I tried,' she moaned in her dream. 'I swear I tried. Let me go past now.'

But just as she was walking by her, the woman's head pivoted at an angle that made it impossible to keep looking at her, and her eyes filled with ink. A huge flock of black birds began to whirl in the sky, shrieking in the most horrible way, and the woman began to laugh – a hysterical, ugly laugh which woke Christine up. Her heart was racing like a horse.

*The letter.*

She was sorry she had left it in the car; she would have liked to read it again. To think it over. To try and guess who had written it, and to what purpose. A blue night light was glowing on the night table, vaguely illuminating the ceiling. Through the open door, the light in the corridor was shining, its glow extending along the floor. She ventured one leg outside the duvet and felt the icy air on her bare foot. It was freezing cold. Beyond the blinds it was still pitch black, but a rumble of traffic was already audible beneath her window – a web of sound made of cars, scooters and delivery vans. She looked at the clock radio. 7:41 . . . *Shit! She'd overslept!* She threw back the duvet and gazed at the empty room, which could easily have been a hotel. A place to sleep, nothing else. And yet when she'd first seen the flat a year ago she had succumbed to its charm, its high ceilings, the marble fireplace in the sitting room. And the neighbourhood that was both secretive and trendy, where she immediately felt at home, with its narrow medieval streets, its restaurants, its bistros, its health food store, launderette, wine shop and Italian deli. Naturally the price was steep. She'd be in debt for thirty years. But she had no regrets. Every time she woke up she thought it was the best decision she had made in years.

Iggy's little claws clicked on the floorboards and he jumped up on the duvet and crossed the bed to come and lick her with his little pink tongue. Iggy was a mongrel with a caramel and white coat, pointed ears, and big brown eyes that were round and watchful and reminded her of a famous rock star – hence his name. He tilted his head to one side to gaze at her; she ruffled his fur with a smile and got to her feet.

She put on an old cashmere polo neck and a pair of thick woollen socks and followed him into the kitchen-sitting room.

'Hold on a sec, Mr Furry,' she said, while he was already scrabbling imperiously in his bowl as she tried to empty the tin of food.

The room was bare, apart from an old leather sofa, an IKEA coffee table and a flat-screen television on a stand next to the fireplace. Only the kitchen area had been decorated. A solitary rowing machine had pride of place, with weights next to it. Christine liked to exercise while watching television. A breakfast show was currently playing, with the sound muted. The television had stayed on all night – like every night. There were piles of books, newspapers and magazines on the floor by the fireplace: Christine was one of the star presenters on Radio Five, a private radio station; her time slot was from nine to eleven a.m. every day except Saturday – when the programme was pre-recorded – and Sunday. *Mornings with Christine* was a cocktail of news, music, games and comedy – with decreasing news coverage and more and more comedy as time went by. In less than an hour she had to be at the studio for the Christmas special.

She wondered if this would be a good opportunity to mention the letter to someone. She had a friendly rapport with Bercowitz, the psychiatrist. He took part in the programme once a week, generally

23

on Wednesdays, though this week they had brought his feature forward a day to have it on Christmas. Because he was good. Because he sounded good on air.

Yes, Bercowitz would tell her whether he thought the letter was authentic or not. Perhaps he might even know what to do.

But he might also criticise her for not doing anything – for the very fact that she'd waited too long. In the end, she and Gérald had not notified the police. She hadn't had the courage to spoil the evening any more than she already had. Gérald's parents had clearly tried to make everything perfect. They did not seem to be upset when they arrived two hours late. Gérald's father was an older version of his son, a model that had improved with the following generation but whose principal characteristics were already present in the original concept: elegance, sturdiness, self-control, warm brown eyes, a direct enveloping gaze, a discreetly charming temperament. A brilliant mind, but one that could be rigid, too, with little inclination towards subtlety or lightness. And an unfortunate tendency to view women as subservient to men.

His mother's genes had visibly had a harder time finding their way into the boy's DNA, but Christine wondered whether the fact that his mother never dared contradict his father, and the way she always agreed with her husband, explained why Gérald so disliked being contradicted – particularly by his future wife.

They had showered her in presents. A tablet computer, a Bluetooth dock that enabled her to directly connect her phone to loudspeakers (she suspected these presents were her future father-in-law's idea, because he was just as avid as his son about technology), a sweater (Gérald's mother). And they seemed enthusiastic about everything she said. Only Gérald's gaze (which she had caught watching her several times while she spoke) had seemed to her a touch more critical.

*It was surely because of their argument in the car . . . you should have been less pushy . . .*

Once Iggy was noisily poking in his bowl, she went over to the counter and prepared a cup of coffee, a glass of mango and passion fruit juice, and spread some low-fat butter onto pieces of Swedish crispbread. She was perched on one of the stainless steel bar stools, dipping them in her coffee, when she heard the little voice in her head again: *If you actually believe your parents are going to make things easier for you, you really are kidding yourself. You will never be Madeleine, Chris. Never . . .*

A sudden rush of acid, a cramp in her stomach.

*Childhood: it doesn't last long but you never get over it*, the voice went on. *That broken child is still there inside – isn't that so, Christine?*

*The child who is afraid when night falls . . . the one who saw what she should never have seen . . .*

Her glass of fruit juice shattered on the tiles at her feet, and she jumped off the stool to pick up the pieces of glass. A sharp pain when a tiny splinter as brilliant as a diamond lodged in her forefinger. *Shit!* Her finger immediately began to squirt blood. It mingled with a puddle of fruit juice like a cloud of pomegranate in a cocktail. She instantly felt her heart begin to beat faster. Her mouth went dry. Tiny drops of sweat formed on her forehead. *Breathe.* She couldn't stand the sight of blood. *Breathe.* Bercowitz had taught her an abdominal exercise. She closed her eyes, let her diaphragm relax and her thorax open to the maximum, then she exhaled without forcing it, pulling in her stomach. She stood up straight and tore a paper towel from the roll with a trembling hand, then fashioned a bulky bandage, careful not to look at her finger. After that she grabbed the sponge and wiped the spot from the floor, also without looking.

Then she peeked at her finger. And immediately regretted it.

The large makeshift bandage was already soaked with red. She gulped. *Good job you're on the radio and not the television.*

The clock on the wall said 8:03. *Get a move on!*

She hurried to the bathroom, pulled off her sweater and her socks. The globe light on the ceiling was blinking: the bulb was about to go out. Every tiny moment of darkness was like an infinitesimal cut with a razor on her skin, every flicker of light a splinter in her flesh. *Phobias*, said the exasperating little voice. *Not only a phobia of blood, but also of the dark, of needles, vaccinations. Injections, pain . . . Nyctophobia. Algophobia. And they each had a name. And the ultimate fear: of going mad. Because of all these fears. That too had a name: dementophobia – the fear of mental illness.* She had managed to control these phobias, to keep them within reasonable bounds with the help of tranquillisers and therapy, but she had never managed to banish them completely. They were there, somewhere, always ready to resurface. She clenched her teeth. She was only half pleased with what she saw in the mirror, distorted by the strobe effect: a woman in her thirties. Chestnut hair, one blonde strand falling to the side of her face, short behind the ears. Green eyes. She was pretty, there was no doubt about that. But her features had hardened over time. And there were little wrinkles, still faint, at the corner of her eyes. Her body, however, was exactly as it had been ten years earlier: narrow hips, flat chest.

She slipped into the shower, careful to keep the bandage away from the spray. The hot water relaxed the tension in her muscles. She thought about the letter again. About the woman who had written it. Where was she? What was she doing right now? She felt a gnawing ache of apprehension in her belly. Ten minutes later, after she had gratified Iggy with one last caress, she was locking her door, her hair still wet from the shower.

'Good morning, Christine,' said Michèle, her neighbour from across the landing.

She turned to the little woman – exceptionally slender, weighing less than fifty kilos – standing in the shadows. She had long grey hair, far too long for her age. Christine knew she was retired, and something about her bearing, her diction, and her vision of the world made Christine think she must have worked for the Ministry of Education. Since retiring, Michèle had been spending her days as an activist, campaigning for associations in support of undocumented immigrants or the right to housing, and she took part in all the demonstrations denouncing the city's policies for being not far enough to the left.

Christine was sure that Michèle and her friends criticised her programme behind her back, because she gave equal time to both union leaders and company bosses, or to council representatives and even the local right wing, and – and this was something she herself deplored – serious topics were becoming increasingly rare.

'What is the topic of today's programme?' asked her neighbour, in an astonishingly loud voice.

'Christmas,' answered Christine. 'Along with solitude, for people who dread this period. Merry Christmas, by the way.'

She immediately regretted her effort to defend herself. Her neighbour shot her a sharp glance.

'In that case, you should have broadcast from the squat on the rue du Professeur Jammes. There you would have seen what Christmas really means to families who have neither a roof nor a future in this country.'

*Fuck off*, thought Christine. It occurred to her that her pint-sized neighbour might have a tiny little mouth, but far too much came out of it.

'One day I'll invite you, don't worry,' she called as she hurried down the stairs without waiting for the lift. 'And you'll have all the time you like to express your views, I promise.'

The cold outside air did her good. It was roughly minus five degrees, and she nearly went flying on the slippery pavement. The smell of exhaust and pollution lingered in the air. There was snow on the roofs of the parked cars, on the windowsills and the dustbin lids, and yet there the homeless man was still, manning the fort on the opposite pavement. Amid his pieces of cardboard. Even in this kind of weather he preferred to sleep on the street than in a shelter. He peered out of his cocoon of rolled blankets. His beard was white on the sides and black in the middle, like the coat of an old animal. How old was he? It was hard to say. Between forty-five and sixty . . . He had been sleeping in the doorway of the building across the street for some months. She seemed to recall he had shown up in the spring. When she had time, she took him a hot coffee. Or some soup. But not this morning. Nevertheless she crossed the road, a coin in her hand.

'Good morning,' he said. 'Not too warm today. Mind you don't slip.'

He held out his hand. His fingers and short nails were almost the same colour as the black fingerless glove he was wearing. Not twenty centimetres from his pieces of cardboard and the bulbous pile of plastic bags, the pavement was covered in snow.

'Go and get yourself something hot to drink,' she said.

He nodded. A shrewd gleam flickered in the grey eyes beneath thick black brows; he gave a slight frown, which formed an entire network of sooty creases around his temples.

'Are you sure you're all right?' he said. 'You look preoccupied to me. It's the weight of all those worries, isn't it? All those responsibilities . . .'

She could not help but smile. He was sleeping outside and it was minus five, he had nothing but a few meagre possessions crammed into black bin liners which he dragged around with him wherever he went like a snail with its house, with neither family nor roof over his head, and an even bleaker future, as far as she knew – and he was worried about her. That was what had surprised her, the first time

27

she went up to him to give him some change. He had spontaneously struck up a conversation, and she had been floored by his poised, clear, quietly self-assured voice. The sort of voice you want to listen to in the middle of a hubbub of conversation. The sort of voice that indicates a certain level of education and culture. He never complained. He often smiled. He spoke about the weather and the news with her as if they were old neighbours. Thus far she had never dared ask him where he came from or how he had ended up here, what his story was. But she had promised herself she would one day, if he was still in the neighbourhood.

'Are you sure you want to stay here? Isn't there an emergency shelter somewhere?'

He smiled at her indulgently.

'I don't suppose you've ever set foot in a shelter. Don't take it the wrong way, it's just that those places aren't very . . . you know what I mean. Don't worry about me. I'm as tough as an old coyote. And the good weather will soon be here again, it's just a rough period to get through, my fine lady.'

'See you this evening then,' she called as she walked away.

'A good day to you!'

She went to her car, which was parked in a nearby street, treading carefully (*I've had enough to worry about already*), opened the passenger door and reached for the de-icing spray in the glove compartment. It had not snowed a great deal overnight; the layer on the body of her old Saab 93 was no thicker. She walked around the bonnet.

And froze. For half a second, she stood with her arms limp at her side, her breath coming out in little white clouds. In the film of snow covering the windscreen, a finger had written:

'MERRY CHRISTMAS, YOU FILTHY BITCH.'

Christine shuddered. Then looked all around her, slightly dizzy. The panic returned: the evil finger that had written those words must belong to someone who *knew* that the owner of the car was a woman.

She squirted the de-icer onto it. Then put the canister away and locked the Saab. She didn't have time to make the journey by car, in any case. Not with this snow. She rushed towards the nearest Métro station, careful not to slip. *She was late.* In seven years, this had never happened.

Not even once.

# 3

## Chorus

Eight thirty-seven. She came through the door of Radio Five almost at a run. The building where the radio station was based, at the top of the allées Jean-Jaurès, was much more modest than the shadowy giants leaning irritably over a runt that taunted them with its slogan:

BE VOCAL, BE POWERFUL

In the entrance by the lifts a sign indicated that Radio Five was the second most popular radio station in terms of listeners in the Midi-Pyrénées region. Before they even reached the floor where the studios and editorial offices were located, visitors were already fully aware of the importance of the mission being fulfilled here. *If the mission was so important, why was she so badly paid?* On the ground floor she nodded to the receptionist, then when she reached the second floor, hurried into the little glassed-in room which contained the coffee machine and water fountain to make herself a 'One hundred per cent fair trade Arabica' macchiato.

'We're late,' whispered a voice in her ear. 'So we'd better get a move on. The boss will blow a fuse.'

A familiar perfume, 'Little Black Dress', and a presence very near – too near – her back.

'I overslept,' she replied, dipping her lips into the froth.

'Hmm. Having a good time, was that it?'

'Cordélia . . .'

'Oh, you don't want to talk about it?'

'No.'

'Did you know you're very secretive? I've never met anyone so secretive. You can tell me everything, you know, Christine.'

'No, I don't think so.'

'We've been working together for ten months and I still know

29

nothing about you. Apart from the fact that you're a very professional, hard-working, intelligent and ambitious woman. Ready to do anything to climb the ladder. Like me, basically. Except that in my case, it's you I'd like to—'

Christine spun around to face a woman roughly one metre eighty in height but who weighed no more than sixty kilos.

'You know I could have you sacked for that?'

'For what?'

'For saying things like that: it's called harassment.'

'Harassment? Oh my God!'

The young intern looked deeply shocked, her lips forming a comical round O, punctuated by two tiny steel beads planted in her lower lip.

'Oh my God! I'm nineteen, I'm an intern! I earn peanuts! You wouldn't really do that, would you?'

'You're not my friend, you're my assistant. And at your age, I didn't meddle in the lives of adults.' She stressed the word *adults*.

'Times have changed, babe.'

Leaning forward, Cordélia put her arm around Christine to drop a coin in the machine behind her. She pressed the *cappuccino* button. Their faces were nearly touching. Her breath smelled of coffee and tobacco.

'What have you done to your hair?' asked Christine, hurrying to finish the coffee, burning her tongue.

'I dyed it. The same colour as yours. Do you like it?'

Before, Cordélia had had platinum blonde and black hair. She also had a cigarette perpetually tucked behind her ear, like an old lorry driver, far too much kohl around her eyes, and wore long-sleeved T-shirts that declared things like *Even the Paranoid Have Enemies*.

'Does it matter if I like it?'

'You have no idea,' replied the young woman, pushing the glass door open, her coffee cup in her hand.

'Have you seen the time?'

Guillaumot, the programme director. Guillaumot didn't work for the radio: he had married the radio. In other words, he had married the owner of Radio Five before becoming programme director. As his superior and the person who paid his salary happened to be his wife, he had developed an ulcer, which he treated with sucralfate.

He had also gone bald and wore a toupee worthy of the Beatles circa 1963. From Christine's perspective, as an unmarried woman between the ages of twenty and sixty, he was anything but attractive. He was even a bit repulsive.

'Happy Christmas to you, too,' she replied, rushing towards the noisy labyrinth of the editorial room. 'Where do we stand with the press review?' she called to Ilan. 'Happy Christmas, by the way.'

'Happy what?'

Ilan was seated at his desk, next to Christine's. He flashed her a smile. Then he pointed to the articles cut out and pinned up next to the clock on the wall, where the seconds ticked by in the form of luminous dots.

'It's ready,' he answered. 'We were just waiting for you.'

She grabbed a felt tip and a biro and quickly read through the material. As usual, Ilan had done a great job. 'That's very good,' she said, reading the article from *Le Parisien* which described a maternity ward in Bethlehem located a stone's throw from the Church of the Nativity and run by a Catholic order, where ninety per cent of the patients were Muslim Palestinian women. She leafed through the other articles. Foie gras banned by the House of Lords in England ('God Save the Queen' by the Sex Pistols as background music). A giant Christmas speed-dating event in South Korea ('Any idea what all these singletons asked for from Santa Claus?'). Several dozen flights cancelled due to bad weather at Blagnac airport ('Check with your carrier before you travel').

'A branch of the Popular Relief has been threatened with closure – aren't you interested?' barked someone behind her.

She swung around on her seat. Becker, news director. He was peering up at her from the full height of his one metre sixty. Stocky, muscular, but also some fat beneath his brown sweater. He was going bald, too; but he didn't wear a wig. Like all radio journalists, Becker was of the opinion that he represented the true nobility of the profession, and he was on a mission: to his mind, presenters were merely entertainers, public clowns. Moreover, there were no women on his team.

'Hello Becker, happy Christmas to you, too.'

'The words "solidarity", "exclusion" and "generosity" are not part of your vocabulary, Steinmeyer? Or maybe you'd rather talk about the stampede of gift buying, or who's made the most beautiful crib?'

'That branch of the Popular Relief is in the north of the country, in Concarneau, not Toulouse.'

'Oh, really? Then why is it that even the TV news of a nationwide channel reported on it? I suppose it isn't funny enough for your listeners. Nor did I hear anything about the authorisation of the sale of prescription drugs on the Internet, or about the total ban on the sale of alcohol to anyone under twenty-five.'

'I am delighted to learn that you listened to my press review.'

'You call that a press review? I call it a joke. The press review should be done by real journalists,' he said and his gaze went from Christine to Ilan, then up to Cordélia, where it lingered. 'That's the problem with this bloody station: people forget that radio is, above all, about news.'

She watched him walk away and felt no emotion. Radio Five was no different from any other radio station or television channel on the planet: the relationships between the newscasters, programme directors and star presenters were often tense if not downright hostile. They denigrated each other, were full of scorn and insults. And the more the Internet got in the way, the more conflicts were likely to arise.

She sighed, collapsed into her chair then swung round to face her assistants.

'Okay, let's go. Ready?'

'What's our headline?' asked Ilan.

He had his back to her. She could see his yarmulke. Christine smiled: he was wearing a 'holiday' one with smileys on it, out of solidarity with his colleagues.

'"Not only Jesus was born in Bethlehem",' she replied.

He nodded enthusiastically.

'Oh, by the way,' he said, 'this came for you.'

She followed his gaze. A padded envelope on the corner of her desk. Christine opened it. Inside was a CD: an old opera CD. Verdi's *Il Trovatore*. She hated opera.

'This must be for Bruno,' she said.

Bruno was the music programme planner.


'With us is Dr Bercowitz – neurologist, psychiatrist, ethologist, and psychoanalyst, author of many definitive works. Good morning, Dr Bercowitz. Today you are going to speak with us about people for whom Christmas is an ordeal.'

32

One minute past nine, 25 December. In the studio, the psychiatrist waited for Christine's question before speaking; Bercowitz was a professional, at ease with radio appearances. A specialist in communication. He liked what he was doing there and you could hear it in his voice, which suggested a warm personality and indisputable authority; his vocabulary was neither too professorial nor exaggeratedly familiar. But above all he knew how to create a bond with his listeners – as if he were in their kitchen or sitting room and not behind a microphone. Bercowitz was the perfect guest and Christine knew he had recently received an offer from a nationwide broadcaster.

'Doctor,' she began, 'it is holiday season once again. Lights, children's eyes shining with joy . . . But it's not only children's eyes that are shining, the adults' are too: why does this time of year get us so emotional?'

She hardly listened to his answer. His opening argument was sufficiently slow for the listeners to get used to his voice. Christine only heard bits of what he said: 'Christmas reminds us of our own childhood'; 'the fact that almost everywhere on the planet billions of people are celebrating the same thing at the same time gives us an exalting and reassuring sensation of being connected to others'; 'that same feeling of communion that one feels at major sporting events, or even sometimes with events as terrible as war'. As usual, his tone was just a fraction too self-satisfied, she noted, but that wasn't a problem: she was already concentrating on the next question.

'Can you explain to us why this period, which is a source of joy and celebration for most of us, can lead to anxiety and torment in others?'

'Paradoxically, it is *because* people feel connected to one another that the feeling of exclusion is equally strong for those who are alone,' he replied with a touch of carefully measured compassion. 'We mustn't forget that our senses are called on more than usual during this season, with shop windows, street decorations, advertising . . . Our subconscious is bombarded with stimuli. For people who don't like Christmas because they know they will be alone – because they are separated or widowed or have no means of support – these stimuli are a permanent source of conflict between society's injunction to be jolly and their actual situation. Moreover, it is not only the joys of childhood that Christmas brings to the surface, but also its shadows.'

At these words, she felt a little seismic tremor in her gut.

'Obviously, you can't go to sleep on 23 December and wake up on 2 January,' she emphasised. 'So what can people like this do, in spite of everything, to get through this period without becoming too depressed?'

'Above all, they must try not to be alone on the day. They can find themselves a substitute family. They can celebrate Christmas with friends rather than family, or with neighbours with whom they get along well. If the people you are close to enjoy your company, no doubt they will be only too pleased to invite you. Providing, that is, that they know you are alone: don't be ashamed to tell them. You can also practise charity and solidarity: it will give you great satisfaction to feel useful, and to do something that matters. Charities, food banks, homeless shelters always need volunteers. Otherwise, you can always try a change of scene. Go away if you can. It will enable you to focus your attention on new things.'

*Go away* . . . go away rather than confront her parents, Christmas, the dinner. The shrink's words fell heavily into her thoughts like coins in a collection box at church.

'And what about people who have neither the means to go away nor friends to take them in, people who no longer have the strength or the health to become volunteers: is there something that *we* can do?' she asked, her throat suddenly tight.

Shit, what was the matter with her? She saw the woman in her dream again: *You did nothing.*

'Of course,' replied Bercowitz, looking her straight in the eye, as if he had noticed that she was upset. 'There is always something you can do.'

Behind the glass separating the studio from the technical cabin, Igor, the director, a bearded thirty-year-old with long greasy hair, leaned over his microphone.

'A little faster, Doc,' he said into the headphones.

The psychiatrist nodded. He turned to face Christine.

'More than ever we must be on the lookout for signs of distress. A solitary neighbour. Ambiguous words that might be a call for help.'

*You let me down*, said the woman in her dream again. The room – a cage of four metres by four, with a glass wall separating them from the technical cabin and another wall hidden by blinds from the editorial room, with no other ventilation than the air-conditioning – suddenly seemed like an oppressive box. As if the temperature in the studio were rising.

Bercowitz was talking.

Staring at her.

His little lips were moving. But she didn't hear him.

She heard another voice.

*You did nothing.*

'Ten seconds,' said Igor in the headphones.

She almost didn't notice that the shrink had finished. For a split second she went blank. It was nothing on the scale of a day or a life. But to the listeners it was an eternity. Behind his glass Igor was staring at her. As was Bercowitz: at that very moment, he looked like a rugby player desperately waiting for his partner to get into position to receive the ball.

'Um, thank you,' she said. 'Now we will, um, take a few questions from our listeners.'

Nine twenty-one. She blushed, stared at her Mac, while Igor, baffled, started the jingle. Three listeners were displayed on her screen, which was blinking impatiently: line 1, line 2, line 3. There were also text messages. The listeners could either ask their questions this way, or leave a message, or request to ask it live. In which case the co-ordinator would speak to them first in order to evaluate the quality of the connection, the pertinence of the question and their ease with expressing themselves, then she would add brief comments for Christine.

Christine immediately noticed number one on the list. Thirty-five years old. An architect. Unmarried. The coordinator had added an enthusiastic evaluation: 'Intelligent, pertinent question, pleasant voice, speaks with ease, slight accent: perfect.' As usual, she decided to keep him for last. She motioned to Igor to connect line 2.

'First question,' she said. 'We are speaking to Reine. Good morning, Reine. You live in Verniolle, you are forty-two years old, and you are a teacher.'

The listener on line 2 provided a few basic biographical details, as requested, then she asked her question. The psychiatrist pounced on it eagerly. His voice was purring. Christine would be sorry when he left for his nationwide destiny.

She asked the shrink to answer a text message. And then she called on Samia, on line 3.

'Thank you,' said Christine, once the shrink had answered yet again. 'One last question? Let's hear from Mathias.'

35

Line 1.

Nine thirty.

She motioned to connect the line.

'It doesn't bother you that you let someone die?'

For a fraction of a second, she was too stunned to move. His voice was powerful and ingratiating. Low-pitched, warm and deep at the same time, an inflection with a faint hiss. Without knowing why, she got the impression that the guy was speaking in the dark, from a place without light. A long shudder went through her and she wondered whether her brain was simply distorting much more innocuous words. No, because the voice continued, 'For all your fine words of solidarity, you let someone commit suicide on Christmas Eve. Even though that person had called out to you for help.'

Her gaze met the shrink's. He opened his mouth and closed it again without speaking.

'What . . . is . . . your question?'

Her own voice seemed detached from her body. Toneless. It had nothing in common with the supple, compliant, almost erotic instrument she ordinarily played.

'So what sort of person are you, then?'

She could feel the sweat on her damp palms; she could see Igor's eyes popping out of their sockets behind the glass window; she could see her own reflection, aghast. She finally raised a hand to tell him to cut off the line.

'Um . . . Thank you . . . Thanks also to Dr Bercowitz for his insight . . . Happy Christmas to everyone.'

The theme music began to play: 'Notion', by Kings of Leon. She pressed her back against her seat, stunned, as if the blood refused to circulate through her veins. She couldn't breathe. The small space was oppressive, the man's words still echoed.

She saw Igor lean in towards his microphone. His voice erupted in the headphones:

'Can someone tell me what the fuck is going on? Christine, for Christ's sake, were you asleep or what?'

'You should have cut him off right away,' said the programme director, his tone full of blame. 'Right from the start. When he took that familiar tone with you. You shouldn't have kept him on the air.' Guillaumot

36

was giving her a dark look. His voice reached her through a filter, a thick layer of stupor.

'Christine, what is the matter with you today?' asked Salomé, the coordinator. 'It was a real shambles.'

'What do you mean?'

'The way you behaved . . . Shit, you left a huge pause! You seemed completely absent!' Salomé's eyes were shining with reproach behind her glasses. 'Don't forget you are the image of this station, my dear. Or rather its voice. Listeners have to picture a cheerful, positive personality . . . someone professional, not someone who doesn't care, and who has the same problems they do!'

Christine was nettled by the unfairness of her comment.

'Thank you, but I've been doing this job for seven years. And the one time I screw up . . . Besides, who let that sick idiot on the air?'

She could see the fury shining in Salomé's eyes. There had been a blunder; there would be a report.

'Could I . . . could I listen to him again?' she asked.

All their programmes were recorded. The recordings were kept for a month. Then sent to the broadcasting regulatory body. Any incidents were subjected to a debriefing like this one.

'What?' exclaimed Igor with a shake of his head to clear his long curly hair from his face. 'What's the point, for Christ's bloody sake?'

The programme director gave Christine a suspicious look.

'Do you know that person? Do you have any idea what he meant with this business about a suicide?'

She shook her head. Could feel them staring at her.

'We have his telephone number on file. We'll notify the cops,' said Salomé.

'And then what? What do you expect them to do? Arrest him for assault over the airwaves?' said Igor. 'Just drop it. It was only another lunatic. What was it Audiard said? "Blessed are the cracks, because they let in the light."'

'I am taking this very seriously,' replied the programme director. 'That was the Christmas programme, for Christ's sake! And we get a guy live on air who accuses us of letting people commit suicide! In front of half a million listeners!'

★

37

'Gérald?'

'Chris? What's going on? You sound funny.'

She was standing by the coffee machine, out of earshot of the editorial office.

'That letter. Do you still have it?' she asked.

'*What?*'

She could sense both his surprise and his annoyance.

'Yes . . . well, I think I do,' he said.

'Where is it?'

'Well, it must still be in the glove compartment, I suppose. Dear God, Chris, don't tell me that—'

'Are you at home, now?'

She sensed a moment of hesitation.

'No, no, I'm at the office.'

He had paused for a fraction of a second; his voice sounded odd. As if he had been about to lie and finally decided against it. She felt her alarm system switch on. She had begun to recognise Gérald's little lies – like the time when she was downloading a film and discovered that he had downloaded some porn the day before. He had sworn it was a mistake, that he thought he was getting something else. But she knew it wasn't true.

'At the office? On Christmas Day?'

'I had – I had something urgent to deal with. Chris, are you sure you're all right?'

'You haven't forgotten we're supposed to meet at my parents' in two hours?'

On the line she heard a laugh that sounded like a snort.

'That isn't the sort of thing I'm likely to forget.'

# 4

# Baritone

Click. She's not sure what she saw. Mirage? Autosuggestion? Fact? Click. Her mind goes over every detail. Like a camera. Click. Click. Sweeping over the entire scene. Click. And comes back each time to the same place, to *their hands*.

Then lines of dialogue fill the black screen of her mind: *their hands, did you see them, yes or no? They were next to each other. Close, even very close, just as you went through the door . . . but close in what way?* She had been humming 'Driving Home for Christmas', a song by Chris Rea that no one ever sang any more, all the way down the deserted corridors of the Higher Institute of Aeronautics and Space, and then she went through the door. She still had snowflakes on her white anorak and her cheeks were on fire from the cold.

'Hey,' she said, stupidly, when she saw them.

While she was surprised to see Denise, she could see equal astonishment in Denise's eyes. And in Gérald's. Then she had caught that movement. Lower down. Their hands . . .

Holding the edge of the desk, his left hand, strong and tanned, very close to Denise's right hand, slender and elegant, with perfect nails. Who had moved their hand first, that she couldn't say: she had just grasped the movement. *Had they been holding hands when she came into the room?* She couldn't be sure. She was sure, however, that they were embarrassed. Of course it didn't mean anything, protested a more reasonable voice inside. If she'd been in a room with another man, about to touch him, and Gérald came in at that very moment without warning, she would surely feel embarrassed as well. Yes. Except that this was not the first time these two had found themselves close together, at a party or a barbecue. Except that they happened to be alone together in a building that was virtually deserted. On

Christmas Day. And they weren't supposed to be here. Christine had decided to surprise Gérald and, what do you know, as far as surprises went, it certainly was one – for everyone concerned.

'Hey,' she said again, and nothing else.

She stayed silent, speechless.

And yet she had knocked. She made a mental note of the time, from the clock hanging on the wall. 12:21.

'Hello, Christine,' said Denise. 'How are you?'

Denise might have an old-fashioned name, but that was the only old-fashioned thing about her. She was twenty-five, rather petite but with beauty on her side, a smile to put a dentist to ruin, and the well-crafted brain of a PhD student. Her eyes were the same deep, troubled colour as Gérald's favourite drink. Caipirinha eyes. Gérald was her supervisor at the Institute. Christine was used to classifying Gérald's female friends into three categories: harmless, interested or dangerous, but Denise needed a category all to herself: supremely interested / absolutely not harmless / *very* dangerous. *How do you think I am?*

Gérald probably didn't see things that way – men never saw things that way. She gave him a quick sidelong glance. In return, he flashed her the smile she could define in two words: *laid-back*, a smile that was so good at making her feel warmer, at calming her down, but not this time. Oh, no. This time, she noticed that his smile was more automatic than laid-back – a simple reflex. With a touch of nervousness; or was it annoyance?

'I thought we were supposed to meet at your parents'?' he said.

As if this were a signal, Denise moved back from the desk, leaning on her lovely arms.

'Well, I'd better get going. There is a life outside work, after all. And besides, it can wait until Wednesday. Merry Christmas, Christine. Merry Christmas, Gérald.'

Even her voice was perfect. Husky and veiled just to the right degree. Christine heard herself reply the same thing, even though deep down she did not wish her such a merry time of it. She watched Denise pass, saw her bottom – perfect as well – pressing against her tight jeans. Through the closed door she could hear her heels fading along the silent corridors of the Institute.

'What's going on?' asked Gérald. 'Still something to do with that letter?'

He seemed irritated. Maybe because he'd had other plans for the hour ahead? *Oh, stop it.*

'Have you got it?'

He wavered evasively.

'I told you, it must still be in the car. I didn't check. Good God, Christine, let's not go into all that again!'

'It won't take me long. I'm taking the letter to the police station and then we'll meet at my parents' as planned.'

Now it was his turn to move away from the desk, looking resigned. He reached for his woollen coat and scarf.

'Don't you think this is going a bit too far?' he asked as they walked down the corridor.

'What were you doing here on Christmas Day?' she couldn't help but ask.

'What? Just a last-minute thing to attend to.'

'And Denise, was she here because of the same thing?'

It just slipped out, and she was already sorry.

'What do you mean by that?'

If his voice had been a thermometer, the mercury would have plummeted.

'Nothing.'

He went through the glass door that led to the car park; the brisk wind, once again laden with snow, seized hold of them.

'No, you must say what you think. What are you suggesting?'

He was just a bit too angry. Gérald got angry whenever he felt he was being accused of something.

'I'm not suggesting anything. I just don't like the way she hangs around you, that's all.'

'Denise does not hang around me. I'm her supervisor. And Denise is passionate about things. *The way I am.* And that is something you ought to understand: you love your work too, don't you? You've got that assistant: that . . . Ilan, who eats out of your hand. And you were working on Christmas Day too, if I'm not mistaken?'

His arguments lined up logically, but the logic was slightly skewed, and his tone was just that little bit forced. He unlocked the SUV, leaned inside, then stood up with the envelope in his hand; gusts of wind made his fringe flutter in front of his glasses.

'See you later,' he said curtly.

He walked back towards the buildings. She unlocked her Saab

and sat in the driver's seat. It was cold inside; she could feel the icy leather through her jeans. She switched on the ignition and the radio came on along with the wheezing blower of the heating system. She glanced behind her at the back seat with its piles of gift-wrapped packages. The day before, after the broadcast, she had gone to several boutiques and shopping malls. She had bought a warm, elegant winter coat for her mother, and a box set of all Stanley Kubrick's films for Gérald, with the book *The Stanley Kubrick Archives* as a bonus, and she'd also got a naughty outfit for herself (she had imagined the effect it would have on Gérald as she gazed at herself in the mirror in the changing room, and the thought of opening the door to him like that had made her smile and titillated her at the same time, but now that she had seen Denise the idea seemed far less sound). For her father, the search had taken longer. She remembered just in time that for two years in a row she had given him a pen, so in the end she settled on a tablet: the cheapest one on offer.

At her mother's request she had also bought oysters, figs, Parmesan cheese, Christmas buns filled with candied fruit, a sweet white wine to go with the foie gras, and some 'holiday coffee'. She pictured the garlands and candles, the apple and oak logs in the fireplace, and like every time she went to visit her parents, which was less and less frequently, she felt a wave of nausea. Then she noticed Denise's car, a red and white Mini, still in the car park. Without warning, she suddenly felt slightly dizzy.

She turned and looked over at the building.

An inner voice told her to wait for them to come out, but another, stronger voice told her to do nothing of the kind, to get out of there instead. She decided to listen to the second voice. She set off, driving slowly over the fine layer of snow that covered the car park like talcum powder. The second voice reproached her for her lack of confidence: she was paranoid, that's what she was. She had no reason to be jealous. Denise was neither the first nor would she be the last woman to hover around her man, after all.

*She had to learn to trust other people. And Gérald in particular.* She knew only too well where her lack of confidence came from: how could she trust anyone, when she had been betrayed by the only person in the world who should not have betrayed her? Yes. It all came from there. From that black hole, which for so long had absorbed all the light. Denise's presence in Gérald's office didn't mean a thing. Of course it didn't.

*That's a lie*, answered the other voice, the one she had inherited from the dark years. *Stop telling yourself stories, girl. Did you see their hands, yes or no? You are fully aware, deep down, that it's not even a question of trust, is it, Christine? No, it's something else: once again, you're afraid to face the truth.*

'Why did you wait?'

The cop was looking at her, his face impassive. Undecipherable. His fingers were fidgeting, playing with his tie. Which was ugly. She hesitated.

'It was Christmas Eve. I – I had to meet my fiancé's parents for the first time. I didn't want to be late.'

'Right.' He looked at his watch. 'But now it is one fifteen. You could have come sooner.'

'I work at Radio Five. I had a broadcast this morning. And I've been waiting forty minutes for my turn.'

His interest seemed piqued.

'What did you have to do with the radio broadcast?'

'I'm the presenter.'

He gave a faint smile.

'I thought I recognised your voice from somewhere. I have a meeting in half an hour, so unfortunately I don't have much time to give you.'

He focused his attention on the letter open in front of him. As if the fact that she was a public person changed everything.

'What do you think?' she asked, when the silence began to seem endless.

He shrugged. 'I don't really know. I'm no psychologist. In any case, no suicides were reported last night. Or this morning, if that will reassure you.'

He said the words as if they'd been talking about a simple burglary, or a snatched handbag.

'The letter is strange,' he added finally. 'There's something not quite right about it.'

'In what way?'

'I don't know. Something about the tone. It doesn't ring true. Who talks like that? Who calls out for help in such a way? Nobody.'

She told herself he was right. She herself had had the same feeling reading it for the ninth or tenth time. The strange feeling of something peculiar, abnormal, even a threat that was not actually a threat of suicide.

Now he was staring at her.

'And could it be this letter was not put in your mailbox by mistake?'

'What do you mean?'

'What if the person who wrote it meant for *you* to read it?'

She felt a shudder go through her.

'That's absurd. I don't know what they're talking about, or who they could be.'

He was still staring at her. Little prying cop's eyes.

'Are you sure?'

'Yes.'

'All right.'

He folded up the letter. 'Are there any other fingerprints on the letter besides your own?'

'My fiancé's. So, are you going to look into it?'

'I'll see what I can do. What is the name of your programme?'

Was he flirting with her? She looked for a wedding ring. He wasn't wearing one.

'*Mornings with Christine.* On Radio Five.'

He nodded.

'Oh, right. I like that station.'

# 5

## Concertato

'What exactly do you do, Gérald?'

Her mother's blue eyes were full of curiosity. Like in the days when she used to host her programme on Channel One, where she would invite everyone who was anyone in the country: actors, politicians, singer-songwriters, intellectuals. There weren't so many comedians in those days. And reality TV, that televisual equivalent of an open sewer, did not exist.

Christine looked at them. Her oh-so-perfect parents. Sitting next to each other on the sofa, holding hands like they'd just met, after forty years of marriage. The Steinmeyers made a point of cultivating a perfect image. Perfection in every detail. Even their clothing matched: shirt and trousers in almost identical colours, impeccably ironed, the harmony of their taste in fashion, food, art . . . Christine noted Gérald's slight hesitation when he started on an explanation that was meant to be both simple and didactic, but which only managed to be boring.

*You certainly didn't expect to find yourself in the family equivalent of a television studio: that's my fault, I should have warned you. Oh dear – and to think I wanted to surprise you.*

'But this must all seem, well, rather boring to you,' he concluded, blushing. 'Even so, I must confess, it is a – how to put it – fascinating profession. In my opinion, um, at any rate,' he thought it best to add.

*Oh for the love of Christ, Gérald! Where has your bloody sense of humour gone?*

He glanced over at her, seeking support. Her mother's smile was full of indulgence. Christine knew that smile. She also recognised the quick look her mother gave her. It was there, in her eyes, the look she would have given twenty years earlier, on the set of her programme, to any guest who was singularly lacking in charisma. The show had started at five p.m., every Sunday. After that there had been a fallow period, then she had been in charge of a weekly magazine show that was already in decline – a relative decline that transformed into a slow death with the advent of the Internet.

'No, no, no,' lied her mother, brazenly. 'It is truly fascinating, honestly.' (One should always be wary of people who used *truly, honestly, frankly* all the time: she was the one who had told Christine this.) 'Even though I must confess I didn't understand everything. Why are you waiting to invite him onto your radio show, my darling?'

Laughs of complicity from both sides. *To send my listeners to sleep?* thought Christine. *No, that was too cruel.*

And her father, in the meantime? He was smiling. Nodding. He let the conversation continue, his gaze absent.

'I – this wine is excellent,' said Gérald.

'Grand-Puy-Lacoste 2005,' said her father laconically.

He leaned over to refill their glasses. Christine wondered when he would bring up Madeleine. And how. Because sooner or later he would talk about her. Even in passing, even in an allusive way – with a slight tremor in his voice. It was as inevitable as turkey at Christmas. Madeleine had died nineteen years ago. Ever since then, her father had been in mourning. A constant, permanent, almost professional mourning. *What is your profession? I've been a journalist, writer, a television and radio man – surely you've heard of that show,* What a Racket . . . *And now? Mourning, put mourning.* His Wikipedia entry indicated that Guy Dorian, whose real name was Guy Steinmeyer, was a French writer and journalist born on 3 July 1948 in Sarrance, Pyrénées-Atlantiques, who for twenty years had presented the most famous daily radio programme in France, launched on 6 January 1972, with 6,246 broadcasts in all, in the course of which he had interviewed every single artist, politician, sports personality, writer and scientist in France – including three presidents, two of them while they were in office. Then he'd moved to television, with the same success.

'We are so happy to meet you at last,' said her mother. 'Christine has told us so much about you.'

(*Oh really, when?*)

Gérald shot her an embarrassed look.

'Yes . . . she has also told me a great deal about you.'

A big fat lie that sounded like one.

'And we are so glad that she has finally found a suitable match.'
(*Oh, no, have mercy, not that.*)

'Christine is someone who knows what she wants,' her father declared at last.

The perfect couple turned their heads towards her, like a pair of synchronised robots.

'That is why we are so proud of our daughter,' echoed her mother.

Another quick look in her direction. It was not so much pride Christine saw there as her mother's effort to convince herself.

'She wants to follow in our footsteps. She's been working so hard at it.'

'We are very proud of her,' insisted her father. 'We've always been proud of our daughters.'

'Christine has a sister?' (This from Gérald.)

And so, there they were. She could feel the bile in her throat.

'Madeleine was Christine's older sister,' said her father hastily and, for a fraction of a second, his voice cracked like an adolescent's. 'She died in an . . . *accident*. Maddie was so very talented, so gifted. It wasn't easy for Christine to live in her shadow. But she has come through. She's shown us what she is made of.'

A memory, like a brutal flash. The summer of 1991. The Bonnieux house. Friends around the swimming pool. So many of them were so familiar from seeing them on TV that it was as if they were actually on set, with Madeleine in the middle. Madeleine was only thirteen but she looked sixteen, with her womanly breasts under her T-shirt, her womanly hips, and her little round womanly buttocks in tight shorts. Madeleine was helping to serve, attracting all the men's gazes, flaunting her charm with a joyful recklessness, testing her precocious power over the male libido (had she really *seen* her like that? When she herself was only ten? Or was her memory reconstructing the scene after the fact?), a nymphet, an ingénue, mimicking and eclipsing the adult women. Ladies and gentlemen, I give you the queen of the party. And not just that party. Madeleine was the queen twenty-four hours a day – whereas Christine was relegated to the role of lady-in-waiting.

She met Gérald's gaze. Could see his bewilderment. *You never told me about your sister. Never told me who your parents were either, that they were famous. Dear Lord.*

47

She was grateful that he kept his mouth shut.

'When she was little,' said her mother with a smile, 'Christine tried desperately to compete with her sister.'

(*Oh no, please, not you, Mum.*)

'Like the time when her father taught her how to swim.'

She laughed. But her father didn't laugh. Didn't look at her. He was looking at his long hands.

'It was a very long process. But she finally got the hang of it. She wouldn't give up. Ever. That's Christine – she hangs on. All through her childhood she had this model there before her who was difficult to equal.'

Yes, it was her father who had taught her how to swim, and he was the one who had helped her discover *The Call of the Wild* and *20,000 Leagues under the Sea* and *The Jungle Book*, and he was the one who had gone with her to the cinema for the first time. And yet, no matter how tender and indulgent and mischievous he had always been (*Well, what? I have the right to a kiss, too, don't I, not just your mother, you little monkey?*), he was always slightly less so with her than with her sister. With Madeleine, there was something else. They had a bond she could only qualify as . . . superior. (*Stop that at once*, said the voice inside.) But it was true, wasn't it? 'Do you love me?' she had asked her father one day – she remembered it was the day of her tenth birthday. *Of course I love you, little monkey.* She loved it when he called her that. But he didn't say 'my' . . . Whereas with Madeleine, it was always *my* darling, *my* hummingbird, *my* sunbeam. Madeleine had never asked her father if he loved her before. Because she didn't have to. She knew.

Her father, even if he protested it wasn't true, even if he hid it and was convinced he was distributing his demonstrations of paternal love evenly (*Good God, girl, the way you express yourself, sometimes!*), constantly favoured Maddie. Already by the age of ten, with her immature little brain, Christine understood this, instinctively.

Which made it all the more ironic that physically, she looked more like him than Maddie did. How many times had people pointed this out to her: *You have your father's face, you talk the way he does, you have his eyes, you have* . . .

Back in the car, Gérald was fuming.

'Bloody hell, you could have warned me!'

'Warned you about what?'

48

His eyes were as round as marbles. 'That your parents were famous!'

'Famous? How many people remember them?'

'Well me, for a start! I remember my mother glued to her radio when I came home from school, listening religiously to your father interviewing some politician or artist or intellectual. Do you realise that his programmes changed the way we saw the world? That they influenced an entire generation? And your mother! How many times when I was a teenager did I switch on the TV and get her show! Why don't you use their name?'

'Steinmeyer *is* my name!' she protested. 'I see no reason to change it!'

'Still, you could have warned me.'

'I'm sorry, I wanted to surprise you.'

'Well, you did that. Your parents are incredible. *Incredible.* They are just the perfect couple. How many months have we been together? And you never talked about them. Why not?'

*Good question.*

'It's not my favourite topic.'


Fucking hell . . . She locked the Saab and crossed the snowy street towards her building. A landscape full of bumps, new contours and traps, as strange as walking on the moon. She felt herself succumbing to an onset of nausea, her stomach full to bursting. She told herself there was something indecent about this yearly gorging on food.

*Obscene.*

As obscene as her father's sorrow. Sometimes Christine felt a boundless rage towards him, that endless mourning he'd wrapped himself up in. She felt like screaming in his face: *But* we *lost her too! We* loved her too! You don't have a monopoly on sorrow! He'd already had one operation for cancer of the saliva glands. When would the next one be? For a moment, Christine wondered whether you could commit suicide through the intermediary of cancer.

She was so upset that twice she miskeyed the front door code. The hallway was cold and dark, enclosing like a tomb. She shivered. She walked over to the mailbox. She felt apprehensive as she unlocked her box. *No letters.* She exhaled. She saw an *Out of order* sign on the cage to the lift and swore. Then she shrugged: it was the logical conclusion to a catastrophic day.

She took the stairs; like the rest of the building, they were completely silent. She felt tired, demoralised. The entire day had been nothing but a huge waste from beginning to end.

'Your parents are incredible . . . just the perfect couple!'

*My dear Gérald, you're such a comedian.*

No sound came from her landing, but that was normal, her neighbour was as quiet as a mouse – except when she opened her nasty mouth. She was two steps from the landing when she first noticed the smell.

She pinched her nostrils.

What a strange odour! Floating in the air. It wasn't the usual unpleasant smell of the worn, dusty carpet on the stairs.

It was a strong smell.

Of ammonia.

Christine gulped. It was the stink of urine. *Yuck, how horrid.* She kept going towards her door. That was where the smell was coming from. She pressed the button for the timer light and bent down, trying to breathe through her mouth rather than her nose, repressing a wave of nausea: the bottom of her door and her doormat were soaked. There was a puddle underneath the mat. Some animal had pissed on her door not long before. *Shit.* It had to be the poodle from the top floor. Couldn't he have waited until he got to the street? This was the first time, but his owner could have mopped it up . . . Christine would mention it the next time she saw her.

On the other side of the door her landline chose that very moment to start ringing. She fumbled in her handbag to find her keys. Which, of course, were all the way at the bottom. Beneath a jumble of tissues, headphones, mint-flavoured chewing gum, pens and lipsticks. The phone went on ringing – imperiously, impatiently – inside the flat.

She unlocked the door. Stepped over the dark spot on the doormat. Tossed her open handbag onto the sofa and hurried over to the phone.

'Hello?'

Slow breathing in the receiver.

'Hello?' she said again.

'You could have saved that poor woman, Christine. But you didn't. It's too late now.'

She gave a start. A man's voice. Her heart was pounding.

'Who is this?'

No answer. Just his breathing, but she'd recognised the voice: warm, deep, vaguely sibilant, an accent – and that impression that the man was in the dark, speaking to her from a deep dark place.

'Who are you?' she asked.

'And you, Christine, do you know who you are? Who you *really* are? Have you ever asked yourself the question?'

The man was calling her Christine. He knew her. She recalled what the cop had said: 'And could it be this letter was *not* put in your mailbox by mistake?'

She heard the echo of fear in her voice when she said, 'Who's speaking? I'm going to call the police.'

'And tell them what?'

The man on the line did not seem the least bit perturbed. His tranquil confidence merely aggravated Christine's sense of panic.

'I did what I could: I gave the letter to the police,' she said to justify herself, her temples throbbing, as if it was normal to have to justify herself to a stranger. 'And you, what did you . . .'

(*It doesn't bother you that you let someone die?*)

'. . . do? And how did you get my telephone number?'

He tutted. 'I'm afraid that's not good enough. Not good enough at all. I think you could have done a great deal more – but you didn't want to spoil Christmas, did you?'

'Tell me who you are, or else . . .'

(*For all your fine words of solidarity, you let someone commit suicide on Christmas Eve.*)

'. . . I'll hang up. What do you want from me?'

A swarm of wasps in her brain.

'You like this game, don't you, Christine?'

She didn't answer. What game was he talking about?

'Christine, do you hear me?'

Oh, yes, she heard him. But she did not have the strength to say a thing.

'Do you love him? Because it's not over. Oh, no. It's only just beginning.'

# 6

## Soloist

His throat dry, Servaz looked at the package. He felt as if clawed fingers were caressing his neck, digging into his chest. And yet the package was much smaller than last time. The postmark indicated that it had been posted in Toulouse, but that didn't mean anything, of course. In any case, it could not be an insulated box, given its size: roughly eleven centimetres by nine. Nor was there a fake sender's name like Mr Osoba . . .

He hesitated, then tore off the wrapping paper; a sharp rustling sound. He knew he shouldn't have done that; he should have called forensics to have them examine it from every angle, cover it with a developer powder, place it under seal in a plastic bag and take it to the lab. But they hadn't found a thing on the previous package, and he was convinced there would be nothing to be found on this one, either.

.The box was made of rigid pearl-grey cardboard, with a tight-fitting lid. He looked out at the snowy landscape beyond the window, took a deep breath, then slowly lifted the lid with trembling fingers and plunged his gaze into the box. His lungs filled with air as the relief washed over him: it wasn't what he'd expected. *A finger, that's what he had feared.* Instead, he was looking at a little white plastic rectangle with a red logo representing a crown, a key and the letters 'T' and 'W'.

*Grand Hôtel Thomas Wilson:* it was written directly underneath, in fine print.

An electronic hotel key. There was also the room number. 117. And a piece of folded paper underneath on the red satin in the box. He unfolded it.

*Meeting tomorrow in room 117*

Round, flowing, easy handwriting. Blue ink . . . *A woman's?*

He wondered what sort of woman might want to arrange a meeting at a luxury hotel with a depressed policeman. And what sort of meeting it might be. Romantic? What else, in a hotel room? Charlène? She had come to see him twice during his 'convalescence'. Charlène Espérandieu was the most beautiful woman he had ever met, but she also happened to be his assistant's wife. Four winters ago, they had grown so close that they had been on the verge of committing the irreparable. Charlène was a very captivating woman. Not to mention the fact that she had been seven months pregnant when they were drawn so irresistibly to each other, and that Vincent was his best friend . . .

Was this her, suggesting they meet? If so, why suddenly out of the blue? Why now?

Or did the key have another meaning?

He looked at it again and shuddered. Servaz had already been to that hotel on the Place Wilson, one of the most luxurious in Toulouse, for an investigation. There was a telephone number beneath the name. He took out his mobile.

'Grand Hôtel Thomas Wilson.'

'I'd like to book a room.'

'Yes, sir. Standard, luxury, or suite?'

'Room 117.'

A pause on the line.

'What days would you like to book?'

'Tomorrow.'

He heard typing on a keyboard.

'I'm sorry, sir, the room is already booked. But I can offer you a very similar room—'

'No, thank you. That's the one I want.'

'Well, in that case, I see only one possibility: I have your telephone number; if there is a cancellation, I will notify you immediately, Monsieur . . . ?'

'Servaz,' he said.

'You said Servaz, S-E-R-V-A-Z?'

'Yes, why?'

'Well, I really don't understand: that is the name on the reservation.'

# 7

# Vibrato

She dreamed she was running through a forest, pursued by something terrible. She didn't know what it was, but there could be no doubt about the monstrosity of the thing behind her. She saw an old farm with outbuildings among the trees. Exhausted, she collapsed only a few feet from the door, in the snow. When she lifted her head, her father was standing on the threshold, in his vest, high-waisted trousers with braces and farmers' clodhoppers. 'There's a letter for you,' he said. He tossed it on the ground in front of her and slammed the door. That was when she woke up.

Fear. Sweat. Pounding heart.

She sat bolt upright, opened her eyes and mouth wide: her heart was racing wildly in her chest. Her armpits, her brow, her back: all soaking. The sheets were damp with sweat. A pale winter sun was forcing its way like a fever between the slats of the blinds. How long had she slept?

One minute past eight.

Oh, no, not again! Her mouth felt furry: she remembered she had taken a sleeping tablet the night before. The first in a long time. A sleeping tablet and a gin and tonic. No: two gin and tonics. She stretched, her eyes puffy with sleep; the moment she moved, Iggy rushed over to the bed to lick her cheek and collect his ration of morning cuddles. She stroked him mechanically. Vague memories floated in tatters through her mind: the Christmas dinner, the call during the programme, the puddle of urine on her doormat and, finally, the man on the telephone.

She forced herself to breathe more slowly. She listened to the silence in the flat. As if there might be someone there. She listened more closely.

Nothing. Only Iggy getting impatient. His round, tender eyes were staring at her, not understanding. His little pink tongue appeared beneath his black nose. She got up. Left the room and hurried to the bathroom, amid mountains of T-shirts, rolled-up sheets, knickers and damp towels, until she reached the sink, where she filled a tooth glass with water and drank it down in one gulp. The ceiling light was still flickering. It made her nervous. She hurried into the kitchen-sitting room to pour some coffee into a bowl. As she was about to open the fridge, she realised she wasn't hungry.

She thought again about the puddle of urine.

She hadn't had the courage to clean it up the night before. She had merely closed the front door and double-locked it. Now she headed to the door, unlocked it and opened it. The stink was still there, but had faded to a vague ambient smell which made you want to hold your nose. She had no time to take care of it now. She decided it would be simpler to throw out the doormat and replace it with a new one. Tonight she would take it straight down to the rubbish area: it was out of the question to bring *that* – whatever it was – into her flat.

Suddenly a thought occurred to her – unpleasant, unhealthy – *what if it wasn't animal pee?* Her telephone had begun to ring at the very moment she stood outside the door. *It couldn't be a coincidence.* Someone had waited for her, spied on her. Was it the same man who had called her at the radio? Could he have *pissed* on her door? *And did he also cause the lift to be out of order? Or was she getting completely paranoid?*

*The radio.*

Time was ticking. She had never been late – never, in seven years – and now she was about to be late for the second morning in a row.

In the shower she suddenly realised that the only thing separating her from that stranger was an old, probably not very reliable lock. She should have it changed and add an inside bolt immediately. She dried off and hurried to her computer, a towel wrapped around her, and went to the online yellow pages. The first three locksmiths she managed to reach told her they could not come for a few days. She looked at the clock. 8:25. *Hurry up!*

'Tonight at five o'clock, will that work?' said the fourth.

'Perfect.'

She gave him the address and hung up. Got dressed as fast as she could. No make-up today – no time. Iggy was sitting by the door, happily wagging his tail. Christine felt her heart sink. She hadn't taken him out the night before, and he had weed like a good boy in a box filled with newspaper for such emergencies. Last night she had felt panicked at the thought of going out into the street after what had happened, and he had waited for his walk in vain, pacing back and forth between her and the door and looking increasingly incredulous.

Iggy had not been out for over twenty-four hours.

'I'm so sorry,' she said to him, scratching his thin little scalp, her throat tight. 'I promise you tonight we'll go for a long walk, okay?'

But in all honesty, she was terrified at the thought of having to go out into the deserted streets at night when there was a psycho out there.

'Christine, for Christ's sake, what the hell are you doing?'

'I'm sorry, it won't happen again!'

She tried to rush past Guillaumot, the programme director, but he grabbed her by the wrist.

'Come into my office.'

'What? But we're already late: the show starts in less than twenty minutes!'

'It doesn't matter. I have something to show you.'

His tone tipped her off. He stepped back to let her go past, then closed the door to his office behind her. There were posters on the walls boasting of the station's achievements, there was a coffee machine, and a computer playing their programmes on a loop. He went over to the coffee machine.

'Would you like one?'

'Do we have time?'

'Espresso or Americano?'

'Espresso, with sugar.'

He set the cup down before her and returned to his seat. He crossed his fingers. Then looked straight at her.

'I – I'm really sorry I'm late,' she began.

He waved her excuse away, a kindly smile on his lips.

'Don't worry about that; you've always been on time, Christine. How many years have we been working together? Six? Seven? And I've never seen you arrive late. You're not coming down with the flu, I hope? There's a lot of it around, these days.'

'No, no, not at all.'

He nodded, reassured.

'Good, good. And what about the working environment these days?'

For a moment she wondered what he was driving at.

'Well, I'm not telling you anything new if I say it's a radio station,' she said. 'Look, thanks for the coffee, but I have to—'

He stopped her with a gesture, opened a drawer and took out two bottles of medicine, which he handed to her.

'What's this?' she asked.

He gave her a probing look.

'You tell me.'

She looked at the labels. Xanax. A powerful tranquilliser. Floxyfral. An antidepressant used in cases of severe depression and to treat obsessive-compulsive disorder. Heavy-duty chemistry for major problems. She stared again at the two bottles, then at the programme director, not understanding.

'I don't get it,' she said, frowning.

'Forgive me,' he continued, 'I shouldn't have been rummaging in your drawers, but I was looking for the list of upcoming guests, and I just found them. Are you sure you don't want to talk about it?'

'Are you telling me you found these in my drawer?'

He gave her the look that TV cops wear when culprits deny the evidence.

'Come on, Christine. I'm your friend. You can—'

She felt her face flush crimson. 'I don't know how this stuff got into my drawer! Someone must have got the wrong desk. They're not mine!'

He could not hold back a sigh.

'Listen. We all have our ups and downs—'

'They're not mine, shit! How do I get through to you?'

She had raised her voice. He looked at her and cocked his eyebrows. Before he could say anything more, she had slammed the door and was headed to her desk, every gaze in the open space office trained fiercely on her.

'Christ, Chris, where were you?' exclaimed Ilan. 'Have you seen the—'

He stopped when he saw her expression.

'Shut up, all right?'


'Debriefing in five minutes, Christine.'

This time he didn't even bother to look at her. He vanished into his office. She clenched her teeth and scrolled through the emails on

57

the screen of her Mac. She'd screwed up, yet again. But how could she concentrate when that psycho's words were eating away at her brain? And how had those drugs ended up in her drawer? She sighed, closed her eyes for a moment, then opened them again.

In her pocket her phone vibrated. The screen displayed an unknown number.

'Yes?'

'Christine Steinmeyer?'

A man's voice – but not the one from the night before: a voice with no accent, not as deep, not as ingratiating.

'This is she,' she said cautiously.

'This is the police station calling. Regarding the letter you brought us yesterday.'

Her admirer: he hadn't wasted his time.

'Could you come by and see us?'

'Well, the thing is, I'm at work.'

'Well then, come as soon as you finish work. Ask for Lieutenant Beaulieu at the reception desk.'

She thanked him and hung up. And saw a new email had arrived in her inbox. She clicked on it. The subject was: Game. The sender's address, malebolge@hell.com, was unfamiliar, and she almost sent it straight to the trash, but at the last minute the message it contained caught her attention.

*Have a look at this*
*Gérald*

She frowned. Why was Gérald writing to her from a strange email address? Was this a joke? If it was, he'd picked the wrong time.

She clicked on the link.

Pictures in a jpg format.

The first was of an outdoor café. Patrons seated at round tables, on the pavement, with their backs to the window: she did not see any familiar faces. A slideshow had started and after two seconds a second photo replaced the first one. Christine swallowed. A siren began wailing in her mind, like a submarine that's made sonar contact. *Action stations, everyone to their station!* The second photograph showed Gérald and Denise sitting behind the window at the same café, face to face. *Torpedo approaching!* shouted the sonar operator in her brain, hysterically. The photographer had zoomed in on them. They were leaning towards each other, laughing as they looked into each other's eyes. The alarm was still sounding in her mind, and Christine hardly had time to let the impact of the image take effect before the slide-show sent the next torpedo. Their position had hardly changed, they were still just as close to each other, although the distance might still allow a certain doubt – and therefore hope – regarding their attitude and their intentions. *Except that now Denise's gloved hand was caressing Gérald's cheek.*

A wave of sheer hatred went through her. Even at this distance, with a telephoto lens, Denise's youth and beauty were dazzling. And Gérald seemed to be totally under her spell. He was devouring her with his eyes.

Her beloved fiancé. Her future husband.

She rubbed her face, held back the tears welling in her eyes. Who had taken these pictures, and why? Who had sent them? To what end?

'Christine. *Christine.*'

She realised Ilan was leaning over her, his eyes wide, and that he'd been calling to her for a moment already.

'They're waiting for you. For the debriefing!'

Fortunately, from where he was standing he couldn't see her screen. In the final photo, Denise was holding Gérald by the arm, as if he were that bitch's fiancé and not hers! And Denise was laughing, whispering something in his ear. Gérald was smiling, the smug, complacent smile of the guy who has the prettiest girl on his arm.

*Bloody bastard.*

She thrust her chair aside as she leapt up and ran off to the toilets, while her assistant watched, flabbergasted. She shoved open the door to the ladies' – so roughly that it bashed into the hand dryer on the wall. There was no one inside. She rushed into one of the stalls. She bent over the bowl, coughing. For a moment she thought she was going to throw up, but nothing came out. Just a hiccup and a spasm. She felt like crying but something inside her refused to. *She was terrified, too.* What was going on? Who was sending her these pictures, calling her on the phone? She didn't understand a thing. There was a vibration in her jeans: a text message. She took the phone out of her pocket and saw the little envelope flash to the top of the screen. She swiped her finger over it.

*You still feel like playing, Christine?*

She almost shattered her smartphone against the wall.

'FUCK OFF, YOU BLOODY IDIOT!'

She had screamed. Her voice reverberated through the empty space.

There was bound to be an automatic acknowledgement of receipt for the message. It was him again. The guy on the phone. The one who had pissed on her door. She thought about the message on her windscreen. '*Merry Christmas, you filthy bitch.*' Was that him, too? What did he want? Why was he hounding her? Because she hadn't reacted quickly enough after the letter? But how did he know that, too?

'Christine. Christine, what's going on?'

Cordélia's voice. She started and turned around. The tall intern was standing in front of her, eyes drowning in two black puddles of eyeshadow, staring at her worriedly.

Christine hadn't heard her come in. Cordélia put one hand on her arm, and with the other she stroked her cheek. Her expression was curious, tender, preoccupied.

'What's wrong? What's going on?'

Her voice was soft, calming. Christine could not suppress a sob, and at last the tears rolled down her cheeks.

'Tell me what's going on.'

Cordélia's perfume in her nostrils, her hair smelling of tobacco.

'You know you can trust me . . .'

Could she? Christine hesitated. She would have so liked to let go, to confide in someone.

Cordélia's arms encircled her, rocking her. It did her good, in spite of everything, to surrender. Then the young woman leaned closer and placed a kiss on her cheek.

'I'm here . . . I'm here.'

Another kiss – more tender this time – at the edge of her lips. Then the intern tilted her head to one side, her mouth seeking Christine's. And finding it. Christine froze, as if she had just put her fingers in a socket.

'Let me go!'

She gave the tall, angular figure a violent shove. Cordélia's back bashed against the wall of the toilet stall. On her face was a predatory smile. Any trace of tenderness had disappeared.

*Could she be the one who . . . ?*

But in that case, who was the man? Christine rushed out of the stall and hurried to the door. As it closed behind her she could hear the echo of Cordélia's laughter.

She went into the police station feeling as if she were up against a wall. A wall of anger and frustration. Of sadness. Of resignation. The queue went all the way from the security door to the counter; all the nearby seats were occupied. Some of the gazes she met were as hard as stone, others were lost, frantic; others still were more tired than used tissues. At the reception desk, an assistant security officer was trying to deal with the crowd.

'I have an appointment with Lieutenant Beaulieu,' she said, when her turn came.

The assistant security officer picked up her phone without looking at it, spoke briefly into the receiver, then motioned to the left with her chin. At no time did their eyes meet. Christine felt as if she were an insect.

She went through the turnstile and found herself by the lifts.

A few seconds later, the doors to one of the lifts opened and a man in civilian clothing came out.

'Christine Steinmeyer?'

He was in his thirties, brown eyes, thick curly hair and the lower half of his face somewhat soft: not the same policeman as last time. The only thing they had in common was their ugly ties.

'Lieutenant Beaulieu,' he said. 'Please come with me.'

He turned around and took out his magnetic badge, and they entered the lift. She felt his gaze on her as they went up, and eventually she looked at him. He did not stop staring at her even then. He seemed to think it was part of his prerogative to stare at people. He had bags under his eyes, and he looked like someone who is no longer as thrilled by his profession as he was at the beginning.

They got out on the second floor.

In an office cluttered with files, Lieutenant Beaulieu removed a stack of documents from a chair and invited her to sit down. The telephone rang. He gave a number of monosyllabic answers before slamming it down again.

'Excuse me,' he said.

But his tone was anything but contrite. He stared at her again without flinching, with his big protruding round eyes.

'Have you had any personal problems lately?' he asked point blank.

61

The question caught her unawares.

'What do you mean? I'm here regarding the letter I gave you, aren't I?'

'Precisely.'

'In that case, what does your question have to do with the letter?'

He studied her, with a sullen, suspicious look.

'What did you do on Christmas Day?' he asked. 'Were you on your own, or with family?'

'What? I was with my fiancé.'

As he said nothing, she thought it might be helpful to add, 'We had Christmas dinner at my parents'.'

She wriggled on her chair, wondering if she should mention the man on the telephone. And the urine on her doormat. But her little voice told her that for the time being it wouldn't be a good idea. Lieutenant Beaulieu did not seem very receptive. She wondered whether his colleague had told him about her profession but, in any case, she doubted whether that would have inclined him more favourably towards her.

'Fine,' he said. 'Let's talk about that letter. You found it on 24 December, Christmas Eve, in your mailbox. Is that correct?'

'Yes. We were meant to spend Christmas Eve with Gérald's parents. We were late. It was a bit . . . tense.'

'The letter was in an envelope?'

'Yes. Which I gave to your—'

'I know. And you have no idea who might have written it?'

'No. That's why we asked around, among the neighbours,' she explained. 'Because we figured the person must have got the wrong mailbox.'

'Okay, yes. And your fiancé, what does he think?'

She hesitated.

'He wasn't all that keen on the idea of questioning the residents on Christmas Eve.'

Lieutenant Beaulieu raised his eyebrows.

'He didn't want us to be even later,' she explained.

'Ah. And other than that, things are fine between you?'

'Yes, why?'

'No tension? Major arguments?'

'What does that have to do with the letter?'

'Please, just answer.'

62

'I just told you: everything is fine. We're getting married soon.'

'Oh!' He gave a faint smile, lacking in conviction. 'Congratulations. When?'

She hesitated; she was beginning to get the unpleasant feeling that he was trying to trap her, but why would he do that?

'We haven't quite agreed, um, on the date,' she acknowledged.

Beaulieu's eyes opened slightly. He nodded absently, as if two people with diametrically opposed opinions were arguing in his head. She was immediately sorry she had confessed this to a stranger who, clearly, was in danger of misinterpreting it.

'Look,' he said, massaging his eyelids between his thumb and forefinger, 'don't take this badly but . . . not a single suicide has been reported for the twenty-fourth, or the following day, or even – fingers crossed – today. Which we obviously should be pleased to hear. And that is a miracle in itself, believe me.'

She felt a deep sense of relief. Since nothing had happened, she was not guilty in any way, in the end. And the man harassing her had no reason to make her feel guilty.

'But do you have any way to find out who that person was?' she asked, insisting all the same. 'Just because she hasn't gone through with it yet . . . well, to me the threat does seem serious, don't you think?'

'Hmm. Is that what you think?'

'Yes. And you don't? Well, I don't know, I'm not a psychologist,' she said, blushing under the intensity of his gaze. 'But from the way the letter is written, I don't think it's just pure fantasy.'

The cop's expression suddenly grew alert and he seemed to emerge from his apathy.

'What makes you think it could be fantasy? The fact you even entertain the idea – that says a lot, don't you think? How did this idea occur to you?'

She fingered the collar of her blouse, and stiffened.

'Well . . . I don't know, you never know.'

'You think that someone might have written a fake letter and then put it in your mailbox? Why would they do that, in your opinion? Isn't that a rather . . . *strange* idea?'

She frowned slightly. She had just noticed something in his voice that hadn't been there before.

'Yes . . . maybe. I – I don't know. I've tried to imagine every possible explanation.'

'In that case, wouldn't it be far more logical to imagine that the letter was written by someone who wants to attract attention?'

'Yes, of course. But the two explanations don't rule each other out.'

'Someone who is seeking, unconsciously or not, to make others talk about him – or her – to draw attention to their situation, their distress . . .'

Christine grew even more puzzled. The cop was not talking off the top of his head, she now realised. He was drawing ever smaller concentric circles around the true aim of the conversation – the one he himself had determined right from the start.

'I'm sorry,' he said, leaning forward, looking at her from under his brows, 'but there are no fingerprints on the letter or the envelope other than your own. What sort of printer do you have?'

'What?! What do you mean? You're not implying that—'

'Is it your fiancé who wants to delay the date of your marriage, Miss Steinmeyer? Has he said that he would like to take a break? That he is having second thoughts? Has he ever mentioned . . . splitting up?'

She couldn't believe her ears.

'Absolutely not!'

He raised his voice. 'Have you ever been treated for psychiatric problems? Don't lie. You know it's very easy for me to find out.'

She felt as if the ground beneath her feet were slipping away. Right from the start this was where he had been headed. This moron thought she was the author. He thought she was making things up, that she was out of her mind!

'Are you insinuating that I wrote that letter myself before I brought it to you?' she asked, incredulous.

'Because isn't that what you did? Do you have something to say on the subject?'

'Go fuck yourself,' she answered, pushing her chair back and getting to her feet.

'What? What did you say?' She saw him sit up straight and turn red in the face. 'I could have you prosecuted for insulting behaviour—'

'See me to the door,' she interrupted. 'We have nothing more to say to each other.'

'As you wish.'

# 8

# Melodrama

Servaz went through the emblazoned doors of the Grand Hôtel Thomas Wilson at one o'clock. He crossed the lobby towards the reception, from one carpet to the next, surrounded by leather, wood-work, more woodwork, more leather, and placed the electronic key on the counter. He took out his warrant card.

'This is one of your electronic keys.'

It wasn't really a question. The young receptionist looked at both the key and the speaker. He took note of the open collar of her white blouse and the lace on her bra. Then she checked the computer.

'Yes. But the key must have been deactivated, as I see that someone was staying in room 117 this morning. Where did you find it?'

'Do they often disappear?'

She made a face.

'It happens. They get lost, stolen. Or the guest forgets to turn in the key before taking his plane back to China.'

'Is room 117 booked today?'

She looked again at her screen.

'Yes.'

'Under what name?'

'I don't know whether I can—'

'It's Servaz, isn't it?'

She nodded. She was quite pretty, as it happened.

'When was the reservation made?'

'Three days ago. On the hotel website.'

He looked at her the way a junkie looks at a dealer.

'Do you have an email address? A credit card number?'

'Both. And a telephone number as well.'

'Can you print that out for me? Now, right away?'

'Um . . . Perhaps I should speak to the manager, first.'

He watched as she picked up the telephone, and they waited. The hotel manager appeared two minutes later. He was tall, with round glasses. He shook the policeman's hand ceremoniously.

'What is the matter?'

Servaz considered the situation. He was on sick leave. He did not have the right to be there asking questions, let alone a warrant.

'An investigation for the Criminal Affairs Division,' he lied. 'Identity theft. Someone booked a room in this hotel in the name of another person without informing them. And they have committed several criminal acts in his name and with his credit card. I asked your employee to print out a copy of the reservation.'

'Hmm. I see. No problem. We'll get that for you.'

He turned to the employee. 'Marjorie . . .'

Marjorie sent the document to the little printer beneath the counter, bent down to take the sheet of paper and handed it to them. The manager glanced at it briefly before giving it to Servaz. Not without a faint frown, which Servaz duly noted.

'Um . . . there you are.'

'Thank you. This room 117,' said Servaz suddenly, 'is there anything special about it?'

The young receptionist and the manager looked at each other. Their silent exchange set off his inner alarm.

'Well, that is,' said the manager after clearing his voice, 'there was, um, indeed something that happened a year ago.'

He wiped his hand over his face, then over his curly hair.

'A woman committed suicide.'

His voice went strangely shrill and there was a tremor in it, as if he had a cold. Followed by a murmur not unlike a rustling of leaves.

'It was horrible. Terrible. She . . . she . . . Well, let's just say that first she, um, broke all the mirrors in the bathroom . . . and in the room . . . And then, and then, she slit her wrists and she, um, tried in vain to, to . . .' His voice was now so faint that Servaz had to lean closer. 'She tried to cut open her stomach with a piece of mirror then, because she couldn't do it fast enough, she slit her own throat.'

He looked around to make sure the businessmen sitting in the armchairs a bit further away had not heard the story. Servaz felt as if two large veins were throbbing in his temples. He saw his dream again: Marianne, naked and disembowelled in that hut. It made his head spin. Fear was pounding under the skin of his brow: the icy, familiar voice of terror.

'May I see the room?'

It seemed to him that his own voice was no longer so firm and confident. The manager nodded. Servaz held out his hand and the receptionist placed a plastic card in it, identical to the one Servaz had received.

'Come with me.'

In the lift, their reflections in the mirror watched them, like frightening clones. Servaz could see the moisture at the roots of the manager's auburn hair in the overhead light. The only sound was the manager's uneasy breathing. The doors opened onto a carpeted corridor.

'This is a platinum room,' said the manager, walking down the silent corridor. 'Thirty-two square metres, king-size bed, an LCD screen, fifty channels, minibar, safe, coffee machine, bathrobe, slippers, free broadband and WiFi, and a bath big enough for two.'

Servaz thought to himself that the man was reciting the inventory in order to cling to something reassuring and familiar. He must not come to room 117 very often. He must leave it to the cleaning women and the hotel porters. Was he the one who had found the body?

'Do you remember her name?'

'It's not the sort of thing you forget, unfortunately. Célia Jablonka. An artist.'

Servaz had already heard the name. Or read it. He seemed to remember articles in the newspapers, a year ago. Suicides were not the responsibility of the crime division, but of Public Safety. However, the manner in which the young woman had killed herself, and her profession, meant that people had talked about her at the time.

The manager stood still.

There was a click inside the door of room 117 when he ran the key card over the gilded lock. In the room there was the same smell of floral perfume, cleaning products and fresh linen as in every luxury hotel. A little hallway with a luggage rack and two white bathrobes on hangers. The door to the bathroom was slightly open. *And here's the bedroom* . . . The silver-coloured headboard was made of large padded diamond shapes, and reached all the way to the ceiling; bright red pillows, a grey laminated floor, ebony walls and little chrome lamps, whose light traced a pattern against the gloom.

Very kitsch.

It was like being inside a box of chocolates with a double layer of pralines separated by silver paper.

Silence. Except for the manager's laboured breathing behind his back. The double glazing muffled the noise from the circular piazza below, and the walls were thick – in proportion, no doubt, with the price of the rooms. Servaz peered out through the blinds, between the thick curtains, at the white swirl of snowflakes.

'Show me. Which mirrors she broke. Where she was found. How she went about it. What she did.'

The manager was wheezing. 'Yes.'

He walked over to the door, pressed a switch and the bathroom lit up. Servaz slipped inside. A bubble of light. A double washbasin with waterfall taps, a basket full of shampoo and little soaps, clean towels carefully folded, a large mirror: in the blaze of light the two men looked dazed, stupid.

'This mirror,' said the manager. 'There were pieces of glass everywhere, and blood. It was . . . awful. The basins, the floor, the walls: everything was splattered with blood. It was unbearable to see. But that's not where we found her.'

He went back out into the room.

'We found her lying on the bed, her arms outstretched.'

The manager sounded like a diver preparing to dive, holding his breath.

'Naked,' he added.

Servaz didn't say anything. A wind from Poland was sweeping through his brain. The howling of wolves. Blood on the snow. A hut in the night. He gulped. Felt his knees shaking. *He wasn't ready*. It was too soon.

'Who found her? Was it you?'

The manager could tell from his voice that he was upset. He shot him a look of surprise. Surprise, no doubt, at the fact that a cop from the Criminal Division could be this emotional. For a brief moment their eyes met; a horn sounded outside.

'No. It was the hotel porter. The door to the room was open and music was blaring. We could hear it all the way down the corridor. He thought it was strange, so he pushed open the door and called out. No answer. And that music, blasting, it was, it was *opera* . . .'

He said the word as if it were something insane.

68

'Opera?'

'Yes. We found the CD case on the bed next to her. Wagner's *Flying Dutchman*. The opera where Senta, a young woman, jumps off the top of a cliff. Committing suicide,' he added, in case the cop hadn't understood. (In his opinion, all cops must be thick, like in films.)

Another thought occurred to Servaz. Music, here. Music in that psychiatric institute, up in the mountains, four years ago. He could feel a vice tightening around his heart.

'The poor boy, he went closer. First he saw her feet.'

The manager's speech was more and more halting. As if his words were keeping pace with the hotel porter's steps.

'Then her legs, her lower body . . . It was the wound to her stomach that caught his attention. She'd really gone at it, cut it several times over: it was a mess, but she hadn't managed to damage any vital organs. Then as he got closer, he saw her slit wrists and, finally, her throat . . . a shard of glass had stayed in her neck . . . the blood had splattered everywhere, on the bed, the walls, the floor. The headboard had to be changed; it was irreparable. According to the doctors, she initially tried to perform hara-kiri by ramming a glass triangle into her abdomen, and when she didn't succeed she finally cut her throat.'

Servaz stared at the empty bed. Trying to reconstruct the scene, what the hotel porter had found. The ugly wounds to her stomach, her wrists, her throat. The jagged piece of mirror planted in her flesh. The opera pounding in her eardrums. Her dead gaze, her open mouth.

'Does the porter still work for you?'

'No, he resigned. In fact, he didn't come back the next day. We never saw him again. But of course we weren't about to sack him . . . given the circumstances. He emailed his resignation a few weeks later.'

'What about you, did you see her?'

A hesitation.

'Yes . . . yes; I saw her. The porter came to get me.'

He obviously didn't want to say anything more. Servaz could understand why. And in any case, he could get the details elsewhere.

'I don't see any CD or MP3 player,' he said.

'She had brought it with her. There are music channels and radio stations on the television, but there's no player.'

'So you're saying that she came with her own? Just so that music would be playing when she took her life?'

'I suppose she wanted to die to it,' said the manager, in the sort of tone a cop might have used. 'And she knew she wouldn't find that sort of thing in a hotel. Who knows what was going through her head at the time.'

'In that case, why not commit suicide at home?'

The manager looked at him as if to say, *You're the police, not me.* 'No idea.'

'Do you remember how long she'd been here?'

'She'd arrived that day.'

*A deliberate decision.* There must be something significant about the hotel. According to Célia Jablonka's staging of the event, it was important. As was the opera. Did the people from Public Safety pick up on these details? Or had they merely wound up the case in no time at all? And who had been in charge of the autopsy? Servaz hoped it was Delmas: he might be irascible but he was very professional. *The way I used to be, too, before . . .*

Finally, the two most important questions: who had sent him this key one year later? And why?

# 9

# Intermission

The leaf came loose from the branch, fluttered for a moment in front of him, inscribing invisible arabesques, and finally fell just by the tip of his shoes in the dirty snow on the pavement. How had it managed to cling on until then on the bare tree, when all the other leaves had fallen long before? His cigarette trembled in similar fashion between his lips, and he had a sudden overwhelming vision of his own fragility, his own struggle. His soul, would it see in the spring?

He took the cigarette from his lips, hardly smoked, and with a shrug of his shoulders crushed it with his heel next to the shrivelled leaf. A little ritual on the part of the repentant smoker. *Eight months.* Before crossing the cobblestones to seek refuge in the warmth of the entrance hall, he took out his mobile and rang Delmas.

'An artist named Célia Jablonka who committed suicide last year in a room at the Grand Hôtel Thomas Wilson: does that ring a bell?'

'Hmm.'

'Does that mean yes or no?'

'Yes. I'm the one who performed the autopsy.'

Servaz smiled.

'Suicide or not suicide?'

'Suicide.'

'Are you sure?'

'Am I in the habit of talking through my hat?' said the pathologist, defensively.

Servaz's smile widened.

'No,' he conceded.

'There could not be the slightest doubt.'

'And yet,' he insisted, 'you have to admit that that business with the opera and the way she cut her throat with a piece of mirror . . .'

'Listen. Incredible as it might seem, that girl did it herself. And no one helped her. Full stop. You have no idea what people can inflict upon themselves. The kind of wound, the absence of any marks on her wrists: if someone had wanted to force her to cut her throat, she would have struggled, believe me; the toxicological tests, the projections and splashes, the wounds before death to the right hand . . . I can't remember the details but everything matched up, there were no grey areas. It was all clear and precise.'

'What was found in the toxicological analysis, do you remember?'

'Yup. She had taken a sleeping tablet roughly fifteen hours earlier, and there were also enough antidepressants and tranquillisers in her blood to knock out an elephant. But no drugs: that I remember because, given the ferocity of her attack on herself, I initially thought she must have taken something hallucinogenic, then I suspected decompensation because of the benzodiazepines. No doubt with prior thoughts of suicide. Are you back at work?'

'Uh . . .'

'That means no, I suppose. With all due respect, allow me to point out that one, the case was closed ages ago and two, you are on sick leave and as such, I am not supposed to be sharing details like this with you. Why the sudden interest in that poor girl? Did you know her?'

'Not until an hour ago.'

'Right, I see. If you don't want to tell me, don't tell me. But when the time comes, I really would like to know why you've taken this sudden interest in her. And exactly what the hell you're up to, Martin.'

'Later. Thanks.'

'Take care of yourself. Do you really think you're ready?'

Ready? Ready for what? he wondered. All he was doing was gathering information.

'Listen,' he said, 'this conversation never took place.'

Silence.

'What conversation?'

He hung up. So the girl had committed suicide. There was no slipping past Delmas. In that case, why had the key been sent to him, a cop in the Criminal Division? Suicides were not his remit. And why did they choose *him*, when he was on leave, put out to pasture, supposedly treating his *mal-être* in a rest home, as useless as a boxer who hasn't trained in months? He took the rectangular key from his pocket and stared at it: the logo and the letters 'T' and 'W', and the paper with its message in blue ink:

*Meeting tomorrow in room 117.*

# 10

# Soprano

Christine watched as the young man busied himself with her door, his toolbox open next to him. He had already replaced the old cylinder lock with a three-point one, and installed a safety chain, and now he was drilling through the door to install a spyhole. He had explained that the ideal thing would be to replace the old door with a steel bulletproof one, with joints integrated into the doorframe and soldered hinge guards, but despite everything, she had no intention of turning her flat into an impregnable fortress.

The phone rang behind her and Christine instantly froze. She could feel the goosebumps on her skin and anything resembling a coherent thought vanished. The young locksmith was staring at her. No doubt he noticed the sudden change in her expression. She headed reluctantly to the phone on the kitchen counter. It kept on ringing, piercing the silence. She reached for the receiver as if it were a venomous snake.

'Hello?'

'Christine?'

A woman's voice, familiar.

'It's Denise.'

A huge wave of relief went through her chest. Then instantly, a question: why was Denise calling her here? She suddenly remembered the pictures on her computer: their tête-à-tête through the window of the café – and a wave of anger mingled with concern created a knot in her stomach.

'Denise? What's going on?'

'Christine, I have to see you.'

Her voice made Christine think of that elastic she used to play with when she was a little girl, stretching it all the way to the point of breaking.

74

'What's it about? Is it so urgent?'

'Yes. I think it is.'

There was a touch of authority in Denise's voice. And hostility as well. Christine immediately felt on her guard. Something had happened. Her nerves jangled.

'What's the matter? Can't you tell me what this is about?'

'You know very well what it's about.'

This time, it was more than authority. It was an accusation. There was anger, defiance. Did she want to speak to her about Gérald and herself?

'I want to see you, *now.*'

Christine felt herself go hard inside: who did this bitch think she was?

'Listen, I honestly don't know what you're talking about. But I really don't like your tone of voice. So let me put it this way: I've had a rough day and I intend to speak to Gérald – about you, about him, and about me.'

There, she'd said it. She waited for a reaction.

'In half an hour, at the Wallace on place Saint-Georges. I think you ought to be there.'

Good God! Not only was this idiot giving her orders, she had even hung up on her!

The Wallace Café was noisy and crowded when Christine walked in. It had a lounge décor, with fake stone walls lit from underneath, little square armchairs, and a bar with blue light like an aquarium. Eighty per cent of the customers were students. The music was a typical indie rock compilation: Asaf Avidan, Local Natives, Wave Machines.

'Hi,' she said, narrowing her eyes as she sat down.

Looking down at her glass, Denise seemed more nervous than she had on the phone. She made a great show of stirring her cocktail with the fluorescent stick before slowly raising her lovely green eyes. *Caipirinha* . . . It's a little early for alcohol, thought Christine. Perhaps the young PhD student needed some Dutch courage. But why?

'You see,' she said, 'I came, as you asked. So why do you want to see me? Why that tone on the telephone? Why all the mystery?'

Denise looked around the room before settling her gaze on Christine, apparently reluctantly.

'Yesterday, you – uh – saw us together at the Institute, Gérald and me, in his office.'

Christine felt her stomach contract even further.

'You almost said *caught*,' she noted coldly.

'Caught, saw: it doesn't matter.' The hostile tone was there again. 'It's not what you think. Not at all. We were there for work. Gérald as much as me. As it happens, he is my thesis advisor and—'

'Thank you, I know that.'

'—and it's not just about my thesis. It goes further than that. You have to understand that we are working on a very ambitious project: we are going to propose a new approach for the acquisition of GNSS signals, that is, in the domain of satellite navigation. Until now, we have had the American GPS, the Russian GLONASS and the Chinese BeiDou. Since 2005 the European Union has launched four satellites and the Galileo system should soon be operational. The method we are using enables us to increase the frequency resolution of the Fourier transform without an excessive increase of the design load within the positioning sensor.' She gave an apologetic wave. 'I know, I know – it sounds like gibberish, and I'm not trying to drown you in scientific jargon, but we are on the verge of producing a very important article, so important that it could earn us the prize at the ION GNSS conference, the biggest and most prestigious international conference in the domain of satellite navigation.'

Her voice was beginning to betray a certain nervousness.

'I know that, viewed from the outside, it seems terribly boring. But in fact it's a fascinating area, and Gérald and I love our work, the research we are doing. Gérald had the idea for this study, and he's a terrific thesis advisor.'

She paused.

'That's why we couldn't care less whether it's Christmas Day or not. I suddenly had an idea, and when I spoke to him on the phone, he got very excited and told me to meet him at the Institute at once.'

'Uh-huh.'

Christine understood the hidden meaning behind her gush of words. *Stop imagining things, girl: you can't understand, because you're not intelligent enough, not clever enough, and you didn't go far enough with your studies. Your future husband and I share this world, and you will never have access to it. You may as well get used to the idea right away, sweetheart.*

Denise looked at her again, and all her nervousness and concern were gone: her gaze was merely accusing.

'But you're imagining things, Christine. Because I'm pretty, because Gérald values my work, and because we get along well. So I don't know what you've gone and got in your head, but . . .'

Christine really didn't like the way Denise formulated those last words. Her allusion to the intellectual compatibility and complicity that existed between her and Christine's future husband. Christine wondered if Gérald ever compared the two of them. At the same time, she felt relieved. She had been afraid of something else on coming here. What, exactly? A bad surprise like the medication found in her desk drawer? The revelation that Gérald and Denise really were having an affair? She couldn't put her finger on it – she had simply had a terrible premonition on hearing Denise's voice on the telephone.

'Denise,' she said. 'Everything is fine. I'm not imagining things, I promise you. I know how much Gérald loves his profession – and how he values your work. It really isn't a problem.'

*Really? Are you sure?*

'Well then, can you explain this to me,' came Denise's icy voice from the far side of the table.

Christine froze. Denise pushed a printed sheet of paper across the table.

'Hello!' said the waiter with professional enthusiasm. 'Would you like something to drink?'

'What is this?' asked Christine.

'You really don't know?' hissed Denise in the same voice, trembling with anger.

The waiter beat a hasty retreat. Christine leaned over. An email. She skipped the heading to read the text.

*Dear Denise, if you think I haven't figured out what you're up to . . .*
*keep your hands off my guy. Take my advice.*
*Signed: Chris, showing her claws*

She felt as if the table and the entire room had begun to spin. *It can't be . . . this can't be happening . . .*

She read the email again. Close your eyes. Open them. She was gobsmacked: none of this could be real.

'I didn't write this.'

'Oh, come on, Christine, please. Who, apart from you or I, could know that Gérald says that about you when you're angry?'

'What?' She shook her head. 'Are you saying that this is some nickname Gérald has for me?'

Denise was looking at her, her expression wavering between impatience and scorn.

'As if you didn't know.'

'Denise, I don't know what is going on, I swear. I didn't send this! When did you get it?'

Silence.

'Last night.'

It was *him*. Who else? But how could he know all this about her?

'Christine,' said Denise, in the tone of a professor speaking to a particularly obtuse student, 'the email has your address in the heading. This message came from your computer. And that signature . . . that's already pretty damning, don't you think?'

'Have you told Gérald about it?'

A cautious look from across the table.

'Not yet.'

'Please, don't say anything.'

'So you admit you wrote it?'

She hesitated. She could deny it. She *had to* deny it. She could tell her about the urine on the doormat and the incident on her radio programme and her visit to the police and the message on her windscreen . . . And then what? She knew precisely what sort of impression it would leave: that she was suffering from rampant paranoid psychosis. She could just imagine Denise gushing to her friends: *The poor woman is a complete nutcase – certifiable, if you want my opinion. I don't know what Gérald sees in her.*

'Yes,' she confessed.

Denise looked at her, her face full of consternation. Christine felt undressed, judged and convicted – all in the blink of an eye. Denise nodded. Her face was inscrutable.

Then she shook herself and Christine could guess what she was thinking: *Aren't I the lucky one, fuck, to be sitting here with this nutcase.*

'I really like Gérald,' said Denise quietly.

There was so much conviction in her words that Christine wondered if she ought to change two of the letters in the word 'like'.

'No, really, I like him a great deal. He's a good person – and a fantastic boss. Let me stress: there is nothing between Gérald and me. But I do like him a lot, it's true.'

*Enough, you already said that, I understand. Let's talk about something else.*

'And I wonder if . . .'

'If what?'

'If you really are the right person for him.'

Christine felt as if she'd been slapped.

'What did you say?'

'In any case,' continued Denise as if she hadn't heard, 'even if there had been something between us, that's no way for you to behave. You should see a shrink.'

Christine was staring at Denise now, not moving a muscle, as if someone had pressed pause. Several seconds went by before she began to speak.

'How dare you?'

She spoke loudly. The male students at the next table turned their heads, aware that something interesting was going on between the two good-looking girls at the table behind them.

'*How dare you speak to me like that?*'

Heads turned. Denise backed down:

'I'm sorry; it's none of my business, after all. You're right.' The young woman raised her hands in a sign of surrender. 'Gérald is old enough to know what he wants to do with his life.'

*Too late, sweetheart.* Christine felt her good old anger was back. And it was out of the question to try to contain it.

'Indeed, it's none of your *fucking* business. And it's true – since the moment has come to lay our cards on the table – that I find you just a little bit overzealous for a PhD *student*.' She stressed the word. 'A little bit too – how should I put it? – familiar, if you know what I mean?'

She stared at her for a long time. Denise seemed too stunned to reply.

'So, yes, I'm going to give you some advice: from now on mind your own business, and focus on your thesis. Just your fucking thesis. Before I go and ask him to give up being your supervisor.'

She got to her feet.

'Stay away from my man.'

★

79

On her way out, Christine walked past a man sitting at the table next to them, less than a yard away. The man folded his newspaper and took a sip of his beer. He watched her leave. His eyes were expressionless, like two black pebbles.

He was small, really very small. Five foot four. A height, for a man, that is likely to inspire a good number of jibes, half-smiles and condescending looks. He was well proportioned, with a muscular body and a slim waist, but his head didn't help. It was almost feminine, with a delicate nose, thick lips, high cheekbones and an effeminate cast to the rest of his face. Moreover, he had almost no eyebrows and, conversely, long pale blonde eyelashes. Even his head, which was completely shaved, made one think of a young woman's perfect head. The only thing that wasn't feminine about him was his gaze: big, dull, empty eyes, like two windows open onto a void. Not particularly hostile or piercing, just *empty*.

He was wearing a khaki parka over a black hoodie and a grey T-shirt, and were it not for his diminutive size and effeminate face, he would not have looked any different from the students around him; apart from his age, perhaps: he was several years older.

He watched Christine go out the door. With his dull eyes he examined her hips, her back, her buttocks, every curve and contour of her body. Satisfied with his examination, he took another sip of his cool beer and noted that none of the men in the café had followed his example: they were all trying not to get involved in other people's business. He reflected that most people were stunningly naïve, like angels or eunuchs: they knew nothing about the individuals they spent their days with, they knew nothing about real suffering, or torture, or agony, or the varying degrees of hell that exist in the world; they knew nothing, he thought, of the tears that are as impossible to stem as the sap pouring from trees, and a smile spread across his feminine mouth. They knew nothing about the moment when the brain rips apart and is left in fragments under the effect of pain . . . nothing about the slow drip of time in the depths of a cave smelling of sweat and piss and shit . . . nothing about people who, their shirts stained with blood and vomit, suddenly understand – too late – that hell does exist here on earth, that we walk by its gates every day, that we pass its servants in the street or on the Métro, and we don't see them.

He recalled some lines by a poet from his country:

*And the cold water grows blacker*
*Death grows purer, misfortune saltier*
*And the earth more terrible and truthful.*

He turned his attention back to the second young woman.

The one who was hellishly pretty and, at the moment, terribly pale. She was biting her lower lip and staring into space.

She had just got to her feet. She looked very angry.

Perfect; it had all gone according to plan. Almost too predictably for his liking. He let her leave – she was not his target.

His target was the first woman who had gone out. The one who had raised her voice, attracting the other customers' attention. *Christine Steinmeyer*. That was the name he had been given. With the address and a host of details.

Furtively, his fingers squeezed his hard penis through his corduroy trousers. Just thinking about Christine Steinmeyer – and what he was going to put her through in the days ahead – set his nerves on edge. She had no idea what was coming.

And to think he was getting paid for this: in every era, under every regime, there was work for people like him. Gifted, zealous practitioners. Experts in confession. He was capable of wresting the truth from anyone, about anything, under any circumstance.

The little man finished his beer. No one was paying him the slightest attention. People weren't curious in this country. They spent so much time staring at the screen of their tablet or their smartphone and avoiding other people's gazes that they became like zombies. And yet there were a few details that might have aroused someone's attention. For a start, the scar that left a pale furrow beneath his chin. Then there were the tattoos. The first one, emerging above the right side of his collar, was only partly visible, but it looked like the face of a sad Madonna of the kind one sees on Russian icons. Without his clothes, more would be visible: from his neck to his chest, where his missing nipple had been replaced by a scar, a virgin with child – and innumerable other designs: Orthodox domes, stars, skulls. Each one had a specific meaning. The Virgin with child, for example: the child meant that he had been to prison very young; the Madonna symbolised loyalty to his clan; each point of a star was for a jail term; the stars on his knees meant he would never kneel before anyone.

The backs of his hands and his fingers were similarly covered with images.

His illuminated hand reached for the gold pen next to the newspaper, which he opened again. He found an empty space and made a quick drawing. A fairly accurate portrait of a woman in her thirties. Then he drew a crown of barbed wire around the woman's brow, and underneath it he wrote:

*Chris, showing her claws*

He folded the newspaper over the drawing and left it on the table when he went out.

# 11

# Crescendo

The next day, Servaz got up before everyone else. When he went down to the dining room, it was deserted. Seven a.m. Most of the boarders had difficulty sleeping so they caught up in the early morning.

Servaz poured himself a bowl of coffee, took a little capsule of cream and went to sit at one of the tables. He liked being alone. He liked the silence; he was fed up with people's tirades. All these worn-out cops, battered by their chaotic lives, their traumatic experiences: all of them, or almost all of them, revelled in their memories of the past. Since coming here Servaz had felt as if he were constantly bathing in a warm pool of nostalgia.

'Would you like a hot croissant?'

He turned his head. Élise was standing by the door to the kitchen. Servaz smiled at her. She came up to him and his mouth watered at the smell of the croissant, which she set down in front of him. She sat down across the table.

'Already up?'

'I have something to do in town,' he replied, taking a large bite from the croissant with its rich buttery taste.

She looked at him, puzzled.

'Say that again. I must have misheard.'

He scraped the windscreen, poured hot water on it, and put the heating on full. Once he was behind the wheel he pulled slowly out of the car park. No salt spreaders had been this way, and the fierce wind blew the snow from the fields whirling onto the road. He drove across the white plain until he reached the A66, then took the A61 to approach Toulouse from the east. While he drove, he thought about Hirtmann. The prosecutor from Geneva. The man who haunted his dreams. The man who had abducted Marianne. In moments of lucidity he told himself he would never hear anything about him again, that Hirtmann had surely died in some seamy street in Latin America or Asia. And all he could do now was forget him. Or at least pretend to.

He was up to the challenge during daylight, but as soon as evening drew near, and the light receded from the furthest rooms in his head, he felt once again as if he were trapped in the lugubrious vice of his thoughts, and his soul cried out in fear. In the old days when he'd been investigating a particularly horrible crime, he would go home and listen to his beloved Mahler, the only antidote for the shadows, and things would shift back into place. But Hirtmann had stolen even that sanctuary from him: the Swiss man was also an admirer of the Austrian genius. A strange similarity which right from the start had underlined their dangerous spiritual proximity, back in that cell at the Institut Wargnier, the music soaring. He recalled Hirtmann: tall and thin in his overalls, his collar open onto his translucent skin, and above all the shock of that unflinching electric gaze – a shock as if from a taser. Then there was the way, too, that in a split second Julian Hirtmann had seen straight through him. Had deciphered him. Servaz had rarely felt that naked in the presence of another person.

He had received a postcard from Irène Ziegler from New Delhi, where she'd been sent. The gendarme was now Attaché for Interior Security at the Department for International Cooperation, a network of 250 police officers and gendarmes deployed in 93 embassies, and whose mission was to investigate various potential threats – terrorism, cyber crime, drug trafficking – that might be organised beyond the borders of France. There were only two sentences on her postcard: *Do you still think about him? I do.*

He sometimes wondered whether Ziegler had applied for that position with the secret hope of one day picking up Hirtmann's trail.

Once Servaz was in town, he headed for the Grand-Rond, then the Capitole. The streets were covered in snow: you could barely tell the pavement from the road, and the vehicles' roofs wore thick white duvets. He left the car in the underground car park and walked across the place du Capitole; he needed another coffee. He drank two in a brasserie opposite the Hôtel de Ville while waiting for his appointment.

He set off again at nine thirty, slipping in the slush of ice and mud, which was transforming the square into a skating rink. He had never seen such a winter sports atmosphere in Toulouse. Fortunately, Charlène Espérandieu's art gallery was not far away, on the corner of rue de la Pomme and Saint-Pantaléon.

The glass doors opened with a whoosh before him and his soles left damp prints on the pale parquet floor. There was no one there. The walls, lit by spotlights, were bare, and large cardboard boxes, most probably containing the artwork for the next exhibition, were scattered across the floor.

Servaz headed towards the rear where a narrow spiral staircase led to the mezzanine.

The sound of heels on the floor above.

The metal steps vibrated with his weight. His head emerged first, at floor level – and he saw a pair of high-heeled burgundy boots, slim legs in jeans, then the grey parka she had not yet removed, and finally the cascade of ginger hair gathered asymmetrically to one side of her face.

'Martin?'

She was almost forty, but looked ten years younger.

'What are you doing here?'

'Oh, I'm getting into contemporary art.'

She smiled.

'You look well,' she said as he emerged from the staircase. 'Much better than last time I saw you, in that sinister place. You looked like a zombie.'

'Back from the dead,' he confirmed.

'Really well,' she said again, as if she were trying to convince herself.

'*Non venit ad duros pallida cura toros*: "pale concern does not approach hard beds".'

'You and your Latin authors. This is—'

Charlène kissed him and her fingers pressed his arm fervently.

'— really good news.'

Her cheek, still cold, lingered a moment too long against his own. He was wrapped in the scent of her hair and a light perfume. Then she stepped back. The cold air had made her cheeks red and her eyes were shining. She was still just as confoundedly beautiful.

'Have you come home or are you still staying there?' she asked.

'I'm fed, housed and watered – it's not so bad,' he replied.

'I'm glad. Glad to see you, Martin. Glad to see you like this. But you haven't come just to visit me, have you?'

'No.'

She hung her parka on the coat rack, turned on her heels and went over to her desk at the far end of the long room, in front of the upper part of the round arch opening that also served as the entrance to the gallery below.

'Does the name Célia Jablonka mean anything to you?'

She turned her head, still with her back to him, giving him a view of her profile and her slender neck emerging from the mass of curly red hair.

'The artist who committed suicide last year? Yes. She had a show here not long before.'

This time she spun around to face him and leaned on the desk. She gave him a piercing look.

'Aren't you fed up with being interested only in dead people?'

He decided to conclude that the double meaning was not intentional. That she was talking about his profession, and nothing else. Nevertheless, for a split second, his pain returned.

*He wasn't ready.*

He had thought that when he left the rest home he would leave his anxiety behind, but fatigue, doubt, and weariness were dogging him.

'Tell me about her,' he said. 'What sort of person was she? Did she seem depressive?'

Charlène gave him a curious glance.

'She was a funny woman, cheeky. With heaps of talent.'

She turned to a low bookshelf, virtually the only piece of furniture in the immense room other than the little seating area and her desk, and pulled out a voluminous, glossy catalogue.

'Here, have a look.'

He went closer. And read, 'Célia Jablonka or Absent Art.' She opened the cover and began to turn the pages. Photographs of homeless people. African families living five to a room of ten square metres. A man who had died from the cold being taken away by the emergency services. A stray dog. A filthy child rummaging in a skip. Another one begging in the Métro. And, alternately, supermarket shelves spilling with food, high-tech gadgets, toys, clothing on sale, shiny brand-new cars, people queuing outside multiplexes, crowded fast food chains, piles of video games in shop windows, rows of petrol pumps, overflowing dustbins, tips, incinerators . . . The message was clear, direct and basic; there was no need to think.

'She refused any sort of sophistication or subtlety. She categorically refused to let her art take on any aesthetic or cathartic function. It was the opposite effect she hoped to produce. The message. Unfiltered.'

Servaz pulled a face. He hadn't come to listen to considerations about art. And his favourite style was international Gothic.

'Where were these pictures taken?'

'In the street. And in a squat. Part of the exhibition was held there. Célia wanted the visitors to do more than just look, she wanted them to *enter* into the photographs, was how she put it. So there was a sound device inviting them to continue their visit at the squat, where they would see the remainder of the exhibition. Célia had stuck little posters all along the route to make it easier for them.'

'And did it work?'

It was Charlène's turn to pull a face.

'Not really. A few brave souls went all the way to the end, but the clients from my gallery are not, well, not exactly the kind of people who are into soup kitchens.'

Servaz nodded.

'I don't know if I'm the best person to talk about her,' she said apologetically. 'I didn't know her very well. But while the exhibition was on, at any rate, we talked quite a bit, and it seemed to me that her mood became darker as the days went by, that all the joy and enthusiasm from the beginning were progressively disappearing. Towards the end she seemed to have lost all her joie de vivre – and that's why, well, her suicide didn't really come as a surprise to me.'

Servaz was suddenly on his guard. This information alone should have reinforced the theory of suicide. And yet there was something not quite right about it. Or was he imagining things? Was he looking for something to cling to at any price – and what better opportunity for an investigator that an investigation that had missed the most important thing? There was nothing to substantiate this hypothesis. Except the hotel key.

'You said you noticed a change in her over the course of your relationship?'

'Yes.'

87

'How long did it last?'

'We met for the first time roughly nine months before her suicide, when she was planning the show at the gallery.'

'And what was she like at that point?'

A crease came to Charlène's brow.

'Not at all in the same state of mind. She was full of energy and enthusiasm; she had loads of plans – and a dozen ideas a minute! But towards the end, she didn't care about anything. She dragged herself from place to place. You had to constantly repeat things to her. She was like a ghost.'

What had happened in the meantime? he wondered. In the space of only a few months Célia Jablonka had succumbed to depression. Was it the first time? Or was it a relapse?

'Do you have the address of the squat?' he asked.

'Why do you want to know all this?'

A question he should have asked himself. What exactly was he looking for? Célia Jablonka's suicide wasn't even his remit. The case had been closed long before.

'I got this the day before yesterday in my mailbox,' he said, taking the plastic square from his pocket.

'What is it?'

'The key to the hotel room where Célia Jablonka ended her life.'

Charlène looked at him, not understanding.

'And do you know where it came from?'

'Not the slightest idea.'

He could read the growing bewilderment in the eyes of his assistant's wife.

'And you don't think that is completely *freaky*?'

He stopped outside the entrance to the squat. A banner was hanging above the door: 'Self- Managed Social Centre. Occupy – Help Each Other – Self-Manage.' The windows on the ground floor were walled up. The facade, which had seen better days, was graffitied with a colourful mural.

Servaz went into the courtyard, where weeds were breaking through the pavement. He headed towards the entrance at the back, next to which bicycles and cars were parked. As soon as he went through the glass door he realised the place was full of life: he could hear children shouting, mothers scolding; there were naïve drawings and posters on the walls, and coats hanging from rows of pegs; there were voices, laughter, footsteps coming and going.

On the yellow walls, posters proclaimed: 'The police are in control, the law locks us up', 'Against evictions, for social self-defence and a popular offensive – on with the struggle', 'They won't keep us quiet!' 'Fuck the mayor!' An atmosphere of imminent insurrection reigned in this country; underground currents were at work, a counterweight to the resignation of broad swathes of the population.

Behind his back, a young woman called out, 'Can I help you?'

He spun around. He had expected to see a young woman with dreadlocks and a rasta cap, smoking a joint, but standing before him was a woman wearing jeans and a jumper, with an intellectual's glasses and her hair in a tight chignon.

'I'd like to see the director of the centre.'

'The . . . *director*? And who are you?'

Servaz took out his warrant card and the young woman suddenly seemed to have noticed a bad smell.

'What do you want? Isn't it enough that—'

'I'm investigating the death of Célia Jablonka, the artist who held an exhibition here. It has nothing to do with your squat.'

'It's not a squat, it's a place where people live. A self-managed social centre where we try to make up for the shortcomings of the administration and the state.'

'Right.'

'We have taken in twenty-five homeless families here. We give them a roof, financial aid, and access to legal counsel. We relieve them of their isolation, and teach them how to confront the hostile environment of French justice, and to overcome their fear of cops' – she accentuated the word – 'prison guards, and judges. This is not a squat.'

'Got it, it's not a squat.'

'Wait there.'

She vanished up the stairs. A little black boy came riding in on a tricycle and stopped to look at him. 'Hello,' said Servaz, without getting a reply. The child pedalled across the vestibule and disappeared. After he had waited for five minutes, he heard footsteps on the stairs. He looked up. The man who appeared was over six and a half feet tall and incredibly thin. What struck Servaz above all was his face – hollow and wrinkled, but burning with the flame of an ever-present youth. The flame was in his huge, deep-set light eyes, and it was of a feverish purity; it was in his smile as it broke into a radiance of wrinkles. He had a beaky nose and a certain beauty tinged with melancholy.

'Do you want to have a look around?'

His eyes twinkled with amusement. He was proud of what he was doing here. And Servaz felt a rush of spontaneous liking for this man who was certain he had chosen the right battle.

Someone who was neither resigned, nor cynical, nor apathetic.

'All right,' said Servaz.

An hour later, they had seen all the workshops; one of them repaired bicycles, another was a screen-printing workshop. Servaz had expected to meet undocumented African families, but he also met Georgians, Iraqis, poor or laid-off workers, students, and an elegant young Sri Lankan couple whose English flowed easily; and then there were the children bundled up in warm winter clothes, ready to go out and play.

'The thing is, everything you've just seen could stop from one day to the next,' said the director of the centre finally, collapsing into a battered leather armchair by a window that looked out onto the courtyard.

Servaz sat down in the other armchair. He knew there was no winter truce where evictions from illegal occupancy were concerned.

'So you have come here because of Célia?'

'Yes.'

'What do you want to know? I thought the case was closed.'

'It is.'

The man gave him a puzzled look.

'I'm trying to understand what it was that drove Célia to want to end her life.'

'Why? Since when do the police ask that sort of question?'

Good point.

'Let's just say there are some grey areas.'

'What do you mean by grey areas?'

'Tell me about her,' he said, to put a stop to the questions. 'Did you notice a change over the last months?'

The grey eyes probed him once again, then the man delved into his memories.

'During the last few days, Célia had completely lost her mind.'

He lit a cigarillo and blew out the smoke without inhaling it, never taking his eyes off the policeman across from him.

Servaz no longer felt the cold.

'She had gone completely mad,' reiterated the giant, looking him right in the eyes, his own eyes two spheres of concentration.

'She thought she was being persecuted; her behaviour was increasingly paranoid. She was convinced someone was following her, spying on her, that they were after her. Even here, she had stopped trusting people. Including me,' he added with real sadness in his voice. 'In the beginning, I didn't pay too much attention to her behavioural problems. But as the weeks went by, her symptoms got worse. She was more and more hostile and suspicious; she challenged my loyalty and accused me of plotting against her; the slightest little thing out of the ordinary would make her completely freak out. As if the entire planet had it in for her.'

Now Servaz was hanging on the fellow's every word. He might have forgotten the cold weather, but another sort of shiver went down his spine.

'And do you know what she was afraid of?' he asked.

Once again, that focused gaze levelled at him. The sound of a car horn from the street.

'Not what, but *who*. Not long before her suicide, she claimed that someone wanted to hurt her, someone wanted to destroy her life.'

He remained silent for a moment. His eyes narrowed.

'Why are you coming now, one year later, to question me about Célia? Have you reopened the case? Because I find it all a bit *strange*, to say the least. I get the feeling your investigation is just a touch, as it were, unofficial – or am I mistaken?'

'No.'

'So why does Célia Jablonka's case interest you? Did you know her?'

'Not at all.'

'What department are you in? I don't remember seeing you among the investigators last year.'

'The Criminal Affairs Division.'

The man frowned. 'You will understand why I'm puzzled: since when has the crime squad taken an interest in suicide? Unless, of course, it wasn't really a suicide.'

'Célia Jablonka did commit suicide. There's not the slightest doubt about that.'

'All right, all right, and if she did . . . then it's a very strange business,' said the tall, thin man. 'And you don't look like you're doing all that well yourself, if you don't mind my saying so.'

Night was already falling, dark and bitter cold, by the time Servaz got back to his own centre. It was just after five. Bloody December.

He switched off the ignition, climbed out of the car, and the gravel crunched beneath the snow as he walked towards the entrance, where he was greeted by the echo of voices from the grand salon. Here, too, there were workshops: drama workshop, belote workshop, gossip workshop, tirade workshop, memory workshop . . .

He climbed the stairs two by two to his room under the eaves. The little room was thick with shadows and chill, and he switched on the desk lamp rather than the ceiling light, which only gave off a paltry and infinitely dreary clarity.

Then he turned on the computer, and clicked on the icon with the portrait of Gustav Mahler in one corner of the screen. The music immediately filled the air, fluid, pure and limpid, falling into the silence like drops of icy water. The peace that emanated from this music was contagious. One lied. *Ich Ging Mit Lust.*

He checked the time. Five sixteen p.m. He took out his telephone.

'Hey, Martin,' said the voice on the line.

Desgranges, a cop from Public Safety whom he'd been teamed with in the past, before he ended up on the crime squad. Desgranges was a thorough, methodical officer, with a sense of smell worthy of a bloodhound. He was also a discreet person, and Servaz trusted him completely.

'It's been ages,' he said.

He must have heard what had happened to Servaz. The story about the box sent from Poland had made the rounds of all the departments. But he was too tactful to mention it directly.

'I'm on sick leave,' said Servaz.

No comment on the line. Purely out of politeness, Servaz asked for news about his daughters. Desgranges had two girls, both as pretty as pictures. They had grown so quickly they would soon be towering over him, and everyone around was charmed by their presence.

'You haven't called me just to talk about my daughters, have you, Martin?' said Desgranges when they had said all there was to say about the children.

Servaz took the plunge.

'Célia Jablonka, does that name mean anything to you?'

'The girl who slit her own throat at the Hôtel Thomas Wilson? Of course.'

'I'd like to see the file.'

'Why is that?'

Straight to the point. Servaz knew that his former colleague was expecting an equally frank reply. He decided to tell the truth.

'Someone sent me the key to the room where she killed herself.'

Silence on the line.

'And do you have any idea who?'

'None whatsoever.'

Another silence.

'A key, you say.'

'Yes.'

'Have you told your superiors?'

'No.'

'For fuck's sake, Martin! You can't keep that to yourself! You're not going to reopen the investigation just because of that?'

'I just want to clarify a few points. If it's worth it, I'll have the information sent up to Vincent and Samira. In the meantime, I just need to verify a few facts.'

'Which ones?'

'What?'

'Which facts?'

Servaz hesitated.

'To be honest, I really want to find the man or woman who sent me this key. And I figure the answer might be in the file.'

Desgranges didn't say anything and Servaz realised he must be thinking it through.

'Hmm. That makes sense. Up to a point. And you didn't ask yourself the other question?'

'What other question?'

'Why *you*? I mean, you weren't even on the investigation. It's not the sort of matter you habitually deal with and this – this person knew very well where to find you, apparently. A depressed cop isn't the sort of information you can get from the papers. Don't you find it strange?'

So Desgranges knew about his depression. As, in all likelihood, did virtually every police officer in Toulouse . . .

'That's precisely why I want to see the file,' he said. 'The person who sent me this thing seems to know as much about me as about the case.'

'At the same time, you've been in the headlines more than once recently, between the case in Saint-Martin and the one in Marsac. If I were a resident of this city looking for a competent cop, you would probably be at the top of my list. I'll see what I can do. Just drop by tomorrow. We'll go for lunch. And talk about the good old days.'

It was almost six p.m. when Christine typed in the security code, pushed open the heavy glass door and hurried to switch on the lights in the shadowy hallway. Her heels rang out on the tiled floor as she walked over to the rows of mailboxes.

As on the previous night, she held her breath on opening her box. Just the new set of keys from the young locksmith, she saw, relieved. She closed it again. Headed over to the lift. The tiny cabin came down to her, screeching and rattling in its wire cage, the cables curling under the floor like snakes hanging from branches. She pulled the metal gate abruptly, entered the tight space and pressed the button for the third floor. The cabin set off again. She watched the patches of shadow that carved shapes on the stairway as it wound its way around the lift shaft – a weave of light and darkness that for a second made her think of the heart of a prison. Her heart, already heavy, began to beat more quickly. And yet she had had a quiet day. At last. Since yesterday and the incident with Denise, life seemed to have gone back to normal. The lift stopped after one last judder and she pushed the gate. As she went out onto the landing she listened carefully. Nothing, except a vague sound of classical music from somewhere deep in the building. She went up to her door.

And stopped with her hand on the lock.

Opera.

*From inside her flat.*

The voice was coming through her door. For a split second she almost turned around. She put in her new key, unlocked the door and stood on the threshold: the music was coming from the living room, from *her* stereo. The woman's voice was vibrating loudly throughout the flat, accompanied by violins. A soprano.

She switched on the light, took a hesitant step forward, leaving the front door open. Ready to beat a hasty retreat. There was no one in the living room, but she saw it right away. On the coffee table: a CD. It hadn't been there this morning, she was sure of that. She would have put it away before leaving. And besides, she hated opera. She didn't have a single opera CD in her entire collection.

She breathed slowly. Took a step and stopped. *Tosca*, Puccini. She thought about the CD that had been addressed to her at the radio station.

So it wasn't a mistake.

It was part of the plan.

*The nightmare – here again.*

Her first thought, as she rushed over to the kitchen, was that he was still in the flat. She opened the top drawer in haste and grabbed the biggest knife she could find.

'Show your face, bastard!' she cried. 'Go on, come out!'

She went from one room to the next, the blade held out before her, trembling like a divining rod at the end of her arm.

The gloom of winter had flooded the rooms and every time she flipped the light switch she froze, expecting to see a figure rise up and jump on her.

*Where are you, fuck?*

*And how do you know these things about me?*

He seemed to know her perfectly. What was even more worrying was that he had managed to get into her place in spite of her new locks. She thought again about the young locksmith. Was he in on it?

*You are getting paranoid, girl.*

Then she remembered the new keys had been left in the mailbox. What an idiot she was! She went back to the door, looked at the inner bolt and bolted it – something she had obviously not been able to do on leaving. Finally, she went and kicked open the door to the bathroom. A final shudder of disgust and horror when she saw that someone had urinated without flushing – something she never forgot to do – and that a solitary, taunting cigarette butt was floating in the middle of a yellow puddle. Furious, she flushed the toilet. She bent double while the water was rumbling beneath her. She gagged, and gagged again. But as in the toilets at the radio station, she couldn't throw up.

She stood up straight, her face damp with sweat.

Empty. The flat was empty.

Then she suddenly realised something, and it was like a fist to her stomach: *Iggy . . . he wasn't here.*

'Iggy? Iggy? Iggy! Please, answer me! Igggyyyyy!'

The silence still vibrating with her cry bounced back like a squash ball with the echo of her fear. She went on throwing open cupboard doors, then drawers, which she tossed to the floor, as if her tormentor might have trapped Iggy in one of them.

'You scumbag,' she moaned. 'If you have done anything to my dog, I'll kill you, you bastard . . .'

She pounded her fists on a door. Spun round, disorientated. She had searched through everything. She had even opened the shoe boxes at the back of the wardrobe. She had looked under the sink. She had opened the recycling bins. She had looked everywhere. Or almost everywhere. *The fridge. Oh, no, no, no, anything but that . . .* She took a deep breath. Walked around the bar of the open-plan kitchen, summoned her courage and reached out towards the fridge handle.

As she pulled the door, the magnets offered a brief resistance. She closed her eyes.

And opened them again.

Her lungs filled with air and relief. Nothing but packs of yogurt, sugarless fruit desserts, two bottles of semi-skimmed milk, low-fat butter, cheese from Chez Xavier, a bottle of white wine and another of Coke Zero, microwave dinners, and then tomatoes, radishes, apples, mangoes and kiwis in the salad drawer.

Then her gaze dropped lower down: the door to the freezer. She pulled on it gently.

The drawers were full of food, items she had recently had delivered by an online supermarket.

Nothing else.

She had to face facts. *Her dog was nowhere to be found.* Christine rushed to the front door, opened it, called out to Iggy several times, but the only answer was the distant, indifferent sound of someone's television. She slammed the door and went back into the living room. Her gaze fell upon the litter tray full of clean newspaper. Something inside her snapped, like a spring giving way, and she let herself slide limply down the wall until she was sitting on the floor. Her face distorted, she could not hold back her tears, which began to flow as they had not done since that day she had come back from the secondary school at La Teste, not long after the Easter holidays. She had been thirteen years old, they were living by the seaside, and her father still went up to Paris three times a week to record his last programme worthy of the name. Thunder was rumbling above the sea that afternoon, the storm was threatening, and she had hurried home on her bicycle, pedalling flat out. So she did not understand why her father and mother, who were waiting for her in the kitchen, looked so sad, and why her father was holding her so tight that he almost suffocated her, why her mother had that ravaged, unrecognisable face. Until her father, holding back his tears, informed her that Madeleine had had a terrible accident. There had been a strange gleam of madness in his gaze, and she instinctively understood that she would never see her sister again. She thought she would never get over the grief. The kind of grief that could break you in two, that could make you want to die.

She wept. With her chin on her chest, and her arms around her knees, she wept.

Her mind had begun to wander. Forty minutes after she had swallowed a double dose of sleeping tablets, they were beginning to take effect: she felt her eyelids grow heavy, and her head was bobbing as her anxiety gradually released its grip. Perhaps, too, because she was exhausted, at the end of her tether, because sorrow and fear had completely scoured her mind and all that was left was stupor and apathy.

Before she would no longer be able to, she pressed the button on the phone one last time.

The one that corresponded to Gérald's number.

And got his voicemail, yet again.

For a brief moment fear overcame the effect of the sleeping tablet. Why wasn't he answering? *Because he is with Denise,* answered the nasty little voice inside her, becoming further and further away the more the chemical hypnosis performed its tranquillising massage on her neurons. *Because he is fucking the bitch. And, consequently, he cannot pick up, sweetheart.* There was a knot in her gut. But the Stilnox had not said its final word – and she felt the knot come undone, irresistibly, under the cottony fingers of sleep.

The police.

She should call the police. She was in danger. But what would she tell them? That her dog had disappeared? After the incident with the letter, she knew what they would think. *That you're raving . . . certifiable . . .* A last sob, like a spasm, then an immense peace came over her. Fucking blissful pharmaceutical peace, but peace nevertheless.

One last thought.

*Had she locked the door?* She frowned, while her head grew heavier and heavier. Yes. Yes, she must have done. She even thought she could remember shoving a piece of furniture in front of it. Had she actually done it, or only intended to? She wasn't sure any more. She was overcome by indifference. She put the telephone back down on the night table. And yawned. Put her neck on her pillow.

Closed her eyes.

At last.

# 12

## Leçon de Ténèbres

From deep in the night, from deepest sleep, come voices we hope never to hear. They are like reminders of childhood fears – how, once the light has been switched off and the door is closed, every object in the room, every shape can change into a monster; when, snuggled deep in one's bed – that life raft upon the disquieting waters of night – we become horribly aware of how very small and vulnerable we truly are. These voices remind us that death is part of life, and that the void is never far away.

That night, Christine had nightmares where she heard voices. She tossed and turned in the damp sheets of her night sweat; she moaned and pleaded in her sleep. Then she opened her eyes wide. All of a sudden. Something had woken her up.

A sound. *A yapping!* Christine threw back the duvet. She concentrated with all her strength and again she heard it: far away but distinct, indisputable. A clear, imploring little bark. There could be no doubt: it was him. *Iggy!* She leapt out of bed.

The sound was muffled, but real. It sounded as if it was coming through the wall. Yes, that was it. She tried to get her bearings. *The kitchen.* Iggy went on barking. *Yes, it was coming from over there.* She slipped behind the counter; it was coming *from behind the wall*! Her neighbour: Iggy was calling her from her neighbour's! Her neighbour who hated animals. Christine was filled with panic at the thought.

'Iggy!' she called, her face against the wall, her lips a few inches away. 'I'm here! I'm here, my sweet!'

She realised all the same how absurd the situation must seem: it was after three o'clock in the morning and Iggy was in the flat next door, barking. It simply didn't make sense. How could Iggy have got from her flat to the neighbour's? And yet . . . She placed her ear against the wall once again and she could hear him very distinctly. Beyond a doubt. That was Iggy – right there, behind the wall. She had to get him out of there, right away! She could not bear to wait until morning. She knew it would cause a fuss, but it was out of the question to leave Iggy even a minute longer. *Who knew what that old bag might do?* She went back to her room, put on a jumper and a pair of jeans and headed to the front door, barefoot. All the same, once she was on the landing, she had a moment of doubt: the barking had stopped.

She went up to her neighbour's door, took a deep breath and pressed hard on the bell. Once. Twice. Her thumb was crushing the bell for the third time, and she could hear the shrill echo of the ringing in the silent flat, when finally there was some noise inside.

'It's your neighbour!' she shouted, her face up against the door.

She could hear the security chain being removed, the click of the bolt in the lock, and then the door opened a few inches. A patch of face showed in the gap, sleepy and worried, framed by a prickly bush of grey hair.

'Christine? Is that you? What's going on?'

*Shit, that's a good question*, she thought: *What is going on? Maybe you can tell me?*

'I – I'm sorry to wake you up this early.' She realised how furry her mouth felt, and her elocution was approximate, given the sleeping tablet and what she was about to say – it was crazy, ludicrous, absurd. 'Well, um, my dog is in your place.'

'What?'

The door opened wide. Christine could read the stupor and incomprehension in her neighbour's eyes.

'Iggy . . . he's not in my flat. I can hear him barking for help. It's coming from your place, I'm sure of it.'

Michèle's eyes narrowed.

'Christine, you're imagining things. You're not in your right mind, are you? Have you been drinking? Or taking drugs?'

'Of course I haven't! I just took a sleeping tablet, that's all. Iggy is in your flat, I can hear him.'

'There's no dog here, don't be ridiculous!'

'Let me come in . . .'

She pushed her way through the door and past the little woman at the same time.

'. . . I'm sure he's here.'

Before her neighbour had time to react, Christine was inside, headed towards the source of the sound.

'Stop! You have no right to barge into someone's home like this!'

'I just want to get my dog!'

'What's going on here?' asked Michèle's husband, a round, bald little man, blinking his eyes like a barn owl.

'She's gone completely mad!' yelped Michèle behind Christine's back. 'She says her dog is here. Charles, either you get her out of here, or I'm calling the police!'

*The barking* . . . she could hear it again.

'Listen! Can't you hear it?'

They all fell silent.

'It's coming from your place,' said the little man, his tone severe. 'The bloody dog is at your place: you're losing your mind, my girl!'

'No, he's here!'

She rushed in the direction of the sound, her legs shaking.

The master bedroom. The bed unmade. Slippers on the bedside rug, old-fashioned furniture, clothing tossed here and there on chairs. A smell of old people. The furniture, as in the rest of the flat, was like a collection of museum pieces from the 1960s, when there were only two television channels, one telephone per house, and children put Banania in their milk at breakfast.

'I'm calling the police!' shouted Michèle. 'Get the hell out of here!'

It occurred to Christine that it was a bit rich to hear Michèle going on about calling the police when she spent the rest of the time bad-mouthing them and anything else that represented the state. She felt another wave of despondency: Iggy was nowhere to be seen.

'So you see,' said her neighbour, once she had gone around the room.

She nodded; she felt lost, nauseous.

'Go home,' said Michèle without animosity, her voice almost compassionate – and her compassion horrified Christine more than anything else.

Her head was spinning. She felt as if she were about to pass out.

She retreated hurriedly, breathlessly, to the entrance of the flat. The yapping had stopped. She was going mad. She went across the threshold, wanted to apologise but couldn't find the strength. She turned on her heels.

'Go and see a psychiatrist,' said Michèle gently. 'You must get treatment. Would you like me to call a doctor?'

She shook her head. The door closed again behind her. The door to her flat had stayed open and a ray of light fell from the vestibule onto the landing. Guided by it, she dragged herself inside, then bolted the door.

Silence.

Here, too, the yapping had stopped.

Christine walked into the living room and collapsed on the sofa. An invisible, invincible force was crushing her. At what point had she triggered it? Why? Who could possibly have it in for her like this?

She curled up on the sofa, her knees folded against her belly with a cushion between them. One solitary lamp was lit, and a strange apathy came over her. It was almost four o'clock in the morning. In less than three hours, she would have to get ready to go to the radio station. At that moment, the last thing she cared about was whether she would be up to it or not. Then she suddenly sat up.

*A bark* . . .

And another one.

Iggy . . .

He was still here! Somewhere. Alive. And he was calling for help. She shook herself. It was still coming from the same place: the kitchen. The wall she shared with her neighbours. For a moment, she was tempted to go back there. *Or could it be* . . . She rushed behind the counter, leaned over the worktop and the sink and gave a violent yank on the metallic flap of the rubbish disposal chute. Iggy's voice rang out: clear, shrill, heart-wrenching.

Carried by the echo of the chute.

*Iggy was downstairs*
*in the rubbish area*
*in the cellar* . . .

She almost burst out laughing; she almost thanked the heavens. Why hadn't she thought of that earlier? Quick, she had to get him out of there! He must be so frightened, alone in the dark, shut inside a place he didn't know. The urgency was like a tonic. But her thoughts were confused, interrupted by a discordant voice. That little voice told her that he didn't get in there all by himself, that he hadn't opened the rubbish disposal with his little paws before diving in with all the unconscious joy that went into making him the dog he was – and that to go down to the cellar at a time like this, with all that had already happened, would be a bit like going too close to the bank of a river full of crocodiles. She was not mad. She had proof of that. If she was not mad, if she accepted this basic premise, she must draw the following conclusion: *she was in danger.* And down there, no one would hear her scream.

*Do you really want that?*

Then Iggy's pathetic little bark came out of the chute again, calling for help, and she knew she could not possibly let him spend the rest of the night alone down there. She leaned over the opening.

'Iggy, Iggy! Do you hear me? Don't move, I'm coming!'

Her voice was amplified by the echo. The mongrel stopped barking for a moment, then barked even louder – hoarse barking that reverberated along the wall, followed by pitiful whimpers that broke her heart.

She opened the top drawer and took out the longest, most solid-looking knife. Then she went back to the front door and opened the box where her keys were kept. She took down a ring which had two keys on it: one for the cellar and the other a spare mailbox key. She put on a pair of fluorescent trainers. Her hand was trembling slightly when she unlocked her door for the second time that night. The darkness on the landing aroused her fear, which spread through her brain like a cloud of ink, her heartbeat suddenly dangerously irregular.

*You'll never manage, you haven't got the guts.*

Her hand found the timer for the light and very slowly she began to breathe again. Without realising, she had pressed the button for the lift: it was already there. For a fraction of a second she hesitated, then she opened the cage and stepped inside. The rattling of the lift as it went down reassured her somewhat, but when she was out on the ground floor, standing in front of the low door leading to the basement, she came very close to giving up. She was at the foot of the main stairway, separated from the actual hallway by a double glass door framed in wood, and the greyish light was so weak that it erased any details and gave her the impression that she was gazing at the scene through special glasses made for watching an eclipse.

The silence had returned and fear slammed into her like a wall. She had only been down to the cellar once: when she first visited the flat. She seemed to recall that the rubbish bin room was at the bottom of the steps to the right. She turned the key in the lock, the door opened with a groan when she pulled on it and a pungent odour of mould and cellar rose from the dark depths.

Two flights of stairs, she recalled. She flipped the light switch and a yellowish glow lit up the peeling walls.

She felt very close to crying out, calling for help, waking up the entire building. Then she remembered her neighbour. If someone found her wandering around in the common area with a knife in her hand at four o'clock in the morning, and they found Iggy in the dustbin room after the incident with the letter, the antidepressants at work, and the fuss she'd just made at her neighbours', it would leave no doubt: she would be entitled to immediate and automatic committal at the kind of institute whose motto was 'we-repair-your-brain-or-send-it-at-no-charge-to-the-scrap-yard-but-in-the-meantime-you're-not-about-to-get-out-of-here'. *Come on, Christine, you just need to grit your teeth* . . . She went down the last steps, stopped, and listened. Nothing. She had reached the first landing. She looked ahead and felt all her courage abandon her: at the bottom of the steps, the corridor leading through the cellar was nothing but a well of darkness, a black, opaque tunnel. Once again, panic spread through her chest like a bouquet of poisonous flowers. *Iggy, forgive me, I haven't got the courage. It's too hard . . . forgive me . . .* She was about to go back up, had already turned her back on the darkness, when a faint noise came to her.

'Iggy?'

No answer.

'*Iggy!*'

This time, she could clearly hear him barking. So near . . . She hurried down the last steps without thinking. Her feet touched the ground, the dirt floor. She looked around: the row of doors to the individual cellars to her left – black holes full of useless old things, cobwebs, memories, and rats – and the dustbin room to her right, behind a metal door painted green.

Her hand on the doorknob, she pulled open the heavy door.

'Iggy, here I am!'

The dog barked in the dark. Where was the bloody light switch? The obscurity beyond the door was as terrifying as if she had come upon a crevasse while walking on a glacier. She felt as if she were plunging her hand into a shark's jaws. Her fingers groped their way along the rubble stone and cement joints until they met a plastic box. There was a flood of light, as sooty as winter twilight, the bulb on the ceiling casting more shadows than it banished, and Christine saw several large shapes, squat and dark, lined up against the wall to the right. The rubbish bins . . . Iggy's barking came from the last bin, not the one overflowing with black bags that was just beneath the mouth of the rubbish chute, but another one, seemingly empty, its lid open and resting against the wall. She went closer.

The slam of the door caused her to jump out of her skin. Two more steps. Now she could see part way into the inside of the tall rubbish bin, but she couldn't see her dog. She could hear him, however, and the deep container acted as an echo chamber. There were thick shadows between the other bins, and she thought fleetingly that someone could hide in there.

*Don't think about it. You're nearly there.*

She took another step.

In the depths of the bin she could see Iggy's nose raised towards her, his soft gaze shining with hope in the gloom, and she held back her tears yet again. He barked and wagged his tail. Then he moaned plaintively the moment he moved. His claws were clicking on the plastic wall of the container but when he tried to straighten up, he again let out a heart-rending whimper. *Dear Lord, what has that bastard done to you?* She was already thinking about how she could get him out of there: the tall container stood chest-high; her arms were too short to take hold of Iggy, and she couldn't dive in there head first. There was only one way: to lay the container flat on the ground and crawl inside. She put the knife on the floor and grabbed hold of the dustbin.

The rear wheels made it harder than she had expected, and Christine struggled until she was finally able to tilt the container then lower it gently to the ground. After that, she slid inside. Iggy yapped joyfully from the bottom. Then whimpered. And yapped. He was barking stridently, fit to burst Christine's eardrums in the sound box the dustbin made. She had the vague impression that she had heard the metal door to the room open, and an icy chill went all down her spine. She froze. She could feel her heart beat faster. She had left her knife outside, out of reach. But there were no other sounds, only the blood in her veins. She slid further forward and her fingers finally reached Iggy's rough fur. She went even closer and wanted to take him in her arms, but the dog reacted by recoiling and growling defensively when she touched his right hind leg.

*What had that bastard done to him?*

Christine groped cautiously with her fingertips along his little paws and felt his curved claws and rough pads, then as her fingers moved up, his hard muscles, the thin bones apparent through his fur, and when she reached his shinbone Iggy began to growl again. She immediately stopped what she was doing.

'Calm down, Iggy, it's only me. There's no danger now.'

As best she could, straightening up and kneeling inside the rubbish bin, with her back curved and her neck against the plastic, she gently lifted the dog, without touching his injured paw, and she held him against her. His warm, rough tongue licked her cheek in thanks. Tears welling in her eyes, she buried her face in his thick curly coat, then she crawled backwards, knees rubbing against the plastic, until she could finally stand up again.

When she inspected his hind leg in the weak glow of the light bulb, she almost passed out: not only was it broken, but a piece of bone was sticking out of the matted fur. The rest of his paw hung loosely, disjointed, like a doll's broken limb held in place only by an elastic band. Iggy must be in agony . . . She wondered if her dog's paw had been shattered when the man threw him in the dustbin, or whether the monster had deliberately broken it.

Another thought occurred to her: the sort of person who could treat an animal so cruelly – who knew how far they would be prepared to go? This was no joke, now. *Yet another hope evaporating, my dear: your I-scare-women friend is clearly more damaged upstairs than you would have imagined – and yet you have a great deal of imagination, as a rule.*

She looked all around her, trembling. She hurried to pick up the knife.

Then with Iggy in her arms she went to the door, pushed the metal bar with her elbow and hurried up to the ground floor. It was only once she was back in her flat, with all the bolts and locks securely home, that she began to breathe. She realised her hands were shaking violently, and she sat for a long while on the sofa, with Iggy on her lap, and his terrible wound – but he seemed peaceful now, curled trustingly against his mistress.

She couldn't leave him like this; his paw must be seen to urgently.

Before the damage was irreparable.

*Gérald* . . . Gérald had a friend who was a vet.

She hunted for her phone, but once she had found it, the sight of it made her freeze. What if Gérald didn't answer? Or even worse: what if he were with someone else? She looked at Iggy out of the corner of her eye as he dragged himself pitifully to his litter box, head lowered, hind leg dangling – and she pressed the button.

'Christine? What's the matter?'

For a fraction of a second, she merely listened and didn't say anything. She tried to make out any voice, breathing, or movement next to him.

'It's Iggy,' she murmured.

'What?'

She was about to tell him what had happened when she realised what he might think. That she was going crazy. Since that's what her torturer wanted: to isolate her, to make her seem crazy, depressive, both to her friends and her family; she must avoid making the task any easier for him.

'Iggy broke his leg,' she said. 'He's in pain . . . He has an open wound, it's really nasty, the bone is exposed. He can't stay like this. And no vet is going to answer at this hour. Except, except, maybe, that friend of yours – if you call him.'

'Christine, for God's sake, it's four o'clock in the morning!'

'Please, Gérald, he seems to be in terrible pain.'

A long sigh down the line.

'Denise told me everything,' he said suddenly. 'Your *encounter* yesterday. Oh, for Christ's sake, Christine . . .'

An invisible hand pulled the plug deep in her guts, draining away the last bit of courage she had left.

*That little bitch!*

'Christine,' hissed Gérald's voice down the line, 'I can't believe you could have written that email. What the fuck came over you? Have you gone mad or what? Did you really threaten her? Did you really say, "Stay away from my man"? Answer me, please: did you say it, yes or no?'

That was why he hadn't picked up the phone earlier that evening. Because he was angry with her. Upset. Strangely enough, she found it reassuring. Gérald's anger was something she knew how to manage.

'We'll talk about that later,' she sighed, contrite. 'Please. I'll explain everything. Believe me, it's more complicated than you think. There's something going on here that's very hard to understand.'

'So it's true, then? You really said that? Fuck, I can't believe it!' he said. 'And you really wrote that bloody message?'

'No, I didn't write the message. Later, please. Call your friend – for me. Afterwards, we'll talk; please, *sweetheart* . . .'

An abnormally long silence. She closed her eyes. *Please, please.*

'I'm sorry, Christine. Not this time. I need to think. We can't go on like this.'

She froze.

'It would be better for us not to see each other for a while, the time it takes to find out where we stand,' he continued. 'To take stock. I need a break.'

She could hear the words, but her mind refused to grasp their meaning. Had he really said what she thought he'd said?

'As for Iggy, I'm really sorry, but surely it can wait a few more hours. I'd be grateful if you don't try to contact me for the next few days. I'll get in touch with you.'

She stared at the telephone, unbelieving.

He had hung up.

# 13

## Opéra bouffe

When dawn broke she was asleep. It was Iggy licking her face that woke her up. She'd been dozing for an hour, no more. Once exhaustion had got the better of her nerves and her tears.

She almost wrapped her arms around Iggy, who was curled up against her chest, but then at the last minute she remembered his broken hind leg.

She stole a cautious glance in his direction and saw he had been bleeding again, on the duvet, although not a great deal. She concluded that he must have slept, too – in spite of the pain. A vet: it couldn't wait any longer.

She slipped cautiously from the bed and this time the little dog did not follow her. Downcast, he watched her leave the room. It was heartbreaking, the way he was sadly licking his wound. It was too early to call, so she headed to the kitchen. On her way she passed the shoe rack, which she had pushed against the front door before going to sleep, perching a vase on it in a precarious position so it would shatter noisily if someone tried to push against it. In the living room it was cold. She turned up the radiator and with a shiver pulled her dressing gown tighter around her, then made herself a black coffee and some buttered crispbreads.

Strangely enough, she was hungry. She was exhausted but famished. While she ate, perched on the bar stool, her heels on the foot rest, she began a thought process which surprised even her. The sorrow and horror of the night she had just endured had drained her of all her reserves of self-pity; unlike her dog, she had stopped licking her wounds. She felt something of a return to a familiar emotional state. It was still only a faint quiver, but she knew what it was: Christine's Great Rebound. Christine's Great Rebound usually happened after an ordeal – and she had been through a fair number of ordeals in her life (*I know what you're referring to*, said the little voice. *Don't even think about it, sweetheart.*) It happened when she was really at rock bottom. And each time it led to increased determination, a fierce desire not to give in to despair, a surge of energy. It was as if at times like this her brain manufactured a particular kind of antibody.

At that very moment, in spite of her extreme fatigue, all her thoughts were focused on her tormentor. If there was some connection that had led him to her – and that connection must exist, given everything he knew about her – it must also be possible to work her way back to him, to trace him as he had traced her.

*Think.*

There were at least two things: 1) he had found a way into her office, or else he had an accomplice there; 2) he was sufficiently close to Gérald and Denise to know what they said to each other, or else he had been spying on them. She remembered the photographs on her computer: yes, that was certainly what he had done. He must have listened to their conversations that day or another day. But one question remained, always the same: his motive. Why? Why *her*? Once she could figure out the motive, then she would have him.

She lifted the mug of coffee to her lips.

Yet another thought:

*He is isolating me.*

Yes. That was what he had gone on doing that night, alienating her from Gérald and her neighbours. In the same way that he had alienated her – now she got it – from the police and, to some degree, from her boss, after that incident with the antidepressants. She didn't know why he was doing it, but that was also part of his plan. *You have to break the isolation. Whatever the cost.* She had to find an ally. But who? Her mother? (*A-ha*, said the little voice, *you are joking, aren't you?*) No, of course not. Her mother would wrinkle her pretty nose and train her sapphire eyes upon her and wonder whether her daughter had suddenly gone mad or had always been so.

Her father? Even less likely. Who, then? *Ilan?* Why not? Her assistant was reliable, hard-working, discreet. But could he be anything more than a good assistant? She had no choice: she couldn't think of anyone else. At that very moment, with unpleasant clarity, the little voice piped up once again:

*No one else? Really? No girlfriends? Someone you can trust besides your beloved fiancé? Hmm . . . doesn't this say a lot about certain aspects of your life, sweetheart?*

There was something else she must do.

She reached for her laptop, opened it on the counter and switched it on. She set about deleting all the cookies and changing her passwords, then she began to download a complete new security package with anti-viruses, firewalls, anti-spyware, anti-phishing and the whole caboodle, and then she went to take a shower. When she came out of the bathroom, she got rid of the old system and launched a quick scan. She glanced at the clock. She would perform a more thorough one at the office. From a drawer in the cabinet under the television she took out binders where she kept bills, receipts, credit card slips and her chequebooks, and she placed them all in a khaki canvas holdall, a relic from her student years. She would open a safe deposit box at the bank and store everything there until she had found a satisfactory solution. Henceforth her flat could no longer be considered a safe place. Finally she called the vet. His assistant put her on hold for a moment then came back to chirp that her boss had agreed to see Iggy immediately: she must come at once.

'Thank you for choosing our services. No potentially dangerous software detected', said a synthetic voice from her computer. The scan was finished. She put her laptop into the already heavy satchel, fetched the wire dog carrier and went back into the room, where Iggy waited for her with a disarming mixture of tenderness and trust.

It was eight twenty. Late again. But nothing in comparison with the previous days. And besides, she had been going in early for years: a few one-off instances of coming in late wouldn't erase all that, surely?

After she came out of the lift she went to grab a coffee from the machine. In spite of everything, she felt relieved: Iggy was safe now, they had given him a tranquilliser, and there was nothing left in her flat that her torturer could use against her. She hadn't had time to drop off the binders at the bank – she still had them with her – so in the meantime she would lock her satchel and computer in her desk (*except your drawers aren't safe, either*, said the voice). Yes, but until now she had never locked her drawers. This time, she would make sure the key never left the pocket of her jeans. So what if her neighbours in the open-plan office saw what she was doing and wondered what she was up to.

She stifled a yawn and thought about her guest for the day: the director of the Toulouse Space Centre. Gérald knew him well. It wasn't the first time she had invited a representative of the industry onto her programme: the city's space and aeronautics focus had long been at the heart of its industrial and economic development. And besides, she may as well admit she had a particular relationship with space, for better or for worse, through the men in her life, and . . . But she stifled that thought too.

*It's no time to be thinking about that.*

She left the glassed-in room, her steaming cup in her hand, her satchel over her shoulder, and headed through the open space towards her desk and Ilan's. She would ask to speak to him after the programme. Right now it was the press review that was urgent. The sight of her assistant's empty desk jarred her from her thoughts.

Ilan was nowhere to be seen.

Where was he?

Ilan was *never* late. Not once in three years.

She saw a yellow Post-it stuck on her telephone. She leaned closer and read:

*Come to my office. Right away.*

Guillaumot's handwriting.

The tone was rather threatening but coming from the programme director this was nothing unusual. Christine looked all around the room. Everyone seemed absorbed in their work. Too absorbed.

*Something was up.* She went to the door of the little office and paused on the threshold.

Guillaumot was standing across from Ilan and Cordélia, who were listening to him attentively. He spotted her, interrupted what he was saying and motioned to her to come in.

The other two turned to look at her.

'Close the door,' said the programme director.

The cautious neutrality of his tone did not bode well.

'What's going on?' she asked.

'Let's sit down, for a start,' he said.

'We have a programme to prepare, I think,' she replied, pointing to her two assistants.

'Yes, yes, I know, sit down,' he repeated, his tone unchanged.

She raised her eyebrows. The programme director, already seated, was looking at her insistently over his glasses. He had a notebook open in front of him. He read quickly what he had written, then looked up again, with a pen in his hand, once they were all seated.

'Well, um, I don't quite know where to begin. This is a fairly unusual situation. I would like to speak to the three of you. As programme director, it is my job, as you know, to make sure the service runs smoothly. And to make sure that no one in this service, um, suffers in any way because of other people's behaviour.'

Christine's gaze went from Cordélia to Ilan. Cordélia's expression was impenetrable and Ilan studiously avoided her gaze. She felt a draught of cold air all down her neck. Guillaumot was staring at her without flinching.

'Cordélia came to see me this morning,' he began.

Christine glanced over at the intern; their gazes met in silence. The blood pounding in her temples, she understood: this was where the next attack was coming from.

'She has complained about you.' He took a deep breath before continuing. 'About your behaviour. Well, shall we say harassment, on your part. That is the word she used. Cordélia asserts that for weeks you have been sexually harassing her: making passes, inappropriate gestures, and even threatening to have her fired if she doesn't comply. She doesn't want to file a complaint but she wants it to stop. This internship is very important to her, and above all, she doesn't want any problems: that is what she has said. She would like for us to deal with the issue amongst ourselves.'

Christine gave a sarcastic little laugh.

'You think it's funny?' said the programme director, immediately indignant. 'You really think this is a laughing matter?'

She restrained her anger.

'Don't tell me you believe all this rubbish?' she said, leaning closer. 'Honestly, have you looked at her?'

They both glanced at Cordélia. That morning, she was wearing an ultra-short plaid kilt and black tights, with a sweatshirt proclaiming ALCHEMY on the chest and high-top black trainers with silver studs. Her nails were painted blood red like her lips. The piercings on her lips sparkled. How could anyone believe a girl disguised as Cruella before they believed Christine?

'She says that you, um, fondled her several times in the toilets,' continued the programme director, blushing slightly. 'That you, uh, tried to kiss her. That you invited her over for a drink and that—'

'That's bullshit.'

'That you have been flooding her inbox with emails of a, um, sexual, or even, um, pornographic nature.'

'Oh, honestly, the girl is completely delusional! Shit, look at her!'

'Exactly.'

'Exactly what?'

'Exactly, you must have figured no one would believe her.'

She looked at him as if he had gone mad.

'This is a joke,' she said. 'You've all gone bonkers!'

And, as he was staring at her without answering, she added, 'Do you know who you're talking to? You're talking to me, Christine, who's been working here for seven years – do I look like a pervert?'

'She said that she's uncomfortable being around you.'

'Oh yeah? Well then, let her show us those emails. Where are they?'

Guillaumot looked hard at her, then shoved a pile of printed pages across the desk.

'Here.'

There was a long silence.

'This is absurd.'

She looked at the printed pages.

*Cordélia, forgive me. I didn't want to threaten you. You know I don't mean you any harm. I think about you all the time, I can't help it. This is the first time I have felt something like this about a woman.*
*Christine*

*Cordélia, what would you say to dinner, just the two of us, on Saturday evening? Please say yes. It doesn't commit you to anything, I promise. Just dinner between friends. I promise you no one will know about it. Call me, please.*
*Christine*

*Cordélia, you haven't been answering my emails. I'm forced to conclude that you disapprove of my attitude. That you're hostile. Cordélia, you know your future is in my hands.*
*C.*

*Cordélia, I'm giving you 24 hours to reply.*

There were dozens more in the same vein. A flock of black birds fluttered through her mind. She felt dizzy; her palms were hot and damp.

'It's impossible,' she said slowly, skimming the messages with an unbelieving gaze. 'This is absurd. I did not send these emails. Honestly, can you really imagine me writing this sort of thing? And signing them on top of it!'

Guillaumot looked annoyed.

'Christine, we double-checked: that is your IP address, from your computer.'

'But – what the hell? Anyone could access my computer, you know that very well! All anyone has to do is spy on me while I'm typing in my password. I'd be willing to bet this little tart sent them herself.'

He nodded slowly. Stared at her coldly. A look of a sort she had never seen on his face before, even in his angriest moments.

He turned to Ilan.

'Ilan,' he said, 'are you ready to repeat what you told me?'

Christine felt a chill all down her spine. She looked at her assistant. He was red as a lobster.

'I would like to start by saying that Christine is a true professional,' he said, his voice almost inaudible. 'We do good work and, um, we've always got on well. I've been very happy working with her, she's someone I respect . . . and I would like to say that I believe her when she says she didn't write this . . . insane stuff.'

'Fine, Ilan,' said Guillaumot. 'We've taken note of your objections. But that wasn't my question. Did you, too, receive inappropriate messages?'

'Yes.'

'From the same IP address, is that right?'

'Yes.'

'And were they signed?'

'Um, yes.'

'Can you tell us by whom, Ilan? "Christine", is that right?'

'Yes,' said Ilan. 'That's what it said, but it doesn't mean—'

'When did you get these emails?'

'Well, last month, but they stopped very quickly. And I'll say it again, I like working with Christine very much, I cannot fault her on anything. I'm sure she's been framed. I can't see any other explanation.'

He shot a suspicious glance in Cordélia's direction.

'What sort of emails?' continued the programme director, unperturbed.

'Um, well, you know, *inappropriate*, as you said . . .'

'Overtures?'

'Yes.'

'Sexual stuff?'

'Yes, that sort of thing; but it didn't last long, as I said.'

'How many were there, do you have any idea?'

'Well, I don't know, maybe twenty.'

'More?'

'I don't remember.'

'Fine, Ilan. All right. Let's suppose it was about that many. How long did it last, can you say?'

'A week, ten days; no more, that I'm sure of. I told you, it stopped very quickly.'

'And you got several of them per day, right?'

Christine felt as if the ground were shifting beneath her feet, like an earthquake.

Ilan's ears had turned purple. 'Yes.'

It was more than she could take. She leapt to her feet and leaned across the desk.

'That's enough now! Stop this bullshit! It proves absolutely nothing: someone could easily have used my email when it was open on my desk! I will not tolerate this slander one more minute, do you hear? This business is grotesque, it's gone on long enough. And I cannot understand why you would even begin to believe it.'

The programme director ignored her outburst.

'Those emails, Ilan,' he asked, 'did you get them during the day or at night?'

Silence.

'Both,' said the young man, embarrassed.

Another long silence. Christine was still on her feet; she felt drained, nauseous, groggy. Guillaumot glanced at his watch.

'Thank you for being so honest. You and Cordélia may go back to work. I thank you both; go and see Arnaud about the programme. He will fill in for today. Get a move on.'

Cordélia and Ilan left the room, Cordélia glaring back at Christine. Christine looked at Guillaumot, stunned.

'Frankly, I cannot understand how you can believe her claims for a minute. How long have we been working together? I've always done my job, you know that. I've never had any personal problems with colleagues until today; I'm not hysterical like Becker, or tyrannical like you, or a layabout like some people around here. I'm professional, reliable, and everybody enjoys working with me—'

Guillaumot rushed to grab the line she had tossed him.

'Everybody enjoys working with you? Open your eyes, for Christ's sake, Steinmeyer! Everyone here thinks you're a pain in the arse, an arrogant, difficult drama queen! Everyone thinks that you've been getting above yourself lately. I cannot count the number of times you've come and pestered me about trifles.' He shot her a look that was heavy with resentment. 'Need I remind you what I found in your drawer? Not to mention all the times you've been late, or your very unprofessional behaviour on the air lately.'

Suddenly she understood. *Guillaumot didn't like her, either.* And for him this was the dream opportunity. She felt as if the ground were moving; a storm was raging inside her mind, thick and dark.

'Do you really think people worship at your feet?' he continued in the same vengeful tone. 'And that we cannot manage without you? That you are indispensable?' He rolled his eyes. 'Of course that's what you think. That's your problem, Steinmeyer; you're completely disconnected from reality. And now this. Who do you think you are, for fuck's sake!'

She couldn't believe her ears. She had always thought that they appreciated her work, respected it, along with her professionalism, and that apart from a few differences of opinion and a few enemies – it was normal to have one or two in an environment so fraught with competitiveness, and where so many employees coveted others' positions – she got along well with the editorial board.

He made a show of checking his watch.

'I have a meeting with shareholders and management in one hour. Go home. I'm going to think about what we do next. In the meantime, stay home tomorrow, Arnaud will handle the programme for now.'

She almost said something, then thought better of it. She was on the verge of exhaustion, of a breakdown. She placed her hand cautiously on the back of her chair to keep from stumbling.

Guillaumot's voice grew softer, as if he'd realised he had gone too far: 'Go home, Christine. I'll keep you informed. Whatever I decide, you will be the first to know.'

She beat a hasty retreat. The door to the office had stayed open after Ilan and Cordélia had gone out: consequently, everyone had heard Guillaumot's outburst. She rushed to her desk, head down. Through a totally silent room. She could feel all those gazes converging on her.

'Christine, I—' began Ilan.

She raised her hand and he fell silent. Her fingers were trembling so violently that she had to try twice to get the little key into the lock of the drawer. She took out her satchel, hitched the strap over her shoulder and hurried to the lift.

'Good riddance,' said someone as she went by.

# 14

## Coloratura

There were woods behind the centre, a short distance away, and miles of poplar trees ahead – on the plain, lined up like halberds in a painting by Paolo Uccello. As he sat down, he realised he was beginning to like this place. He might not like the other boarders, with a few exceptions, but the place itself was not without charm. Or peace and quiet. He realised he was in no hurry to leave, that he was afraid of returning to the real world. Did that mean he was still a long way from being cured?

To Servaz the word sounded somewhat suspicious. *Cured* . . . The language of shrinks and doctors. He didn't trust any of them. He looked at the white plain, wondering when this snowy season would end. And suddenly he understood that this icy plain was the reflection of his brain: something inside him had frozen after Marianne's death. His soul was waiting for a thaw; his soul was waiting for the spring.

The Cactus was not the sort of bar you would find in a guidebook, but it had a loyal clientele who chose to go there the way cats decide to live in a particular place. And it had a story. It had been built by the previous owner, an indomitable man who chose who he wanted to frequent his establishment, any hour of the day or night: whores, trannies, yobs – and cops. In a neighbourhood that wasn't particularly fond of the police.

Upon his death he had left the bar and its legacy to his employee, and since then the *patronne* – who wrote poetry when the mood took her – steered her ship with a steady but gentle hand, knowing that those who came on board also did so for her sake.

Desgranges was sitting in his usual place, with a big glass of beer in front of him. Servaz felt a few gazes upon him as he sat down, friendly as a polar bear's: he knew that the police could also discriminate against their own kind, that they would treat those who cracked like pariahs. He noticed, too, that nothing had changed: the same old faces perched in the same spots.

'You're looking good,' said the policeman soberly.

'I spend my time sweeping dead leaves, doing sport and resting . . .'

A chuckle reached him from across the table.

'This business with the key came along at just the right time, it looks like. It's good to see you, Martin.'

Servaz did not respond to the expression of affection. It was pointless. 'And how are you doing?' he asked instead.

'Not bad, not bad. I've been assigned to Gambling. You want to hear my latest adventure? A gallodrome . . .'

'A what?'

'The Maracaña of cock-fighting, old man. In Le Ginestous, among the Rom . . . A ring with terraces for spectators, a treatment room for injured fowl, another one that's air-conditioned for the bloody birds before they enter the arena. They even had fucking moving walkways, like in a gym, that worked with a washing-machine motor, so the champions could exercise their little claws. They were not in a good way, the champions, when we found them . . . It was downright foul, forgive the pun. Bloody bastards . . .'

Servaz recalled reading about it in the paper.

'To the health of cops who fly to the rescue of cocks,' he said, raising his glass.

'And who fly at their abusive handlers,' added Desgranges.

'Do you still keep a copy of all your cases?' asked Servaz.

Desgranges nodded. He reached for the cardboard folder next to him.

'You're in luck. They could have given it to someone else. I had a look at it before coming . . . Martin, have you any idea how many dodgy suicides there have been over recent years in Toulouse? You know as well as I do how fine the boundary is between suicide and crime in this city.'

Desgranges had lowered his voice. Servaz nodded: he knew what his former colleague was referring to. The 1980s and 90s. The darkest pages in the city's history. 'Suicide' was the word that had shown up inexplicably time and again in autopsy reports. The list was as long as a day during Ramadan: young women who disappeared between their workplace and their home, prostitutes whose murders in windowless Toulouse hotel rooms were never solved, botched autopsies, slapdash instructions, more cases dismissed than you could count, others filed away without follow-up, crazy rumours about corrupt policemen and magistrates, prostitution and drug networks involving celebrities, ultra-violent S&M parties, sex, porn, violence, murders . . . In all, over one hundred unsolved cases between 1986 and 1998 had fallen under the jurisdiction of the Toulouse county court alone. Murders written off as suicide. The individuals implicated had been cleared, but the suspicion still hovered, nauseating and indelible. It was as if behind each pink brick city wall, behind each doorway in the sun there was a wall, a doorway, of shadow.

'When gathering facts, before concluding that it was suicide, the cops who were first on the scene initially thought it was a murder, given the very unusual circumstances. Consequently they placed a number of things under seal, and among these was . . .'

Desgranges reached into the cardboard folder and took out a pink notebook.

'What's that?'

'A diary.'

'Why do you have it?'

'When I wanted to restore the belongings to the family, I called Célia's parents. They came to get them. I gave them everything except this.'

'Why?'

'Just in case . . . I was intending to get beneath the surface a bit more but, when they proved it was a suicide, I dropped it.'

'But you still kept the diary.'

'Yes. I wanted to check something, and then I no longer had the time.'

'What did you want to check?'

'I told you: I only had time to start nosing about a little before they concluded it was suicide. It only took me a few hours to iden- tify all the names in here. All except for one: Moki.'

'Moki?'

'Yeah. All the others were Célia's friends, colleagues and relatives. Except this one.'

Their gazes met: Servaz was on the alert. How many cases like this one, sleeping in cardboard boxes, kept their secrets locked forever in the pages of a forgotten case file? He tasted longing in his mouth.

'Well! It's been ages,' said the *patronne,* standing above him. 'Back from the dead?' He wondered if even she was in the know. Did he have the depressive's mark of infamy on his forehead? But her pretty smile was full of warmth. He realised that he had missed a lot of things here; he ordered a steak and salad.

Desgrange's podgy fingers turned the pages of the notebook.

'Here. Look.'

He spun the diary around in front of Servaz and read, 'Moki, 16.30', 'Moki, 15.00', 'Moki, 17.00', 'Moki, 18.00' . . .

'Are you sure it's a person?'

Desgranges raised his eyebrows.

'What else could it be? In any case, none of Célia's acquaintances was able to tell me who it was.'

'And that's all?'

Desgranges smiled. 'What did you expect?'

'Have you got a theory?'

'A married man,' answered Desgranges immediately. 'The times indicated are typical for an affair. That must be the nickname she gave him. One thing is certain: the guy never turned up. Which also supports the theory of a married man.'

'It could be anything,' said Servaz. 'A place, a bar, a fashionable new sport—'

'There's something else.'

A fleeting thought crossed Servaz's mind: he hadn't felt this alive in a long time. Desgranges took a receipt out of the folder and slid it across the table.

'Not long before committing suicide, Célia bought a few things that were . . . of a rather particular nature.'

Servaz leaned closer. A receipt. The Toulouse gunsmith. He read: *Guardian Angel, defence bomb, pepper cartridges* . . . Apparently, Célia Jablonka had wanted to protect herself, not commit suicide.

He narrowed his eyes to read the date on the receipt: roughly two weeks before her suicide.

'That's strange, for someone who wanted to end their life, don't you think?' he said.

'Hmm,' said Desgranges, doubtfully. 'Who knows what goes on

in people's heads? If depressive people behaved logically, we would understand them better.'

'It does give the impression, all the same, that she was afraid of something.'

'That is indeed the impression it gives.' Desgranges stabbed his fork in his salad. 'But it's still only an impression.'

Servaz got the message. In every investigation there were always elements that looked meaningful and then turned out to have nothing to do with the case.

In the long run an investigation was like deciphering a new alphabet: some words were more important than others but at the start you had no way of knowing which these were.

Suddenly Desgranges frowned.

'This business with the key, it bothers me. Do you think that the person who sent it to you knows something?'

'Maybe they just want us to reopen the investigation somehow. But there's another question: how did they get the key?'

'By staying at the hotel,' said Desgranges.

'Exactly. Do you think they keep a list of people who have lost or forgotten to hand in their key?'

'I'd be surprised, but it might be worth a try.'

As soon as he left The Cactus, Servaz called another department at his former employers (who were still his former employers until further notice). Operational Documentation was a team of four people who were in charge of 'live' files, in other words all the files that dealt with people even remotely connected to ongoing procedures – witnesses, suspects, and so on – without waiting for them to be implicated. They cross-checked and cross-referenced facts (something investigators didn't necessarily have the time or the wherewithal to do) between all of these files and the specialised brigades' files. Operational Documentation was run by Lévêque, a chief brigadier who had once worked for the crime squad and had had both legs crushed in a hit and run accident. He had a limp, which got worse when it rained, and he'd been invalided out of active public service. After training at Europol, Lévêque had become a criminal analyst, in order to put his intuition and his experience to good use: he no longer had the right to investigate, but he made up for it by rummaging in other people's investigations – and nothing gave him greater satisfaction than turning up a detail that his colleagues had missed: a name or a telephone number that came up in several unrelated cases; a green Clio spotted on the scene of an attack and then again at a hold-up . . .

'Servaz here. How're the legs doing in this weather?'

'Pins and needles. And not just in this weather. How are you getting on? I thought I heard you were on sick leave.'

'I am. I suppose I have pins and needles in my legs, too.'

'You haven't called just to talk about pins and needles.'

'I'd like you to check a name for me.'

'You just told me you were on sick leave.' Silence on the line. 'What's the name?'

'Moki. M-O-K-I.'

'*Moki?* What's that supposed to be: a person? A brand name? A goldfish?'

'No idea. But if you can't find anything, try associating it with "rape", "domestic violence", "harassment", "threats", and so on.'

'I'll get back to you.'

He had an answer within the hour:

'Nothing.'

'Are you sure?'

'Are you trying to hurt my feelings? Your Moki didn't show up anywhere. I processed the name everywhere, I associated it with everything I could think of – there's nothing, Martin. And it came back to me: someone already asked me the same thing last year.'

'I know. Thanks.'

She put her glass back down on the table, her gesture hesitant, like a captain drowning his sorrows in the storm while the bilges fill with brine with every roll of the ship. Drunk. By the time Christine realised, it was already too late; the alcohol had had the time to go from her stomach to her intestines and from there to her entire circulatory system.

She turned to look out of the steamy window. While the snow had briefly stopped falling, a bitter wind was blowing, sweeping the white pavements of the allées Jean-Jaurès where cars were slowly making their way, wheels in the black tracks left by others before them.

The Radio Five building was across the street, a Tom Thumb of brick among all the fifteen-storey blocks. Every time Christine looked over that way, she felt nauseous. She had thought the alcohol would anaesthetise her pain, but no such luck: it had just made her wearier and more disheartened.

'Are you sure you're all right?' asked the waiter.

She nodded and ordered a coffee, her voice unsteady. Her mind was wandering. She couldn't focus. In the space of four days she had lost her fiancé and her job; she wondered if these losses were irrevocable.

*And in your opinion?* said the little voice; didn't it love rubbing salt in the wound. *Maybe you supposed he would really like to spend his life with a crazy woman?*

As she stirred the sugar in her cup, she wondered whether it had all started with that damned letter. It was absurd, of course. Irrational. And yet she had the feeling that the cataclysm had begun at around that time. And then she saw her. Cordélia. Leaving the radio station, taking great strides from the rue Arnaud-Vidal onto the allées Jean-Jaurès.

Mechanically, she checked her watch: two thirty-six. Christine watched Cordélia go alone up the pavement in the direction of the boulevard de Strasbourg and the Métro, four hundred metres away. She kept her eyes glued on the dark shape. She could feel the hatred burning inside her, like an onrush of bile. *Keep calm; above all don't succumb to impulses.* But when the bundled-up figure was about to leave her field of vision, Christine grabbed her satchel from the next chair and got up.

'How much for three beers, two cognacs and a coffee?'

The bartender looked at her from over his glasses and hastily did the maths.

'Twenty-one euros.'

Her hand trembling, she pulled out a twenty and a five and left them on the counter.

'Keep the change.'

The wind was howling as she emerged into the cold, but the alcohol kept her warm. There were very few pedestrians. She could see Cordélia a hundred metres further on; she readjusted the shoulder strap of her satchel and began walking quickly, her gaze trained on her target; careful not to go flying in places where the slush and melted snow had frozen.

When Cordélia reached the entrance to the Métro station – outside the former Hôtel de Paris, rebaptised Citiz Hotel – Christine was already crossing the central reservation, near the big well that over-looked the open-air atrium. She reached the top of the steps just in time to see Cordélia head down the escalator to the platform for line A. She followed in turn, down the slippery concrete then the escalator leading to the lower level. Cordélia was going through the turnstile. From where she watched, Christine could see her cheeks flushed with cold, her shameless' young bitch profile, and her long slender form. Hatred and anger burned inside her. When she reached the turnstiles, she glanced down at the platform below her and saw that the intern was headed in the direction of Basso-Cambo.

Now things were getting tricky: if she went down onto the platform right away, Cordélia might see her. She let a crowd of passengers go by. When the train pulled in two minutes later, she hurried through the turnstiles and down to the platform. As expected, Cordélia entered the train without looking behind her. Christine boarded two doors further down. She stayed by the window, hidden by a young man who was listening to Zebda full blast in his headphones, and another man in his forties who would have to choose between rapid weight loss or a bed in the operating theatre for heart surgery. Christine was aware, however, that if Cordélia was the kind who liked to look around at other passengers, she would eventually see her.

She glanced over to where the intern was standing and what she saw reassured her.

Totally indifferent to everything around her, the gangly girl was tapping away at great speed on her mobile. Two stations further along, she saw Cordélia put her smartphone away and move closer to the doors: Esquirol. Christine did not know where the young woman lived, but it couldn't be in that neighbourhood. It was too expensive. Unless she still lived with her parents. The most probable theory was that she was going to meet someone. The neighbourhood was popular with the city's young crowd.

She suddenly wondered why she had decided to shadow Cordélia. She had given in to an impulse. Maybe it was time now to think about the situation she was in. The truth was she had no idea what she was doing. And she was probably acting against her better judg-ment. Still, when the girl got out at place Esquirol, Christine followed her.

When Christine found herself at street level, she saw Cordélia a hundred metres ahead of her. She followed in her footsteps, keeping well behind. Cordélia went through the door to the Unic Bar. She walked over to a table where three young adults sat, a boy and two girls. They were all dressed in the same way: black clothes, silver necklaces and bracelets, Goth make-up, red or purple hair; even the boy had black pencil around his eyes.

Christine looked around.

Opposite the brasserie were a boulangerie-pâtisserie and a waxing salon: not the sort of place where she could hang out. If she stayed on the pavement, they would eventually notice her. The only decent lookout was a little café next to the one where Cordélia had gone in – but the risk of being noticed was even greater, because the two enclosed terraces were separated by a single transparent glass wall. Christine spun around.

*Think.* She glanced cautiously in Cordélia's direction: the young woman had draped her long black coat over the back of the chair, so she would surely be there for a while.

Christine walked up the rue d'Alsace-Lorraine, a major shopping street, with lots of clothing boutiques. Two hundred metres further along, she went into one of the boutiques, found a winter parka with a hood as unattractive as it was warm and comfortable, and hurried to the till. Not four minutes later, she went back out with the hood pulled up over her hair, the belt tied around her waist, and her coat inside her satchel. She had chosen a colour that wouldn't draw attention, avoiding the reds and yellows that were trendy that winter. *Couldn't you have found something uglier?* said the sarcastic little voice.

Back on the place Esquirol, she made sure Cordélia was still there, and she went into the adjacent café without removing her hood. She ordered a hot chocolate. The waiter had only just returned with her order when she saw Cordélia get up, put on her coat and kiss her companions.

Christine hurriedly paid, dipped her lips in the chocolate and felt her empty stomach contract, but the girl was already weaving her way between the tables towards the door.

Christine took two more quick sips, burning her tongue, and followed Cordélia back to the Métro station. There was only one line, she thought: that limited the possibilities. Both clocks on the square indicated 15:26.

That was when she felt it. The change taking place in her, beneath the dark hood of her parka. *She had changed from prey to hunter* . . . This reversal of perspective filled her with a burst of energy; her blood was seething with impatience; questions came hurtling one after the other. Was Cordélia the person harassing her? If so, why? Christine had always treated her well; at least she thought she had: the programme director's outburst had made her understand that she was not as well liked at the radio station as she had thought, that some people actually detested her, and this revelation had upset her deeply. But if Cordélia was her tormentor, then who was the man on the telephone? Her boyfriend? Christine figured that she was sure of at least one thing: *Cordélia was lying.* That was something she knew for a fact. And if Cordélia was lying, that meant that at the very least she was also an accomplice – unlike Ilan, who had understood the truth regarding the emails.

Another certainty immediately struck her, like an unexpected thunderclap. *Even if it was not her, Cordélia must know who was harassing her.* Through Cordélia, Christine had the means to trace that person.

She was electrified at the thought.

She went along the corridor as far as the stairway leading down to the platform and, as before, she waited at the top of the steps until the train pulled into the station. Direction Basso-Cambo, once again. Once she was in the Métro, she observed Cordélia discreetly from the protective shadow of her hood. The intern was again frenetically tapping away on her phone. This time, the journey lasted a bit longer. Eight stations, to be precise. After Mirail-Université, the young woman began to move. Christine looked up at the display. She immediately felt vaguely apprehensive, as if an unusual alarm signal had flashed up on a car dashboard: Métro Reynerie. She had never set foot in this neighbourhood, but she knew it by reputation: gangs, violence, trafficking, assaults. It was often mentioned in the local news.

She stepped out onto the platform, behind Cordélia and several other passengers – women, which reassured her somewhat. But once everyone had emerged onto the immense deserted esplanade, swept by an icy wind, and she saw the choppy black water of the little pond and the huge soot-coloured clouds drifting above the rows of faded tower blocks, her excitement for the 'hunt' evaporated all of a sudden.

Christine saw Cordélia make her way up the snowy pavement with a hurried step, then veer off to follow a footpath where the snow was well trampled in the direction of the rows of concrete dwellings. The wind was blowing hard and the temperature had dropped even lower.

In a few seconds the passengers from the Métro had vanished into the twilight and Christine was alone. She left the pavement to take the footpath. As she climbed a little hill she could not help but count the number of figures lounging at the foot of the concrete block: eight. She was grateful for the hood pulled over her head, because she thought it made her look like someone who would live in this neighbourhood. Then she remembered what she had in her satchel: invoices, receipts, credit card slips, chequebooks – and she went pale.

Cordélia had made her way past a row of cars parked at the foot of the central building, and Christine looked in her direction just in time to see her disappear through a glass door. What if she needed a code? She could hardly see herself asking one of the shadowy figures hanging around outside, or waiting for someone to show up and let her in.

A few solitary flurries drifted down through the gloom and, looking up, she saw that the sky was growing darker and darker, swelling with clouds above the bare branches.

She could hear dogs barking somewhere further away, and a voice calling, 'Booba, come here!' Hip-hop from one of the cars with an open sunroof, and youthful laughter and voices calling and echoing like tennis balls being batted back and forth in the dusk:

'Hey, man, it's bloody freezing out here, forget your fucking car.'

'I don't give a fuck. Go on, step on it.'

'Hey, man! Whatta fuck you doin'? That's not the way, man!'

'That's not the way? Not the way? Whatta fuck d'you know?'

'Ey! I been working in a garage, after all!'

'Fuck, hear that? Bro's been workin' in a garage. Two weeks and they got rid of you! Fine job! I woulda been pissed off. Fuck it man, I woulda fixed him, that fat bastard. But you went home to Mummy with your tail between your legs, boo hoo hoo . . . Know what? They been pissing on you, bro . . . That's what they done.'

'Hey, don't you go talking to my little brother like that, you hear? For starters, he's the one who left that shit garage – he packed it in, you got it?'

'Got it, bro. Easy.'

'No, it in't easy. It's anything but easy, even. If I hear you telling any more lies and talking shit like that to my little brother, I'll bust your face and put it on YouTube.'

★

The snow reflected the lights of the buildings, but the trees, even with their bare branches, retained the darkness. Christine drew level with the cars and made her way past. Her instinct told her that she was being watched, so she hurried across the trampled snow. The voices around the car had fallen silent. Her pulse began to beat erratically. She was relieved to see that the door had stayed open and she hurried into the hallway, panicked at the thought that the kids outside might follow her, or that there might be others inside. But it wasn't kids waiting for her in the entrance. It was the old codgers. Sitting on folding chairs, despite the lack of space. Half a dozen of them. They stopped talking the moment she crossed the threshold.

'Uh . . . Good evening,' she said, surprised.

There was a murmur of voices and a few smiles when they saw she was not a dealer. They immediately lost interest in her.

Their conversation resumed and she went discreetly over to the mailboxes. She leaned closer and quickly read the names.

*Shit . . . no Cordélia!*

She looked again, increasingly nervous. One name caught her eye. *Corinne Délia.* Fourth floor: 19B. She hurried to the lift and glanced over at the little committee of observers, but they were no longer paying attention to her. In the lift she forced herself to breathe calmly. Every fibre in her body told her she ought to get out of there as quickly as she could.

The long corridor was empty. She pressed the timer for the light and began walking past the doors. She could hear the sounds of television and dishes, electro music, a baby crying, children shouting, their cries echoing down the endless corridor . . . She turned a corner. Then another. Graffiti on the wall. She came to the last door.

19B.

She stopped to listen. Music came through the door; the sort of R&B pop you could hear on channels like MTV Base. She took a deep breath and pressed the buzzer. A shrill sound rang out beyond the door. She thought she would hear Cordélia's footsteps, but there was nothing. The music continued. But someone was there.

The light went out.

She was plunged into darkness. Only the luminous little eye of the spyhole broke the pitch black. Then even it disappeared and Christine realised she was being watched. And what if someone else opened the door? The man who had threatened her on the telephone, for example?

Her panic was starting to overwhelm her: she could already recognise the symptoms in her gut.

Then the door opened wide, flooding her with light and sound, and she started.

She looked up.

And realised that her mouth was open, forming a perfect O.

*Cordélia.*

*Standing on the threshold, naked.*

Her tall figure stood against the light of the flat behind her. Christine wondered where the light in her eyes came from, because her face was still in shadow. And then her gaze dropped lower down and she shuddered: the intern's arms were completely tattooed from shoulder to wrist. It was as if she were wearing transparent lace over her skin. Christine realised she had never seen her bare-armed at work. On her right bicep was a ruddy sunset illuminating burgundy skyscrapers; the Statue of Liberty and blue waves veiled her forearm. On her other arm was a yellow, laughing skull, its eyes lined in black; a spider's web; scarlet roses and a huge cross. She was also tattooed on her thighs and hips. A rudimentary alphabet, which must have had a particular meaning for the woman wearing it. Christine thought with a shiver that it was a bit like walking around with your life story printed on your skin. Her gaze then took in Cordélia's tiny breasts, and her navel, where – contrary to what she would have expected – there was no piercing; her firm stomach muscles, and her slim boy's hips. Finally her gaze came to rest on her groin: as smooth as a shell.

Again she felt a shiver down her spine.

For a moment she could not take her eyes off Cordélia's labia minora which, in the shadow, formed a veritable seam of flesh, but what drew her eye was the dull metallic gleam of a semi-circular genital piercing, ending in two tiny balls that shone on either side of the young woman's clitoris.

She realised that her blood was flowing more quickly. Her head was spinning.

'Come in,' said Cordélia.

# 15

## Duet

A baby was screaming.

A furious, famished wailing rose from the room next door, then Cordélia's calming voice could be heard, 'Hush, my angel . . . hush, my sweetie . . . my lovely, my lovely . . .' The wailing subsided then gradually stopped.

Christine looked around her.

IKEA furniture, cheap trinkets, film posters: *Lost Highway, The Crow, Eastern Promises.* The music was too loud – pounding bass, binary techno for the dance floor; there was a smell of candles, the baby's screaming, the alcohol, the vision of Cordélia's nudity: Christine was struggling against the painful throbbing in her head.

It was too hot in the flat. For a brief moment, she felt a raging desire for air. She put down her bag and hurried out onto the balcony. Above the buildings, the last light of day was fading in an ultimate burst of colour beneath a veil of low, dark clouds. Four floors further down, the hooded shadows were still calling to each other in loud voices. Christine pictured herself heading back to the Métro station and shivered.

She went back inside.

Contrary to what she had expected, she was the one who had been surprised, not Cordélia. She wondered if Cordélia was in the habit of wandering around her flat naked or whether the girl had greeted her like this in order to unsettle her. She had to pull herself together very quickly. She would never have imagined Cordélia as a mother. The girl wasn't even twenty years old. She had no steady job, just a poorly paid internship. Where was the father?

The young woman came out of the bedroom and closed the door behind her. This time she was wearing a dressing gown as black as all the rest of her wardrobe. Only the cuffs were red, as were the words written on the sleeves: FUCK ME, I'M FAMOUS. The dressing gown stopped at the top of her long skinny legs.

'What the fuck are you doing here?'

'I came here to try to find out why you lied,' declared Christine.

The two women stared at each other. Christine calmly took a seat on the sagging sofa, and crossed her legs.

'Get out,' hissed Cordélia. 'Get out of my house. Right now.'

Christine did not move, merely sweeping the room with her gaze, feigning nonchalance in spite of the ping-ponging in her chest.

'Well?' she said, looking up after a while, as if she was surprised Cordélia was still standing.

Cordélia's eyes, ringed in black, now became calculating: clearly she was weighing up the situation. Hunting for a response.

'You have no right to be here,' she said. 'Out. Piss off.'

'Oh,' said Christine, her tone casual. 'What are you going to do – call the police?'

She thought she could detect a flicker of doubt in Cordélia's eyes. It lasted only a fraction of a second, and then she heard a nervous laugh.

'Right,' she said, her tone indicating that she had not lost all her sense of humour, or her sang-froid.

She left the room and Christine, more nervous than she would have liked, heard the sound of a fridge door opening and closing. The young woman came back with two bottles of beer, opened and covered in condensation, and she put one down in front of Christine before flopping into the remaining armchair.

'Well, *Madam-I'm-taking-myself-very-seriously*, what do we do now?'

Her tone was spiteful. Christine noticed that Cordélia's dressing gown had ridden up and that she was making no effort to hide what was underneath. The young woman reached for her beer and took a swallow. Christine did likewise.

The alcohol she'd drunk earlier that afternoon had made her thirsty.

'Who told you to lie?' she asked, putting her beer back down.

'What difference does it make?' Her pupils were dilated: Christine wondered if the girl was on drugs. 'You came all this way just to ask me that? In this neighbourhood? Weren't you scared? Jesus, what are you wearing: where did you dig up such an ugly thing? And what are you dragging around in there, anyway?'

'Who is the man on the telephone, Corinne? Your boyfriend? Your . . . pimp?'

133

A flicker of anger in the girl's eyes.

'What? What did you say?' Her tone was dangerously unstable. 'Don't you fucking dare talk to me like that. Who do you think you are, anyway, you bourgeois slut!'

'Where is the baby's father?' continued Christine, unperturbed.

'None of your fucking business.'

'Are you bringing it up on your own? Who looks after it when you're not here? How do you manage?'

Cordélia scowled at her. But her look was no longer quite as hard or confident as before.

'I don't have to answer your questions. What is this, some fucking interrogation?'

'It can't be easy,' continued Christine, her tone more conciliatory. 'Could I – could I see the baby?'

The young woman shot her a suspicious glance.

'What for?'

'Just because. I like children.'

'Well then, how do you explain the fact that you still don't have any?' hissed the intern through her teeth.

Christine pretended to ignore the attack, but she felt the blow, her belly contracting as if someone had just punched her.

'What's his name?' she asked gently.

A pause.

'Anton.'

'That's a nice name.'

'Don't treat me like I'm an idiot! If you think you're going to win me over pretending to be all nice . . .'

'Can I see him or not?'

The young woman hesitated. Finally, she stood up, never taking her eyes off Christine. She went into the next room and came back with the sleeping infant in her arms.

'How old is he?'

'A year.'

Christine stood up herself and went over to the mother and her son.

'He's lovely.'

'That's enough,' said Cordélia.

She took the baby back into the other room.

'And now you get out of here,' she shouted as she came back into the living room. 'Out. Right now!'

'Who told you to lie?' said Christine, not budging an inch.

'You are fucking pissing me off. I told you to get out!'

The young woman's face was only a few inches from hers, and her fury was so intense that Christine felt as if she were staring at a wall of flame. Cordélia was a good six inches taller than her.

'Quiet! You're going to wake Anton. Not until I get an answer.'

She sat back down, trying to hide the trembling of her knees and hands.

'I know an excellent private kindergarten and primary school,' she added.

'What?'

'For your son. The head is a friend of mine. It's rather expensive, but we might be able to come to an arrangement. Or would you rather Anton grew up in this neighbourhood? Can you imagine what will happen in a few years? When you won't be here to keep an eye on him? And the guys downstairs start offering him money to be the lookout. Or drugs. That's the way it starts. How old will he be by then, eight years old? Nine?'

She saw a gleam of terror flare briefly in the young woman's eyes.

'I'm offering you a solution so that your son can attend a good school, and have a better chance in life, a chance to get away from what is waiting for him just outside this building.'

'This is some sort of fucking joke, isn't it?' said the young woman. 'You really think I'm going to swallow something like that? Even if I give you the information, once you leave here you'll be trying to forget us as soon as possible!'

Christine noted her use of *us*. She repressed a smile: she'd found her way in. She took out her mobile, switched it to speakerphone and pressed a button.

'Alain Maynadier, Crédit Mutuel,' said a voice on the loudspeaker.

She introduced herself.

'Hello, Alain, It's Christine Steinmeyer, I'd like to make a transfer to another account,' she said. 'How do I go about it? Is it possible over the phone?'

The bank employee outlined the procedure. She thanked him.

'I'll call you back in fifteen minutes.'

Cordélia was staring at her. Something had changed in her eyes. 'Well?'

135

'How do you know that whoever asked me to lie hasn't offered me an even bigger amount?'

'And did they also offer you a future for your child?'

*Touché.* Cordélia recoiled, as if she had just burned herself. She sank deeper in her chair.

'Are you – are you that determined to know the truth?'

'Someone is seriously fucking with my life. So, yes: I am determined.'

She saw Cordélia think. *Give her time.* She picked up her beer. The silence went on. Cordélia took two more sips, looking pensive. Never taking her eyes off Christine. She glanced at her own bottle; she had already drunk half of it, just like that.

Finally Cordélia spoke.

'I didn't want to do it. I didn't want to . . . but they forced me.'

*That's a lie*, thought Christine, but she didn't say anything.

'They forced me. And they gave me money. They told me that if I didn't do it, I'd be out on the street. They're threatening to evict me. With my baby.'

Cordélia crossed her legs and once again Christine had to force herself not to look lower down.

'I got this flat thanks to a friend who's subletting it to me. I moved out of my parents' place. And Anton's father went away without leaving an address.'

'Why did you leave home?' asked Christine.

'My father was drinking, my mother was drinking, my brother was drinking . . . My father is unemployed, so is my brother . . . When I was fifteen, my dear brother tried to fuck me and since I didn't want to, he broke my tooth. Four people in fifty square metres; a family of nutcases. I didn't want my baby to grow up in a place like that.'

*Is that where you grew so hard? Is it because of them that you became so cold? So calculating? Or is this just another lie? Another one of your inventions?* It seemed so much like a lie that it might actually be the truth. It reeked of social deprivation, intellectual poverty, filth and alcoholism. No books, or hardly any – but there was bound to be a game console and a satellite dish, just to be sure their brains were steeped in vulgarity as well as alcohol . . . was that too much of a stereotype? But just look outside: the streets were full of stereotypes.

'The internship,' said Cordélia suddenly. 'Ilan and you, you have no idea what it means to me. To work at a radio station. To learn. To come from where I come from and wind up there . . . It was as if for the first time I could imagine a future.'

'How did you get the internship?'

She hesitated. But she had begun. So why not carry on to the end?

'I faked my CV. But I deserved the position. While my parents were sprawled in front of the telly, and my bastard brother was playing *Grand Theft Auto IV*, I was borrowing books from the library and devouring everything I could get my hands on. I had the best marks in French all through school, even if I dropped out when I was sixteen. I lied, that's true. But I do good work, don't I? At least as good as anyone else . . .'

*That's not altogether true*, thought Christine. More than once she'd been surprised to see the gaps in Cordélia's knowledge and wondered how the girl had wound up there.

'All I ask is for a chance to improve,' insisted Cordélia. (Had she seen the flash of doubt in Christine's eyes?) 'I know I can. I work hard and I want to get ahead, and you know it.'

Christine nodded. It was true that the girl wanted to get ahead. There was a hint of sincerity in what she had just said, something that rang true. And it touched her. Christine told herself she mustn't be taken in, that she had to keep a cool head. The girl was trying to win her over.

'The person's name,' she said, setting down her beer.

'If I tell you, they'll make me pay. A lot.'

'Think of your son. You have my word that I will help you. Provided you help me.'

She could see the inner struggle in Cordélia's frightened eyes. And she came up with another idea.

'Listen, here's what I suggest: tell Guillaumot everything. I'll stick up for you, I'll tell him you were the victim of blackmail. I'll tell him to keep your position for you, that you do good work. Not only will I not file a complaint, but I'll help you – financially, too. All you have to do is tell Guillaumot everything. The name you will only tell me. That's my business, and I won't tell anyone about it.'

'They'll hurt my child!'

Seeing that her pupils were once again dilated, Christine understood that she was terrified. She wasn't bluffing.

'I – I'll – listen, we'll find a place, for you, for you and your son . . .'

Good God, what was happening to her?

All of a sudden her words were sticking to her gums like toffee, refusing to leave her lips. She reached out towards the coffee table and her gesture seemed terribly slow. As if her brain wouldn't co-operate. Or it was just the opposite: her body was rebelling. Her fingers hit the beer bottle and it fell over, rolling across the table with a strange, smooth, distorted sound, before it fell silently onto the carpet.

'What is . . . what is wrong with me?'

Cordélia was staring at her. Her lips tight.

Christine concentrated. *Get a grip, come on.*

*Christiiinnneeee . . . are you suuuure you feel aaalll riiiiight?*

What sort of voice was that? She must have taken something to speak like that . . . what a ridiculous intonation . . .

Christine restrained a nervous laugh; they were both completely stoned.

It was as if her veins were running cold, and the room and the sofa were pitching like the deck of a ship.

She looked at Cordélia and got a shock: she was removing her dressing gown. Her long body, covered with tattoos, like a hieroglyph, once again unveiled.

*Cordéliaaaaa . . . what are you doing?*

*I don't feeel weeelll . . . not weeelll at aaaalll . . .*

She saw the girl get up and come around the coffee table. Her sex filled Christine's field of vision. Stunned and fascinated, once again she gazed at the sparkling genital piercing – then Cordélia's still-childish face replaced it, obstructing her visual field, and a warm, moist mouth pressed against her own.

*Doooon't mooooove . . .*

Christine tried to struggle. She was blinking, shivering; her face was soaked. She tried to struggle, to get up and leave, but she couldn't budge an inch.

She concentrated on Cordélia's gestures. The girl had her back to her, she had opened a laptop computer on the coffee table. She was typing something.

Christine saw her round buttocks, her long athletic back and her prominent shoulder blades. Her tattoos were going blurry.

*Heere weee gooo . . .*

Cordélia turned around. Christine knew she was about to pass out.

Blackout . . .

# 16

# Recitative

A noise sliced through her brain like a blade. She woke up instantly.
The noise came again, scraping over her nerves, and she realised it
was a car horn.

The sound of conversation in the street below; the sound of a
motor – and then silence. Christine sat up.

It was almost completely dark, only grey filtering between the
slats of the blinds, and her fear of the dark returned. She tossed
this way and that in sheets as black as her surroundings, which
seemed to be a strange unknown place until she realised it was her
own room. The feeling of silk on her skin: like a shroud. *She was
naked.* An image came back to her with the sudden intensity of an
electric shock: Cordélia, naked too, kissing her, her tongue in her
mouth.

Trembling, she groped for the switch on the bedside lamp but
when she found it and pressed it nothing happened.

Something was shining in the darkness, all the way at the end of
the bed. A rectangle of grey only slightly paler than the ambient
darkness: a screen.

Its faint luminosity indicated that it was on sleep mode. She
wondered, with a cruel feeling of vulnerability, how she had ended
up here, who had undressed her and switched on her computer?
*And what had they done to her while she was asleep?* Instinctively, she
crawled across the bed to the screen to turn on the computer:
anything but this dense gloom. Terrified, leaning on one elbow, she
clicked on the trackpad. The computer came to life. The sudden
brightness of the screen dazzled her, bringing relief, casting shadows
all through the room. A video session was about to begin. A big
triangular arrow in the middle of the screen was waiting for her, but

something held her back: the certainty that what she was about to discover would plunge her even deeper into her nightmare.

Her fingers slid over the trackpad, hesitated, then finally started the video.

She recognised it right away.

The door to flat 19B.

A view of the interior of the little flat. A webcam, set up facing the front door. The shrill sound of the doorbell. The one she had made pressing the button. Then Cordélia's tall form entering the camera's field of vision. From behind. Naked. Her round, pale buttocks, separated by a deep groove. She unlocks the door. Pulls it open and Christine appears, seen from the front. Strangely familiar and strangely different from the picture she had of herself.

On her MacBook Christine saw Christine looking at Cordélia, then Christine's gaze running along the young woman's body, stopping to stare for a long while at her groin. Christine felt her face flush. On the video, Christine's eyes were open wide, her gaze glowing. There could be no doubt about the object of her fascination. Then Cordélia's voice saying calmly, 'Come in,' and Christine following the intern into the flat.

*As if she expected you,* she thought. *As if you had been there before.*

The next image.

Christine sitting on the sofa with her back to the camera.

Only her neck and shoulders are visible; Cordélia is standing in front of her. In an eminently suggestive pose. She spreads her thighs, her fingers with their nails painted a neon yellow spread the lips of her vagina, in a gesture that is shockingly immodest and disturbingly intimate. Christine doesn't move. She is as motionless as a statue.

With her back to the camera, her attitude suggests that she is staring at the young woman's genitals, the way she did in the doorway.

The next image. Christine started: Christine and Cordélia naked on the sofa, facing the camera this time. *They are kissing.* Christine has her eyes closed, her hand is buried between the intern's thighs, and they are kissing. The young woman is moaning. Christine is not moving – for good reason.

The final image: Christine sees Christine on the sofa, once again with her back to the camera; Cordélia is facing her and counting a wad of bank notes:

'Eighteen hundred . . . Nineteen hundred . . . Two thousand. Okay,

I'll withdraw my complaint. But it's not just because of the money, it's because you were so good at making me come.'

Snow on the screen. The little private porn film was over.

She gulped. Her temples pounded. She now had a partial answer to what had happened while she was unconscious.

*Trapped.* If Guillaumot or anyone at the radio station happened to see this video, it would confirm everything Cordélia had said. And her career would be well and truly over. *Was this blackmail?* Was this the next stage? Is this how things were going to end? But she had already lost her fiancé and her job . . . What did she have left to lose?

The drug she'd been given must still be in her blood, because her brain felt all foggy and her arms and legs were heavy.

Suddenly she remembered her satchel and she looked anxiously all around her, then felt intense relief when she saw it on a corner of the bed. Next to it on the black sheet there was a white rectangle. She grabbed the piece of paper and held it up to the glow of the screen.

A receipt for a bank withdrawal. She was overcome with panic.

She recognised the first few and last few digits: it was her bank account. On it was written: '*Withdrawal, date: 28/12/12, time: 10.03, cashpoint 392081*'; a sum of €2,000 had been debited from her account that very morning. Then she made the connection with the images on the video where she'd seen the girl counting a wad of bank notes.

A double trigger trap . . .

There was something else on the sheet next to the MacBook. A plastic CD case. She grabbed it.

*Madame Butterfly*. Opera, naturally.

She recalled with a shiver that Madame Butterfly commits suicide at the end. Fear was working its way into every corner of her brain. Was that what they were trying to drive her to? A dreadful memory came to her: her father holding her so tight that it hurt, his strangely shrill, erratic voice saying over and over: *Oh, my darling, there has been a terrible, terrible, terrible accident.*

She only learned the truth much later: Madeleine had hanged herself.

At the age of sixteen.

She closed the video player and saw that her email had stayed open on the screen. Or rather that someone had opened it while she was sleeping. Shit, she had downloaded an entire security package, erased all the cookies, changed her password – how was this possible? Her gaze scrolled mechanically through the emails that had come in since the last time she had checked. There was one from the vet entitled 'Iggy', there were several messages from online shops, then she froze: malebolge@hell.com. The subject of the message was 'OPERA'. She held her breath and clicked the trackpad.

*I hope you like opera, Christine.*

Nothing else.

*Bloody fucking bastard!*

She grabbed the MacBook with both hands and with a gesture that was both liberating and vengeful hurled it with all her strength against the wall of the room, and watched as it smashed then fell to the floor, no longer functioning but almost intact: MacBooks are virtually indestructible . . .

In the little speakers, the first movement of the Ninth Symphony – light violins, hazy horns and sparkling harp – was like the mournful stillness of an autumn morning in the forest, when suddenly a storm of brass and strings burst forth after a thunder of pounding kettle-drums. At this new surge of music in the little room beneath the eaves, Servaz looked up from his reading for a moment – not at something specific but in order to listen more attentively, his eyes lost in contemplation of the wall, that passage where the percussionist strikes the rhythm with dull thuds, as if signalling approaching tragedy. He'd heard it hundreds of times, yet he always felt it in his blood, those hammered blows of destiny.

Relegating the music to the background, he re-focused his attention on the printed words. He still had trouble reading on screen, so he'd gone to the library before coming home. He didn't know exactly what he was looking for, to be honest. But he had eventually unearthed a few books. And now he was immersed in titles such as *The Manipulators Are Amongst Us* or *Moral Harassment: Perverse Violence in Everyday Life*.

What he gathered from these books was that certain encounters can change your life for the better and others can drive you to the brink, or even constitute mortal danger. Within society there were perverse, manipulative minds, people who every day caught in their nets weak and vulnerable individuals, men and women whom they went to great lengths to control, debase and destroy. Was this what had happened to Célia Jablonka? Had she fallen in with a bad lot? When he got home he typed *Moki* into an Internet search engine and discovered that the Blue Moki was a perciform fish native to New Zealand, the Moki Bar was a concert café in the 20th arrondissement in Paris, and the word was also used to refer to a type of haiku in Japanese. But there was no one by the name of Moki in either the White or the Yellow Pages – no Moki at all other than in Célia Jablonka's diary.

In his reading, Servaz discovered there was a first stage, called *breaking and entering*, when the manipulator did everything in his power to penetrate the other person's psychic territory, causing them to lose their bearings, and invading their thoughts and replacing them with his own. Then came control and isolation: from family, friends, loved ones. *Like in a cult*, thought Servaz. At the same time, denigration, humiliation and acts of intimidation were destined to bring on a collapse of identity in the victim's mind, and to destroy their self-esteem.

If the victim resisted, showed opposition and didn't react as predicted, then out came threats, physical violence and, when the victim was a woman, sexual violence – including rape, or murder. Once again, Servaz wondered if this was what had happened to Célia. Should he dig deeper or was he wasting his time? She hadn't been married, but maybe she'd had a boyfriend, a companion at the time of the event. Had he been interrogated? There was virtually no information in the file that Desgranges had given him. The case had been closed very quickly.

He went on reading.

According to these texts, psychological violence was deeply egalitarian, transcending social class. Domestic and professional tyrants were everywhere, hidden behind an innocuous social masquerade.

Finally, when it came to couples, the bully knew his victim very well – her weaknesses, her flaws: this gave him a considerable advantage. In this case, psychological violence consisted in humiliating, debasing, provoking a feeling of shame, and making the victim lose all self-confidence: 'What would become of you without me?' The partner was terrorised by indirect aggression perpetrated against animals or children; she was cut off from former friends and family; her defences were methodically undermined by a continuous barrage of minor attacks until she ended up losing any ability to discriminate, until she was immersed in a state of mental confusion, having lost all bearings, incapable of distinguishing what was normal from what was abnormal. *Until she reached a point where she tolerated what was intolerable.* She would be held captive in a climate of permanent tension and anxiety: the victim never knew where the next attack might come from, or when. Whereas the partner remained two-faced: smiling, affable and likable on the outside; unstable, intimidating and scornful within the four walls of home – so much so that it was the victim who eventually ended up seeming difficult and antisocial in the eyes of others, when sometimes she could no longer help but overreact at odd times.

With the spread of the Internet, stalkers could now choose their targets outside the family or the workplace. The Web had made this activity, too, more democratic: it was no longer only celebrities who fell victim to stalkers; anyone could be a target now.

Servaz stood up and went to the window.

Night was falling on the expanse of snow and woods as it melted into the greyness, slowly turning to midnight blue.

He went back to Célia.

If someone had driven her to suicide, Servaz didn't believe that they were acting without motivation. Unmotivated crime didn't exist. Serial killers struck because of their sexual drive, crimes of passion were driven by jealousy, fraud by the lure of money; even a stalker only became a stalker because at a given moment something about his victim had drawn his gaze: there was always a motive. And that motive, if it existed, if Célia Jablonka wasn't simply depressive and paranoid, must be hidden somewhere in the details of her life.

Behind him, the adagio came quietly to its almost tentative coda, slow and furtive like a deer's footsteps in the forest, light and fragile as smoke – and everything was consumed. Everything except silence.

# 17

# Walk-on

Xanax, Prozac, Stilnox. Why did all these meds have names straight out of some science-fiction film, names that in and of themselves implied danger? She had wondered as much the night before, training her glassy gaze upon the unbelievable number of legal drugs that inhabited her medicine cabinet.

She had stared at them in the palm of her hand: the two-colour capsule, the big blue divisible oval tablet and the little white rod, also divisible (but she hadn't cut either one). One antidepressant, one tranquilliser and one sleeping tablet: memories of an era when her demons had occupied such a space in her life that only a chemical carapace could keep them at bay – and she had wondered whether the solution might be simply to increase the dose by ten or twenty right there. Then she had stuffed all three in her mouth before lifting the tooth glass to her lips, her hand trembling so violently that she had spilled half its contents. After that, she went to curl up under the duvet in a ball, her brain feeling as if it were a landing strip for suicidal thoughts.

Now that morning had come to her aid, Christine could not remember exactly what those thoughts had been (she remembered, rather, the sort of semi-coma which preceded her terrifying plunge into a sleep resembling a black and lifeless abyss), but she knew she was in danger. Greater danger than any she had ever known. The thought was so chilling that her teeth began to chatter, despite the fact she had bundled herself up in the sheets and duvet, leaving the rest of the mattress bare. She stood up with the duvet still over her shoulders, just like the homeless man down in the street, and she walked hesitantly into the living room. It wasn't just an impression: it was cold in the flat. She must have turned the heat down without noticing.

Now she turned it up as high as it would go before heading over to the kitchen. She happened to look at the clock, and in a moment of distraction she told herself she had to get ready to go to work, and then the memory of Guillaumot's words came back to her, leaving her stunned. She swayed. She had to reach out for the kitchen counter to keep her balance.

She saw Iggy's empty bowl and this was like another punch in the stomach. She hurried to the bathroom. Quick, another capsule, another tablet.

Clinging to the sink, she forced herself to look in the mirror and saw her terrified face. *And now? What's going to happen?* The oval tablet, the two-colour capsule – like ice cream with two colours – were already in the palm of her hand. The little voice, however, hadn't had its final say: *You are reacting exactly as they expect you to*, it said acidly. *You are behaving just as they predicted.*

*And so what?* was what she felt like replying. *What fucking difference does it make? Have you got an answer? No? Then shut up!*

She gazed at the tablets, then put them on the edge of the sink for the time being.

She went back into the living room with an effervescent aspirin dissolving in a glass, sat down on the sofa and stayed there for a long time without moving. She had lost her bearings: she was a ship come loose from its moorings – adrift, constantly in danger of shattering on the rocks . . . It was so much easier to let oneself go . . . *The truth is, I have no options left; I've lost my job, my man – and no doubt it won't stop there.*

She felt crushed by the truth. *In the meantime, it doesn't stop you from thinking,* insisted the little voice all the same, the one she had just sent packing. She obeyed. Her first thought was that now she had to make her way through a world that was radically different from the one she had always known. Like after a tornado, everything that had gone to make up her life before had been swept away and in this new devastated, unrecognisable world the rules had changed. If she wanted to survive, she had to adapt. Except that this new world was like a swamp without any solid ground to stand on. And she had no compass, no map to help her find her way. Then she remembered that there *was*, in fact, still a little corner of solid ground, the same one that had been there before: Cordélia. The thought that had occurred to her while she was shadowing her had lost none of its pertinence: *Cordélia must know who was behind all this.* Because Christine no longer believed she could be the instigator. It was too elaborate. Too complicated. How could Cordélia have orchestrated and implemented such a plan with a part-time job and a baby on her hands? The young woman was surely motivated solely by the prospect of financial gain. Someone had promised her – or already given her – a hefty sum.

A second thought flashed through her mind: how could she find out more about Cordélia without attracting the attention of whoever was constantly watching her? Answer: she couldn't do it on her own. Some obscure hunch told her there were at least two people on the other side: Cordélia, and the man on the telephone, and perhaps more. All alone, she could not manage. She had to get help from someone who could act on her behalf. But who? Gérald was out of the question; and Ilan, too, now. The same went for her father and mother.

And then an idea formed: she thought of two totally unexpected people, whom her tormentor or tormentors could not possibly know; the first one was just downstairs from her apartment.

Christine suddenly felt buoyed by an abrupt, paradoxical bliss: the idea was so absurd that *they* could never envisage it. A considerable problem did remain, however: how to convince the person in question.

She went to the window and looked at him, sitting there on his patch of pavement among his cardboard boxes and the bin bags containing all his personal belongings.

He was turning his head from left to right, sweeping the street with his piercing gaze. The ideal person. She recalled their conversations. He had always seemed lucid, calm, sensible, and astonishingly quick-witted in spite of his situation.

*If he's so quick-witted, can you tell me what the fuck he's doing on the street?* asked the little inner voice, so fond of contradicting her.

*Shut up.*

Christine saw him smile and thank a woman who had just dropped a coin in his cup, then watch her as she walked on down the street.

Christine backed away from the window. First she had to wake up.

An almost icy shower got her blood flowing. She made a very strong coffee, and dressed quickly. When she went out into the street, she felt strangely cheered. She greeted him from across the road, and he waved back. She hurried to the nearest cashpoint, on the place des Carmes. When she stood in front of the machine, Christine did some rapid maths. The maximum withdrawal authorised for her credit card was €3,000 over a period of thirty days; her tormentors had withdrawn €2,000 the previous day and she felt a moment of apprehension as she placed her card in the slot. What if they had taken more? Would that mean she had no more credit? Nothing of the sort happened, and she looked with relief at the pile of bank notes the machine spat out. She then stopped at the boulangerie to buy two croissants – the baker gave her a filthy look when she paid with a fifty-euro note. Back in her flat, she wrote a note, which she folded and slipped in her pocket. For a split second she wondered whether she was completely out to lunch. She decided she wasn't, poured some black coffee into a Tupperware cup and put the croissants in the microwave. She then put a plastic lid on the coffee, returned the hot croissants to their paper bag and headed for the lift.

'Here, this is for you,' she declared two minutes later, down in the street, as she handed him everything.

She saw a smile spread through his greying beard. Yellow, crooked teeth appeared in the middle of his craggy face, as well as several metal stumps shining in the corner of his mouth.

'Well! I'm being spoiled! A proper breakfast.' There was astonishment in his tone.

'What's your name?' she asked.

He shot her a surprised, wary look.

'Max.'

'Max,' she said, slipping the folded paper inside a twenty-euro note into his coat pocket, 'I can help you. I just put a note in your pocket. Be careful no one sees you read it. It's very important.'

This time, his look was more cautious than surprised. He nodded, without smiling, and she felt his gaze upon her back the entire time it took her to cross the road and go back to her building. When she got home, she went to her bedroom window. He was already looking up towards her window; he knew very well where she lived. Even from this distance, she could gauge the bewilderment in his eyes. He slowly raised his cup, as if drinking a toast. Never taking his eyes off her. Unsmiling. Only later, once he'd finished the coffee and eaten the croissants, did he lie down and disappear beneath his cardboard and his blanket.

Christine could recall every word she had written:

*The building code is 1945. There's another entrance on the street at the back. Wait for an hour. Then come in the back entrance and go up to the third floor, to the door on the left. I have some work for you. Trust me, it's nothing illegal, however it may seem.*

It was only once she left the bedroom that she realised how afraid she was. Was it wise to invite someone like him to her place? What did she actually know about him? Absolutely nothing. He might be an ex-convict, a strung-out junkie, a thief, a rapist.

Too late. She had given him the code.

Having said that, she could always refuse to open the door. She walked over to the door and checked that it was locked. Then she went back to her bedroom. Now he was sitting again, staring up at her window. And at her. He made no sign to communicate whether he accepted or refused her offer. He just went on observing her from down there, his face upturned, unreadable.

Suddenly she felt very uncomfortable: he must take her for a madwoman.

*Then what will he think when you've explained what you want from him.*

Every five minutes she went back to the window, more and more impatient, but he still hadn't moved. After roughly an hour, she went to the window again and froze. The pavement was empty: he had left his post. When the doorbell shattered the silence of the flat, she stiffened. And yet he was doing just what she had asked him to do.

*Dear God, you are completely crazy.*

She took a long deep breath. And covered the distance to the door, unbolted it and opened it.

# 18

## Verismo

Her first thought was that he was very tall. At least one metre ninety. And very thin.

'I'll stay here if you want,' he said with a big ironic smile, sensing her hesitation. 'I can take my shoes off, too, but I don't advise it.'

His voice was calming, relaxed; she felt ridiculous.

'No, no, come in.'

She stepped aside and he walked past her. Then the smell reached her nostrils: a mixture of rancid sweat, filth, unwashed feet, and in the background the sickly sweet but insistent stench of alcohol oozing from every pore. Perhaps in the street he did not stink as much as some of his fellows, but here, in the confined space of the flat, his stench enveloped her like a cloud of acetone. She could not help but be glad she did not have five noses like an ant. She wrinkled the only one she had and pointed in the direction of the living room, keeping her distance. As he made his way calmly through the room, she eyed his mud-encrusted shoes clumping across her floor.

'Would you like a coffee?' she said.

'Do you have any fruit juice?'

*The fermented and distilled kind?* asked the nasty little voice inside, but she stifled it. She went to fetch a bottle from the fridge and pointed to the sofa.

'You're not afraid of germs?' he joked as he sat down and took the glass, three quarters full, in a big hand that was almost as black as his fingerless glove; his white nails looked like pale pebbles set against charcoal.

She watched his Adam's apple bob up and down as he took great gulps, as if he were dying of thirst, with no regard for the noise he was making, greedily sending the liquid down his throat then licking his chapped lips with an agile tongue that concluded the operation with a light-hearted click.

'Thanks for the drink,' he said. 'But I'm not prepared to do just anything for money.'

Plunging one hand into the pocket of his stained coat, he set the twenty-euro note in front of him on the coffee table. He put her message next to it.

'If there's nothing illegal about it, why all the mystery?'

His tone was friendly enough, like someone who is curious and entertained by the situation.

'Are you crazy?' he asked, since she didn't answer.

The question made her start. Although his tone was relaxed, he seemed to expect a reply.

'I don't think so,' she said.

'What's your name?'

'Christine.'

'Go on, Christine. Tell me.'

After that, he leaned back into the sofa and crossed his legs. She almost smiled at the thought that in spite of his filthy clothes and his long hair that had not seen a pair of scissors in ages, he made her think of a shrink.

'How did you end up where you are?' she asked, instead of answering. 'What did you do before?'

She saw him hesitate, then his features hardened.

'I was a French teacher,' he began, 'in a private school.'

He frowned and let out a sigh.

'I also used to take the kids on outings at the weekend, or during the autumn or Easter break. In those days, I was a believer. I went to Mass every Sunday with my wife and kids. I was an important member of the community and I had a lot of friends.' He paused for a long time, staring at her. 'I lost my faith the day a little boy's parents filed a complaint against me for *inappropriate behaviour* with their child. According to them, I had shown him my penis. Rumours spread very quickly. It was a small town. Other parents questioned their children, and then they began to spread stories that were even worse. I was taken into custody. I was confronted with the little boy's testimony. There were details that didn't add up. Loads of details. Far too many, in fact. He admitted that he'd made the whole thing up, and I went home. But things didn't stop there. Emails started going around clandestinely. They said that videos with child pornography had been found on my computer, that I masturbated on the sly, looking at the children, during the weekend trips, and that I always found a way to be there whenever they were going to the toilet or taking a shower . . . They said I had even made . . . inappropriate advances to my own children.'

He choked on his last words and when he looked up, Christine could see that his eyes were moist. A little muscle was throbbing beneath the skin on his right cheek. She looked away.

'According to those who spread the rumours and forwarded the emails, the fact that the gendarmerie didn't have sufficient proof clearly didn't mean that I had done nothing; the little boy had withdrawn his testimony so he wouldn't have problems later on, the investigation had been closed because of a simple technical detail, and so on.'

He was perspiring. It occurred to Christine that he must not be used to being indoors any more.

'It was more than suspicion. I was guilty. Someone will always think you're guilty, won't they? There were too many rumours, and too many clues, you see? So all those would-be dispensers of justice, ordinary bastards convinced they are in the right, the sort who are just waiting for an opportunity to give free rein to their violent impulses, they decided to take the law into their own hands. We lived in a pretty house, my wife and kids and I – just outside the village, near the forest. One evening when we were watching television someone threw stones through the living-room window. It happened again two days later, through other windows. Once, twice. A noise like thunder, insults screamed in the night, cries like animals . . . The children were terrified, of course.'

He pointed to his glass and she refilled it. He drank it as thirstily as before, but this time without clicking his tongue. He was no longer in the mood.

'The incidents accumulated. Our cat was poisoned and died, our tyres were regularly slashed, friends stopped seeing us. More and more friends. My children became outcasts; they were treated like pariahs; they had no one to play with. So they played with each other, my son and daughter, twins – they were seven years old that autumn, when it happened: seven years old, can you imagine?'

He shot her a sad smile.

'And then one day my wife looked right at me and said, "You did

152

it, didn't you?" Even she ended up believing I was guilty. You understand: that many people could not be wrong. Something must have
happened, *there's no smoke without fire*. She left me. She took the
children. I began drinking. The headmaster was just waiting for me
to make a wrong move in order to sack me; he too was convinced
there was no smoke without fire. The house was not paid off, so I
lost it. I went to stay with the last friend I had left, then even he said,
"You have to go now." I don't hold a grudge: his wife had said it
was her or me. He made me promise to stay in touch, he gave me
some money, and he said, "Call me whenever you want." I never saw
him again; I never tried to get in touch, and nor did he. He was a
very good friend, the best friend I've ever had.'

He closed his eyes, tight, all his wrinkles converging towards the
corners of his eyes, and then he reopened them. They were bright
and dry again.

'Well,' he said in a firm voice, as if he had just related an amusing
or entertaining story, 'that's enough about me: what do you want
from me, Christine?'

How old was he? He looked close to sixty but given the time he
had been living on the street, he could be ten or even twenty years
younger. He gave an impression of serene strength, in spite of the
terrible story he had just told. She wondered if he had been telling
the truth, if he really was innocent. Or if he had committed at least
some of the acts he was accused of, and had rewritten the story. How
to find out? She decided not to beat about the bush.

'Do I seem in any way unbalanced to you, mentally unstable or
neurotic?'

'No.'

'If I tell you that I have good reason to believe that someone is
following me, or having me followed . . .'

'I believe you.'

'That they are having the building watched.'

'It certainly sounds quite serious.'

'It is. You spend your time on the street, opposite my door. I would
like you to notify me if you see anyone going up and down the street
a bit too often or who seems interested in this building, do you
understand?'

'I'm not an idiot,' he replied good-naturedly. 'Why do you think
someone is having you followed?'

'That's not your business.'

'Oh yes it is. I told you: I'm not prepared to do just anything for money.'

She hesitated. In a way, his profession of faith reassured her. If he was not being driven solely by greed, it might mean that he would not sell his services to the first person who came along.

'Fine,' she said. 'It all began with an anonymous letter six days ago.'

He listened to her without moving, just nodding from time to time, unreadable and patient. Because patience was something he knew well; he spent his life on the street waiting for a coin here, a coin there. However, the further she went with her story, the more she saw his eyes narrow with interest and astonishment. From time to time as he listened to certain details she could see a brief flicker of disbelief, but it vanished almost immediately: he'd seen worse.

'That's interesting,' he concluded simply when she had finished.

'You don't believe me, do you, Max?'

'Not yet. But I don't think you're crazy. How much?' he asked.

'One hundred euros to start with. Then we'll see.'

'See what?'

'The results.'

He smiled.

'One hundred euros and something to eat and another hot coffee, now, right away,' he said.

She laughed for the first time in days.

'Deal.'

He gave her an intense, probing look and shook his head.

'Christine, you don't know me, and yet you opened your door to me without hesitation: I could have used the opportunity to rob you or assault you. You're a pretty woman. And very much on your own, by the looks of it. Why take such a risk?'

She replied, wearily, 'I've already had my share of bad luck; I don't think I could have even more. And besides, I know you: for weeks we've been chatting nearly every day. I have colleagues I talk to less than you.'

He shook his head.

'Don't you read the papers? There are people who live alone and invite people like me into their homes, then one night, for no apparent reason, they end up with their throats cut while they sleep.'

'I'll lock my door after you leave, if that will reassure you,' she teased. 'You don't believe my story, do you?'

The frankness of his answer surprised her:

'For the time being, I see above all the opportunity to earn a little money fairly easily. I will keep my part of the bargain and then I'll decide whether I should believe you. And I have no objection to some soup, a hot coffee and a snack from time to time. Deal?'

She nodded and they smiled at the same time. As if a warm and cosy current had begun to flow between them, she sensed a sudden complicity. It was good to be able to confide in someone, someone who would not judge her, who would give her the benefit of the doubt. For the first time in days she began to feel hopeful again, and she wondered if perhaps her luck was at last beginning to turn.

'Fine,' she said. 'If you notice anyone suspicious, come and tell me and describe them to me. In the meantime, if you think the coast is clear and no one is watching my door, put the cup you use for your coins to your left. If, on the other hand, you notice something fishy, put the cup on your right. Is that clear?'

He nodded and gave a faint smile.

'Cup on the left: coast is clear; cup on the right: danger. Hmm, I like it.'

She suddenly thought of something and got up.

'Do you know anything about opera, Max?'

'A little,' he said, surprising her once again.

She handed him the CD she'd found on the bed.

'What's the connection between *Il Trovatore*, *Tosca* and *Madame Butterfly*?'

He examined the case.

'Suicide,' he answered, after giving it some thought. 'In *Il Trovatore*, Leonora takes poison after promising to give herself to the Count di Luna in order to save Manrico. Madame Butterfly commits hara-kiri after Pinkerton abandons her. And Tosca throws herself into the Tiber from the top of a tower in the Castel Sant'Angelo.'

She was left speechless by his knowledge of opera, but even more so by this revelation. Of course. She should have known. The message was clear.

'Max,' she murmured as gently as possible, 'have you seen your children again?'

A moment of silence, then:

'No.'

# 19

## Tenor

She took out her telephone. She had a second person to call. She took another quick look at Iggy and once again felt close to tears.

She had gone to fetch her dog. Around his head he now had a ridiculous collar in the shape of a funnel, which prevented him from pulling off his dressing. Kept in place by a splint and a thick bandage, his hind leg was as stiff as a pirate's peg leg. Frightened and disorientated, the poor animal spent his time shaking himself in order to try and get rid of these instruments of torture, and banging into the corners of doors and furniture as he moved around.

'You know how much I love you,' she said to him.

The mongrel replied with a whimper that broke her heart. He gave her a pleading look. As if he were thinking, *how can you do such a thing to me?* The vet had asked her why she hadn't come to collect her dog sooner; Christine had stammered that she had family problems, but she could tell she wasn't terribly convincing. The vet gave her a challenging look and said, 'How did you say this happened, again?' She had replied, her voice as diaphanous as an autumn morning, that Iggy had been hit by a car after breaking his lead; there was a hard, sceptical gleam in the vet's eye, and her cheeks flushed with shame.

Christine went back over the plan that had been ripening in her brain. Leave nothing to chance. Anticipate. She looked at her mobile, and the number she was about to call. What if his phone was tapped? *Well, let's see: it must be the CIA behind it, love, with help from the KGB – no, wait, nowadays they call it the FSB . . .*

She walked over to her bedroom window. Max was back at his post, and the cup was on her new ally's left-hand side: the coast was clear. She put on some jeans, running shoes, a jumper and a black sweatshirt, and she pulled the hood up over her face before putting on her sunglasses.

In the street she ignored the homeless man and went straight to the nearest Métro station. When she sat down on the train she examined all the passengers one by one. Young faces and old, and most of them vacant . . . One man in his thirties caught her attention: he had looked at her when she boarded the train, then averted his gaze when she had looked at him in turn.

Christine got off at the Palais de Justice station. While the long escalator was taking her to ground level, she stood still and turned around, and from the shelter of her dark glasses she studied everyone around her in detail: the young man was not among them. When she reached the top of the escalator she immediately took the other one back down, turning around again to make sure no one was doing the same. Satisfied, she briefly admired the vast tapestry with the unicorn, where LIBERTÉ, EGALITÉ, FRATERNITÉ were embroidered in big capital letters, then she hurried down the last few steps before jumping onto the first train heading in the opposite direction. She got out three stations further along, at Jean-Jaurès.

Once she was out in the open air, she wove her way through the crowd milling by the kiosks and the morris column, went round the fountain and the carousel with its wooden horses, crossed the central reservation on the place Wilson and hurried down the rue Saint-Antoine-du-T. She walked as far as a mobile phone shop, entered, removed her hood and her dark glasses, and waited for a salesperson to show some interest in her. Five minutes later, she left with a prepaid mobile, then went into the nearest café.

She threaded her way among the tables and settled at the back, making sure no one had come in behind her. She looked up the number she wanted to call on her old phone, then dialled it on the new one.

After that, with the phone glued to her ear, she waited for someone to answer, someone she had thought she would never call again.

Servaz was sweating profusely. All his muscles were saturated with lactic acid. They were burning so intensely that he felt he was on the verge of paralysis. A vision came over him: his corpse lying on the treadmill, and the electronic coach's voice squealing, 'Get up! Get up! This is no time to be resting, lazybones!'

He switched off the programme and reached for his towel. His soaking T-shirt clung to his back and chest and his lungs were making a noise like a bellows. And yet he did feel a wave of well-being come over him. He wondered why he had waited so long to start getting some exercise. The truth was, he had waited until he was forced to: here, exercise was obligatory, as were all the daily chores – it was part of the therapy. In the beginning Servaz had been very reticent to comply with such discipline, but now he appreciated its routine nature, and the benefits he gained.

He took a quick shower. As he was leaving the former barn that had been made into a gym, he saw Élise wave to him from one of the windows in the main building. His hair was wet and he hurried across the snow-covered lawn in his tracksuit.

'There's a parcel for you,' she said, meeting him in the hallway.

He glanced at the package she was holding. For a split second he was back in the Polish forest. Then something jarred him and he remembered the hotel key.

'Would you like me to open it?' she asked.

'No, it's okay. I'll do it.'

He took it from her hands. He checked the postmark: posted from Toulouse, like last time. 'Thank you,' he said, and she understood he wanted to be alone; she gave him one last look, nodded, and went away.

He waited until she was out of sight to tear off the paper. The same little box in hard cardboard, roughly eleven centimetres by nine. He took a deep breath and lifted the lid. His gaze went straight to the bottom of the box. *A photograph.* At first he didn't understand what he was seeing. Some sort of giant Meccano set. Floating in orbit around the earth, and the earth itself clouded with a cold, blue halo. Huge wings made of solar panels, white cylinders and cross struts, portholes: he was staring at a photograph of the International Space Station.

That was it. He picked up the print. There was something underneath: a little piece of graph paper torn from a spiral notebook, and a few words written in ballpoint pen:

*Another clue, Captain. Time to make headway.*

He focused on the photograph again. First they directed him to room

117, the room where an artist called Célia Jablonka had committed suicide, and now, very clearly, they were pointing towards outer space.

What connection could there be between the two?

He slipped the photograph in his pocket and took out his telephone.

'Charlène?' he said when she answered. 'It's Martin. I have another question for you about that artist you exhibited.'

'Go ahead.'

'Before the exhibition, did Célia Jablonka show any interest in space?'

'Yes. It was the theme of her previous show. Why? Have you found something?'

That familiar tingling.

'Could she have met someone during her research?'

'What do you mean, met someone? Célia met loads of people through her work; she considered herself to be both an artist and a sort of journalist.'

'But you don't know about anyone in particular, that she mentioned?'

'No . . . I didn't have anything to do with that exhibition.'

He thanked her.

'Martin, are you sure you're all right? Your voice sounds funny.'

'I'm okay,' he said. 'But thanks for asking.'

'Take care of yourself,' she said. 'A hug from me.'

He took out the photograph and gazed at it. Space exploration . . . a sensitive domain, at the crossroads between science and politics. How many people were there in Toulouse and the surrounding area whose work was closely or remotely connected with the space industry? Probably thousands. And Servaz didn't even know what he was looking for.

'I can't believe it, it's snowing again!' said a familiar voice behind him.

Servaz turned around. He smiled. The young man in the wrinkled Burberry brushing himself off in the hallway had the slightly chubby face of a kid who is overfond of sweets, with chestnut hair sweeping across his brow and the slovenly look of an adolescent who spends too much time on the computer, or with his video games and graphic novels. And yet at the age of thirty-two, Lieutenant Vincent Espérandieu already had two children – one of whom was Servaz's godson – and he was married to one of the most beautiful women in Toulouse. The very same woman whom Servaz had just called on the phone and recently dropped in to see.

'Hey,' said Vincent. 'Charlène told me you stopped by to see her and ask about that artist who committed suicide. What's this about? Do you have something new?'

Servaz looked at him. He reached into his pocket for the little pearl-grey cardboard box that he had just opened, and handed it to him.

'Here. Could you take a look at this? See where this thing was made, and where it's sold? There's the make inside.'

His assistant frowned and took the box without looking at it.

'What is this? An official request? Are you investigating? Are you back among us?'

'Not yet.'

'I checked into it. That case is closed, Martin. They concluded it was a suicide.'

'I know. Like the Alègre affair.'

'Except that in the case of our girl, it was Delmas who did the autopsy.'

'I know that as well. And he was categorical: as far as he's concerned, it was a suicide.'

'Did Delmas talk to you?' Espérandieu did not hide his surprise. 'When was that?'

'It doesn't matter. And what if someone drove her to commit suicide?'

'You talked to Delmas?' insisted Vincent, puzzled. 'What are you playing at, exactly?'

'What if someone was behind all this?'

'What do you mean?'

'Hounding, harassing, manipulating . . .'

'Do you have any proof?'

'Not yet.'

'What the hell is going on, for fuck's sake! Are you investigating? Don't you know you're on sick leave? You're not supposed to be investigating anything at all!'

'You came all the way here just to tell me that? You could have done that over the phone. I'm not investigating: I'm just checking a few things.'

Espérandieu shook his head.

'Thanks for the welcome. How are you?'

Servaz was immediately sorry he had got carried away. Vincent was the only person who came regularly to see him.

'Didn't Charlène tell you?'

'Yes. She thought you were looking well.'

Servaz nodded slowly. Espérandieu pointed to the box.

'What is this?'

'I got it in the post today. There was this photograph inside.'

He handed the picture of the space station to Vincent.

'And four days ago I got an electronic hotel key. In an identical box. The key to the room where Célia Jablonka committed suicide.'

He saw Vincent's eyes light up like a thousand-watt bulb.

'So that's why you started on this investigation, then?'

Servaz nodded.

'Do you have any idea who might have sent them?'

He shook his head.

'Martin, if anyone finds out—'

'Do you want to help me or not?'

'Go on.'

'I need to find out whether Célia Jablonka had filed a complaint for harassment, or whether she felt threatened, or whether she spoke to any of her friends: there is nothing in the file. And also whether she had any depressive tendencies, or had already attempted suicide. And I want to know if this sort of box is mass-produced, or manufactured on a small scale, and where.'

Espérandieu nodded.

'Suppose I do agree to help you, you can't just go showing up all over the place saying you're a cop and you're in charge of an investigation – eventually it will get back to our superiors.'

'He's right, boss.'

Servaz swung round in the direction of the voice belonging to the extraordinarily unprepossessing face that had just come in, now emerging from a hood with a fake fur lining. Samira Cheung was the only member of his team who called him 'boss'. The daughter of a Hong Kong Chinese father and a French-Moroccan mother, she was also the youngest on the team. And quite clearly one of the brightest.

'I've been all round the place,' she said. 'It's quite cosy here, you feel like you're in a retirement home.'

Servaz had not seen Samira in months. He realised he must no longer be accustomed to her looks because, once again, they shocked him like the first day she had shown up to start work in his department. Although she did have a certain paradoxical charm, something unattractive people often have. Now she took a handkerchief out of her pocket and blew her nose noisily.

'Why haven't you come to see me earlier, Samira?'

She gave a twisted smile like a grimace and he saw her blush.

'I heard you weren't doing too well, so they said,' she answered in a nasal voice, her nose still in her handkerchief. 'I didn't really feel like seeing you in that sort of state. You're sort of a father figure to me, if you don't mind me saying so. I haven't quite worked out my Oedipus complex, know what I mean?'

She said it with humour, and he smiled.

'I'm not that old, am I? A father figure – really?'

'Well, something like that. A sort of Jedi master.'

Her stuffy nose was the colour of an aubergine and her eyes were watering. She trumpeted once again into her handkerchief.

'A what master?'

'Like in *Star Wars*,' explained Vincent.

Servaz looked at them both, then gave up trying to understand.

'What's this?' she asked, pointing to the photograph in Vincent's hand.

Espérandieu repeated what Servaz had just told him. Servaz looked from one to the other. When they had started in his department, both of them had been subjected to attacks, some less veiled than others: anti-Arab or anti-Chinese racism, or both, in Samira's case; and homophobia in Vincent's, because some of the older cops suspected that despite his wife's beauty, he wasn't attracted solely to women – probably simply because Espérandieu had certain mannerisms and sartorial habits that could be deemed somewhat effeminate. As for Samira, some of the men in the brigade found it extremely difficult to admit that a young woman with an immigrant background was better at her job than they were.

'Do you have any idea what this picture might mean?' asked Vincent, waving the photograph as if it had just come out of the developing bath.

'None whatsoever.'

'Do you know whether Célia Jablonka was in any way connected to the milieu of space research?'

'According to Charlène, the subject of her penultimate exhibition was space research, yes.'

Espérandieu stared at him, and Servaz recognised an expression he knew well: that of a collector looking at an interesting piece.

'I don't get it, boss,' said Samira, putting away her handkerchief. 'Did the girl commit suicide or not?'

'As surely as you've got a cold,' he answered.

It had been the absolute hot ticket of the holiday season that year, 2010. The Salle des Illustres at the Capitole. A long gallery laden with the bourgeois and pretentious gilt, paintings and stucco that were the fashion in the nineteenth century, a place where people crowded together and greeted one another and congratulated themselves on their presence. On having climbed sufficiently high, on having a long arm, on being important enough to have been invited. There were true celebrities and the only mildly famous, politicians and lawyers, architects and journalists, artists and athletes, people of influence and parasites. Christine knew that she herself was exaggerating her role as a popular local radio presenter. She went from one subject to the next the way she went from one guest to the next, serious when she had to be but not excessively so; light-hearted and cheery the rest of the time.

A butterfly.

And naturally, because it was the purpose of the soirée, all the way at the back, clustered around the mayor, were the upper crust from the European space endeavour. Engineers, directors, researchers. With, as their star attraction, the space cowboys. The company showcase. With strings of diplomas, even more than most of their fellow guests, and yet as virile as any Hollywood actor, they sent the needles of the members of the fair sex zooming into the red. Christine had already noticed a certain number of women looking their way while she herself was gazing at the painted ceiling high above. For the time being the space cowboys joined the crowds around the buffet, but the moment they began to scatter, the available ladies (and even those who were not available) would swoop down upon them like a cloud of locusts on a field. That was what she was thinking, her glass of champagne in her hand, when a voice called out to her:

'Don't tell me that you, too, only have eyes for them.'

She turned around to look at the gentleman with thick glasses who was definitely anything but her image of a spaceman.

'And who are you?'

'Gérald Larchet, professor and researcher at the Higher Institute of Aeronautics and Space.'

'Then you're like me, Gérald: you merely look at the stars from down below.'

She'd left the bespectacled man there on the spot. She'd gone around to shake a few hands and kiss a few cheeks, she exchanged a few words of no importance, and then the voice once again resounded in her ears.

'And who do you think *you* are, for God's sake!'

'I beg your pardon?'

'Do you always give people the brush-off like that?'

He seemed very agitated. His eyes were flashing through his lenses. And they were actually quite attractive, those eyes. His anger almost made her smile. And on closer inspection, the effect of his glasses was deceiving: she could tell that there was a muscular physique beneath his wool coat, grey jacket and blue shirt. He was tall. He had pleasant features. He was good-looking, even.

'You should change your glasses,' she said.

'Is that another nasty remark?'

'No, anything but: it's a compliment.'

That was how it had begun. An hour later, she knew almost everything there was to know about him; that he was single, for example, and above all that he had a *true* sense of humour (there were quite a few *fakes* in the room; you could hear their laughter, triggered on demand). And she also knew for certain that she fancied him.

Except that the story didn't end there.

It was also on that evening that she made the acquaintance of Léo: Léonard Fontaine. A real, handsome celluloid hero. A space cowboy. He was, in fact, the most famous of them all: the star turn of the evening, the poster boy for the European Space Agency. She was the one who had gone up to him. To invite him onto her show. She had had to elbow her way through the horde of admirers (seventy-five per cent of whom were women). She had expected to encounter a fairly insufferable, self-assured type, but he was just . . . relaxed. With an athletic build, a pleasant face with wrinkles that lent him charm, and a smile that had clearly been arranged by his dentist. Fifty-five years old. The archetypal cool guy . . . *married, two small children,* the little voice inside reminded her. And yet she was flattered and even a bit more when he began to come on strong.

She had felt only the briefest flare of guilt: he had called her back the next day, to her great surprise, to tell her that he would appear on her programme, and he had invited her to dinner at the same time. They had slept together that very evening. He was very enter-prising and direct – and she liked that. He was a good lover. Imaginative. During that time, she had let Gérald pursue his court-ship in due form, taking his time. Léo was rarely free in the evening; he had his family life. So as a rule they met at a hotel in the afternoon. He had warned her right from the start: he had no intention of leaving his wife. He had been honest. Or at least that was what she had thought at the time. Today she told herself that it had been, rather, a supreme form of dishonesty: he was in the clear, knowing all the while that even if she agreed to his conditions his partner was bound to suffer. In this way, he was at peace with himself and could play the game however he liked. No promises he could not keep, no responsibilities; in the beginning she had felt more in love with Léo than with Gérald but gradually the scales had tipped in Gérald's favour. So why hadn't she ended the affair sooner? Why had she waited so long? Almost two years! She only gave Léo up one month ago: when Gérald showed her an engagement ring.

Could Léo be behind all this? She had wondered – but she had immediately concluded that he couldn't: Léo was both the most egocentric and the most well-balanced person she knew. Besides, at no time during their two years together had she ever thought he was truly in love. Bizarrely, it was perhaps for this reason that she had waited so long to leave him: because she had hoped, with a secret appetite for revenge, that the right moment would come, the moment when she would manage to break through his shell, and reach his heart – and make him bleed . . .

But that moment had never come.

What would happen, on the other hand, if Gérald found out that all through the first two years of their relationship she had been seeing another man? That she had been constantly lying to him and hiding the truth from him? That when she snuggled up in his arms, she had just left those of another man? She shuddered; for a brief moment she was filled with panic at the thought. Now that Gérald seemed to have gone cold on her . . . *for how long*? she wondered. She was in love with Gérald. It was Gérald she wanted to spend her life with. Even if the thought of her afternoons with Léo still made her feel warm inside.

Yet now, as she listened to the ringing on the line, she was preparing to resume contact with the man she had banished from her life scarcely a month earlier.

'Christine? Have you changed your mind?'

There was no bitterness in his voice. Or surprise. If anything, he sounded jokey. She felt a twinge of sorrow at the thought he could joke so easily about an affair that had lasted two years and ended only a month ago – and it was also the sound of that warm, deep voice. Then she told herself it was his way of dealing with their break-up. Of digesting it. That just because he wasn't showing his emotions didn't mean he did not have any.

'I'm sorry,' he said, his tone more serious. 'How stupid of me. What's up, squirrel? How are you?'

She faltered for a moment: *squirrel*. One of the nicknames he used to give her. One month later it had lost none of its potency.

'I have to see you, Léo, it's important.'

'You sound strange. What's the matter?'

She replied that she would rather talk about it in person. She could tell from his silence that he was surprised. She closed her eyes. She tried to drive the doubt from her mind: how could she explain what she had been through over the last few days? How could she make him understand how distraught she was? If anyone could help her, it was Léo: this man who was stronger and more sure of himself than anyone else.

'Please,' she murmured, her voice almost inaudible.

'Of course,' he said. 'Is it that bad?'

'I'm in danger, Léo. My life is in danger.'

A very long silence.

'Where, then?' he asked solemnly.

'Our usual hotel, the usual room, you reserve it. In one hour.'

'Fine. I'll be there. Christine?'

'Yes?'

'I don't know what's going on. But trust me: we'll take care of it.'

She hung up, vastly relieved. Léo's final words had filled her with hope. Yes, she'd been right to call him. The soft touch of a flannel winter shirt. The smell of lemony aftershave. A knot in her belly, and her blood stirring, just there – precisely there – along the body's meridian to the sensitive spot between her abdomen and her groin: Léonard Fontaine was a remedy almost as dangerous as the affliction.

She paused as she emerged from the side street. Her sharp gaze looked all around the square. Then with her hood still pulled over her head, her hands deep in her pockets, she quickly crossed the square and went around the frozen fountain in the direction of the Grand Hôtel Thomas Wilson.

Inside the revolving door she removed her hood, but she still sensed the receptionist staring at her as she headed towards the lift. The doors opened on the first floor and she walked down the long silent corridor, her steps hushed by the carpet.

She stopped outside a dark door with a big gold electronic lock. Knocked discreetly. The door opened almost immediately and she went into room 117.

The familiar little corridor with its panelled walls, luggage rack, two white dressing gowns on their hangers, the bathroom door open a crack to their left: she immediately recognised it all. And the scent of cleanliness and floral perfume that drifted through the room. Léo closed the door behind her and swung her around to face him; she let him kiss her, but then quickly ended their embrace.

'Please, Léo . . .'

She held herself ramrod straight.

Then she turned around and walked across the room. The king-size bed, the television with its LCD screen, the desk covered with black leather, the coffee maker, the minibar, the bedstead of silver diamonds, the red pillows, the little chrome lamps subduing the darkness of the ebony walls.

How many times had they come here? Thirty? Forty? Fifty? At least once a week for two years, except during the holidays: that would add up to a hundred times they'd met.

One hundred!

He went over to the desk and she saw he'd had some champagne sent up.

'No, thank you,' she said.

'Are you sure? Christ, it feels strange to be here.'

She was surprised by the tenderness and a slight weariness she heard in his voice: yet Léo was not the kind of man who would dwell on the past. When their gazes met, she saw the familiar tender glow in his eyes. He took the bottle from the bucket and she saw he had already drunk from it while waiting for her.

'I didn't come here for that, Léo.'

'Christine, relax. We're going to talk; you're going to tell me what's going on. You are in no danger here, all right?'

He sat on the edge of the bed, with a full glass. He was wearing a faded denim shirt open over his tanned chest, and his sleeves were rolled up as if it were summer.

She pulled a chair over in front of him and sat down. He stared at her, frowning.

'I'm listening,' he said. 'You seemed upset on the phone. Apparently, you still are. Take your time, I have all the time in the world . . .'

'I'll have half a glass after all.'

He got up to pour it for her. She took the opportunity to start talking, in a slow and measured voice, while he had his back to her. She summarised what had happened as honestly and objectively as possible. He showed no expression during her entire story. When she had finished, ten minutes or so later, he let out a whistle. His eyes were veiled – as if he had gone inside himself and was searching through his considerable experience for something remotely similar.

'It seems serious,' he said finally, giving her a worried look.

She knew that with Léo the word 'serious' meant 'grave', 'worrying', or even 'dramatic'.

'Are you absolutely sure it all happened exactly the way you've told me?'

There was a hint of scepticism in his voice that Christine did not like.

'What are you insinuating by that? That I'm making it all up?'

'And you are sure you don't have the slightest idea who is behind it all?' he asked, ignoring her reaction.

She hesitated.

'For a moment, I thought it could be you.'

She saw him raise an eyebrow.

'Me?'

'Mmm. I left you hardly a month ago, I told you that it was all over between us and then suddenly someone started fucking up my life.'

She gave him a defiant look.

'You don't honestly believe what you're saying, Christine?'

Well, well, she'd managed to break through the shell after all: his voice was trembling with anger.

'No, of course not. I know nothing, Léo. But I can't imagine Cordélia is acting on her own; I think she's doing it for money and nothing else.'

He seemed preoccupied.

'In any event, this business has already gone much too far, don't you realise? You have to go to the police.'

'After what happened with the letter?'

'Yes. Even after that. There's no alternative. If you want, I'll come with you.'

She paused to reflect. What would the cops think of her if she showed up with a married man who was not her fiancé – a man who, on top of it, was almost instantly recognisable?

'No, it's better you don't come with me.'

He looked deep into her eyes.

'Christine, you have to go to the police. You've waited too long already. You have virtually lost your job. And what happened with your dog: I don't like that at all. This is much more than simple harassment. Somewhere, there, outside, there is someone walking around who really has it in for you. Someone has already broken into your place. And hurt your dog.'

She frowned and screwed up her eyes. As if she didn't know. Suddenly she had a terrible sense of apprehension: she was desperately seeking a way out and all he could suggest was going to the police? If a man like him could see no other alternative, what course of action did she have left?

He must have sensed how terrified she was, because he put a hand on hers.

'Don't worry. We'll find a solution. We have to act methodically,' he continued. 'For a start, go and stay at a hotel for a while.'

'And what about Iggy?'

'Take him with you. Or give him to someone else for a while . . . to your parents, or friends.'

*What friends?* she almost said.

'Why don't you come and stay at my place for a few days?' she suggested. 'Just tell your wife you're on a business trip.'

She knew that Léo's life after leaving his career as a spaceman had been very busy. He had spoken at length about his new direction when he had appeared on her programme at Radio Five: for a while he had been in charge of the astronaut training centre in Cologne, in Germany; he had worked as consulting astronaut on the ATV project, an uncrewed cargo spacecraft whose purpose was to supply the International Space Station; he had created his own company, GoSpace, a branch of the National Centre for Space Studies, which organised scientific flights on the reduced-gravity Airbus 300 ZERO-G; he had also become one of the principal sales representatives for the European Space Agency, promoting human spaceflight and space exploration to a wider public as well as to government officials and universities.

Now he gave her a sharp look.

'No, I can't do that. But we have to act. You were right to come and see me. Who else have you spoken to?'

She had a picture of Max in her living room, with his dirty clothes, filthy beard and long greasy hair.

'Nobody. Gérald, given the present state of our relationship, would not believe me.'

He gave her another keen look.

'He has never found out about us, has he?'

She shook her head.

'Here's what we're going to do,' he said. 'You go to the police; I'm going to start asking around.'

'Asking around?'

'I have a few contacts at public security. I'll see if any other women have been experiencing the same thing as you in Toulouse or nearby, and if they were taken seriously, if there were any suspects.'

He got up, walked over to the desk, tore off a sheet of hotel letterhead and picked up the pen nestling in a little leather portfolio. Then he sat back down.

'We'll start by putting together a list of all the people you've been in contact with over recent months and with whom you've had the slightest disagreement. Even the ones you don't really have any reason to suspect. I'll see what I can find out.'

'How will you go about it?' she asked.

He gave an enigmatic smile.

'You know, I know a lot of people.'

She gave it some thought and a few names came spontaneously to mind: Becker, the macho bastard who was head of news at Radio Five; Denise; her next-door neighbour. *Other names.* It wasn't exactly heartening to realise she had more enemies than friends. Paradoxically, as the list grew longer, her hopes rose: the guilty party was bound to be one of them.

'Well,' he said, when they had finished, 'it looks like you have a gift for making friends. Look at these names: I'll be damned if your tormentor isn't among them.'

He was right. She should have started there. All you had to do was think and act logically.

'Tell me: how are you going to find out about these people? I want to know.'

He gave another of his enigmatic smiles.

'I know a private detective. He owes me one: a few years ago, he got caught while he was illegally investigating my company – industrial espionage, pure and simple. He had been hired by a rival company abroad. I caught him red-handed and, rather than send him to jail, I offered him a deal: if he stopped his snooping, I would not file a complaint, but perhaps one day I would need to call on him. I thought I could use his services for, shall we say, commercial, rather than private, purposes. But never mind.'

A detective; friends who were cops. Yes, she had been right to call Léo. He was always resourceful, not the sort who gave up easily. She wondered fleetingly how Gérald would have behaved in his place, but then banished the thought. She felt a wave of gratitude come over her.

'Relax,' he said again in a gentle voice. 'Everything will be fine.'

He had got up, and took her empty champagne glass to refill it. He placed it in her hand. Then he walked around her chair and put his hands on her shoulders.

'Let yourself go.'

'Léo . . .'

'What?'

'Thank you.'

Léo's strong, gentle hands kneaded the muscles in her shoulders. As they used to do at times when she was stressed. Relaxing one by one the knots in her neck and upper back, exerting pressure as firm as it was precise. She closed her eyes. She wanted to let herself go. She could feel her muscles getting warm and more supple. Her neck began to relax. She lifted the champagne to her lips. It was good. The little bubbles went straight to her head.

'Do you remember that hotel in Neuchâtel, on the lake, the suite on stilts?' he said. 'In the morning, all we could see were sails, birds and the mountains in the distance.'

Of course she remembered. It was one of the rare weekends they had spent together. She would have liked to stay there for a month, a year – instead of two days.

'Give me some more,' she said.

All of a sudden she felt like being drunk. She took a long sip of champagne, and the bubbles tingled her palate and tongue.

'I've missed you,' he said.

He planted a kiss on her neck, which gave her goosebumps, then another one near her mouth. She turned her head, parted her lips and he slipped his tongue between them. She took him in and they began to breathe more quickly. Before they even knew what was happening, they were on their feet and she had her jeans around her knees, her thighs bare. He slipped one hand into her knickers and she was immediately wet at the contact of his fingers. She spread her legs. She moaned when his fingers caressed her more closely. She wanted to feel him inside her, *there, now.* She let him go, and tenderly clasped his smooth, hard cock. They moved apart to get undressed more quickly, then once they were naked she passed her hands all over his sides, his chest, his back, his buttocks – and then her hands moved further down and she again caressed his rigid cock. They made love on the bed and she took him, moving rhythmically, their hips gently colliding. She was panting and fluttering her hands from his sides and shoulder blades to his buttocks and hips. She dug her fingers into his hair when he pinned her to the mattress and came.

She felt a sudden pang of remorse and when he collapsed by her side she knew she'd been betrayed. Not by him, but by herself: by her body. She got up and hurried to the bathroom to clean up. When she came back out and reached for her clothes, he asked, 'Where are you going?'

'I'm leaving, we shouldn't have done that.'

'What?!'

She finished getting dressed. She thought briefly about kissing him or saying something more; then she changed her mind and hurried to the door.

'Go to the police!' he called, to her back. 'Christine, do you hear me? *Go to the police!*'

She slammed the door. Found herself alone in the corridor. Her head was buzzing.

She walked quickly along the silent hallway, from shadow to light and light to shadow, the little wall fixtures interrupting the darkness with theatrical effect. A parade of doors, all the same. A fleeting thought occurred to her: how many adulterous couples were behind them? *Was she adulterous?* Gérald had decided to distance himself from her: did that free her of any obligation of loyalty? She imagined him finding out she had been fucking someone else in a hotel only a few hours after their argument.

And what about him? *Wasn't he fucking Denise?*

In the lift, she felt her knees go wobbly. A wave of ugly, naked fear washed over her. The fear of losing everything. She felt deeply unhappy. The blood was pounding in her head, and she rushed out of the lift the moment the doors opened.

A man was standing there. She collided with him, violently. He was extraordinarily small for a man, smaller than her. His head was shaven and he had a strange face – *effeminate*, she thought in a fraction of a second – but when she rammed into him he hardly moved, and she almost fell over backwards.

'For – forgive me,' she stammered, her voice betraying anger more than anything else. 'I'm so sorry!'

The little man stepped aside with a smile. She caught a glimpse of the tattoo emerging from his collar. A Madonna with a halo, of the kind you see on Russian icons. *How strange*, she thought, rushing towards the revolving door. The unusual image left an imprint on her brain – the way certain dreams do when you wake up – as she ran across the lobby, pushed the revolving door and fled into the snow, which had started falling once again.

# 20

## Operetta

The female cop looked at her computer screen, then at the wall behind Christine, then at her pen, then her nails, then finally Christine.

'You say you found urine on your doormat: couldn't it have come from your own dog?'

Her tone was so obviously, blatantly sceptical that Christine tensed.

'No,' she replied firmly.

'What makes you so sure?'

She shrugged.

'I didn't take my dog out that day. So I don't see how he could have—'

'You didn't take him out? Where did he do his business?'

'He has a box for emergencies, when . . . I don't have time to take him out.' The cop gave her a stern look. 'Listen, let's not dwell on this for hours, all right? Far worse things happened.'

The woman checked the notes on her screen.

'Yes. Someone got into your place and left a . . . an opera CD, but they didn't take anything. This same person called you at the radio station where you work and at your home. You were drugged and undressed at the home of this young woman, Corinne Délia, who is an intern at Radio Five, and then you were taken home unconscious, and woke up there naked. Oh yes, I almost forgot: these people also withdrew two thousand euros from your bank account, but without stealing your bank card. And they, uh, left some anti-depressants at your workplace in order to discredit you.'

Her gaze went from her screen to Christine. It was a hostile gaze. Not only sceptical but also exasperated.

'You look exhausted,' she added. 'Have you seen a doctor?'

Christine took a deep breath. She was sorry she had come. *Calm down. If you throw a wobbly now, it will only confirm what they already think.*

'I printed out the messages he sent me,' she said, placing one hand on the cardboard folder she had picked up at her flat when she stopped for a shower. 'Do you want to see them?'

The woman did not say yes or no.

'"He"? So you think it's a man? Just now you said it was your intern who was behind it.'

'What I meant . . . I think there are at least two of them.'

'A regular conspiracy, then.'

The words stung her. She knew what the woman cop was driving at.

'You think I'm crazy, don't you?'

Once again the woman answered neither yes nor no.

Christine put her hands on the armrests.

'Right. Looks like I'm wasting my time here all over again.'

'Stay there.'

That was an order, no doubt about it. Christine sat back down.

'A few days ago, you came here with a letter supposedly written by a person announcing their intention to commit suicide. It turned out there were no fingerprints on the letter other than your own – not the slightest one – and no postmark.'

'Yes, and moreover, I thought I would be int— questioned by the same person who saw me about the letter.'

'Today you say you went to see Mademoiselle Délia at her house and she drugged you, is that right? You say she filmed a compromising video where both of you are naked, and it was clearly with the intention of blackmailing you?'

Christine nodded. This was at least the third time she found herself answering the same questions.

'A letter, a phone call, your dog in the dustbin, urine on your doormat, this video . . . where is the logic behind any of this?' said the cop. 'Why would anyone do this? It doesn't make sense.'

She took a small key out of her pocket, locked her desk drawer, and stood up.

'Please come with me.'

'Where are we going?'

No answer. The woman cop was already at the door, and went out without turning around. Christine hurried to follow her, thinking that Léo had been way off the mark: coming here had been a mistake.

A corridor with brick walls, then a corner; Christine saw a man sitting on a cement bench in an alcove lit by translucent squares. Another corridor. The woman cop was walking quickly, greeting colleagues.

She walked past a photocopier, stopped, and opened the door.

'After you.'

A little room with brick walls; a table and three chairs. A neon bulb gave off a harsh light. There was no window. Christine's heart began to beat faster. The woman pointed to the single chair on one side of the table.

'Sit down.'

She went back out, leaving Christine alone. After a long while, the door opened at last and the woman cop reappeared, together with a second person: the policeman from last time, with his round protruding eyes, thick curly hair and ugly tie. His expression was neutral and he did not even greet her. Christine saw this as a very bad sign and she swallowed. He put a file down on the table and sat opposite her on the remaining chair, to the right of the woman, never taking his eyes off Christine.

There was a long and very awkward silence, then Mr Poodle (*Beaulieu, Lieutenant Beaulieu,* she remembered) removed some photographs from the folder and slid them across the table to Christine.

'Do you recognise this individual?'

Christine leaned closer. Opened her eyes wide. The picture was like a slap in the face.

Cordélia.

A close-up of her face: clearly the pictures had been taken with a flash and at very close range, because the pale white light shone on her cheeks and forehead. And there was no way to ignore any of the sinister details. Her left eye was puffed up and almost closed, her eyebrow was swollen, and there was a big bruise veering from mustard yellow to green and black all around the eye. Her nose had doubled in size. There was a huge bruise on her right cheek and her lower lip was split. The skin on her chin was ragged and exposed, as if someone had gone over it with a grater.

Cordélia had been photographed full face and in profile. Christine swallowed. She could not take her eyes off the pictures. She shuddered. Never before had she seen such naked and unrestrained violence in real life. She repressed a wave of nausea. The plans she had made with Léo not even two hours ago suddenly seemed very far away.

'Oh my God. What – what happened to her?'

When she looked up, the cop's eyes were gazing right into her own. He had leaned across the table and was staring at her intensely, now – his two globular brown eyes like those of a sunfish only a few centimetres from her own.

'You ought to know. You're the one who did this to her, Mademoiselle Steinmeyer.'

The neon light blinked with a brief buzzing sound and she suddenly saw the two motionless faces across from her lit with a stroboscopic effect. Bzzzz-bzzzz . . . Their gazes vanished then re-appeared a fraction of a second later. Once, twice. Just like the photographs of Cordélia on the table. Every flicker, every fraction of darkness was like a nail driven into her flesh. She struggled against rising panic. She felt drops of sweat pearling on her forehead.

'Bloody neon,' said Beaulieu, standing up, his movement abbreviated by the stroboscopic effect.

He went to the light switch and played with it. She scarcely had time to see the female cop's gaze disappear and then it was there again in the same place: focused on her, expressionless. The man came and sat back down. He no longer looked at all like someone who didn't find any excitement in his job. He glanced at his colleague, then turned again to Christine.

'Right. Well. She alleges that you offered her a very large amount of money to make love to her – two thousand euros – and she said she went along with it because she desperately needed the money for herself and her baby, and because you are an attractive woman, after all, and she likes doing it with women, or so she declared. But afterwards you wanted your money back, you told her that she had climaxed, and you weren't in the habit of paying for that. And since she refused and was getting annoyed, you began to hit her, isn't that right?'

His words echoed in a room that was silent, apart from the neon, which was no longer blinking but whose light throbbed with a faint buzzing sound; absurd, impossible words.

'That's ridiculous. There's no truth in any of that.'

'You did not go of your own volition to Mademoiselle Délia's house?'

'I did, but—'

'And when she opened the door, she was naked?'

'Yes.'

'And you went in anyway?'

'Yes.'

'Why?'

'I told you, I—'

'That letter: you're the one who wrote it, aren't you?' interrupted the woman.

'No!'

'So how do you explain that it ended up in your mailbox?'

'I can't explain it.'

'We've questioned the inhabitants of your building: not one of them has the slightest idea who the author of the letter could be.'

'I know, I myself—'

'Your next-door neighbour,' interrupted the man, 'maintains that you're insane. You showed up at her house at three o'clock in the morning, insisting that your dog was in her flat. You forced your way into the home of two elderly people. You searched their flat without their permission, and terrified them.'

The slight vibration coming from the neon lights was giving her a headache. Or perhaps it was the smell of the detergent.

'I—'

'In fact, your dog was in the rubbish chute, with a broken paw, is that correct?'

'Yes.'

'Did you put him in the rubbish chute, Mademoiselle Steinmeyer?' asked the woman cop very distinctly.

Christine shot her a desperate look.

'No! He was in a rubbish bin next to the chute!'

'Next to what?'

'Next to the rubbish chute.'

'But you said—'

'Listen, I—'

'This was not the first time you have tried to intimidate someone, and have threatened them.'

He slid a sheet of printed paper across the table to her. Email messages. Christine recognised them immediately:

*Cordélia, you haven't been answering my emails. I'm forced to conclude that you disapprove of my attitude. That you're hostile. Cordélia, you know your future is in my hands.*
*C.*


*Cordélia, I'm giving you 24 hours to reply.*

'Mademoiselle Steinmeyer, did you write these emails?' asked the woman cop.

'No!'

'And yet, they were written on your computer?' asked the man, growing impatient.

'Yes, but I already explained that—'

'Were you recently let go at your work because of your behaviour?' asked the woman.

Christine did not reply. She felt as if a deep abyss had opened up beneath her feet.

'We have spoken to your boss, who is also Corinne Délia's boss,' said the man.

Christine was speechless.

'Did you hear me?' asked the woman.

Christine still said nothing.

'It is eighteen forty,' said the man, rubbing his eyes. 'From now on, you are in police custody.'

# 21

# Ensemble

Christine did not sleep that night, except for an hour towards morning, when she dozed. That night she understood that a city contains various sorts of hell, of varying sizes and aspects, but that the principal form of torture, as Jean-Paul Sartre put it, comes from the other people who inhabit that city.

The night before, she had given a start when Lieutenant Beaulieu uttered the time-honoured phrase: 'It is eighteen forty. From now on, you are in police custody.'

She had listened while he explained the charges brought against her and read her her rights, and she had watched him go through the initial gestures of police liturgy, then put through a call to the prosecutor of the Republic. The female cop went out. Beaulieu asked her, among other things, if she wanted to consult a lawyer. She figured that the fewer people knew about this, the less chance there would be of a leak to the press (she could already imagine the article's introductory paragraph: 'Radio Five presenter in custody for assault'). She could certainly survive a night in a cell. She replied that she did not want a lawyer, because she had done nothing. He shrugged, and at about seven o'clock, invited her to go with him. It wasn't really an invitation. They made their way to another lift, not the one she had taken, but one directly opposite. The cop swiped his magnetic badge and the doors to the lift opened. Once they were inside, he swiped the card again and the lift began to go down, vibrating.

When the doors opened again, the cold, clinical aspect of the place made her begin to tremble. They turned to the right and immediately came to a corridor with many doors on either side. The place was vast and echoing and poorly lit, as were some of the cells; others were completely dark. She saw men lying near the ground, their heads close to the window, like puppies in a pet store, and she began trembling again. On the other side of the corridor, in a room that was entirely glassed-in, several guards in light-coloured uniforms were observing her; two of them stood up and left the room to join them in an adjacent space where there was a metal detector. There were no windows at all. Anywhere. A basement. She swallowed hard.

'Hey,' said Beaulieu, 'I've brought you Mademoiselle Steinmeyer. How are things this evening?'

'Calm,' replied one of the guards. 'But it's still a bit early: the D&Ds aren't here yet.'

Beaulieu saw her worried look.

'Drunk and disorderly,' he explained. 'See that she gets an individual cell – if that's at all possible.'

The man nodded and looked at her. The other guards were also staring. She shrivelled beneath their gaze.

'She's in your hands,' declared Beaulieu. 'See you tomorrow. Night, lads.'

'Please go through the metal detector,' said one of the guards politely.

She obeyed. A woman in uniform joined them soon after. She greeted the men then began searching Christine – a superficial search, but the guard's hands displayed a repulsive absence of restraint which gave her goosebumps.

'Follow me.'

She opened a door onto a little room with forty or more lockers. Christine noticed that there were motorcycle helmets lined up along the top. The woman in uniform – small and stocky – grabbed hold of a large deep wooden box and placed it on the table.

'Please remove all your jewellery: watch, rings, bracelets, earrings and your belt, and put them in the box,' said the woman. 'Along with any money, papers, keys and mobile phone.'

Christine did as she asked, with the impression that she was losing a bit more of her identity with every object she relinquished. The guard drew up an inventory, out loud, while writing it down at the same time in a big ledger; then she took a piece of paper, looked at Christine's ID, and wrote, *Christine Steinmeyer, 31/4817.* She placed the box in one of the lockers, locked the door and stuck the paper with her name on the door.

'Where shall I put her?'

When she had an answer, they went through the glass door and the woman walked ahead of Christine down the long, poorly lit corridor. The cells had Plexiglas facades and metal posts painted blue-grey. The men behind them were lying on brown blankets in the harsh light, on blue plastic-coated mattresses. Christine made an effort not to look in their direction.

'Hey! What time is it?' called one of the men as they walked by. 'Hey, babe, first visit, is it? Watch out for that vicious guard: she likes pussy!'

The woman stopped two doors further down, turned the key, then gave the short vertical bar a sharp tug. The powerful clang of metal resounded down the entire corridor – a sound out of a film, a prison sound. Christine was trembling so violently that her shoulders abruptly drew level with the base of her skull.

'Take your shoes off.'

She obeyed. The woman opened a drawer in the glass and metal facade, just below the bunk, and she shoved them into the dark.

'Go in.'

She trembled as she stepped forward in her socks over the cold concrete. She looked around at her cell: an off-white cave of two metres by three, a concrete bench with a partitioning wall, behind which the toilet must be hidden. Rounded corners everywhere. A mattress. A sink in a niche at the back. That was all.

'In a short while, two people will come to take you for finger-printing. In the meantime try to get some rest.'

'It's cold here,' said Christine.

'I'll bring you a blanket. Do you want something to eat?'

'No, thank you.'

She wasn't hungry: she was cold, she was frightened – she was terrified.

Once she had the brown blanket over her shoulders, she closed her eyes and tried to close her mind to the place as well, to forget where she was – and how she'd got there. *After all, it's not so terrible. At least here no one can get at you. You'll see: in an hour or two, you'll feel better – even if it won't be easy to sleep on this thing.* She spent the next hour curled up on the thin, hard, plastic-coated mattress, wrapped in a musty-smelling blanket, and she was sorry she had turned down the food, because her stomach was contracting with cramps.

After an hour had gone by, two people – a man and a woman

who were younger than her – came to fetch her and led her into a windowless, neon-lit room (near the lift, which gave her a brief, cruel flash of hope that was immediately extinguished). There was a table, a computer, a counter behind a glass window and a large device that looked like a cash dispenser. A man with blue gloves, his face protected by a surgical mask, was waiting for her behind the window. He made her sit down, asked her to open her mouth, and with the help of a cotton bud took what she supposed must be a DNA sample; after that, the young woman asked her to go over to the big device for fingerprinting: first her entire hand, then her five fingers one by one. She spoke to her pleasantly, as if this were some simple administrative formality. Finally, in one corner of the room, Christine was entitled to the traditional mug-shots. Once the two young people had accompanied her back to her cell, Christine felt as if this time it really had happened: she was on the other side now. She found it hard to fight against the dejection and despair that were overwhelming her. Her brain, which up to now had not taken the full measure of the situation, was howling with shame, confusion and fear.

*And then it was hell.*

Every dealer, pimp, thief, streetwalker, drunk or junkie in Toulouse seemed to have agreed to meet there. They came in one after the other, between ten o'clock at night and two o'clock in the morning, making an enormous racket. Christine was glad no one could see her behind the canvas blind because her madness was increasing from one minute to the next. And her *anger*: a terrifying tension ran from one end of the corridor to the other, bouncing down it like particles along a collider. It was impossible to sleep: her cell was the next-to-last individual one; two doors further down were the larger cells where between four and ten people were locked up. Noise, fury, havoc: a frenzied Sabbath. By around two o'clock the corridor was as busy as the main concourse of a railway station, transformed into a rowdy, keyed-up, feverish menagerie.

That night, Christine listened to the shrill screaming of wild beasts, their demented howling, their pounding fists and flailing kicks against Plexiglas and metal, the sinister laughter of drunkards, the desperate wailing of junkies, the provocative, querulous insults of whores, languages, accents, locks turning, doors opening and closing, footsteps, calls, ringing sounds, cries. She tried to shut herself off from the anarchy, from all the bestiality and fury that reigned. And couldn't.

At around three o'clock, her body eventually reacted: she was overcome by nausea and she hurried to the hole to vomit, on her knees
on the ground that was covered with industrial surfacing, hidden by
the partition wall, while other newcomers started up with their own
racket. She got up, wiped the sweat from her brow and pressed the
button for water from the tap – and it splattered her clothes. This
time, she began to cry, stifled sobs at first – because she was afraid
someone might hear her – then louder and louder, shaken by convulsions, as all her mental barriers broke down.

'Go ahead and cry, baby, it'll do you good,' said a woman's voice
gently from the neighbouring cell.

The cold woke her up. She had eventually fallen asleep on the hard
mattress, wrapped in the brown blankets, and when she sat up, the
aching in her back was like a thousand nicks with a razor. Her mouth
was furry and she was horribly thirsty. She noticed that it had grown
silent at last. The corridor was calm once again. Loud snoring came
from the cells, as did murmured conversation in low voices. Then
the locks clicked again and there was the sound of footsteps. Doors
opening; people waking, complaining, coughing. Three minutes later
the woman in uniform was pulling up the blinds, unlocking her door
and handing her a tray.

'Here.'

Two sugar biscuits and a carton of orange juice.

'Thank you,' she said, despite everything.

The woman pulled down the blind and went on to the next cell.
Christine looked at her breakfast, which in other circumstances she
would have pushed away disdainfully, but her stomach was cramping
with hunger. She hadn't eaten a thing since the night before, so she
hurried to open the carton of juice, her teeth clenched so tight it felt
as if she had needles in her jaws when she took the first sip. Once
she had finished, far from being assuaged, her hunger and thirst were
even greater.

One hour later, as she was dozing and dreaming, the blind was
raised and the lock clicked again.

'Follow me.'

She went down the corridor behind the woman. Beaulieu was
waiting for her by the guards' glassed-in room.

'Good morning,' he said, going ahead of her into the room with the lockers. 'Please take your things, Mademoiselle Steinmeyer. Make sure everything is there and write, "collected searched items, all complete" here, please.'

The woman in uniform opened her locker, pulled out the wooden box and set it down before her on the little table. Christine felt her chest inflate with hope as if it were an inner tube. She put her watch back around her wrist, fastened her belt and picked up her papers and her belongings one by one, her hand trembling. She did not recognise her uneven handwriting as she wrote across the page, as jagged as the scrawl of a seismograph.

'Follow me,' said Beaulieu.

Hope again, when he went ahead of her towards the lift. As they rode upwards she felt like a diver in the depths who has been freed from imprisoning straps and with a kick of her heel rises to the surface at the last minute, just as her oxygen tank is nearly empty. She would never have believed that a simple lift could symbolise freedom to this degree. Then there came a chilling thought: he was going to interrogate her. And then he would take her downstairs again. *Oh no, please.* She realised she was ready to confess anything rather than go back into that hell. But she was no fool: if she confessed, it would make things much, much worse.

They came out of the lift and Beaulieu led her not to the interrogation room but to his office. He pointed to a chair. She collapsed into it with the same pleasure she would have experienced luxuriating in a soft armchair at some grand hotel.

'You are lucky, Mademoiselle Steinmeyer,' he said, sitting down in turn.

She said nothing. All her senses were on the alert.

'You are being released. You are no longer in custody.'

She almost asked him to repeat himself.

'Corinne Délia has withdrawn her complaint.'

Clearly, this was not to his liking, and Christine wondered if he was joking, if this was some sort of mental torture – like hostages, blindfolded, made to undergo fake executions. She couldn't believe her ears.

'I tried to dissuade her, but she didn't want to know,' said the cop sternly. 'She is of the opinion that she also had her part to play in the matter, and that you have learned your lesson. You really are very lucky. But don't forget we have your name now.'

There was still not a shred of kindness in his protruding eyes. He reached for a sheet of paper on the desk and handed it to her.

'Here, this is a list of psychiatrists who might be able to help you. Now if you'll excuse me, I have work to do.'

He got up to accompany her to the lift, which he activated with his badge. Just as the doors were about to close, he leaned closer to be able to speak in a hushed voice.

'A few words of advice,' he said. 'I have my eye on you. So don't go messing with me, sweetheart. Make yourself scarce.'

The endearment and the threat were like a slap in the face. Her knees shaking, she sought refuge at the back of the lift. With only one thought in her mind: to get out of there.

Thus it was that on an icy, late December morning, Christine dragged herself to the nearest Métro station, feeling ashamed, guilty, unhappy and terrified. She waited for the train and once she was inside, she sat down without a single glance around her. It was a typical early Sunday morning; there weren't many people. Staring at the glass pane in front of her, she tried to evoke some happy memory, but nothing came. She had thought she could resist, put up a fight, but she had to face facts: it was a lost cause. Despair was about to take control of her spirit and win the merciless struggle; its outcome, she now realised, might well prove fatal for her.

As she hurried out onto her street, she slipped on the icy pavement and twisted her ankle painfully, but she didn't even swear. Exhaustion had stripped her of any vague desire for rebellion. She saw her guardian angel sleeping, dead to the world in his cardboard boxes, and she gasped with rage. *Some bodyguard he is!* The thought inspired a sinister little laugh, void of any humour, until she reasoned she couldn't expect him to stay awake twenty-four hours a day, after all.

Christine crossed the street and shook him gently by the shoulder. She needed to speak to someone about what had happened, and he fitted the bill perfectly. After all, he had proved himself more shrewd and attentive than anyone else. But he didn't move. She shook him again. A loud snore came in lieu of an answer and when he opened his mouth full of yellow teeth a powerful fustiness of alcohol, as if a barrel had just been tapped, caused her to recoil. *He'd been drinking . . . he was drunk!* The bastard had taken her money and rushed off to liquidate it, quite literally. He had absolutely no intention of keeping his part of the bargain. The betrayal was like a punch in the stomach and she staggered towards her building.

Her flat was freezing and she wondered if someone had come to turn down the heat. She had an immediate answer: music was coming from the living room, two women's voices woven together like vines, poignantly wrapped one around the other. She pushed Iggy to one side; the dog was limping pitifully, his head in his plastic funnel, but he still managed to wag his tail on seeing her. She recognised the music. *Lakmé,* the 'Flower Duet'.

She saw the CD case on the coffee table. Yet another opera.

*He had been here.*

She was stunned with terror and took a step backwards, dazed, unsteady, while the music soared, filling every corner of the flat.

And yet something else was welling inside her. A devastating anger. As if from a chain reaction, as if her radioactive core had reached a critical mass. Her vision blurred and her anger flared as suddenly as an ember falling onto a bed of dry pine needles. She stepped forward, grabbed hold of her mini stereo and picked it up angrily, yanking the plugs from the sockets and bringing the lament for two voices to an abrupt end. She gave free rein to her fury, yielding to an all-embracing, blinding outburst as she hurled the stereo across the room, smashing it against the opposite wall and screaming, 'What do you want from me? Go fuck yourselves! Shit-faced bastards!'

Servaz was sorry it was Sunday. He had calls to make, people to visit. Well, not that many. But he had always hated Sundays.

He was walking in the snowy woods, following a lane that wove through hornbeams and tall, twisted oak trees. He pondered the meaning of the two clues his mysterious correspondent had sent. Room 117 and the Space Station. Célia Jablonka had briefly frequented the milieu of space research and exploration before ending her days in the aforementioned room. Those were the facts. But what was the connection between the two? Clearly, his anonymous informer knew a certain number of things. Why, then, did he not simply give his information to Servaz? Why didn't he show himself? Was he afraid for his own safety? Could he not do it without breaking some professional secrecy by which he was bound? Servaz probed deeper. A lawyer? A doctor? A fellow cop?

He couldn't think of anything. Had he lost his touch? Deducting, constructing, amassing, extrapolating – elementary operations, but the thing was, you always had to go that little bit further, and then a little bit further . . .

A space station: space, stars, cosmonauts (didn't they call them *spationauts* in this country?). A paranoid, suicidal artist . . . or perhaps not. *A little bit further.* He knew where he had to begin, and how: as if he were investigating a murder and not a suicide. He had to start with that premise. First step: the family.

# 22

# Lakmé

She shook him until he opened his eyes. He shot a wary, probing look at the outside world, then opened his eyes wide when he recognised her.

'Christine? What are you doing here? What time is it?'

Half of his face was hidden by the blanket, like a Bedouin, and the rest of his body was buried in cardboard boxes. Then Christine's gaze went down to the pavement, and she gave a start: *the cup was on the right.*

'Time to get moving,' she replied, a cloud of breath rising from her lips. 'I'll wait for you at my place. In five minutes. There'll be some hot coffee.'

She saw an astonished gleam in his gaze. She turned on her heels and went back upstairs. He rang at the door three minutes later.

'You look bloody terrible,' he said when she opened the door. 'It's so cold! Some hot soup wouldn't go amiss.'

He headed into the living room as if he were a regular visitor, and she repressed a burst of anger. She watched as he sat down on the sofa, and she noted the dirty hem of his coat, crusted with snow and mud, the dirty rag he must use as a handkerchief emerging from one pocket, and a dog-eared book sticking out of the other. She caught a glimpse of the author: Tolstoy.

'You fell asleep,' she said. 'And someone was here.'

Max looked up at her in surprise, scratched his greying beard as if it were itching, which might well have been the case.

'At night I sleep, like everyone else,' he replied. 'If you want someone on guard twenty-four hours a day, you should call a security firm.'

For a split second she resisted the temptation to throw him out.

'You put your cup on the right. Why?'

He nodded, frowning. He suddenly looked preoccupied. He was chewing pensively on the wooden stirrer clenched in his rotting teeth, between his chapped lips.

'A guy went by more than once, and he stood for a long time watching the building. Then he eventually went in. He obviously knew the code.'

'Could it have been someone from the building?'

'No.' He shook his head, firmly. 'I know every single person who lives on this street. He wasn't one of them. It was him, the guy you're looking for.'

She went pale.

'Why do you say that?'

He gave her an intense look, still chewing on his stirrer.

'You're right: you have got a big problem. I don't know who he is, but that guy . . . there's something about him . . . He's a nasty piece of work.'

'How do you know that?'

'Because I grabbed him by the bottom of his trousers to ask him for money. I didn't expect him to give me any, mind you. I know how to recognise generous people. I just wanted to know who we were dealing with, what sort of man he is. So I grabbed him, just lightly, and he stopped and looked at me . . .'

He took the stick from his mouth.

'You should have seen his face. He leaned over and grabbed me by the collar. And told me that if I ever touched him again, he would cut off all my fingers, one by one, with a pair of rusty shears, in a very dark place, once he had gagged me and everyone was asleep. And you know what? The guy wasn't bluffing. Not for one second. His face was a few inches from mine and he was staring at me, looking me right in the eye. He really believed what he was saying . . . Oh, yes. He would even have *enjoyed* doing it. There's no end of violent men on the street, I've seen my share. But this one was worse than any I've ever seen, believe me. I don't know what you did to him, but if he's got it in for you, I think you'd better call the police.'

She shot him a desperate look.

Max didn't know, of course, that the police would be of no help to her whatsoever.

'And apart from the police,' she said in a toneless voice, 'what can I do?'

Once again she saw a gleam of surprise in his grey eyes.

'Why don't you want to call the police?'

'That's my business.'

He shook his head, incredulous.

'Not much you can do. Get out of town for a while. Do something so he can't find you, wherever it is you go. Do you know who it is?'

'No. What did he look like?'

'You're sure you don't know who it is? He's in his thirties, and small, very small, no more than one metre sixty-eight. He looks fucking insane, if you want my opinion. Oh, yes, and he's got a strange tattoo on his neck.'

She gave a start. A memory. She thought of the tattoos covering Cordélia's tall body. But it wasn't that. She'd seen another tattoo, recently.

'A tattoo? What sort of tattoo?'

'Kind of unusual. It looked like a Madonna with her halo.'

She'd already seen that tattoo somewhere. But where? Suddenly, it came back to her: the Grand Hôtel Thomas Wilson. When she came out of the lift, after her meeting with Léo. She'd bumped into a funny little man with a Madonna tattooed on his neck. So he'd followed her. She thought she'd got rid of him, but she hadn't.

The thought brought a surge of despair. Had he found Léo, too?

'What's that?' said Max.

She followed his gaze. He was looking at the CD case.

'Do you know it?'

'Yes. It's another opera.'

She studied him intensely.

'It's another tale of suicide, isn't it?'

'Mmm. Lakmé is a young Hindu woman who poisons herself with datura when she understands that the man she loves, Gérald, is going to go back to his family.'

She was staring at him, as pale as a shroud.

'What's wrong?' he asked. 'What did I say?'

'Did you say Gérald?'

'Yes, why? Do you know someone called Gérald? Good God, Christine, are you sure you're all right? You're very pale . . .'

★

'Here. Drink this,' he said. 'You passed out. We should call a doctor.'

'No, thank you, I feel better already.' She took the glass of water from his hands.

'So you know someone called Gérald, do you?'

She nodded.

'Is he the man with the tattoo?'

She shook her head.

'You don't want to talk about it?'

'Not yet. Thank you for all you've done, Max. And I'm sorry about my comments just now. But I'm not ready yet.'

He gave her a worried look.

'Christine. Up to now I didn't really know what to make of your story. But I saw that man. I saw his expression. I know that kind of man: he won't let you go. What will he do next time, have you thought about that? How far is he prepared to go? Because sooner or later he's going to come after you again. That sort of sicko has a one-track mind. Believe me: I think you should call the police; you need help.'

'I already have your help. And there's someone else, too. Someone strong, someone who is at least as strong as that man.'

She had raised her voice, as if to convince herself of what she was saying.

'Now, if you don't mind,' she added, 'I'd like to be on my own.'

He nodded, his lips pinched. He got slowly to his feet. In the doorway, he stopped and turned around.

'If you need me, you know where to find me.'

Once he had left, she waited a long time for the adrenaline to subside. She didn't understand what was going on, it didn't make any sense. Max seemed to think that the man in question was a professional criminal. What sort of criminal? A member of the mafia? A thief? A hitman? The business with the tattoo reminded her of stories about Russian or Latin American gangs she had seen on television.

Her thoughts returned to Gérald, and it was as if a viper were unwinding in her belly. What did that guy know about her relationship with her fiancé? Was he the one who had photographed Denise and Gérald? And why this reference to Gérald by way of opera? It couldn't be a coincidence. Gérald was part of the equation. She felt the paranoia washing over her again and she thought about Denise. Had Denise hired some crook, some criminal to frighten her, to make her give up Gérald? It was absurd. Ridiculous. The sort of thing that happened only in films. *And in programmes like* Bring in the Accused, said the little voice in her head, with a hint of impatience. *In real life, in other words, my dear.*

What escape routes were left to her? She took out her phone and looked at it. Shouldn't Léo have called her by now? He had said he was going to see what else he could find out, mobilise his contacts. Had he made any progress? She wished she could have had news from him right at that moment.

She was not going to let that fucking bastard poison her life forever.

The thought galvanised her. She would fight back. But not the way the guy expected. Up to now, she'd always been one or two steps behind. But thanks to Max, she had just obtained some precious information. Yes. She was going to pass it on to Léo; he had talked to her about a private detective: he would know how to make the most of this information. Secondly, *she had to get out of here.* Max was right: she couldn't stay in her apartment. But where could she go? Her first thought was, why not pack her suitcase and take refuge with her parents for a few days? But her killjoy inner voice immediately reacted: *Your parents? Are you serious? And what will you tell them – that you needed a change of scenery?*

The voice was right: *Why now?* they would ask – without bothering to hide the fact that their daughter's incursion into their everyday life was not part of their retirement plan. But she couldn't go and tell them what had happened, after all. And if she made up a story, no matter what it was, her father would see it as confirmation of what he had always thought, namely that his daughter was spineless, that she would never be capable of finding her place in the world, that deep down it would have been so much better if she had died instead of her sister (because that was what he thought, wasn't it? When he'd had enough alcohol to find the nerve to assert his . . . *preference*). As for her mother: well, she would look at Christine and wonder where she had gone wrong as a mother, and she would view her daughter's failure as a personal failure.

*Anything but that.*

Christine went back into the living room and poured another full cup of coffee. She had just had another idea. She looked for Ilan's number in her address book; she knew that at this hour he wouldn't have left for the radio station yet. Moreover, when he answered, she could hear children's voices and a commotion in the background.

'Christine?'

She tried to determine whether his voice was hostile or wary, but it was simply surprised.

'I'm sorry to bother you,' she said, 'but I need you to do me a favour. I know I've already caused you a lot of problems and I would understand if you refused – but you're the only one I can count on, Ilan.'

Not leaving him the time to reply, she explained what it was she needed. Then she waited.

He was silent for a long time.

'I can't promise you anything,' he said. 'But I'll see what I can do.'

'Daddy, who is it?'

A little girl's voice by the telephone. And the sound of another incoming call on her own line.

'It's no one, pumpkin.'

With that he hung up.

She took the second call. 'Hello?'

'Christine? Guillaumot here. The police rang me yesterday. They asked questions about you, and they also told me what you'd done. I called Cordélia after that. She explained what happened over the weekend, and that she had filed a complaint with the police and then eventually withdrew it.' There was a sigh on the other end. 'Fuck, how could you do such a thing? It's . . . it's . . . We all knew, here, that you've got a hell of a temper, but that . . . that . . . it's . . . I still can't believe it.' He made a grinding sound on the line, as if he had a sudden toothache. 'There's no point in you coming to the station tomorrow morning. Or the day after. Or any day after that. We are preparing a procedure of dismissal for grave misconduct, and opening legal proceedings against you.'

There was a pause.

'Maybe that poor girl thinks you've been punished enough, but I don't: your behaviour is seriously detrimental to the radio station's image. You'd better find yourself a good lawyer. You are one fucking crazy bitch.'

# 23

# Leitmotiv

Servaz had rarely seen so much snow in the valley. He was driving across an immaculate white expanse, along the lines of trees stripped bare by winter, his only companion the music of good old Gustav. The grey skies formed a second upside-down valley above his head, filled with hills of clouds. In the middle of a long straight stretch, he left the main road for a narrower, poorly maintained one, and, three kilometres further along he saw the farm on his right.

He parked outside a long residential building whose grey cement had never seen a coat of paint, and got out.

He pulled up his collar, instantly feeling the cold and damp.

Before he had even gone in, he had a vision of Célia Jablonka's childhood and youth in a place far away from everything that might enliven an adolescent's long days. He instantly understood the nature of her ambition, her dreams, as a kid with an imagination that was too big for such a stifling background.

A bottle blonde was standing on the threshold. She watched him approach, her eyes narrowed warily, about as welcoming as the hoarse barking of the dog choking as it yanked on its chain.

'Commandant Servaz, Toulouse police. I have an appointment with Monsieur Jablonka.'

With a brief jerk of her chin, never unclenching her teeth, she pointed to a large barn thirty metres away, and Servaz began walking along the deep ruts left in the snow and mud by tractor wheels, past piles of silage covered with white tarpaulins or stored in bales, and a row of silos and agricultural machinery. When he went through the two wide-open metal doors, he was overpowered by the stench coming from drains full of a brownish, steaming liquid.

'Over here,' said a voice.

He turned to the left and saw a man with white hair sitting at a computer screen in a little office. He had a pile of papers and notes in front of him. Servaz went into the little room. There were columns of numbers on the screen.

'If you don't mind,' said the man, 'I just have to check on the robot. See if everything went all right during the night.'

'The robot?'

'The milking robot.' The man turned around for the first time and gave him a sharp look. He had the same suspicious eyes as his wife. 'You're a city cop, aren't you? I can tell. Have you got a card?'

Servaz had expected this question. He reached inside his jacket pocket. The older man, frowning, compared the visitor with the photograph on the card he held in his gloved hand. Then he turned back to the screen.

'Sorry, but I have to check whether everything went all right last night and take care of the cows that are late, according to the robot.'

Servaz nodded.

'Do what you have to do,' he said. 'I have time.'

'Good for you.'

'How many cows do you have?'

'One hundred and twelve. But you didn't come all this way to talk to me about my cattle.'

Servaz looked at him closely. He had blue eyes in a face that was brown and sun-ravaged, but firm.

'You're reopening the investigation? Why?'

'No,' said Servaz, 'we're not reopening the investigation, Monsieur Jablonka. My job is just to examine a few closed cases,' he lied.

'Why?'

'That's just the way it is: administration.'

'Why this case?'

Servaz didn't reply.

'She grew up here, did she?'

The man gave him a twisted smile.

'I know what you're thinking,' he said.

'Do you?'

'Mr Policeman . . . what we do here is what you call concrete. We don't speculate with money that doesn't exist; we don't sell useless products to people who think they need them; we work day and night; we might be the last people to know the real world exists – and that is why others want to see us disappear. But as far as Célia is concerned, I'll have you know that she grew up surrounded by books. If I invited you into that house you see over there – which I won't – you would see that there are books everywhere, dog-eared books, books with notes in the margin, books that have been read. Célia loved books. And we always encouraged her. Her ambition didn't come from wanting to get away from here, or to do better than her parents; on the contrary, it was so that we would be proud of her. Whenever she felt the need to recharge her batteries, to breathe a bit, she came back here. You should see what it's like here in the spring, this countryside – she liked this place better than anywhere on earth . . .'

'And did she come in here often?' asked Servaz. 'Or did she tend to avoid the place?'

Célia's father give him a hard look.

'Célia was against putting in this machine,' said a woman's voice behind his back. 'She said it was inhuman to keep the cows inside all the time. Maybe she was right.' The look the woman gave her husband was not kind. 'Célia was a very intelligent young woman. And well balanced. At least until she met that guy.'

Servaz turned around. The blonde woman was staring at him.

'What guy?'

'I don't know. We never met him. I think he was married. Someone important. That was why she didn't want to talk about him. All she said was that she had met someone. An exceptional man, by the sound of it. At least in the beginning . . . before her mood began to change—'

She broke off.

'I think towards the end she was depressed. But she refused to talk about it. During those final days, she seemed to be afraid of her own shadow. Something was terrifying her. Something or someone . . . But I would never have thought that she would . . . she would . . .'

Servaz felt as if time were decelerating, flowing infinitely more slowly than the milk in the robot's greedy hoses.

'Are you sure she didn't say anything about this man?'

'She did say one strange thing, once,' Célia's father replied. 'Just the once. She said he was a real cowboy: *a space cowboy*. Or something like that. I don't know what she meant. But she was like that, Célia; she often talked in riddles.'

Servaz stared at him, thinking of the photograph in the box – the photograph of the space station – and he shuddered. Célia's father's eyes were lowered. When he looked up again, Servaz was struck by the intensity of the fierceness of his gaze.

'If she really did commit suicide, what are you doing here one year later?' he asked.

'I told you, a routine check.'

'Don't try and have me on. What's the point of all your questions? Have you reopened the investigation or not?'

'No, sir. The case is closed.'

'Closed?'

'Yes.'

'Right. Then get the hell out of here, Inspector, Lieutenant, Commissaire, or whatever your bloody rank is: you get the hell out of here, right now.'

Servaz slowed down outside the entrance to the Space Centre, which made him think of a motorway tollbooth surmounted by a huge symbol clearly representing a planet and a rocket launcher. The Space Centre was located at the heart of a vast university science complex consisting of laboratories, engineering schools and aerospace industries, to the east of Paul Sabatier University and south of the city. The two guards at the entrance, in blue uniforms, were bickering; they looked about as efficient as a pair of extras on a reality TV programme. He rolled down his window. He explained that he had an appointment with the director. The guard took his ID card and in exchange gave him a visitor's badge that indicated the name of the person he was going to meet (just in case he was tempted to *wander off* inside), and then he was told to leave his car on the left-hand side of the car park, just beyond the entrance.

Servaz did as he was told, switched off the ignition, got out and looked all around him. A few snowflakes were whirling in the cold air; he saw tall fir trees, high pylons with projectors on top, a rocket, and an enormous satellite dish on the snow outside one of the buildings. All the facades were made of tall vertical strips of concrete separated by narrow arrow slits. He could not detect the presence of any particular security measures on the site, and yet there must be some. He headed in the direction of what they had told him was the 'Directors' Building'. Opposite was the Fermat Building, which housed the control rooms for the Ariane satellites. Just next to it was the CADMOS, the Centre for the Development of Microgravity Applications and Space Operations.

When Servaz had called, he had introduced himself as an investigator from the Criminal Investigation Department, and had asked to speak to the director of the Centre, and he had prayed the director would not get in touch with the CID. He had explained that he was investigating the death of the artist Célia Jablonka, who had used space research as the theme for one of her exhibitions. Over the telephone the director had confirmed that Mademoiselle Jablonka had indeed come to visit the site. He did not see what he might actually add to the investigation (so he said), but he had no objections to meeting with Servaz – although he was, he insisted, quite pressed for time. Well, no, the police had not contacted him until today, and why should they have: didn't Célia Jablonka commit suicide? Servaz already suspected that the director was not exactly the modest sort. A quick glance at his CV had informed him that the man had got a degree from the prestigious École Polytechnique in 1977, as well as a PhD, and an MSc from Stanford.

The large man who welcomed him into his office five minutes later had little eyes that sparkled with humour, and a friendly hand-shake, despite his damp palms.

'Please, have a seat.'

He sat back down behind his desk and adjusted his large polka-dot bow-tie. He gave Servaz a kind, enveloping gaze, then spread his hands.

'I don't know exactly what you expect from me, Commandant,' he began, 'but please, fire away. I will try to answer your questions.'

Servaz decided to beat around the bush.

'Why don't you tell me, for a start, what it is you do here.'

The man's smile broadened.

'The Toulouse Space Centre is the operational centre for the National Centre for Space Studies. Here we design, develop, send into orbit, control and operate the space vessels and systems that are the responsibility of the National Centre for Space Studies. You have surely heard about our various programmes – Ariane, Spot, Helios, and above all the robot Curiosity, which the Americans sent to Mars?'

Servaz did as expected: he nodded.

'Well, the ChemCam – the laser camera that is at the top of the robot's mast, the one that has already fired 80,000 laser shots at the rocks to analyse them – is piloted *from here*, and was designed *here* by the National Centre for Space Studies and the Institute for Research in Astrophysics and Planetology.'

Toulouse and outer space, Toulouse and aeronautics: an old story that went back as far as the beginning of the previous century, with Latécoère's planes, and the legendary pilots from the Aéropostale like Jean Mermoz and Saint-Exupéry: *Wind, Sand and Stars, Southern Mail*, the dunes of the Sahara, the lights of Casablanca, Dakar, Saint-Louis in Senegal – stories that were filled with words and names like Patagonia, wireless, Southern Cross, thanks to which Servaz, as an adolescent, had escaped from his room.

'But you haven't come here to talk about robots and research, have you?'

'Do you remember what Mademoiselle Jablonka seemed to be most interested in?'

'She was interested in everything; she was an intelligent, curious young woman. And very pretty, too,' he added, after a moment. 'She wanted to know everything, to see everything, to photograph everything – naturally, we could not satisfy this last request of hers.'

'Did she strike you as depressed?'

'I'm no shrink,' replied the director. 'And besides, I only saw her on two occasions at the most. Why do you ask?'

Servaz thought of something.

'She had met someone,' he said, disregarding the director's question. 'She talked to her father about a "space cowboy".'

The director frowned.

'If you're interested in the astronauts, you've come to the wrong place: you won't find any here. The training centre for European astronauts is in Cologne – and the headquarters for the European Space Agency as well as for the National Centre for Space Studies are in Paris . . . But she might have been in touch with other people without going through me. Why are you interested in them?'

'I'm sorry, but I'm not allowed to tell you.' He noted with satisfaction the little spark of annoyance in the eyes of the man sitting across from him.

'Listen, I don't really know what you're looking for – or what you imagine – but those men are highly trained, thoroughly prepared, both physically and mentally. You cannot imagine the sort of training they go through: centrifuge, swivel chair, tilt table . . . these men can withstand anything. With a smile. They're incredible. And they undergo a whole series of tests, including psychological ones.'

'Is there any way she might have met one of them here?' insisted Servaz, ignoring his remark.

'I just told you . . .'

The director sounded increasingly annoyed. Then he paused.

'Now that you mention it . . . She was also invited to a gala event which the National Centre for Space Studies gave at the Capitole: everybody who was anybody in the French space industry was there. I invited her to come with me. When she saw all those alpha males in their dinner jackets, she completely forgot about me,' said the big man with a hearty laugh.

'You mean that—'

'Yes, all the French astronauts were there: the *space cowboys*, as you call them.'

'Do you remember the date of the gala?'

The director picked up his telephone and exchanged a few words with his assistant, then waited for her reply.

'The 28 of December 2010,' he said, hanging up. 'If it's an astronaut you're looking for, well then, take your pick. They were all there that evening.'

Night was falling over Toulouse, although the afternoon was only two thirds over. It was 31 December and the city was lit up like a Christmas tree. An icy wind seemed to be blowing in all the way from the Polish steppes.

*Why have you come back into my life?* he thought. I had managed to forget you.

You haven't forgotten me.

But you're dead.

Yes.

I am already forgetting your face.

The way you will forget everything else.

Is that all there is? All those words we said. All the promises. All the kisses, the shared moments, the gestures, the waiting, all the love – will nothing remain?

Nothing.

Then what is the point of living?

What is the point of dying?

Are you asking me?

No.

He looked at the pedestrians, wan and hurried, the Christmas lights and decorations, the pretty girls, all bundled up and laughing on the café terraces: their laughter would fall silent, the Christmas lights would dim, the pretty girls would get old and wrinkled, then die. He dialled the number for the town hall.

'Hello?'

A woman's voice. He gave his name, explained who he was and talked about the gala evening on 28 December 2010.

'Anything else?' said the woman, with a touch of bureaucratic smugness.

'Might you have kept a list of the guests?'

'You must be joking.'

He stifled an urge to make a cutting remark.

'Does it sound like it?'

'I'm sorry, but it's not within my remit. I will put you through to someone who *might* be able to help you.'

'Thank you,' he said, taking note of the word *might*.

He waited patiently, listening to Mozart.

'Yes?' said a second voice.

Servaz explained why he was calling.

'Stay on the line. I'll find it for you.'

He stood up straight. The voice was firm and determined. He heard the woman moving about, addressing someone else in an authoritarian tone. He felt a fresh surge of hope. After all, it was the same in the police – there actually were some civil servants who were competent and eager to help. He heard the footsteps come back a few minutes later.

'I'm sorry, but we don't have it here. I'll put you on to someone else.'

He was about to give up and end the call when a thin little voice answered.

'Yes? Hello? *Hello?*'

He hesitated. What was the point?

He trotted out his story again, wearily.

'Um . . . the list of guests for 28 December 2010?' echoed the little voice, not very sure of herself.

'Yes. Do you see which event I'm referring to or not?'

'Of course. I was there. The evening with the astronauts.'

'That's it.'

'I'll see if I can find it for you. Do you want to hold or would you rather call back?'

He thought about how difficult it had been simply to get hold of her. And if he hung up, he might not have the courage to call back.

'I'll hold.'

'As you wish . . .'

After ten minutes had gone by, he was beginning to wonder whether this person had not forgotten about him and gone off to celebrate New Year's, leaving her phone off the hook on a corner of her desk, when he heard:

'I've got it!' Her voice was triumphant.

'Really?'

'Yes. We have a full archive. Including photographs.'

'Photographs? What photographs?' His mind was racing. 'Stay where you are . . . I'll be right there,' he decided, suddenly.

'What? Now? But I – I get off in half an hour and it's – it's New Year's Eve!'

'I'm only a hundred metres away. And it won't take me long. It's very important,' he added.

The little voice became even thinner.

'Well, in that case . . .'

# 24

## Voice

It was seven forty-six p.m., that 31 December. The temperature had fallen below 2°C, but she nevertheless opened the French windows of her hotel room, and evening sounds rose from the square below. From her bed and beyond the balustrade she could admire the illuminated facade of the Hôtel de Ville, which was perpendicular to her hotel, the Grand Hôtel de l'Opéra, 1, place du Capitole. Fifty rooms, two restaurants, a spa with sauna, a steam bath and a massage parlour, right in the centre of town. Her room was red: red walls, red armchair, red floor – only the ceiling, bed and doors were white.

Iggy had sniffed out every nook and cranny of the place, bumping into the doors because he had still not got used to his plastic cone collar, and then when he'd had enough, he fell asleep on top of the bedspread.

She too had dozed off – after unpacking both her suitcases – once she felt safe, and the tension of the last few hours had finally receded. It was her mother who had found this place for her: 'Get a room at the Grand Hôtel de l'Opéra, the manager is a friend of mine.' She had made her promise not to say anything to her father. But she had had to give her a plausible explanation all the same – her mother was not the type of woman who would be satisfied with feeble excuses. Her explanation boiled down to this: a burglar had broken into her place while she was sleeping, and she no longer felt safe. 'You informed the police, I hope?' Christine lied. Then she added that it was only for a few days, the time it would take to have the locks changed.

The bronze tones of Saint-Sernin and the other churches rang out; the monotonous concert of traffic rose to her windows, broken by solo passages of shouts and laughter, and now and again by the dissonant note of an impatient car horn. She stared at the fan on the ceiling. Bells were ringing, vibrant, fervent. She could also hear strains of more pagan music floating like tattered joy among the evening sounds. She could hear the city's heartbeat. So much activity bringing it to life. So much activity and joy she could no longer be part of.

*Why hadn't Léo called?*

She couldn't stand it any more, so she took out her mobile and looked for his number among her contacts. She heard it ring four times before the voicemail clicked in. Damn! Furious, she hung up and immediately redialled. This time he picked up on the second ring.

'Christine—'

'Yes. It's me. Sorry to disturb you, I'm sure you're at home, but I wondered if you had tried to reach me. The battery on my mobile was dead,' she lied, 'and—'

'No, I didn't try. Christine, you know I can't talk now,' he said in a low voice.

'Who is it?' called a woman's voice in the background, and Christine thought she recognised it – she had met Léo's wife once at a party; they had even got on well together.

'It's nothing. It's about the trip I told you about!'

'Kids!' shouted the same voice. 'Kids, go and get ready!'

'When can I see you?' asked Christine. 'Were you able to get hold of that detective?'

Silence.

'Listen, this is not a good time. What did the police say?'

Should she tell him the truth? Later.

'Nothing,' she lied. 'I got the impression they didn't believe me.'

Another long silence.

'I need to see you,' she added, shivering not only from the cold air that was fluttering the curtains – as if they were taking flight in the room – but from something else besides.

'Christine . . . I need to think . . . I spoke to the detective, the one who owed me a favour. He turned up some stuff about you.'

She gulped.

'What stuff? Did you ask him to investigate *me*?'

'He said that during your adolescence you underwent psychiatric treatment. You attacked your family doctor.'

'I was twelve years old!'

'He was also in touch with his contact in the police: there was a girl you attacked, too. I know all about it.'

'It wasn't me!'

'I have to give it some thought,' he said again. 'I'm the one who'll call you back. Look after yourself.'

He had hung up. She felt the rage wash over her and she pressed the redial button. He couldn't just cut her off like that! She had a right to explain herself. For Christ's sake, it wasn't fair: everyone had the right to defend themselves! He knew her, didn't he? They had been to bed together at least a hundred times!

She heard the call go to voicemail.

It was the summer of the year she turned twelve, the evening of 23 July 1993. That summer – a summer of nightmares and ghosts – she had contracted glandular fever and it had left her so exhausted that she rarely left her bed; most of the time she was prey to a fairly high fever which caused her to break out in a hot sweat, and the glands in her neck and armpits were swollen, while the constant headaches made it feel as though her skull was compressed in a vice. The increase in her white-blood cell count, and above all the complications in her bronchial tubes required the family doctor to come and give her an injection every evening before bedtime. After that, her mother switched off the light. Those nights when she had a fever were memorable for their elaborate nightmares, and she ended up dreading the moment when her mother pressed the switch and darkness fell. Just as she was convinced that Dr Harel's mysterious injections were the cause of her nightmares.

But that evening of 23 July, it was not her mother who came, because she was at the bedside of her own mother, who was ill. It was her father who saw to things. 'Sleep well, monkey face,' he said, as if he knew nothing about her nightmares and fever, then he switched off the light and closed the door.

In the dark, wrapped in absolute terror, she had felt her heart begin to beat wildly. Drowsy, she heard voices coming from the swimming pool just beneath her window. The voices were whispering, but the temperature had climbed to over 30°C at night, and the window was open. She listened out, and then she heard it: the splashing of someone swimming. She turned her wan, feverish face towards the clock radio. Midnight. Her cheek against the pillow was damp from her night sweats. Beneath her skull was a blazing sun. And once again she heard them: the whispering, mysterious voices. She was drawn to them. But the swimming pool at night was a different place from during the daytime: an inaccessible and dangerous place, a *forbidden* place. Nevertheless, she threw back the sheet and went out on the mezzanine: there was no one downstairs in the living room, and yet all the lights were on. She went downstairs.

Barefoot, she crossed the living room to the sliding door that gave on to the patio. She opened it quietly and went out into the warm, starry night. Then a shiver of pleasure mingled with anxiety ran down her skin. Before her lay the lapping, illuminated surface. Someone was swimming. A figure back-lit by the lamps at the bottom of the pool. She immediately recognised her: her sister Madeleine. Maddie was swimming through the translucent little ripples, on her back, her hair undulating around her head like seaweed. And she was completely naked.

'Maddie?'

Her big sister turned towards her and righted herself, waving her arms.

'Christine, what are you doing here? Don't you know what time it is?'

'Maddie, what are you doing?'

The air was trembling above the pool; there was a smell of chlorine tickling her nostrils, and the air was filled with a luminescent ballet of fireflies. They were dancing, sparkling, and Christine, at the age of twelve, felt the full hallucinatory strength of the image: Madeleine naked in the pool and the fireflies dancing all around.

'Go on, Christine, out! Go back to bed!'

The violence – and distress – in her sister's voice were like a slap, but the enchantment, or might it have been the dream, held her there, transfixed.

'Maddie . . .'

She was on the verge of tears. There was something about this strangely enchanted summer night that was deeply sinister and unpleasant. She felt something disruptive, something not as it should be, dizzying. It must be a dream – because then her attention was drawn to something on her right at the far end of the pool. *A shadow.* It was slithering and undulating smoothly under the surface of the water and there were instant associations. *Snake, poison, danger.*

Christine went cold all over. A snake was swimming on the surface of the water, headed towards her sister. She wanted to warn her of the danger, but no sound would come from her throat . . . Then she understood that it was just a shadow. The shadow of a shadow, standing motionless at the edge of the pool, at the far end. She couldn't see his face, but she recognised him. Recognised his shoulders, his torso, the way he stood.

'Daddy?' she said.

The shadow didn't move. Didn't speak.

And yet it couldn't be him: because Daddy was asleep upstairs in his room. It was someone who looked like him. Someone his age. *He was naked, too.* The revelation was strangely oppressive, and made her deeply uncomfortable.

What was Maddie doing naked in the swimming pool with a man Daddy's age who was also naked?

'Please, Chris, go back to bed. I'll be there right away.'

Madeleine's voice, imploring, immensely sad. Christine turned around and went back through the living room and slowly up to her room, moving like a sleepwalker. Behind her the whispering had resumed, and she heard a loud splash. *The swimming pool is dangerous, and I forbid you to go there at night:* her daddy had often said this to her.

The next day her fever was even higher, 39.5°C. Dr Harel opened his box full of syringes. She said no, she didn't want a shot. He smiled – *now, now, you're a big girl.* No, she said again, feeling as if her eyes were popping out of her head because of the fever. NO. *Be reasonable,* said her father before leaving her alone with the doctor. Only a few seconds later her father and mother threw open the door to the room when they heard the doctor scream with pain, the needle rammed into his thigh.

After that, she had to admit, she had gone mad. She had screamed. Spat. Scratched. And when her father tried to calm her down she bit him. It was Dr Harel who suggested the psychiatrist.

*How could Léo simply accept the cops' version?* she wondered. How could he base his reaction on events that had occurred twenty years earlier? They had been lovers for two years. Did that not count for something? Shouldn't he at least have listened to her version of the facts? Who are all these people who come into your life, demanding your love and attention – only to suddenly leave you? (*May I remind you that you're the one who left him,* said the little voice.) If she could not rely on Léo, who was left? Max the wino, with his endless thirst? God help us!

Outside, the bells had stopped ringing. She got up to close the window; the air in the room was icy. Down on the square pedestrians were bundled up, strolling among the Christmas lights. In the crowd she spotted a man on his own, a man in his forties, with a champagne bottle in his hand. As alone as she was . . .

Who else? *No one.* She was alone – as alone as anyone can be: this time, it was for real.

# 25

# Counterpoint

On the evening of 31 December, Servaz entered the Henri-IV court-yard of the Toulouse Hôtel de Ville through the large wooden door that gave out on to the place du Capitole. He walked across the courtyard to a sliding glass double door, turned right once he was inside and went through a handsome wrought-iron gate immediately followed by a tall wooden door that opened beneath a sign declaring in large gilded letters: DEPARTMENT OF ELECTIONS AND ADMINISTRATIVE PROCEDURES. His guide was waiting just beyond: a little woman as wide as she was tall, oddly dressed in a flowing purple overgarment. She led him at a brisk walk down a labyrinth of corridors and offices that were clearly less splendid, then opened a door and he followed her into a tiny space with a computer. She pointed at the screen.

'You've got everything here,' she said. 'The photographs of the party on the evening of 28 December 2010.' She pointed to a bound file. 'And the list of guests is there.'

He moved his finger to the rows of images on the screen.

'How many are there?'

'Roughly five hundred.'

He pointed to the chair.

'May I sit down?'

She glanced worriedly at her watch.

'How long will you be?'

'No idea.'

She seemed somewhat put out by his answer.

'You know, I would like to be on time for my party, actually.'

It had been dark for a while already, and in the little room only one lamp struggled against the encroaching shadows.

'If you like, I'll lock up,' he suggested.

'No, I can't do that. Is it really that important?'

He nodded gravely, looking her straight in the eyes.

'And urgent?'

He stared at her with the same stern look. She shook her head, defeated.

'Well then, fine, do what you have to do. Would you like a coffee?'

'Black, no sugar. Thank you.'

Half an hour later, he was not so enthusiastic: over two hundred guests had been invited, not counting all the extras, and the photographer had been overzealous: he'd snapped away as if there were no tomorrow. The same faces appeared again and again, while others were visible only once, and even then they were blurry, far away, practically off camera. Everyone who was anyone in the space industry was there, if Servaz was to believe the list, beginning with the director of the Toulouse Space Centre, whom he spotted in several pictures, and the director of the National Centre for Space Studies. There were also local and national journalists, guests from all walks of life, the mayor, a deputy, and even a minister. Naturally, he had no difficulty identifying Célia Jablonka; the young woman was ravishing in her bare-backed evening gown, and her lovely neck was emphasised by a chignon dotted with little pink pearls, loose strands of hair artfully arranged on either side of her face, an elaborate hairstyle that must have taken hours at the salon. There were not many women who could compete, and no doubt the photographer found that she captured the light – or that she was good publicity for the evening – because he had taken her picture over and over.

The problem was that she had spoken with rather a lot of people.

Servaz's second angle of attack was the famous Space Cowboys, the galactic boy band. He had the list before his eyes and the photos on screen, and he thought he had managed to locate the thirteen astronauts who were present, although he was not able to match a name to every face. Smiling guys with square jaws and bright eyes, looking as healthy as any California surfer. They were all wearing the same suit, rather like members of a sports team on an official tour. Once he had stamped their faces onto his memory, he went back to the pictures of Célia. She had spoken with three of them. With the first, she only appeared once. With the second, the conversation must have lasted a bit longer, because there were two pictures; the man was in his forties and he was lavishing all his charm on her. Célia was responding – but nothing more. With the third man, she had been photographed in three different places in the room, and on the last picture their faces were clearly closer together. Servaz felt his heart beat faster. Something was happening in this photograph. The photographer had zoomed in and caught Célia at an angle that showed her dilated pupils, all her attention absorbed by her companion. In addition, she had moved close enough for the conversation to take a more intimate turn. It's a question of proximities, the physical distance separating individuals during communication. All space is shared; there is no such thing as neutral territory. Whether it was Célia or the astronaut who had taken the first step, in the end both of them had agreed on a distance that was on the border between personal space and intimate space – a long way, in any case, from simple social space.

Servaz sat back abruptly against his seat, his hands behind his neck. And now? What did this prove?

The town hall employee chose that moment to look in through the door.

'Have you finished?'

'Not yet. Give me just a little while longer.'

'You're not celebrating New Year's, Commandant?'

'Um, yes . . . is it that late?'

'Seven o'clock.'

'Ah, yes. So it is.'

He called to her again.

'Um, Cécile – is that right?'

Her round face and curly hair reappeared.

'Yes?'

He pointed to the screen.

'This man, here, looks familiar. Do you know who it is?'

She slid into the narrow space with the same millimetric precision as she had earlier, as if she possessed integrated radar or sonar, and leaned towards the screen.

'Don't you watch television?' she said.

'I don't like television.'

She looked at him as if trying to determine whether he was joking.

'It's Léonard Fontaine.'

And, as he raised an eyebrow:

'The astronaut.'

He smiled, contrite. 'Ah, yes, of course.'

He wrote down the name.

'Are you married, Commandant?'

'Divorced,' he replied. 'Fancy-free.'

She burst out laughing and again looked at her watch.

'I'll go and get a USB key and put all these photos on there for you. That way you can look at them as much as you like. And you can take the list with you. I'd be very surprised if anyone else asks for it. I'm really sorry but I have to close the office.'

There was a festive atmosphere throughout the city. He didn't feel like going back to the rest home – any more then he wanted to get stuck somewhere with strangers who would slap him on the shoulder in a shower of confetti and streamers while their wives insisted on getting him to dance.

It was better to drink alone than in the wrong company. He had bought a bottle of champagne and a box of plastic champagne glasses, all of which he had thrown into the rubbish except for one, and he filled his glass as he walked across the vast esplanade crowded with people. All around him couples hurried through the freezing night with their winter coats over their evening clothes, some with a bottle, some with gifts. He was sitting on a bench in the square Charles de Gaulle, at the foot of the Donjon, when his telephone vibrated in his pocket. He answered without checking the caller's identity – proof that although he was not drunk, he was no longer in a normal state.

'Where are you, Martin?'

Vincent's voice. A faint smile passed momentarily over his lips.

'I'm just leaving the *mairie*,' he said, figuring that at least an hour and a half had gone by since he had left the town hall employee with her purple overgarment and fluorescent trainers.

'The *mairie*? At this time of night? What were you doing there?'

He didn't answer, his attention distracted by a homeless man who was eyeing his half-full champagne glass.

Servaz winked at him and handed him the glass.

'Happy New Year, mate!' cried the tramp, seizing it.

'Who are you with?'

'No one . . . Aren't you going to celebrate?' he asked his assistant.

A stupid question if ever there was one.

'That's why I'm calling. We're having a party with a few friends; they'll be here any minute. Why don't you come and join us?'

'That's kind of you, but—'

'Listen, Charlène is waving at me, I'll put her on. I hope you'll come,' he added. 'You're not really going to spend New Year's in that sinister place, are you, Martin? Or maybe you've got a date . . .'

He could hear music in the background, one of those rock groups Vincent liked so much. No: something more syrupy, a chick wailing like a cat whose tail has been stepped on – must be something their ten-year-old daughter Mégan had chosen.

'Martin?'

A warm, smooth voice, like a sip of Baileys Irish Cream.

'Hey,' he said.

'How are you?'

'Couldn't be better.'

'Why don't you come?' she said in a loud voice. 'We'd be delighted to have you: your godson has been asking for you, you know.' She must have walked further away, because suddenly she lowered her voice. *'Come. Please.'*

'Charlène.'

'I'm begging you. We haven't had much time to talk lately. I want to see you, Martin. I *need* to see you. I promise I'll be good,' she gushed.

He could tell she'd been drinking. He hung up, and switched off his phone. His stomach in a knot, he raised the champagne bottle to his lips – then stopped when he thought of all the alcoholic policemen who haunted the centre. Then he looked again at the bottle: he had forgotten how much alcohol could depress him. He got slowly to his feet. He looked at the group of homeless men sitting on the ground on the other side of the walkway. The one he'd given his glass to was still holding it, empty, in his hand. He raised it in Martin's direction with a smile. The others followed his gaze and they all nodded to greet him courteously, mainly staring at the champagne bottle, for the fact that it was still two thirds full had not escaped them.

Servaz went over to them and handed them the bottle.

'Happy New Year,' he said.

His gesture was greeted with applause and cheers.

Martin headed for the underground car park where he had left the car.

He switched off the headlights when he drove into the rest home car park. He didn't want Élise or one of the other health-care assistants to notice him and pressure him to join the party. He closed the car door as quietly as possible, but it was unlikely he would be heard: music was pouring out of the building, full blast.

He walked on tiptoe, although the snow muffled his steps, to the hallway, and then crossed it, hugging the walls. Here the music was deafening. Laughter, applause, exclamations. He hurried silently towards the stairway without switching on the light. Even when he had closed his bedroom door he could still hear the bass through the walls. He looked at his watch. Seven minutes to midnight. Okay, he wouldn't be able to sleep, anyway. So he switched on his computer and opened his email. He saw the message at once. It had been sent by a certain malebolge@hell.com. An obvious reference. Dante. *The Divine Comedy*. You could have shown a bit more imagination, he thought. All the same, his hair stood on end, like iron shavings on a magnet, when he opened the message:

*Any progress, Commandant? I've given you a fair number of clues. You're getting soft.*

His features lit up by the screen. His heart pounding. Winded both by the familiarity of the tone and its bossiness. He gazed at the message. Someone impatient, authoritarian – even tyrannical. Someone who knew but who was playing with him, like a cat with a mouse. *Why?* he wondered. Once again, he thought it must be someone who was bound by professional secrecy: a doctor, a cop, a lawyer. But there was something else in the tone of that message: an impression of stubbornness . . .

*Or could it be . . .*

Yes, of course. It must be him. The one who had driven Célia to suicide. And now he was challenging Servaz to find him. His mouth was dry, and he felt as if the idea were taking root in his brain like a tree. Was it an actual possibility or was it yet again he himself who was constructing outlandish theories to suppress his boredom?

Breathing faster and faster, he got up in the dark and rummaged inside his jacket pocket for the USB key Cécile had given him. He plugged it in. His computer took forever to download the five hundred photographs. Suddenly the sound of the music from downstairs grew even louder and he heard the faraway echo of shouts and hearty applause. He checked his watch in the glow of the screen. *Midnight.* A new year . . . He wondered if he would be back on the job before the year was out − and whether he would be better. Suddenly he remembered he had switched off his mobile after hanging up on Charlène, and he thought about Margot. He hurried over to his jacket and switched on the phone. There was one voicemail and one text message. Margot's voice on the first: *Happy New Year, Papa. I hope you're all right. I'll try to come and see you this week. Take care of yourself, my dear Papa. I love you!* He could hear voices and music in the background and he wondered whether Margot was at her mother's or with friends. The text message was from Charlène. *Happy New Year, Martin. You should have come. I hope you're having fun at least. See you soon.* He read it again but the words slid over him; his mind was already elsewhere.

He went and sat back down at the table and started the slideshow. The faces paraded past him again. A crowd of faces. How could he sort them? How could he find the man who mattered? Then he lingered on the picture that had caught his attention: Célia Jablonka and that astronaut, Léonard Fontaine. Very close together. So close they must have been able to feel each other's breath on their faces. Was this a lead? He wasn't at all sure. He typed the name into Google and realised why the civil servant had been so surprised he'd never heard of him. Apparently, Léonard Fontaine was an emblematic figure in the French space industry: the second Frenchman in space, the first to have been on board the International Space Station, and he had also spent time on a Mir station and flown on Soyuz missions as well as the Atlantis Space Shuttle; logged over two hundred days in orbit; he was a commander of the Legion of Honour, a Knight of the National Order of Merit, he had a medal for the Russian Order of Courage, three Space Flight Medals and two Exceptional Service Medals awarded by NASA; he was on the board for the National Air and Space Academy, a member of the American Institute of Aeronautics and Astronautics, of the International Academy of Astronautics, and of the Space Explorers' Association, whatever that meant. Lost in thought, Servaz recalled the photograph of the International Space Station he had given to Vincent and Samira . . .

As happened every time when he thought he was onto something, he was overcome by a slight giddiness. Léonard Fontaine. At the same time, a second sensation, almost the opposite of the first, was nagging at him: the hunch that he had let something slip by.

He had seen something. But what? And when? He couldn't go through those five hundred photographs again!

But that is precisely what he did. Not once, but twice. It was one twenty-three in the morning when at last he came upon the detail that had subconsciously caught his attention. A reflection, in a mirror . . . a huge mirror above the buffet, behind a small group of people: Célia Jablonka was visible there. And she was not alone.

She was talking to a man. Or rather, the man was talking to her, in her ear, while handing her a business card: she held it between her index and middle fingers. She was smiling. Beaming. Servaz looked at the man again. In his thirties, short hair. He was wearing a coat, a grey jacket and a blue shirt. And glasses . . . He didn't look anything like an astronaut with his woollen coat and specs, but he was good-looking nevertheless. A rather intellectual sort of look. *Who are you?* he wondered. In his suntanned hand, the stranger was holding a glass full of a green liquid and ice cubes. *Caipirinha.*

# 26

# Synopsis

Tuesday the first of January. A new year, new hope. Putting his feet on the ground that day, he was eager to get on with his investigation – but his impatience immediately came up against a specific and unavoidable fact: *it was 1 January*. And consequently there was little chance that anyone would feel like answering an investigator's questions, no matter how motivated he was. On the other hand, he did not know how he would spend the day if he had to wait until tomorrow – so he might as well see what he could do.

He tried to remember where he had put the Space Centre director's business card. Once he'd found it, he took a look and a smile came to his lips: there was a mobile phone number. He checked his watch. One minute past eight. A bit early to get a director out of bed, the morning after New Year's Eve.

While waiting for a more appropriate time, he went down to the common room for a cup of black coffee. The room had not been cleaned, and a thick carpet of confetti and streamers cushioned his steps. The tables were covered with a jumble of paper cups, plastic champagne glasses and empty bottles. There was no one in sight. Servaz went over and looked at the bottles. Golden labels on a black background, remnants of gilt paper around the neck – his brain translated: champagne. *Had they really been allowed to drink?* He leaned over one of the bottles. The brand name didn't ring a bell, but the number on the bottom left of the label immediately caught his eye: 0%. To escape the smell of grape juice, he went to drink his coffee in the little room on the north side, as far away as possible from this battlefield. He switched on the telly, then immediately switched it off again when he saw the images of celebration flickering across all the news channels. He turned his head and saw a snowman staring at him through the picture window. *He wasn't there yesterday* . . . He looked sad, with his mouth an upside-down V, and someone had written 'Martin' across his chest.

Servaz went back up to his room.

At nine o'clock sharp, he reached for his phone. The director of the Space Centre was a bit surprised by his call:

'Good God, do you know what day it is?'

'No, what day is it?'

A sigh on the other end.

'Make it quick. What do you want?'

'Léonard Fontaine.'

'Again? You don't give up easily, do you, Commandant? Well then, what about Fontaine?'

'Any spicy titbits? A scandal? Accusations of harassment? Some malicious gossip, for Christ's sake! I thought you were a bit vague last time.'

The silence was abnormally long.

'What are you playing at, Commandant? Look, I will be obliged to submit the matter to your superiors. Not only, as I already told you, does the Centre have nothing to do with astronauts, but I will be the last one to spread gossip about anybody, do you hear me?'

'Loud and clear. Do you mean that there was some – some gossip?'

He heard the dialling tone: the director had hung up. Right, perhaps Servaz had not taken the right approach. Who could fill him in on the astronauts' darker side? The problem was that he did not know where to begin, and he could not go and see his colleagues from the technical service – those who were science and technology buffs – and ask them to give him a hand. An Internet search, typing in the names, one after the other, of the thirteen astronauts who had attended the gala, yielded heaps of information like the stuff he already had, but no new contacts.

As he scrolled through the pages on Google and the dozens of entries that had nothing to do with the purpose of his search, he eventually came, on page 11, to one column that piqued his interest. It referenced a book entitled *The Black Book of Space Conquest*. It had been written by one J.-B. Henninger. Servaz wrote down his name and it took him an additional ten minutes to find an address and telephone number: the journalist in question, although he was French, lived in the Spanish Pyrenees, which placed him just under three hundred kilometres from Toulouse. At last, luck had given him

219

the little nudge that he'd been waiting for. It was time to find out what Henninger was up to on 1 January. The telephone rang for a long time, but no answerphone picked up, and Servaz began to doubt whether the number was still valid, when all of a sudden a strident voice boomed down the line.

'HELLO?'

Servaz held the receiver away from his ear. The man must be deaf.

'Monsieur Henninger?' he asked, automatically raising his voice.

'Yes! That's me!'

'My name is Servaz, Commandant Servaz! From the Toulouse police! I would like to talk to you!'

'What about?'

'About the book you wrote: *The Black Book of Space Conquest.*'

'Have you read it?'

'Um . . . no, I just found out about it.'

'Ah! I thought as much. The circle of my readers is almost as small as that of the astronauts it describes. How can I help you, Commandant?'

'I have some questions for you.'

'What about?'

'I would like to know if any of the French astronauts have been involved in any scandals.'

'Forgive me – what sort of scandals?'

'I don't know . . . violence, harassment . . . that sort of thing – the sort of thing you find almost everywhere but, apparently, not among astronauts.'

There was a chuckle at the other end of the line. 'Reprehensible behaviour, stories that have been hushed up, secrets that are not all that flattering – is that what you mean?'

'Yes.'

'And do you have a name in particular?'

Servaz gave it to him. He waited a long time for his answer.

'Let me give you my address; we cannot talk about this over the telephone,' said the man suddenly. 'And besides, I will need to verify your identity.'

Servaz felt his pulse race. The most excellent Henninger might be deaf, but he did not seem all that surprised by his odd question.

'When can we meet?'

'What exactly is going on, Commandant?'

220

'I will tell you when we meet.'

'Right. Fine. I'll be expecting you.'

'Do you mean, *today*?'

'You're the one who's in a hurry, aren't you? Why? Have you got something else planned? Apparently not.'

The address Henninger had given him was in the Cadi-Moixero Park, the largest natural park in Catalonia. Henninger's house was nestled in the countryside among sylvan pines, birch trees, maples and aspens, and as Servaz stepped out of the car he felt as if he were in Canada. He breathed in the pure, invigorating air, listened to the silence, and almost expected to come upon a dam built by beavers or a bear rubbing itself against a tree. It was a place of extraordinary beauty. A place, he thought, where he would have gladly spent several days or several weeks. Or even years?

He turned to look at the house: it was built entirely of wood, with a south-facing terrace overlooking the valley.

The man who came out of the house did not, however, look anything like a Canadian lumberjack. He must not have been any taller than one metre thirty, and he was leaning on a cane that sank deep into the snow with his every step. Other than that, he had a full beard and was very muscular, and he had a vice-like grip as he shook Servaz's hand.

'Hello! I hope you didn't have any trouble finding it. You're lucky they cleared the road yesterday.'

He spoke as loudly as he had on the telephone. One of the frequent symptoms of achondroplasia – the most common form of dwarfism – is recurrent ear infections, which leave the sufferer with a tympanosclerosis leading to varying degrees of deafness. It was fortunate, thought Servaz, that he had no neighbours. Henninger studied him with a critical eye.

'So you're a cop?'

'In the crime squad, the CID in Toulouse,' Servaz confirmed.

'Since when have the crime squad been interested in astronauts?'

'I hope you don't intend to make me freeze outside?' asked Servaz.

The little man burst out laughing.

'No! But your story aroused my curiosity. I won't pretend that I haven't been bursting with impatience ever since I spoke to you on the telephone.'

The house's interior made Servaz want to stay even more. Wood-panelled walls, chestnut floorboards, old armchairs that looked deep and comfortable, a fireplace where three big logs crackled as the flames bit, a bar with copperware, books piled everywhere and a large window overlooking the forest.

Servaz looked around him.

'Why did you settle here?' he asked.

'You mean, why this side of the Pyrenees? For a very simple reason: when you fly over these mountains from France to Spain on board a commercial airliner, you notice that the cloud cover collides with the peaks the way Saruman's armies collided with King Théoden's fortress.'

'Whose armies?'

'Never mind. Two minutes earlier, you were flying over impenetrable cloud cover, and then once you're past the mountains you suddenly see rivers, roads, villages, lakes, and not a cloud on the horizon. It's the same thing when you go through the Envalira tunnel and Andorra from north to south: two times out of three, you go from an overcast sky to dry and sunny weather. That is why I settled here. To be able to gaze at the stars as often as possible.'

Servaz had already noticed the huge telescope on its tripod waiting for more favourable nights. Henninger invited him to take one armchair while he plopped down into the other, where he looked like a child sitting in a grown-up's seat.

'I often wonder where my passion for space came from. The fact is that by the age of seven or eight I wanted to be an astronaut; I used to draw rockets, spacesuits and planets, I gazed at the moon through my bedroom window, dreaming of the day when I would stand on it. As you can imagine, it was as I grew up – so to speak – that I realised that I would never be an astronaut.' He smiled. 'That merely increased my interest in the profession and in space itself. To know that I would never be able to leave the earth's atmosphere behind, that I would be doomed to dreaming of space from down below, trying in vain to imagine what it must be like to be up there . . . as an adolescent, I devoured science-fiction novels. Last year I was able to fly at zero gravity for the first time on board an Airbus A300 ZERO-G. Of course, I know that means nothing compared to what they experience up there. It is the ultimate human adventure, unsurpassable. There is nothing beyond it: to leave the earth behind . . . but who knows?

Perhaps we will live long enough to see space tourism within our reach. More and more private companies are exploring the possibility.'

Servaz noticed that his gaze had wandered far away. It lasted only a second, then he was present once again.

'But you came here for something far more down to earth, I believe,' said Henninger.

'In fact, the one who interests me most is Léonard Fontaine. When I mentioned his name over the telephone, you seemed to react.'

'Why him in particular?'

*Yes, why him?* wondered Servaz. *After all, Célia might have met another astronaut at the party . . .*

'Him, or someone else,' he corrected. 'Have there been, to the best of your knowledge, any scandalous incidents of any sort involving an astronaut?'

Henninger took some time to think.

'Space agencies are almost as secretive as information agencies, but there are incidents that make it into the press from time to time: we found out that a couple of Soviet cosmonauts had serious psychological problems in the past, or that American astronauts admitted to having suffered from isolation or even slight forms of depression during their stay on the International Space Station. We also know that there have been incidents, situations of tension or crisis on board both the Mir and the International Space Station over the years, but these events have been buried deep within very confidential reports and they rarely see the light of day. But the two most notable incidents, the Judith Lapierre affair in 1999, and the Nowak affair in 2007, both happened on earth.'

He leaned forward.

'From 1999 to 2000, the Russian Institute for Biomedical Problems conducted a series of experiments to test human response in conditions of isolation in space. One of these tests consisted of isolating several trial participants for 110 days in a replica of the Mir station on earth. On 3 December 1999, three international subjects and one Russian were invited to join the four Russians who had already been staying in this confined space since the beginning of summer: an Austrian, a Japanese, and Dr Judith Lapierre, a beautiful thirty-two-year-old woman who held a doctorate in health sciences, sent by the Canadian Space Agency.'

Henninger stood up, went over to the bar, and came back with a little joint, which he lit carefully.

'Would you like some?' he said.

'No, thank you – you seem to forget I'm with the police.'

'And you seem to have forgotten that we are in Spain, and that here, consumption is legal.'

He reached for a Zippo, lifted the lid, rolled the switch and brought the flame up to his joint.

'Less than one month after their arrival, while they were celebrating New Year's, the Russian commander, who was drunk, tried twice to force a kiss on Judith Lapierre, then he touched her and tried to drag her out of sight of the camera in order to have sex with her. This led to a fight between two Russian cosmonauts. It was so violent that the walls were splattered with blood. Judith Lapierre took pictures of the wall with her digital camera and sent them back to Canada via email. As for the Austrian and Japanese participants, they asked their respective countries to intervene in order to bring the Russian commander to his senses. They were told that such behaviour was normal for Russians and that they would either have to accept it or leave the experiment. The next day there was a second incident, where one of the cosmonauts had to hide the station's kitchen knives, because the two belligerents from the day before were threatening to kill each other. Given the overwhelming tension, the Japanese astronaut decided it was impossible for him to continue the mission and he left. As for Lapierre, she was reluctant to give up so easily. After fitting her room with locks, she decided to stay on. Following the incident, Dr Valery Gushin, the project coordinator, blamed Lapierre for spoiling the atmosphere of the mission by rejecting the commander's kiss. Once she was home again, Judith Lapierre took the Canadian Space Agency to court because they had refused to come to her assistance: she eventually won her case after five years of proceedings.'

The little man leaned further forward.

'The second incident involved Lisa Marie Nowak, an experienced NASA astronaut who had flown with the Space Shuttle *Discovery*. On 5 February 2007, Lisa Nowak was arrested at Orlando airport and put on trial for the assault and attempted kidnapping of a female officer from the US Air Force, Captain Colleen Shipman, who was having an affair with another astronaut, William Oefelein, with whom Nowak had just broken up. In Nowak's car they found latex gloves, a wig and dark glasses, as well as a BB gun and ammunition, pepper spray, a knife with a four-inch blade, big bin liners, and a rubber hose. Nowak had sprayed Shipman with the pepper spray in the airport car park, but the victim managed to escape and call the police.' He leaned even closer. 'I was not given access to the file; however, given the gear found in her car, I think it looked more like attempted murder, don't you? However, the prosecutor decided otherwise. He reduced the initial charges, even dropping the attempted kidnapping, and in the end Lisa Nowak got off with two days in prison and a year of probation.'

Henninger took a moment to pull on his joint, narrowing his eyes and focusing on Servaz. The superman image was seriously damaged. Servaz noted that the two 'incidents' had involved both men and women: in both cases, there had been jealousy, harassment and sexual greed.

'Did the . . . did the incident with Fontaine also involve a woman?'

'A woman?' The little man looked at Servaz. 'Yes, it did indeed.'

'When?'

'In 2008. In Russia. At Star City.'

Servaz felt a shiver go down his spine.

'What happened?'

'The European Space Agency had sent Fontaine and a young French-Russian female astronaut to train at Star City, then spend some time on board the International Space Station as part of a Soyuz mission. The mission was cancelled at the last minute. When he came back from Russia, Fontaine wasn't himself any more. I think that when he was there the Russian police had accused him of harassment and violent behaviour with regard to the young female astronaut. Something like that. I don't know all the details. The European Space Agency hushed up the affair in order not to tarnish the image of one of its most famous heroes, and the Russians did the same, so as not to tarnish the image of Star City. Whatever the case may be, Fontaine was never invited again to participate in any other programmes. Since then the Space Agency has just used him for media events, public relations . . . He has become the number one VIP, the agency's Tom Cruise. But as far as being an astronaut is concerned, he's toast.'

'Do you know the identity of the young woman?'

Henninger nodded.

'Of course. I even met her. But she refused to go into detail. It was . . .' He took time choosing his words. 'Bizarre. On the one hand,

I felt she was afraid to say too much; on the other hand, she was aching to relieve herself of a burden. I remember asking her whether it was true he had assaulted her, and she nodded, but when I asked her what exactly had happened, she refused to say.'

Servaz shuddered: perhaps he'd found his man.

'Are you sure about this?' he asked. 'It hardly seems believable that a guy like him could be a manipulative pervert.'

'Not all that unbelievable if you take into account what happened in 1999: Judith Lapierre was almost raped, and two astronauts almost killed each other . . . And if you remember the Nowak affair in 2007 . . . Why should astronauts be any different from other people, Commandant? Why shouldn't they too have their weaknesses, their black sheep? People want to have a certain image of them. But that's not real life.'

Servaz took the time to digest Henninger's words. He felt as if he had torn open part of the curtain and that a starry night was waiting for him on the other side. A night whose depths he had not yet finished exploring.

'Would it be possible to have the woman's address and telephone number?' he asked.

Henninger stood up.

'Yes. No problem. I'll get it for you.'

The journalist went out of the room and Servaz took a moment to make some rapid calculations. Had Célia been beaten or raped in addition to being harassed? He was clearly dealing with a repeat offender: in this case, there might be other victims . . . Henninger came back with a Post-it. Servaz read:

*Mila Bolsanski*
*Route de la Métairie Neuve*

'Mila is a Slavic name,' he said.

'Yes. I told you: she has dual French-Russian nationality. That was the whole problem.'

'In what way?'

'Well, as a rule, at Star City the Russian cosmonauts do not behave towards their Russian female crewmates in the same way as they do towards the female astronauts from other countries. Take Claudie Haigneré: she has always sung the praises of her Russian partners –

"they're so jolly", "they're so kind" and so on – and she always said that everyone danced attendance on her at Star City – even good old General Alexey Leonov, who was her "sweetie". The same Leonov who, in 1975, when he was commander of Soyuz 19 as part of the first joint Soviet-American mission, explained to journalists that the Russian space endeavour did not need women on board. Russian female cosmonauts have often denounced the way they're treated as if they are second-rank cosmonauts, of minimal importance . . . And so it would seem that at Star City, because of her dual nationality, Mila was treated as a Russian rather than as a Frenchwoman.'

He leaned back abruptly in his armchair.

'But if you want to know more, I suggest you get in touch with her directly.' He studied Servaz. 'It's my turn to ask you a few questions. Why is a policeman from the crime brigade suddenly taking an interest in Léonard Fontaine?'

'Well, it's not an official investigation.'

'What do you mean?'

'Let's just say that . . . well, I'm conducting my own investigation.'

For a moment, the two men observed each other in silence.

'Hmm. And this investigation has something to do with Léonard Fontaine?'

Servaz nodded.

'More rape business?'

He shook his head.

'Harassment?'

He nodded.

'Well Christ, that comes as no surprise! Those guys are always at it. Can't you tell me any more?'

'It's too soon.'

'Damn, give me your word that if you solve this investigation, I'll be the first to know!'

'You have my word.'

'This woman,' asked Henninger, 'did the same thing happen to her as to Mila Bolsanski?'

'No. She died.'

This time, the metallic eyes of the man sitting opposite him lit up with curiosity.

'What do you mean, she died? A murder?'

'Suicide.'

# 27

# Diva

At a quarter to four in the afternoon, he was back on the road beneath a darkening sky. The snow had started gently falling again. The mountains were veiled in clouds, challenging him to cross them before nightfall.

Driving with his headlights on, although it was still more or less day, and with the wipers going, he wondered how Fontaine chose his prey. In the case of Mila Bolsanski, chance and the Space Agency had set her in his path, and the encounter with Célia was also by chance – as with so many encounters that did not lead to harassment and violence, he thought. Had there been other victims? Was Fontaine watching them? Was he getting to know their habits? Or, on the contrary, were they always women whom destiny – that great celestial lottery – set down before him?

Servaz found himself stuck behind a coach during the long climb to Andorra. Every time he tried to go round, he would find himself face to face with a car speeding down towards him. Finally, just beyond the tollbooth for the border police, he pulled over and took out his phone to call Mila.

She replied after the second ring – her voice cautious, timid. He had read that for victims like her, the memory of physical violence eventually faded, whereas the humiliation and insults they had endured left indelible traces.

'Hello,' he said. 'My name is Martin Servaz, I'm a police commandant. I need to speak to you. A journalist, a Monsieur Henninger, gave me your number.'

'What do you want with me?'

'It's about Léonard Fontaine.'

She took so long to answer that he had time to count four cars and three articulated lorries passing by.

'I don't want to talk about him.'

'I know that you withdrew your complaint at the time, and Monsieur Henninger told me how reluctant you were to speak about the . . . episode. But there is something new.'

'What do you mean?'

'I'd rather talk to you in person, if you don't mind.'

There was the sudden, momentary blast of a horn.

'Listen,' she said, 'as far as I'm concerned, it's finished business. I don't want to bring it all up again. I'm sorry.'

'I understand, Madame Bolsanski.'

'Mademoiselle—'

'Mademoiselle Bolsanski, what if I told you that there are other women who have been through what you went through, and that Léonard Fontaine has blood on his hands?'

Another silence.

'Can you prove it?'

'I think I can.'

'Are you going to arrest him?'

'Unfortunately we haven't reached that point yet.'

'I see. Thank you, Commandant, but I'd rather stay out of it.'

'I understand.'

'Back then they obliged to me to withdraw my complaint. I was under enormous pressure. Why should it be any different now?'

'Because I'm not them.'

'Well . . . I don't doubt your good faith, or your good will, but . . .'

'All I ask is five minutes of your time. As I told you, it would seem that other women experienced the same thing you did. If I manage to connect their experiences and yours in some way, then perhaps I'll be able to nail him.'

He counted four cars and two more lorries before she came back on the line.

'Fine. I'll be expecting you.'

Night had fallen by the time he drove up the long straight road lined with plane trees. The big house was all the way at the end, in the meadow – almost square, with two storeys and windows that were all identical. Perhaps it was an old farm. A lamp was burning above the entrance. Other than that, all the windows were dark. He slammed the car door in the silence and looked all around: other than a faint little light perhaps half a mile away, the place was completely deserted.

He thought it was a brave choice for a woman who had gone through what Mila Bolsanski had gone through. But he had also read that women who had been victims of repeated violence might eventually shut themselves away, convinced that the outside world was hostile towards them. Years later, they might still fear the smallest event that could re-immerse them in the past. He knew that by coming here he was going to arouse painful memories – if Mila did not throw him out before that.

He could not see her car, but he thought he could make out a corrugated metal garage in the darkness, a dozen or so metres away. The door opened while he was walking towards it.

The woman who stood on the threshold was tall and slim; as the light came from deep within the house behind her, her features remained in shadow. She did not say a single word until he had approached the steps.

'Come in,' she said, her voice sounding firmer than on the telephone.

She went ahead of him down a corridor as endless as the gallery of a mine, a corridor plunged into semi-darkness. The only light came from the room at the end, and her shadow trailed behind her like the black veil of a recently widowed bride. He studied her. Clearly she kept herself fit; her shoulders were broad and she had a long graceful neck. He noticed two old radiators and some even older paintings in the gloom. The room at the back was a large, well-appointed kitchen, brightly lit by two spotlights on the ceiling.

No matter how hard he tried, he could not hear a sound. Given the number of steps they had taken to come this far, and the two storeys above, he figured the house must have at least thirty rooms.

'Do you live here on your own?'

'No. There is Thomas.' She gave him a faint smile. 'My son.'

The light from the spotlights now lit up her face and he thought she must be thirty-five or thirty-six. Brown hair, brown eyes, high cheekbones and a few wrinkles at the corner of her eyes, but a handsome face with a wide, firmly drawn mouth, olive skin and a square jaw. A face full of character. But what made it remarkable was her gaze. A gaze that was penetrating and understanding, with a glow that was both serious and compassionate, as if she had considered all human baseness and pettiness from every angle and decided once and for all to forgive. There could be no doubt that the person standing before him was highly intelligent. She was wearing a thick woollen turtleneck jumper and jeans.

'Coffee? I'm sorry, but there's no alcohol here.'

'Coffee will be fine.'

She turned her back to him and reached into a cupboard above the countertop. She set a cup down on a table big enough for ten and sat down on the other side, a good metre away from him.

'Thank you for agreeing to see me,' he said.

'I will listen to what you have to say. But that doesn't mean I'll answer your questions.'

'I understand.'

'Go ahead, Commandant. Tell me what's new.'

She had taken a deep breath before speaking, as if she were preparing to dive into a void. She had also remembered what he'd said on the telephone.

'Have you ever heard of Célia Jablonka?'

'No.'

'Célia Jablonka was a young woman who committed suicide last year. Before that, she had an affair with Léonard Fontaine. I suspect he had something to do with her suicide.'

'Why?'

'You tell me.'

She had not taken her eyes off him. She did not look either intimidated or fearful. Then her bright gaze grew imperceptibly harder.

'And that's all? That's all you have? A vague suspicion? Is that why you came here?'

Her voice was sharp, now. He could tell that if he did not act more convincingly, she would clam up. He took the magnetic key and photograph from his pocket, and leaned forward to slide them across the table.

'What's that?' she said.

'Did you send them to me?'

She looked at him, not understanding.

231

'Someone sent me this key and this photograph through the mail. Do they mean anything to you?'

She spent a long time looking at the key, then put her finger on the photograph.

'Of course it means something to me: this is the International Space Station. And what's this?' she asked, about the key.

'The key to the hotel room where Célia Jablonka took her own life. Did you ever go to this hotel with Léonard Fontaine?'

She looked again at the plastic rectangle and shook her head.

'Not with him or with anyone else.'

'Someone who clearly does not wish to reveal their identity sent me first the key, then the photograph, along with messages pushing me to reopen the investigation into Célia Jablonka's suicide. The only connection between these two things is Léonard Fontaine. He was Célia Jablonka's lover. And he has been to the International Space Station.'

Silence fell. It was now that she could stop everything, refuse to open the door leading to the past. It was another door that opened. Servaz heard it creaking faintly to his right, and he turned his head. A corridor he had not noticed before was lit up. A shadow moved along the floor then a little boy wearing red and blue pyjamas appeared. Mila's face changed instantly. She motioned to him to come closer, and the little boy climbed onto her lap and pressed his head between her breasts, his features drawn with the fatigue of a busy day. Mila kissed the top of his head through his fine hair.

'Say hello, sweetie.'

'Hello,' said the boy in a sleepy voice, turning to Servaz, his thumb in his mouth and his eyelids heavy.

'Hello, I'm Martin. What's your name?'

'Thomas.'

'Delighted to meet you, Thomas.'

He must have been three or four years old. Servaz couldn't identify the character on the front of his pyjamas. He was fair-haired, and had inherited his mother's lovely brown eyes.

'Mummy, will you tuck me in?' he said.

'Excuse me. I'll only be a minute.'

She disappeared and Servaz heard the mother and child talking quietly, although he could not grasp what they were saying.

Something was bothering him. An alarm signal in his memory.

232

Although they were still blurred by childhood, Thomas's features reminded him of someone. A face he had seen recently either in the flesh or in a photograph. He searched, and then suddenly he knew. The revelation crept into his mind: it threw up new ideas, although he could not yet gauge its full impact.

'How old is he?' he asked when she came back.

'Three and a half.'

2008, he figured. She was staring at him, as if she had guessed what he was thinking.

'Do you really think that woman committed suicide because of Léo?' she asked.

'I'm convinced. And I think there were others. The problem is that you can't convict a person for someone else's suicide, even if that person contributed significantly to their unhappiness. On the other hand, it might be possible to convict him of a crime that is a matter for the law – before the statute of limitations kicks in . . .'

She nodded.

'What happened to you was in 2008,' he continued slowly. 'The statute of limitations is three years for an offence like assault and battery, or sexual assault excluding rape. But it is ten years for a serious crime. The question is whether one was committed.'

He stared at her. Once again she nodded, holding his gaze. It wasn't an answer, but it signalled that she understood what he was getting at.

'And if I knew exactly what happened to you it would allow me to determine where I should look for other victims, which services I should contact, which files I should go through.'

She remained silent and he did not press her. He let her ruminate on what he had just said.

'I won't talk about it,' she insisted after a few seconds. 'I cannot, I told you . . . it's too much.'

'I understand.'

'Do you really think you can charge him?'

'That will depend on what I find.'

She nodded her head for the third time, looking at him closely.

'If I give you something, will you promise me you won't show it to anyone?'

He nodded. 'I promise, Mila.'

She got up and left the room. He heard the sound of her trainers padding along the floor behind him, and a door opened. A minute later, she set an object down in the light in front of him. He looked down. A book bound in leather and tied with a ribbon. He untied it and looked inside. Neat, feminine handwriting. And a date to begin with: a personal diary.

'When is this from?'

'Back then,' she replied.

'Everything is in here?'

'Yes.'

'You were no longer an astronaut after this, were you? They let you go.'

'They made it clear to me that I was no longer welcome. Apparently, it was almost as serious to accuse someone of rape as to commit it.'

A slow intake of breath.

'So there was a rape?'

'It's more complicated than that. Read it.' She pointed to the diary. 'Do I have your word that no one else will ever see it?'

'I'll say it again, you have my word.'

'Now, if you don't mind, I'd like to go and read my son a bedtime story.'

Servaz stood up, the diary in his hand, and smiled suddenly.

'Which story?' he asked.

'*The Little Prince.*'

'"*My star, this will be one of the stars for you*",' Servaz recited. '"*Then you will like looking at all the stars. All of them will be your friends*".'

She shot him a long, puzzled, amused look.

'Who is Thomas's father?'

Her gaze immediately hardened. 'You've guessed, haven't you? It's true he looks like him . . .'

'He refused to recognise him legally?'

For a split second she hesitated, then nodded.

'Why?'

'Read it, Commandant. And now, good night.'

# 28

## Intermezzo

She undressed, brushed her teeth, put on her pyjamas and went back into the room. Iggy was still asleep on the bed, his eyes closed deep inside his collar. A pale glow came in through the French windows. As she went over to them, she saw the moon smiling at her above the Capitole. She wondered what Max was doing at that very moment, whether he was sleeping on his patch of pavement, among his belongings and his cardboard boxes.

*The only company you have left. A homeless man. You never know, maybe he is behind all this, have you thought of that? No, of course you haven't.*

She looked at the two tablets in her palm, and the glass of water in her other hand. She swallowed them all. She had locked her door, and heard the hotel guests going by in the corridor. More and more her life was like that of a hounded man who sought refuge first in one hole and then another, like a rat. How long would this go on? Her mother had insisted on paying the hotel bill, but she could not stay here indefinitely. And Max was right: the man was not about to let her go.

Her mother had come to see her and they had drunk coffee in the hotel bar. 'You look terrible; you look as if you've aged ten years in just a few days.' Fortunately, her mother had had things to do, as always: appointments at the gym, manicure, pedicure, facial, hot stone massage, hairdresser, shrink, the president of her charity, personal development coach, art therapy workshop, auction, and an interview with a journalist on the topic 'Where are they now?' Christine had spent the rest of the day wandering aimlessly in search of an idea, a solution. She had gone into a store that sold firearms and knives (and even sabres and katanas), but also tasers, electric-shock devices and pepper sprays. The salesman was an obese man who stank of sweat, and when he came a little bit too close, she told herself he was precisely the type of man who was capable of taking advantage of a defenceless woman. Of course she knew she was suspecting him because she didn't like the way he looked, but ever since she had discovered that the world is hell for those who are most vulnerable, she felt far less inclined to give others the benefit of the doubt. She realised she was becoming increasingly aggressive. Intolerant.

*Welcome to the jungle, old girl.*

She began to get drowsy, overcome by the medication. She had no idea what she would do tomorrow, let alone the day after, or next week. A tear rolled down her cheek. She brought her knees up to her chest under the duvet and put her arms around them. She put her head down on the pillow and let the cocoon of sleeping tablets envelop her, her fears dissipating one by one like morning mist. Except that she wasn't being drawn towards the light, but towards the night, the darkness, oblivion . . . She closed her eyes and let herself go.

Respite. Until tomorrow.

# 29

## Libretto

Servaz sat at the head of the narrow bed, put some Mahler on very quietly, looked at the full moon outside his window and picked Mila's diary up from the night table.

Perhaps in these pages he would find the answer to all his questions. Who was Léonard Fontaine, really? What did he do that drove these women to suicide, or to living alone with their children cut off from the world? What sort of two-faced monster was he? Mila and Célia were intelligent women, hardly lacking in personality, and still he had managed to keep them under his thumb and break them. How had he done it?

It looked like it might be a long night. Servaz was no coward, but he felt a nagging apprehension at the thought of what he was about to read. He had never forgotten Alice Ferrand's diary. He had found it in the young girl's bedroom, up there in the mountains, five years earlier. Her words were branded in his mind. Now he turned the first two blank pages and started reading; Mila's story began with their arrival in Moscow.

*20 November 2007*

*We got here at eight thirty in the morning. Deplaned in the brand-new terminal C at Sheremetyevo. A long wait at customs. I'm a bit nervous. Léo seems perfectly calm. Gennady Semyonov, the project head for the Andromeda mission, and Roman Rudin, the correspondent from Star City, were waiting for us at the exit. The bus taking us into town has changed, too. There is no longer that terrible smell of exhaust like last time when I came on my own. We drove towards Moscow then took the road northeast leading to Star City; all along it there is a profusion of dachas behind high fences. There are pretty little isbas that look like doll's*

*houses, painted blue or red, or simple huts. They show the Muscovites'*
*deep attachment to their native soil, despite the air pollution, the cranes,*
*the concrete, cars, and hundreds of hoardings disfiguring the landscape.*
*The great enterprise of uniformity is at work here like everywhere else;*
*concrete is surely the work of the devil . . .*

*In the bus I observed Léo. He was talking to Roman and Gennady.*
*He wasn't paying me any attention – or, rather, I got the impression he*
*was deliberately ignoring me. What's going on? Suddenly I felt over-*
*whelmed by a bad premonition and I recalled the scene from yesterday.*
*It had never happened to me before. Just as we were about to go out to*
*a little party organised by the National Centre for Space Studies in our*
*honour before our departure for Moscow, and I was finishing getting*
*dressed and sitting at the mirror, putting on my make-up, he came up*
*behind me and looked at me.*

*'Do you really need to tart yourself up like that?' he said.*

*At first I thought I'd misheard.*

*'What?'*

*'You heard me.'*

*'What are you talking about? Léo, for Christ's sake, are you joking?'*

*Then he put his hands on my shoulders, but his gesture was anything*
*but friendly.*

*'Of course I'm joking. But still: you've been going a bit overboard.'*

*I felt like losing my temper, but I was too stunned. I had never seen*
*him like this. This was not the Léo I knew. In the three months we have*
*been together, he has always been so considerate, so funny, so loving. I've*
*never felt so good with a man before.*

*I have to concentrate on what's ahead, and nothing else. This is the*
*most important experience of my life. We have nine months instead of*
*two years to get ready: that's very short! So I already know that our*
*schedule will be hellish, and this is not the time to start feeling wobbly.*
*But this morning, and during the entire bus trip, I couldn't help but*
*think about what happened last night.*

*20 November, evening*

*Zvyozdny Gorodok, Star City: hardly the right name for it – a grey*
*urban zone with long-deserted avenues and blocks of flats, it looks like*
*a French* banlieue *lost in the middle of the Russian forest. They settled*
*Léo and me into the Prophylacticum, the 'hotel-clinic' for cosmonauts,*
*while we wait for our flat in Dom 4 to be ready. Léo is a star here. They*

*bend over backwards for him. This evening he went out – he had some 'old Russian mates' to see. I'm on my own and I'm looking at the dark lake outside the hotel, and the immense icy forest beyond. What's going on? Since we got here yesterday, Léo hasn't been the same. First there was the argument, and today I found him distant and cold.*

*I'm afraid. It's already hard enough being here. If he leaves me now, I won't be able to stand it.*


*28 November*
*He's at it again. He's accused me of flirting with the Russians. We had gone out for dinner with a little group. On the way back, he suddenly said, venomously, 'You think I didn't see you?'*

*'What are you talking about?' I asked.*

*'Don't take me for a fool. I saw you.'*

*I think I couldn't quite convince myself any of it was real.*

*'What did you see?'*

*'I saw you acting the whore.'*

*That language again. I was stunned, knocked for six.*

*I would never have thought he could be that jealous. I looked at him; I just didn't understand. I couldn't say a thing. He shrugged his shoulders and went to bed.*

Servaz checked the time: seven minutes to midnight. He rubbed his eyelids. The moon kept watch in the night sky. Even if it took him all night long, he would finish reading. Once again, he felt a growing unease when he thought of Mila. There was a feeling of imminent tragedy about her story, of something set in motion that would be impossible to stop. Or maybe that was because of what he knew already? As in Mahler's 6th Symphony, where the clouds gathered from the opening bars, a sinister force was at work here.

He gave a start when he heard a burst of laughter somewhere, immediately stifled by a thick layer of silence. Propped against his pillows, he shuddered.

He went on reading.


Iggy raised his head.

He thought he had heard a sound. In his grey, monochromatic world, the dog surveyed the bed and the room, bathed in silent moonlight. Sound asleep next to him, his mistress was snoring lightly.

In a split second, the little dog's brain forgot what had awoken him, to concentrate on another more urgent sensation: he was hungry. He quickly examined every available possibility. He was not at home: he didn't know this place and it was much smaller than his usual territory, but he had explored every corner (it didn't take long) and he knew that his mistress had put his bowl in the bathroom. The door to the bathroom was open. Maybe there was something left to eat there? No sooner had the thought occurred to him than the dog wagged his tail with pleasure, anticipating imminent sustenance, and he decided to go and see without further ado. He jumped off the bed and trotted over to the bathroom, his short legs barely clicking on the carpet, his hindquarters hampered by the splint on his left rear leg.

In the bathroom, where his mistress had left the light on, his claws clicked more distinctly over the tiles. Now he could see his dish at the foot of the bath. From over here it looked empty, but he couldn't see the bottom. When he reached the edge, he dipped his hypersensitive nose into the bowl, snuffled all around and felt a pang of disappointment: absolutely nothing left to nibble on! Dejected, he drank some lukewarm water from the plastic bowl and went back into the bedroom, tail dragging.

It was as he crossed the threshold to the bedroom that he again became aware of what had woken him up. What was it? He stopped at the edge of the room, listening for a moment. The fur on his neck stood on end. There was something in the room. He had not yet identified it, but his instinct shouted that someone besides his mistress was there. Someone who was not moving: he could only properly detect things that moved. Nevertheless, he could hear slow breathing, and he could associate it with a palette of smells a hundred times richer than any human could detect, and thus create a precise map of his environment – in this case, the bedroom. Conclusion: there was definitely someone here – a living creature, over there, by the window, behind the curtain on the right. A shadow. Hiding in the darkness. It could have been an optical illusion created by a ray of moonlight, but illusions have no smell. He sniffed the air. There could be no doubt, there was a man over there. The mongrel also detected another, less usual smell: chemical, or medicinal; it reminded him unpleasantly of the effluvia at the vet's, and he began growling, timidly at first (his fear had not left him), then a bit more loudly. It was then that a murmur came from behind the curtain – a soothing, gentle, perfectly friendly murmur:

'*Good dog, Iggy . . . good dog, good puppy . . . are you hungry?*'

This last word lit up his feeble intellect. His memory had inscribed it in his cortex long ago among the register of words essential for survival. He crouched down on the ground and, again joyfully wagging his tail, made a yapping sound.

'*Shhh . . . good dog, Iggy, quiet now . . . I'll give you something to eat, okay?*'

Iggy's tail wagged ever faster. He had recognised his name twice over. The intruder came slowly out from his hiding place and the dog was tempted to withdraw into the bathroom, just to be on the safe side. He was not altogether reassured. But the man said again, '*Are you HUNGRY?*' and the prospect of a meal swept away all his doubts. When the intruder headed over towards him, Iggy was waiting joyfully, his tail ticking back and forth like a metronome.

*1 December*
*Six o'clock in the morning: it's still dark out and I cannot sleep, even though I'm exhausted. I cannot stop thinking about what Léo said yesterday. Eight hours of theoretical study and two hours of daily gymnastics, in addition to the sessions in the swivel chair – which is actually an armchair where one is transformed into a human spinning top. The Russian doctors, astonished by my resistance, told me that I'm managing better than most of the men.*

*Proudly, I told Léo about it when we met up again in the evening. He shot me a look so cold it sent a chill right through me, and then he smiled and said, 'These Russians are all trying to hit on you. It's not their fault. You're the one who has to watch how you behave.'*

The man who had been hidden behind the curtain stared at the sleeping form. He stood by the door to the bathroom, as motionless as a statue. As if he had the entire night ahead of him. His face lit by moonlight, he kept his gaze riveted on Christine. He felt calm, relaxed.

It was his moment of triumph, the hum of blood through his veins, the crescendo of sensations. He was nearing the summit. He was wearing nothing but a pair of briefs, his watch and latex gloves. The rest of his clothes were in the bath.

He swept the beam of his torch over Christine's back and shoulders as they rose and fell rhythmically. Then down her spine and waist as it curved alluringly in her nightgown. And along her legs to her feet tangled in the sheets. He was already beginning to feel excited. He turned reluctantly away from the spectacle and headed barefoot to the minibar. Opening the little fridge, its bright interior reflected in his black eyes, he took a miniature of vodka, unscrewed it and lifted it to his lips. He drank the entire bottle in three long, cool, delicious gulps. Then he put it on the desk above the fridge. *Don't forget to take it with you.* He wiped the bottleneck, just in case.

One forty-five.

The man grabbed Christine's handbag, emptied the contents out onto the desk and examined them methodically in the light from the torch: credit card, loyalty cards, wallet, pack of chewing gum, keys, pens, mobile phone. His vacant, lifeless gaze lingered on a much-thumbed photograph. Christine, smiling. Sitting on a wall. A little harbour below her. Who had taken it? Where? He put everything back and reached for a transparent pouch closed on one side with a zip. One by one he removed a syringe, a cutter, two fifty-millilitre ampoules of ketamine and the rubber mask.

He broke the ampoule and dipped the needle into it, filled it with the colourless, slightly viscous liquid, which smelled faintly chlorinated.

Then he tapped on the syringe, and squirted a little liquid out of the needle.

Satisfied, he put the syringe back down, raised his arm and stretched, his legs spread wide, his toes flat on the carpet. He opened the fridge again. Reached for a second miniature. Drank another shot of vodka. Burped. Went to urinate in the bathroom. A smile on his lips. He felt strong, lucid, alert. He would flush before he left. Still smiling, he stopped by the body of the little dog, next to the toilet.

Iggy was still wearing the collar around his neck, but just beneath, a gaping wound showed the cartilage of his windpipe beneath his blood-soaked fur. The animal's eyes were closed, his tongue hanging out. Blood thick as epoxy paint spread in a puddle beneath him.

The man looked at his watch: it was time to move. Grabbing the mask (a hideous grimacing red devil with a long nose, pointed ears and horns), he pulled it over his face until his eyes were level with the holes. He opened them wide beneath the mask, which felt cold against his skin, compressing his chin and hampering his breathing, but he adjusted it as best he could, and through the narrow slits his implacable gaze turned towards Christine.

*7 December*

*The dacha is located in a white, isolated clearing in the forest. It looks like something out of a fairy tale.*

*Surprised and troubled, I looked at Léo. I suppose I should've been enchanted by what I saw, but my first thought was that he was trying to isolate us from the others, get as far away as possible from Star City, even if we are only a few hundred metres away in the forest. I feel more and more cut off, emptied out, mentally drained by these recurring situations. Who could I confide in, here? I don't know anyone, and Léo is doing everything possible to make sure it stays that way. Dare I say it – he frightens me.*

*'Do you know what I want, right now?' he said, once we were inside.*

*I saw the expression in his eyes, full of lust. His new look, staring at me the way you would stare at an object. A toy. He grabbed my arm and twisted it behind my back. I said, 'Léo, no, stop, please,' but he didn't listen. He pushed me against the windowsill, opened the zip on my jeans and pulled them down my legs along with my pants. I didn't move, didn't protest. I knew it was pointless, and above all, afterwards he'd leave me alone. He penetrated me right away, without a single caress, licking my cheek and ear as he thrusted.*

*He climaxed quickly and as he walked away, tears ran down my cheeks.*

*9 December*

*The second phase has begun at last: training on board the simulator. From now on, as a titular cosmonaut, I am working with my double, a young Russian pilot called Sergey. I've noticed that ever since we started this phase Léo has been systematically interrogating me about how I spend my days: he wants to know exactly what I've been doing, and what we've said to each other. It's exhausting. I'm finding it harder and harder to remember everything we have to memorise.*

*But Léo doesn't care. The other night, he came back at around two o'clock in the morning, wafting a thick cloud of various odours: vodka, beer, tobacco,* women. *Instead of going to sleep, or jumping on me, he made me sit in a chair in the middle of the room and he began to*

*interrogate me. About my days, my training with Sergey, my professors,*
*the men I had been working with. Like that, all night long, even though*
*the next day I had a vital test for the next stage.*

*18 December*
*I still can't believe it:* Léo *hit me. I've been saying the words to myself*
*over and over again:* Léo *hit me . . .*

*When I got back last night, Sergey called me about the programme*
*for the next day. I saw the expression change on Léo's face. As soon as*
*I hung up, he wanted to take the mobile phone from my hand to read*
*my messages. I resisted. Then he said, 'You need them all, don't you?*
*You're bored here, with me. You'd rather be there: so they would all be*
*where you could get at them, within reach of your pussy!' I couldn't*
*believe my ears. This time I slapped him. He looked at me, his eyes open*
*wide, and he touched his cheek, flabbergasted. Then a moment later there*
*came a punch in my belly so violent it took my breath away.*

*I bent over and felt a second blow on my neck. I fell to the floor and*
*then he kicked me.*

*'Stupid bitch! Filthy whore! All you're good for is sucking cock! Do*
*it again and I'll kill you!'*

*He threw my mobile across the room. Then he went out, slamming*
*the door.*

*I don't know where he spent the night. This morning, my ribs are*
*horribly painful, my stomach and neck, too. I've got an important training*
*session today. I have no idea how I'm going to make it through the day.*

Dark. Something woke her up. Suddenly Christine was sitting bolt
upright, at the head of the bed. It was *dark! Pitch black!* An icy vertigo,
a falling sensation. She reached for the light, groping feverishly. She
pressed the button. Nothing happened. A power cut . . .

It was completely dark. Someone had pulled the curtains in the
room and switched off the light in the bathroom. She cried out, 'Is
anyone there?' What a stupid question, as if they were about to answer!
To her great surprise, a light came on at the other end of the room,
a dazzling beam trained right at her, which made her blink furiously.
She saw nothing but that blinding eye. She held her hand out as a
screen in front of her.

'Is . . . is that *you?*' said Christine, her voice so faint she wondered
if he had heard her.

She knew very well that it was Him. Who else would it be? Suddenly, the light began to move. It came slowly around the bed, in her direction, wavering, still dazzling. She blinked like an owl, and she wanted to scream, but her throat contracted with fear and her scream was strangled in her mouth. She closed her eyes, squeezed her lids, refused to believe it was real: *there was a man in her room*. The man who had been persecuting her for days, He was there, *with her.* No, no, no – she couldn't believe it.

'Open your eyes,' said the voice.

'No!'

'Open your eyes, or I'll kill your dog.'

Iggy! Where was he? *She couldn't hear him* . . . She opened her eyes and almost passed out. Her chest filled with horror and she gasped, terrified: only a few inches from her face was a grotesque mask. A red rubber mask. Its long, hooked, bulbous nose was almost touching her. And that smile! Those thick lips, those yellow, pointed teeth! She pedalled frantically in the sheets to get away from the thing, she recoiled as far as she could, ground her shoulder blades, her neck and her back against the wall as if she wanted to melt into it. She turned her head away, her mouth twisted, her face disfigured by fear.

'Please don't hurt me, please . . .'

As he didn't speak, didn't react, she regained a tiny bit of courage.

'Why are you doing this?' she asked, although she didn't dare look in his direction. 'What do you want? What do you expect from me? Why are you trying to drive me mad?'

The questions pouring from her lips. A flood of questions.

'Because I was asked to do it,' he replied.

This immediately shut her up. She was finding it harder and harder to breathe. As if all the oxygen were being sucked out of the room.

'Because I'm being paid to do it . . . and I have to finish the job.'

His voice was calm and neutral. *Finish the job.* The words caused her to gasp, horrified. She would like to struggle, to kick him, to punch him, to rear up like a wild horse, scratch his eyes, leap towards the door – but her limbs were like jelly; any strength she might have had had drained away.

'*Oh, no, no, no, no,*' was all she could say.

'Oh, yes.'

'*Please, no* . . .'

245

Suddenly she looked at Him. Because He had just put a hand gloved in latex on her thigh. She avoided looking at the mask; it was too frightening. She looked lower down. She saw a thin, pale body; tattoos everywhere. She thought of Cordélia. She could see his erection and she felt a violent surge of nausea. The gloved hand was moving up her thigh. She could see more tattoos through the translucent latex on his wrist, but not very well: his hand and his fingers were covered with patterns, like ivy.

He grabbed the hem of her nightgown with both hands.

He lifted it up over her shoulders and above her head. He left it there, behind her skull. He ran his gloved hand over her breasts one after the other. Slowly. She found a last burst of energy, squeezed her knees together as hard as she could, and pleaded:

'No, no, no. Don't do that. Please, don't do that.'

She could see his dull eyes behind the mask. Empty eyes. Then he leaned back, put his torch on the night table. He picked up something else instead. A syringe.

This time, she was about to scream when he slapped a hand over her mouth and lifted the sparkling needle into the light, then rammed it into her arm.

'Just wait, baby. It will go straight to your brain. It's Super K, the real top-end stuff. You are going to trip out in a way you've never done before . . . You're going to reach the sky.'

He pressed very gently on the end, and with horror she felt the ultrafine stem penetrating her muscle, her flesh. She was going to pass out, for sure.

'Fifty milligrams to start off with. We'll see how it goes.'

# 30

# Opera Seria

CHRISTMAS

*Over the last few days Léo's attacks have been more frequent and more intense. The man is evil; he wants to destroy me. Everything about him is toxic, malevolent. I should report him. But if I do, the entire Andromeda mission will be jeopardised. And I know they won't give me another chance after this. Space travel is my entire life. I must not give up because of him. I have to resist, one way or another.*

27 January

*The third phase has begun. The one where all the teams are working together. We spend our days in the different simulators. The captain, who is at the heart of the team, running things, is Pavel Koroviev, an experienced cosmonaut. The flight engineer, who sits to his left and who is in charge of controlling all the systems, is usually another Russian, but for the first time two French nationals are going to go on board the Soyuz at the same time, and the role has been assigned to Léo. Finally, I am on his right, the experimenter, and I'm in charge of managing air quality, taking care of the radio, etc. Koroviev is solid, serious, rigorous, and I feel better with him between us. Particularly as we're packed like sardines in there. Now that we're no longer alone, Léo is nervous. But only beneath the surface: on the surface, he is cheerful and jovial, and he gets along well with Pavel. When he talks about me, he cannot help but put me down however he can, but he always hides it with humour: 'Mila's better in bed than in a capsule,' he said today. I blushed with shame. I felt humiliated. But I know that he was trying to make me angry, to pass me off as hysterical. I won't give him the pleasure. This time, emboldened by Pavel's presence between us, I actually dared answer back: 'Quite the opposite to you, my dear.' Léo was silent, and Pavel gave an embarrassed laugh.*

*28 January*

*I shouldn't have provoked him. I still didn't know what he is capable of.*

The man is insane.

*That evening, after the exercise, he told Pavel he had something to do and he went off somewhere. I had a drink with Sergey – he seems to like me, I know that – then I walked back to the dacha. It was pitch black out, and I followed the snowy path through the forest with the glow from my torch. I went up the wooden steps and unlocked the door. Just as I was about to switch on the light, I felt the cold steel of a blade against my throat.*

*'Don't turn on the light.'*

*Léo's voice, in the dark. That sinister voice he's been using when he loses it. He dragged me into a corner of the dusty floor, then switched on a little light. I started. He was naked. There was blood, or paint, on his torso; I don't know where it came from. He grabbed me by the hair and forced me to kneel down in front of him, and he ran the cold blade over my cheeks.*

*'You're ugly and useless, and on top of that you humiliated me in front of Pavel. You make me look like an impotent imbecile. You're going to pay for it, you whore. You know what I'm dying to do now, right now? I'm dying to kill you. I'm going to kill you, you filthy whore.'*

*'No, please! You're right: I shouldn't have said that. It won't happen again, ever. I swear. Never again.'*

*He dragged me by the hair, shook me hard and slapped me. 'You're crazy,' he said. 'You're crazy and dangerous, do you know that much, at least?' And suddenly, before I had time to realise what was happening, he placed the knife in my hand, squeezed my wrist around the hilt and struck himself in the hip with it. He screamed, 'You stabbed me, fuck! You crazy bitch, you stabbed me.'*

*I was stunned. He got out his telephone and took a photo of me holding the bloody knife, then one of his own hip covered in blood.*

*'Don't go getting it into your head to humiliate me again,' he said. After that he went to the bathroom to tend to his wound.*

*That night, he told me to sleep on the sofa. He said he didn't want to share his bed with a prostitute. It was cold in the lounge and I shivered most of the night under the thin blanket he'd left me. This morning since I woke up I've been feeling feverish. I'm overcome with panic: all the cosmonauts are afraid of falling ill. Catch the flu or a virus and they'll dismiss you from the programme. Oh, God: anything but that.*

[Christine looks up. She stares at the man. She is lying beneath him, motionless. She can hear his breathing. How long has she been there? She blacked out, temporarily lost consciousness. The man is not making a single sound, he is toiling away in silence. She can feel his hips sinking into the sweat-soaked sheets every time he penetrates her. Then she notices that the room around her is changing colours: orangey red, fluorescent green, electric blue, fuchsia, lilac, lemon yellow . . .]

*15 February*
*I wonder whether Léo has been bad-mouthing me to his Russian crewmates. Their attitude has changed. Gone is the chivalry, the kindness. I've come in for an increasing number of openly sexual allusions and macho behaviour. The other day, Pavel even placed his hand on my thigh in the simulator. I went completely stiff as if I'd received an electric shock, and he didn't persist. But I can tell they have less and less respect for me.*

[Christine is overcome by a warm, strange dizziness. Her vision goes blurry all of a sudden. She stares at the rubber mask, so near, but she no longer finds it all that frightening, this time. Just . . . *funny*. She laughs without knowing why. The hooked nose emerges from her blurred vision, strangely sharp, while the rest of the horrible leering face is lost in fog. The effect is striking. She loses all notion of time. She realises she feels nothing at all, her entire body is numb.]

*10 June*
*Sergey is furious. He has talked about going to smash Léo's face in. Because at last I found the courage to confide in him. He admitted he's suspected something for a long time. I think he's in love with me. He said, too, that things couldn't go on like this, that everyone at Star City could see I was at the end of my rope, that we had to find a solution. He explained that he knew someone: a* vor v zakone, *a sort of godfather in the Russian mafia. Sergey told me he would talk to him. I'm worried: if something serious happens to Léo, our entire team might be removed from the mission. Sergey could see I was anxious: 'Don't worry, I'll tell them not to mess him up too much, that Moki piece of shit . . .' Moki is the nickname they've given Léo. I think it means 'mocker', because Léo likes to joke around and tease them.*

249

Servaz sat bolt upright. He reread the last two sentences. He put the open journal face down on the grey blanket and swung his legs out of bed. He walked over to the little desk where he had put the diary Desgranges gave him, Célia's diary. He opened it and turned the pages quickly. And stopped. There it was, before his eyes: 'Moki, 16.30', 'Moki, 15.00', 'Moki, 17.00', 'Moki, 18.00'.

'Moki,' he said, 'I've got you.'

*25 June*

*Léo is in hospital. Some skinheads beat him up. It happened as he was coming out of one of the many strip clubs in Moscow where you can sleep with the girls. He has multiple fractures. He lost three teeth, but nothing that cannot be repaired. I'm sure Sergey briefed his cousin so that his goons wouldn't go overboard. Because even though Sergey hasn't said anything, I know he's behind it.*

[She doesn't immediately notice that the wind has picked up, that dry leaves are blowing and animals are fleeing invisible danger. Suddenly the room becomes a clearing swept by an icy wind, and she sees threatening shadows darkening the sky and the earth. She wants to flee, like the animals. But she cannot. Her entire body is paralysed, nailed to this bloody bed in the middle of the clearing. She tries to toss off the man weighing on her, tries to push him away with all the strength of her arms. But he slaps her and when she blinks she discovers, horrified, that she is being ridden by a homunculus, a hideous little creature, who seems to get no pleasure out of what he's doing, totally ignoring her, his gaze fixed straight ahead.]

*3 July*

*Léo left hospital yesterday, on crutches. The Russians have assured him he will be able to resume his training very soon. Our mission has been delayed by a fortnight so that Léo can take part. What a surprise: his behaviour towards me has been almost normal. Might the attack have served as a lesson? Did the men who attacked him threaten him in any way? I acted as if our relationship had never been anything but normal. He went to sleep on the sofa, leaving me the bed I've been sleeping in since he's been in hospital. I hate him, I despise him. If he thinks he can find his way back into my good books, he'd better think again. But if we can just carry on like this until the end of our stay, and focus on the mission, that will be all right by me.*

[She understands at last when he leans close to her ear to say, 'I'm a positive hero.' She croaks, 'What?' And he says again, 'I'm HIV-positive,' just when she feels herself falling into an endless tunnel, where her heart begins beating more and more slowly, beating so slowly it was as if . . . it were about to . . .stop . . . altogether . . . any second . . .]

*4 July*
*The most dreadful thing has happened. I still can't believe it. Sergey has been run over. He died the instant his skull hit the pavement. They didn't find the driver. I'm sure Léo is responsible. How did he find out that it was Sergey behind the attack? Did he run him down himself or hire someone to do it? And where is he now? I haven't seen him all day. It's past midnight. I can't sleep. I can hear the trees rustling in the wind all around the dacha, and I've got my face pressed against the black window-pane as I peer into the darkness.*

*He did come back. Suddenly I saw a little light: no doubt about it, the beam of a torch, coming closer. Out there on the path. I rushed into the main room and locked the door. I went back to the window. It was him. He was striding towards the clearing. His powerful voice boomed into the night: 'Milaaaaa!' I could hear him rattling the doorknob furiously. He shoved against the door, realised that I'd locked it, shook it violently, hammered it with his fists.*

*'Mila, open this door. Open this door, you fucking moron! Stupid bitch! Open up!'*

*He rammed it with his shoulder, forcefully, but the door resisted. Then nothing. Silence. Until suddenly the rear window shattered. I rushed to the front door, turned the key in the lock and tugged on the handle, but it resisted. I tugged harder. The door opened at last. I was about to rush out when suddenly, he had his arms around me.*

*'Where do you think you're going? You're mine, Mila. Whether you like it or not, we're bound to each other from now on. For eternity.'*

At around four o'clock in the morning, Servaz took a break.

He felt tangled in a net of words, drawn ever deeper into Mila's nightmare. He sensed the story could only end tragically. He put the kettle on the boil, tipped some instant coffee into a cup; beyond the dark window it had started snowing again.

In the pages, and weeks, that followed, Mila seemed to grow resigned to the situation, now that Sergey had died. Servaz figured that even though she didn't say as much in her diary, she must have been counting the days until her first space flight. The way a prisoner counts the days until his release. She had also understood that Fontaine could no longer afford to beat her, because of their ever more frequent medical check-ups as D-day drew nearer. Instead, he increased his threats, barking like a rabid dog – but it went no further; they both knew he must not overstep the mark.

# 31

## Grand Opera

*22 July*
*Fourth day, still no period. Dear God, please don't let it be that!*

Servaz stopped reading. With the journal open in front of him, he looked at the ceiling and again saw little Thomas sitting on his mother's lap. The question sprang to mind: why had Mila kept the child?

*It's my fault, I'm so exhausted, upset and on edge that I forgot to take my pill two days in a row. Dear Lord, please make it be no more than my hormones! If it's anything else, I'll have an abortion: no way am I going to keep a child by that dog . . .*

*25 July*
*I'm pregnant. In my pocket is the test I bought at a pharmacy in Moscow. I still can't believe it. If the Russians find out, my place on board the ISS will be fucked. And the entire mission along with it. I don't know what to do. I'm beginning to have the kind of symptoms that, even without the test, wouldn't leave any doubt as to my condition. And I've never felt so tired.*

*26 July*
*Léo found the test. What an idiot! I should have thrown it out. I didn't know he was going through my things. No doubt to find proof of my misdeeds. Bloody fucking maniac . . . He came in, with the test in his hand, and he said, 'What the hell is this?'*
*What do you think it is, fuckwit? A pH test for swimming pools . . . except that his question came with a blow that almost severed my head from my body, and his eyes looked as if they were about to pop out of his skull.*

'I'm pregnant,' I announced.

Another slap.

'Who's the father?'

'You are, Léo.'

'You're lying!'

He grabbed me by the hair and lifted me off my chair.

'I swear, Léo! It's your child! I – I'm sorry!'

He held me by the hair.

'You don't get it, do you, you bloody idiot? Because of you, the mission is up shit creek. You really think they won't notice? You did it on purpose, didn't you? I'm going to kill that child, I'm going to kill it in your belly.'

'I'm going up there, Léo. And so are you. You have no choice: if you tell anyone, our team will be taken off and replaced by our backup. I cannot possibly have an abortion before that, not with the schedule we're on and the doctors constantly breathing down our necks.'

'And what do you suggest?'

'Act as if nothing has happened. Plenty of women can hide their pregnancy up to the last minute. And even if they find out, by then it will be too late.'

'You are not keeping this child,' he thundered. 'As soon as we are back on earth, I'll find someone to give you an abortion – no matter how late it is.'

### D-10, 15 August

We've arrived in Baikonur. Hotel Cosmonaut. I managed to avoid the last sessions of tilt table and swivel chair: I said I'd had a migraine for the last few days. It's too late to go back now, so they've let me off the final exercises.

### D-1, our last evening

I've made my final preparations: my little lists so I don't forget anything, my headphones, opera on mp3. Everyone around us – technicians, doctors, base personnel – is completely euphoric.

I looked over at Léo: his face was expressionless; he's been ignoring me. I can tell he's worried. He's afraid I'll crack. But I feel stronger, more alive than ever with MY child inside me, who is going to go up there with me.

*This is it: the great day has arrived. I'm there. Three hours before depar-
ture, and it was time for the ritual of putting on the spacesuits. There
were people all around us, filming, examining us. Then we got on the
bus, there were the last words of advice, the technicians checking our
spacesuits, and that knot of anxiety in my stomach. When we got off the
bus, at the foot of the launch pad, a little crowd was waiting. More hugs.
I felt strangely alone: no parents, no family to hug me – unlike Pavel
and Léo, who had a lot of people there for them. Just the Russian authorities. It was strange how, at that moment, everything resurfaced: the
taciturn child, the worried adolescent, the foster families, the schoolmates
I never really got close to and who treated me as if I had some sort of
shameful disease . . . And then the love affairs that never went anywhere,
the impossible dreams – until Léo. After he kissed his family, he looked
at me: a hard look full of hatred. But I didn't care. He can't do anything
to me any more: I'm already elsewhere. I'm up here. I've won.*

*And I felt it at last, the impression I'd always wanted, hoped for,
desired – the impression of being* where I belong *at last.*

Servaz stopped, reached for his notebook. Jotted something down. A
feeling, an impression, vague, inconsistent, but that would not go
away. He highlighted it with three question marks.

*I was a bird. I was an angel.*

*But first of all I was an insect.*

*Confined, curled up inside its pupa. Knees bent on my seat, I tried
to relax. 6-5-4-3-2-1.*

*The rocket tore itself away and pushed back against its launchers in
a blaze of fire, a roar of thunder. Shocks, vibrations, sparks, creaking.
118 seconds and it separated from the lateral boosters. Speed: 1,670
metres/second. 286 seconds later, a new, violent shock: the second section
was jettisoned. Speed: 3,680 metres/second. It was still vibrating. More
and more . . . 300 seconds: the third section was jettisoned. Speed: 3,809
metres/second.*

*And suddenly, Soyuz was in orbit.*

*Speed: 7,700 metres/second.*

*The last kick in the butt expelled us in a cacophony of metallic shocks,
then it was a God-like calm . . . Silence, weightlessness. A burst of stars
after the burst of sparks. Objects floating unimpeded through the cabin.*

*I turned my head and I saw IT: the place we came from. Earth. Majestic in its dazzling halo, cold and blue. And all around, the cosmos: black, so much black, black everywhere.*

*28 August*
*The docking with the ISS went well. According to the Russian tradition we shared bread and salt with the crew who were already there – one Russian and two Americans. The station is divided into two clearly distinct areas: the first consists of the pressurised American modules and the European Columbus module. The second, connected to the first by the Unity 'knot', is made up of the Russian modules. Pavel, Léo and I will be staying in the Russian section.*

*4 September*
*We've been on the station for a week now. I spend most of my time in Zvezda – in its work compartment, to be more exact. I've only been to the other part of the station once, though Léo and Pavel have already been there four times. I get the impression that they want to isolate me, keep me apart from the rest of the crew. I also get the impression that Pavel and Léo are plotting behind my back – that Léo has been secretly encouraging Pavel to behave more and more inappropriately towards me.*

*12 September*
*Like every morning, I had my face up against the porthole, fascinated, tears in my eyes, when suddenly I felt someone bumping awkwardly up against me in spite of the weightlessness. As I thought it was Léo, I told him to stop, but then it was Pavel's voice echoing in my ear: 'Léo's gone to see the Americans. The two of us are all alone.' His hands on my breasts through my T-shirt. 'We could try something new: don't you want to know what it feels like to make love in weightlessness? I do.' I resisted but he kept trying. I slapped him hard. He gave me a surprised look and headed towards Zarya, simmering with rage.*

*19 September*
*Things have degenerated still further. Now several times a day I have to put up with furtive groping, salacious jokes, advances . . . I lost my temper with Pavel and he shouted at me the way Léo himself would have done. I couldn't believe my ears. In the end he spat in my face,*

*unbelievably brutal: 'You think I don't see what you're playing at? If ever you tell anyone else what's going on here, you will have an accident.'*

23 *September*
*It's all over. Finished. After what just happened, there's no going back. Game over. This evening, Léo and Pavel were completely drunk. It was Pavel's birthday. They got out several miniatures of vodka they'd hidden in various spots around the module. It isn't the first time that cosmonauts have taken alcohol in their luggage. They drank it with straws. After a while, they made me drink. I refused, but because they insisted, I eventually had a bit of vodka to toast Pavel's forty-third birthday.*

*Then their jokes started to skid off the rails, and their expressions were more and more insistent. When I wanted to go to sleep, Léo said, 'You're right, she's a whore, half of Star City has had her. You want to fuck her, Pavel?' I shuddered. I wanted to leave, but Léo was holding me by the wrists. I told him to stop, that I would scream so loud they would hear me all the way to the other end of the station. So, before I could do anything, both of them pinned me down, with a hand over my mouth. I roared and wriggled, trying to get free, I was panicking, but Léo was holding me tight while we were floating freely in the atmosphere in Zvezda and Pavel was gagging my mouth with his big damp hand.*

*I suppose that in a way what happened next should advance their fucking space science: haven't these two totally drunk cosmonaut bastards just proven that rape is possible in weightlessness, provided there are at least two perpetrators?*

*It's over.*

*My dream of space.*

*It stopped there.*

*What did I do? At the time, nothing: what could I have done, or said? At that point, nothing could have stopped them.*

*I waited until they were sound asleep and then I made my way to Zarya, and went through it clinging to everything at hand. I went through the airlocks, the PMA-1 and Unity, I made it to the quarters where the Americans and Europeans were and where the other Russian, Arkady, had elected to install his sleeping bag: he doesn't like either Pavel or Léo. They were all asleep. I woke them up. I could see the stupefaction in their eyes when they saw the state I was in; my swollen face, my torn T-shirt and pants, my bleeding lip. I asked them to call Mission Control urgently.*

257

*It's over. During the Control conference that followed that night, the Americans and Arkady asked for me to be repatriated urgently.*

*The two Americans and Arkady were terrific when Léo and Pavel came to get me the next day. It almost degenerated, but Pavel and Léo quickly understood that they no longer had the upper hand with me; and finally it was decided that I would stay in the forward section, and Arkady and one of the Americans went to get my belongings from the rear section.*

*Down on earth, they are really freaking out.*

*Operations on board the station are based on a rigorous, delicate division of labour and everything is chaos here now. Besides, they must be scared to death that word will get out. But I feel safe at last, for the first time in a long time.*

# 32

# Boos

*7 December – Paris*

*It was raining in Roissy. There was no one here to greet me. Obviously. What I was afraid of has happened. There were interrogations, then a committee of inquiry. It lasted for weeks. Finally, they said I'd made it all up, staged the whole thing.* Paranoid psychosis: *that was their diagnosis. According to them, Sergey's death was nothing more than a tragic accident, and my accusations regarding what happened up there amounted to no more than ridiculous fabrication.*

*The Russian police closed the case with no further investigation. Their Institute for Biomedical Problems put me through psychiatric tests. Those idiot psychiatrists looked at me as if they'd already made up their minds. The European Space Agency made it clear that there was no future for me in their space programme. Something broke inside me when I heard that. As for Léo, he still has his place, even though apparently the Russians are not particularly eager to see him again any time soon. I am devastated.*

*Devastated, unemployed, without a future, and* pregnant.

Servaz closed the journal. So that was it. That was what had happened up there. Rape. In outer space. It far surpassed anything he could have imagined. Once again he wondered why Mila had kept the baby. He had an idea: when Léo had threatened to kill them, her and the baby, if she didn't have an abortion, something must have rebelled inside her. The proof, in any event, that she was not paranoid, was that Fontaine had done it again: he had driven Célia Jablonka to commit suicide. No one had ever seen the connection between the two incidents because no criminal investigation had been carried out. And even if there had been an investigation, no investigator would

259

have been able to link the two stories without the helping hand of fate.

*Or of someone who knew . . .*

Was it Mila who had sent him the key card and the photograph? She seemed genuinely surprised when he had told her about them. Moreover, she had been living as a recluse with her son ever since the affair. Even if she had heard of Célia's suicide, it was highly unlikely she would have known about her liaison with Léonard Fontaine.

Who, then? Someone, in any case, was guilty. And that was all that mattered for the time being. Now that he had read Mila's diary, he was perfectly aware that it would be difficult or even impossible to bring Fontaine to justice: the Russian committee of inquiry had cleared him. And a guy like Fontaine was not born yesterday. He was not likely to be easily taken in.

Servaz would have to be wilier. As wily as the devil. Because that was what his adversary was, to the highest degree. He put the journal back on the blanket and rested his head on the pillow. His thoughts were keeping him awake. He felt he was back, he felt he was *alive*. At last he had something to fight for. He could not wait until morning to start the fight. He looked through the window at the smiling moon, the unquiet night – and he knew he would not find sleep.

# ACT II

Oh, you hurt me so much,
so much, so very much!
It's nothing, nothing! I thought I was going to die,
but it soon passes like
clouds over the sea . . .

*Madame Butterfly*

# 33

## Queen of the Night

She opened her eyes. It was dark.

'Who's there?'

'Hush!'

'Madeleine, is that you?'

'Yes.'

'What are you doing in my bed?'

'Hush . . . you don't mind if I sleep here tonight?'

'No.'

'Thank you, little sister. I love you, you know. Give me a kiss. You can go back to sleep, now.'

'Why do you want to sleep here? Is it because of Papa?'

'Huh?'

'Is it because of him that you're sleeping here?'

'What are you talking about?'

'You don't want him to find you, is that it?'

'Chris—'

'I saw him.'

'When?'

'The other night.'

'What did you see?'

'I saw him go in your room.'

'Chris, who else did you tell?'

'No one!'

'Chris, listen carefully: you mustn't tell Maman, do you hear me? Ever!'

'Why not?'

'Stop asking questions! And promise me, please.'

'I promise, Maddie.'

263

'Papa was sleeping with me because I had a nightmare, that's all.'

'What's the matter?'

'Huh?'

'You're crying.'

'No I'm not!'

'So, if I have a nightmare, can I ask Papa to sleep in my bed, too?'

'Chris, for heaven's sake. Never, do you hear me? He must never sleep in your bed. Promise me.'

'But why?'

'Promise!'

'Okay, okay, I promise, Maddie.'

'If you have a nightmare, you come and see me, all right?'

'All right.'

'Night night.'

'Night, Maddie.'

She opened her eyes. For real, this time. She wasn't thirteen years old, but thirty-two. Daylight was filtering through the curtains, and all the lamps in the hotel room were lit. The sound of traffic came through the windowpanes. She yawned. Her head was splitting and she had a terrible stomach ache. In fact, she was aching all over. She looked at the ceiling for a moment, then she looked down.

# 34

# Drame Lyrique

It . . . it can't be . . . they couldn't have . . . couldn't have done that . . .

What . . . ?

*Wait, Chris, wait. Don't look. Don't look at it. Otherwise it will scorch your eyes and you'll never be able to forget.*

But she did. She looked. And her mind buzzed and crackled like a phone gone haywire. A direct connection to the switchboard of insanity. Because that was the only word to describe what she was seeing. Dementia. Aberration.

One step closer to her own lunacy. Because that's what they wanted, wasn't it? It was obvious they had no lack of imagination when it came to attaining their ends; they had constructed a hell around her that only she could see, a subtle nightmare. As she emerged from her medicinal sleep, she remembered having a dreadful dream. But now, seeing the hard yellow stains on the sheets, she knew her nightmare was as real as could be. Her gaze ventured further and she felt as if her skull was splitting in two. She did not cry out, and she did not weep. She could not make a single sound. But inside, she was screaming. Iggy's body . . . *He was lying between her legs.* His eyes closed, without his collar; he looked asleep, but the wound to his neck left no hope.

Around Iggy, the sheets were covered with a mountain of tiny bottles of alcohol that had been opened and abandoned in the sheets, along with peanuts, empty beer cans, crisps . . . everything a minibar contained as well as the contents of a bathroom waste bin: cotton buds, paper tissues, clumps of hair . . . The wave of disgusting rubbish spilled over her own toes. Abruptly, she pulled her feet away.

She began trembling as if it were freezing cold in the room. After a few minutes had gone by, she jumped out of bed and hurried to the toilet to throw up. But she must have already emptied everything she had eaten during the night, and the spasms of her empty stomach brought no more up than a bit of bile mixed with saliva.

She had flushed the toilet and was on her way back into the room when suddenly the stench overpowered her. An indefinable brew of smells: alcohol, dried blood, sperm, vomit, sweat – with something vaguely chlorinated in the background. She staggered under the olfactory assault, and abruptly turned around.

First of all, she had to clean off the traces of the man who had contaminated her.

She rushed into the shower, paying little attention to the temperature of the water – which went from icy to burning – and she soaked and scrubbed herself for a long time, everywhere, going over and over the most intimate parts. She washed her hair with masses of shampoo, rinsed off, then came out of the shower to brush her teeth, furiously, until her gums were bleeding. After that, she gargled for a long time with an antiseptic mouthwash.

She wanted to erase every last trace of the Other, of what He had done to her, of what He had left on her, but she knew she would not be able to erase what He had left inside her.

'I'm HIV-positive.'

The words were like a slap. She froze. Her legs went shaky and she had to hold on to the edge of the sink. Had he really said that, or was it part of a drug-induced vision?

*It's just a dream, like the ceiling getting higher, the room changing colour, or the clearing . . .*

No. It was real. She could still hear his voice in her ear – the same voice as on the telephone.

She would have to take the test. She would have to see a doctor. She would have to—

*And Iggy? What are you going to do with him?*

The thought was gut-wrenching. *Iggy* . . . She couldn't wander around the corridors with a dead dog in her arms! And if she left him there, the cleaning woman would find him. Put him in a suitcase? And go where? It was out of the question to abandon him in a rubbish bin, like some common piece of trash. A thought occurred to her
. . . *No need for a test, no need for a doctor, no need for a suitcase,*

266

*either.* . . . She let the thought expand. Suddenly it all seemed so clear. Yes, why not? After all, this was where this thing had been leading right from the start, wasn't it? She sat down at the desk, tore a sheet of hotel notepaper from the pad and wrote a letter. Her hand was trembling so badly that her first effort was illegible. She crumpled it up, tossed it in the waste bin and started again. Then, holding back a sob, she went into the bathroom, picked up two towels fragrant with lavender and set them down next to the sink.

After that she went to fetch him. She felt a surge of nausea when she put her hands under the lifeless little body, with its sticky fur, and she was careful to support his head – she was afraid it might come loose from his body.

With Iggy in her arms, Christine went back into the bathroom. She set him down gently in the shower, reached for the spray nozzle and turned it on full blast. She rinsed him for a long time, cleaned away the blood, trying not to look at the terrible wound in his neck. She turned off the water, picked him up the way she had done before and put him down on the bed of clean white towels. Although she did not know why, it seemed to her that white was the most appropriate colour. She plugged in the hairdryer, picked up a comb and meticulously dried the little mongrel's fur, then went on combing him until he looked normal again, with his curly, tawny coat and black-tipped white nose. Finally, she positioned his head over his chest so that the wound would not show beneath his fur, and she looked at him.

Only then did she scream.

Like a crazy woman. Screamed at death.

And let herself slide to the floor, her back on the tiles, kicking the air with her feet as if kicking some invisible enemy.

She looked down. Three storeys . . . Her legs were trembling from the vertigo. She looked again and instantly regretted it. From up here, the few passing cars looked like toys. She could only see the tops of pedestrians' heads, their shoulders and feet moving forward. Her own feet were on a ledge overlooking the place du Capitole, her back hugging the facade, one hand flat against the wall, the other still clinging to the frame of the French window.

Incredibly, no one on the vast esplanade had noticed yet, but it wouldn't be long.

She took a deep breath. *What are you waiting for? Jump.*

The wind was howling in her ears; all around her the city was vibrating-buzzing-thrilling with energy and an appetite for life. How many people were thinking about her at that moment – other than those who wanted to see her jump? What memories would she leave behind? The only companion who had been unfailingly loyal to her lay dead in the bathroom, where the hotel staff and police would find him after she jumped. She had left a brief note on the desk: *Iggy is to be buried at Beaumont-sur-Lèze, in the pet cemetery: contact Claire Dorian.*

She moaned. She felt crushed by a feeling of solitude so terrible and so total – in this city of 700,000 inhabitants – that she knew she would jump. She would go through with it. It was only a matter of seconds now, the time it would take to find the last ounce of courage still lacking.

Then she heard the little voice again:

*Jump. But if you jump, you'll never know. Not who or why. Don't you want to find out? Is this really what you want, to die without knowing what was behind it all?*

And for the first time in her life, with implacable lucidity, a new clarity, she suddenly understood that this voice that had been talking to her for years was her sister's. Madeleine's voice. A Madeleine who had grown up in secret, deep inside her. An adult Madeleine: sometimes sententious, often exasperating, always requiring her attention, just like the Madeleine from her childhood. But a Madeleine who wanted what was right for her: the only person, perhaps, who truly loved her.

For a long time she didn't move, but sat staring into space, her back against the balustrade, her feet in the room.

When she had emerged from her trance, she had *changed*. She was no longer the Christine of before, the one who had tried clumsily to ward off all the attacks and to understand, the one who had been looking for support and had found only a homeless man who cared about nothing but booze.

*You don't need any support. You can do it on your own, little sister. All you need is one thing: the rage burning inside you.*

Yes. She edged her way upright back to the window, extremely cautiously, her nails scraping against the granular surface, then she stepped over the stone parapet and slipped into the room just as someone down on the square noticed her at last and pointed up.

Now she began to feel the shock set in, the internal impact of the act she had almost committed. She was paralysed to the bone both by the icy wind coming through the window, and the idea that she could, at that very moment, be lying sprawled on the pavement, all her bones broken and her inner organs reduced to a formless stew. But for all that, she felt a new wave of determination filling her veins. They wanted her dead? Fine. Perfect. Perhaps she would die – but they could no longer count on her suicide. They would have to pay. Someone who is not afraid to die and has hatred in her heart makes for an even more formidable adversary. They had miscalculated: they had aroused something in her that had been sleeping for a long time. Without realising, her tormentors had hardened her and prepared her for this moment when the strength and rage waiting inside her would prevail.

*You are strong, much stronger than they realise, much stronger than you thought you were, little sister.* It was a feeling of great purity: they had stripped her of everything she possessed, but thanks to them, she now had nothing left to lose.

As if empathising with her new state of mind, a ray of sun burst from the leaden clouds and came to illuminate the floor of the room in front of her. It sprinkled the red carpet with gold dust and she noticed that it was also lighting up Iggy's empty basket in one corner. This time, her tears flowed profusely: it was impossible to hold them back.

So she let them come, in the knowledge that they were not tears of weakness.

She closed her suitcases and left the room. Two people were waiting ahead of her at reception. When her turn came, the receptionist frowned.

'You're leaving? I thought you were going to stay for several nights. Is anything wrong?'

'Everything's fine,' she answered. 'I'm going home. The workers performed miracles: everything has been repaired. No more leaks.'

'Fine.'

'Please put this on Madame Dorian's account.'

'Yes. Did you take anything from the minibar?'

269

'Yes. Put that on her bill as well.'

She began walking through the streets of Toulouse, trundling her suitcases behind her. She did not live very far away, and she didn't feel like taking the Métro. And Iggy's body was not all that heavy. She had all the time in the world, now.

*That's all well and good*, said Madeleine's voice, *but where do we start?*

She knew, of course. It was perfectly obvious. There was only one way to begin.


At dawn he was already in place. Sitting in his car. The adrenaline flowing through his veins. After finishing Mila's journal he had showered and dressed, then he went down to prepare a thermos of black coffee in the kitchen on the ground floor. He drove silently out of the rest home car park.

With the car stopped on the hill, at the edge of a field, Servaz was sipping strong, if tasteless, coffee. He had seen a light come on downstairs in the fog-shrouded designer house. A big modern house that looked as if it had been designed by Mies van der Rohe himself: an assemblage of concrete cubes with horizontal lines and a flat roof, big rectangular windows and picture windows on the swimming pool side; even a little stable. White fences and meadowland all around. The full round-faced moon was keeping watch over the landscape; the thickets were black and the hills were still a dark blue.

A figure walked by the lit window. Servaz focused his binoculars. It was him. His pulse began to race. It was six thirty: he was an early riser. Servaz watched him calmly drinking his coffee, in a bathrobe, sitting by the window. He obviously wasn't worried that someone might be watching. Then Servaz saw him leave the room and a second rectangular window lit up. For an hour and a half, Léonard Fontaine sat in front of his computer. The sky grew lighter; the countryside emerged slowly from darkness, like a theatre backdrop gradually being illuminated, and Servaz went back to his car to move it behind a cluster of trees, without switching on the headlights. He then stepped back out into the brisk chill and pulled up his collar. He climbed over an electric fence and walked through the melting snow and the tall wet grass to the very edge of the hill. He had his thermos with him to keep warm, but he was dying for a fag, to feel the smoke go down into his infected, eager lungs. By the time he reached the edge of the hill, the bottoms of his trousers were soaked.

At seven twenty-eight the sun came out at last and its pale low rays caressed the frozen landscape, unable to warm up the air. At eight o'clock its rays swung over the hill to light up the bottom of the dale and the picture window at the front of the house suddenly opened. Servaz saw Fontaine take a few strides along the wooden terrace, still wearing his bathrobe, barefoot in spite of the cold. With a new cup in his hand, he was sipping his coffee and looking straight ahead. Servaz could see the steam from the cup through his binoculars. There were little lights shining on the ground.

Once he had finished his coffee, Fontaine walked around the pool in the direction of the pool house. The snow had been cleared, but the wood must nevertheless be slippery and he was walking cautiously. He went into the little building, switched on a light and disappeared inside. All at once an electric hum rose and the PVC cover on the pool began to roll back. Servaz watched this spectacle with the same odd fascination a voyeur secretly inspecting a pretty woman might feel.

*He's not really going to swim, is he?*

Servaz gave a start when he saw the astronaut come back out of the pool house: despite the cold, Fontaine was naked. He crouched down to switch off the security alarm with a key and a moment later, he dived into the water.

*Bloody hell.*

Crawl, butterfly, backstroke. Servaz watched the astronaut doing laps for a good hour. The water was steaming: the pool must be heated. The sun had lit up the dale now; it was a fine winter morning, clear and cold. Servaz was freezing. At last Fontaine got out of the water; he ran to dry off in the pool house, then went back to the main house in his dressing gown. For a good while, Servaz could no longer see him.

When Fontaine reappeared, he was wearing a thick jumper, jodhpurs and riding boots; he walked along the white fence to the stable and disappeared inside. Fifteen minutes later he came back out with a magnificent horse. Servaz observed him as he saddled the horse then mounted it nimbly before setting off in conquest of the facing hillside. Servaz felt a shiver go through him; every fibre in his body

271

told him the house was empty, and that Fontaine's ride would last at least half an hour. He knew that Fontaine was married with small children, but everything told him, too, that this morning he was alone, there was not the slightest movement, the slightest trace of any other presence. It was extremely tempting to go down and explore, but on the one hand, he did not really know how long Fontaine would be absent, and on the other, he would leave footprints in the snow. Unless he parked the car outside the door . . . Fontaine would see that someone had come and gone in his absence, and he would have no way of knowing who. A public figure like him must receive regular visitors.

Hesitating, Servaz studied the house; he saw nothing that looked like an alarm system, not even a projector on the facade at roof level, that might be activated by a motion sensor. There was no one in sight, either. He was perfectly aware that if he went into the house without a warrant (the cops called it a 'Mexican') and was apprehended, his career would be over. He might as well start looking for a job as a security guard right away. He could, to begin with, simply knock at the door. That wouldn't implicate him in any way. He walked back across the sodden field to his car, sat behind the wheel, and set off. He drove slowly down the slope to where the drive met the main road, by two oak trees, then he went up the drive and switched off the engine at the front door.

Now what?

What if the wife and kids were inside asleep? What would he say? That he suspected her husband of being a monster? He got out of the car. Studied the frozen landscape one more time. His breath rose, white, into the cold air. His pulse was beating just a little bit faster. He went up the two concrete steps. Rang the bell. No answer. Pressed the Bakelite button with his thumb one more time. Nothing moved. The door seemed to be mocking him. As did the silence inside the house. A raven cawed in a tree behind him, startling him.

*Go on. Do it. Prove to yourself that you're alive, that you've still got guts.*

A long time ago, he had learned from a thief how to open a lock in thirty seconds. This one looked like a very standard model.

Yet there might be sensors inside the house. If Fontaine had something to hide, he would certainly not have left it in an accessible place. And besides, what did he expect to find? He wouldn't have

272

time to search his computer, in any case. Or his files. Servaz inspected the lock again: it looked new. So much the better. Oxidation and dirt might have seized up the pins.

*What are you trying to prove?* He went back to the car, opened the door on the passenger side, and leaned over to the glove box. He took out a ring of a dozen or so keys wrapped in a rag. These were not ordinary keys, but instruments known as bump keys, used by burglars to pick pin tumbler locks. Logically, he should have had a skeleton key for each different make, but a dozen models were enough to open over half the locks on the market. Servaz got to work. By the eighth key he still hadn't found his way in, and his hands were moist, his face covered in sweat. The ninth key slipped from his damp fingers but it responded favourably. Once he had pushed it in, in the neutral position, he gave it a short bump with his palm and immediately turned it. Bingo. The door opened onto a silent hallway.

He checked his watch: fifteen minutes had gone by since Fontaine had ridden off.

The walls of the long hallway, grey polished concrete with a fine finish, were absolutely bare. The anthracite flooring was magnificent. There was no furniture. Nor any obvious motion detector. He continued walking along the hall. And froze. Stopped breathing for a moment. A dog bowl. Empty. Huge. *Big bowl = big dog*, he deduced. He felt sweat run down his spine: he was terrified of dogs. And of horses. He could still turn around . . . He walked into the big living room, which confirmed his initial impression: black and white abstract canvases on the walls, a modern desk in front of a small bookshelf, a big flat-screen television above an equally large fireplace that ran on bioethanol – its flames dancing on a bed of pebbles . . . The swimming pool was visible beyond the picture window. Through a door to the right, Servaz saw a big bed. No burglar alarm. But a dog . . . *Where was it?* He stood motionless for a moment in the middle of the room. Stairs of pale wood, suspended in space, led up to a mezzanine; the mezzanine overlooked an open-plan kitchen. Servaz looked up the stairs . . .

And saw it.

A monstrous dog. What breed, he could not say, but it had a massive head, a short muzzle, and its thick jowls left not the slightest doubt: he belonged to the category of killer dogs. Pit bulls, Rottweilers, bulldogs and other filthy beasts with jaws of steel and beady, fierce little eyes. He felt himself go cold all over. The animal was sleeping at the edge of the mezzanine; his head was slumped on the floor, overlooking the living room. If he opened his eyes he would immediately check the room and see the intruder. Servaz's throat went dry.

*Get out of here; go back down the corridor the way you came. Now.*

The slightest suspicious noise and the beast would wake up. And Fontaine could show up at any minute. *Get out!* The desk. Servaz headed stealthily towards it: there was a pile of innocuous-looking papers next to the computer, which was switched off. He glanced again at the sleeping monster upstairs. He opened the drawers as silently as possible, one by one. Then he lifted up the papers. Bills, receipts, letters . . . nothing! He turned to the books, pulled out a few, put them back. Incredibly, the mutt wasn't moving: what sort of guard dog *was* this? Servaz walked quickly around the kitchen: there was a big metallic refrigerator, induction hotplates, glass-doored cupboards, a post office calendar. Then he went into the bedroom. An erotic lithograph on the wall. A dresser. A thick shaggy bedside rug. Cupboards. He opened them. A clothes rail. He parted jackets, shirts. Dried his hands on his trousers: they were increasingly damp, and he mustn't leave any traces. He found several uniforms with epaulettes; there was a pilot's cap on a shelf just above: like most astronauts, Fontaine had been a fighter pilot and a squadron leader before joining the Space Agency.

He turned towards the bed and the night table. On it was one book.

Servaz went over.

His blood thickened in his veins like a sauce setting: the book was entitled *Perversity at Work: Harassment in the Workplace and in Relationships.*

There, on the night table. Not even hidden. A book that might be useful to people who were trying to protect themselves from perverts – but also to the perverts themselves.

Servaz felt that strange surge of power, of an investigator nearing his goal. But at the same time he was beginning to panic. He looked at his watch. Twenty-five minutes: twenty-five minutes had gone by since Fontaine had left! *Get the fuck out, right away!* Suddenly, a strident sound broke the silence and he jumped as if someone had

274

set off a firecracker at his feet. The telephone! It went on ringing, then an answerphone picked up in the living room. A synthetic voice invited the caller to leave a message after the beep, followed by a woman's tense voice: 'Léo, it's Christine. I have to talk to you. Call me back.' Who was Christine? His next victim?

The dog: the ringing phone must have woken him up. *Get going, now.* He was walking hesitantly back to the living room when a vibration started beneath his feet, something like an imminent earthquake. Still far away but clear nonetheless. It was moving through the ground. What was it? A boiler or some machinery that had just started up somewhere deep in the house? No, it wasn't that . . . And then suddenly, in an instant, he understood. *Hooves.* Pounding on the ground. A horse approaching at a gallop.

*Out!*

This time he took to his heels, first through the living room, then along the endless hallway. On his way he caught sight of one eye opening on the mezzanine, still sleepy but not for long. The vibration grew stronger. Resounding through the floor, the walls. Servaz was about to open the door when he saw a car pull up on the drive. Shit! He stopped short in the middle of the hall. He glanced towards the living room and the picture window and could see Fontaine dismounting at this end of the meadow, just beyond the swimming pool. He heard the car parking next to his: he was trapped!

He glanced again through the half-open door. A woman was getting out of the car. In less than a minute, she would be inside the house. If only she could have been the fire department, or the postman come for his Christmas box. *The postman.* Of course: that was his last chance. He went back into the living room, rushed into the bedroom, opened the wardrobe and reached for the pilot's cap on the shelf. Then he rushed into the kitchen and tore the calendar from the wall. That was when he heard it: the clicking of claws coming down the stairs from the mezzanine. He walked through the kitchen. And froze. The enormous beast was coming slowly down the steps, looking at him. It reached the floor of the living room and began to move, impassively, in Servaz's direction. Its little eyes stared at him, shining with the brilliance of well-polished coins. His massive black muzzle was the most terrifying thing Servaz had ever seen that close up – except, perhaps, the barrel of a gun.

The dog began growling, showing his fangs: a low-frequency growl that struck Servaz in the plexus, and a row of teeth worthy of a shark. The animal was staring at him. Fifty kilograms of muscle ready to leap up and tear open his neck, and his face along with it. Servaz was trembling, sweating like a pig . . .

'*Darkhan!*'

At the sound of the woman's voice, the dog reacted. 'Darkhan!' she called again, from outside and – oh, mercy! – the monster suddenly lost interest in Servaz and began to bound joyfully towards the front door. Despite his desire to turn and run the opposite way, Servaz forced himself, still trembling, to follow the dog. On his way he picked up the pile of papers from the desk and placed the calendar on top, then walked to the door and reached it just as the woman was coming in, followed by the mutt. In her forties, she was wearing gloves and a winter coat; she looked self-assured and authoritarian. She froze when she saw him, throwing an immediate dart of suspicion in his direction.

Servaz flashed her a smile and held the calendar up briefly in her direction. 'Morning, madame.' His voice was calm and professional, astonishingly steady after what he had just been through. He walked quickly past her, under the watchful eye of the ferocious dog – which did not growl, this time – and he could tell she had turned around; he went down the steps to his car, expecting to be called back at any moment. He could not possibly run away like a thief – because then in all likelihood she would quickly take down his number plate. His heart was pounding like the horse's hooves only minutes before. He tossed the cap and the calendar onto the passenger seat, then calmly walked around the car and got in behind the wheel. He turned the car around and headed along the drive. He looked in the rearview mirror: neither the woman nor the monster was following him. She must be playing with the dog, or telling Fontaine about the odd postman she had just run into. In a few minutes or hours Fontaine would discover the calendar had been taken from his kitchen wall, and that papers were missing from his desk. He would also discover, probably somewhat later, that his pilot's cap had been stolen. They would conclude they had been the victims of an attempted burglary, which she had aborted. She certainly hadn't had the presence of mind to write down his number plate; why should she have? Servaz could consider himself lucky: he could stay in the police, he had confirmation that harassment was a subject of great interest to Léonard Fontaine, and he would not die torn to pieces by the fangs of a pure killing machine.

She called Ilan when she came out of the lift.

'Do you have what I asked you for?'

'Yes.'

'Great. Can you send it to my email?'

'No problem. Christine . . .'

'Yes?'

'How are you?'

She almost told him about Iggy, but restrained herself.

'Fine,' she said. 'Thank you for the recording.'

'Keep me posted,' he said.

'About what?'

He hesitated.

'I don't know . . . about what's going on.'

'Mmm.'

She hung up and unlocked her door. Her apprehension was quickly swept away by the strange feeling of coming home. Since she was no longer safe anywhere, she saw no reason to stay away any longer. And besides, her fear had left her, up there, above the void.

She went quickly around the flat. Nothing to report. No opera CDs, no sign of any intrusion. She opened one of her suitcases and removed Iggy, wrapped in his white towels like a mummy, and set him down in the bathroom. Then she dialled another number.

'Hello?'

'Gérald?'

Silence at the end of the line.

'I know you don't want to talk to me,' she began, firmly. 'And I understand. Everything you've been told, everything you think you know—'

'Everything I *think* I know?' he said, instantly annoyed.

'Yes. What you think you know is not the truth. And I have the proof.'

A sigh on the line.

'Christine, for Christ's sake, what are you talking about?'

'Think. Just think about what you know *exactly*, and what you *suppose.* What would you say if I had you listen to something that will radically challenge all that?'

'Christine, I—'

'Gérald, please: give me five minutes of your time. After that, you can decide for yourself what to believe or not. And I'll leave you alone. For good: you have my word. All I ask is five minutes. You owe me that, at the very least.'

He sighed again.

'When?'

She took a breath and told him. And where to go. Then she hung up. She realised that the pleading tone she had adopted was pure farce, this time. A charade solely for Gérald. He loved to be implored. From now on she would never plead with anyone for anything ever again.

He looked both furious and frightened when she came into the café on the rue Saint-Antoine-du-T. She thought he looked like a little boy.

'Hey.'

He glanced up and didn't say anything. She pulled over a chair and sat down opposite him. She hadn't put on any make-up, had made no effort to be attractive, and she must have looked terrible with the dark circles under bloodshot eyes, but he didn't comment. He only seemed to be in a hurry to leave.

Nonetheless, he spoke: 'The police did come and see Denise.'

She sat up straight.

'About the intern you beat up, they showed her the photographs—'

'I didn't touch her,' she replied firmly.

'You should get help; you're not well, Christine.'

'Quite the contrary.'

The look he gave her through his glasses was hardly friendly. She switched on her smartphone and opened her inbox, then plugged in the headphones.

'Do you remember that letter I got in my mailbox? That was when everything started.'

'They think you wrote it yourself.'

'Why would I do that?'

'I don't know . . . because you're . . . *not well* . . .'

She leaned forward.

'Stop saying that, for fuck's sake!' she growled.

Oh, Lord. He had recoiled in his chair, and he looked like he was really frightened now.

*Gérald was frightened of her!*

'Here, listen,' she ordered curtly.

At first he merely stared at her and shook his head, looking disgusted; then he took the earphones. She began to play the recording from the radio broadcast that Ilan had just sent to her: the part where the man had rung up regarding the letter. She waited for his reaction, saw him frown, then concentrate, his eyes lowered. He removed the earphones.

'So, that call,' she said, 'did I invent that, too?'

He didn't answer.

'That was the programme on 25 December – in other words, the day after I found the letter. You can check; it's still available as a podcast,' she lied. 'Please explain, if I wrote the letter myself, how that man found out about it.'

He didn't say anything. But he seemed less sure of himself.

'And if I wrote it, how did he know about its existence and what it contained, given the fact that the letter was in your possession at the time he was calling?'

Gérald reddened.

'It must be a coincidence,' he ventured. 'He doesn't talk about the letter, just the fact that someone committed suicide.'

She rolled her eyes.

'Oh, Gérald, for God's sake! This is exactly what he says: *'It doesn't bother you that you let someone die? … you let someone commit suicide on Christmas Eve. Even though that person had called out to you for help.'* Of course he's talking about the letter! He says just enough so that I alone can understand, that's all!'

He blinked; she saw a fog of uncertainty cloud his gaze. Finally he shook his head, incredulous.

'Okay,' he conceded. 'You're right. He's talking about the letter. But what you said to Denise . . .'

'Denise told me that I was not the right person for you! And yes, that did set me off. How would you have reacted in my shoes?'

'You seem to forget the email you sent to her.'

'I did not write that email any more than I wrote that letter,' she said, articulating precisely. 'Shit, don't you understand? That guy didn't stop at calling me at the radio station: he got into my email, and he got into my house. He's . . . he's some sort of fucking *stalker*.'

This time he opened his mouth then closed it again without speaking. She saw him thinking.

'When did he get into your house?'

'The night I called you because of Iggy,' she replied. 'He was down in one of the rubbish bins in the basement with a broken paw; I found him thanks to his barking. I even thought for a moment that he was at the neighbours' – and that same neighbour wasted no time telling the police I was out of my mind.'

'How is he?'

'He's dead.'

'What?'

'Someone killed Iggy, Gérald. And I don't know what to do with his body. He's still in . . . in the flat. If you don't believe me, just come and see.'

She watched him taking in what she had told him. Then she saw in his eyes the first signs of panic.

'Christine, for the love of God, you have to go to the police!'

She snorted.

'The police? You just told me yourself that the police think I'm guilty! That I'm crazy! Even you – you believed I beat up that poor girl. Fuck!'

He was looking at her closely now, his gaze increasingly worried.

'What do you intend to do?'

'Two things: find out who, and why. And there is only one person who can tell me.'

'The intern,' he said. 'Of course. What do you want me to do?'

'I think they're watching me. I took every precaution in coming here. So they don't know yet that we're back in touch.'

'You say "they", so you think . . . Yes, of course: the intern, and the guy . . .'

'I think there is someone else,' she added. 'Just an insignificant hard man. He's probably been paid. He had no reason to go after me. Above all, he couldn't have found out all that stuff without someone else's help.'

He looked at her questioningly through his glasses.

'Do you have any idea who it is?'

She stared at him, pensively.

'Maybe. I want you to watch that girl for me,' she said.

'Shit, Christine! I'm not a cop, I don't know how to do that!'

She looked at him, studied his smooth face, his sober, elegant, fashionable yet conservative glasses, his bespoke winter coat, his pretty grey silk scarf. She breathed in his clean smell, with its top note of rich cologne . . . *When will you stop being a well-behaved little boy, Gérald?* She clenched her teeth. And said in a firm voice:

'All you have to do is follow her for a day or two. Tell me if she meets someone, and call me if she is at home alone.'

'Where does she live?'

'La Reynerie.'

'Great.'

He suddenly took Christine's hand in his and squeezed it.

'Forgive me,' he said. 'I'm sorry. I should have looked into it some more. I should never have simply taken it at face value. I'm so sad to hear about Iggy: I want to make up for the way I've behaved.' He gave her a jaunty smile. 'Okay, I'll follow the girl. And those guys in La Reynerie had better behave: they have no idea what a guy who grew up in Pech-David is capable of.'

She couldn't help but smile on hearing his typical Gérald bravado. She suspected he was afraid but that in spite of everything he wanted to help her. He was looking at her, smiling. You can count on me, said his smile, I'm not any braver than the average person, but I'm going to do this for you.

She responded to the squeeze of his hand. She would have liked to lean across the table and kiss him, but she wasn't altogether ready to forgive him yet.

'One piece of advice,' she said. 'Change your clothes, first.'

Servaz watched the planes taking off from the industrial zone at Blagnac at five-minute intervals, with peak periods of one take-off every minute or two. He hated planes.

Something was nagging him. Mila's diary was next to him on the passenger seat and he couldn't stop glancing over at it. *Why did she keep the child? Why didn't she have an abortion?*

He focused his attention on the building, all glass and concrete, that interchangeable architecture that could be found from Tokyo to Sydney by way of Doha, with the letters GOSPACE on the roof. Léonard Fontaine was still inside. Servaz reached for his telephone.

'Vincent?' he said, when Espérandieu had answered. 'I need something else: have a look among recent complaints to see if there were any filed by a Christine; a complaint regarding physical abuse or harassment.'

'Christine? You don't have her last name by any chance?' A pause. 'Forget it.'

# 35

# Encore

The A&E doctor was younger than she was. He was dark, with features that made her think he must be of Indian or Pakistani origin, and he seemed exhausted and stressed out. He was the one who needed care, she thought. When was the last time he'd got any sleep?

'I'm listening,' he said after glancing briefly in her direction. 'You told the nurse you thought you had a cardiac issue last night.' He checked his sheet. 'According to the symptoms I see here, it might be a simple episode of tachycardia.'

'I lied.'

A flicker of astonishment passed over his gaze. Just a flicker: he'd seen it all before.

'What do you mean?'

'It's . . . rather delicate.'

She saw him lean back abruptly in his chair and fiddle with the pen in the pocket of his white coat, pretending to have all the time in the world, which was hardly the case: the corridor behind her was filled to bursting.

'I'm listening.'

'I had . . . unprotected sex, last night. I . . . I had been drinking and had also taken . . .'

'Drugs?'

'Yes.' She pretended to look ashamed and guilty.

'Which ones?'

'It doesn't matter. That's not why I'm here. But because of the . . . possible contamination.'

He nodded.

'I see. You would like to be tested, right?'

She nodded. He stopped to think.

'I can prescribe an Elisa test in three weeks' time: any sooner would be pointless. And a second test to confirm, after six weeks have gone by. But in the meantime, I must ask you, um, a certain number of questions. To determine what sort of post-exposure treatment I should prescribe: perhaps a simple prophylactic treatment would suffice, or perhaps we should already envisage multiple therapies in order to try and ward off infection – do you understand?'

'I think I do.'

'Good. Was the sex oral, vaginal or anal?'

'Um . . . vaginal.'

'What do you know about your partner? Do you know him well?'

'Not at all. He was a – a stranger, you see,' she replied, blushing.

'How did you meet him?'

'Well, in a bar . . . two hours earlier.'

For a fraction of a second, she got the unpleasant impression he was judging her.

'Excuse me. You say you met him in a bar. In your opinion, do you think he might be HIV-positive? That his behaviour suggested risk?'

'He fucked me without a condom,' she replied shortly. 'And he didn't know me. So, yes: I think the probability is hardly zero.'

*Raped*, shouted her inner voice, not *fucked* . . . She saw the young doctor frown and blush dark red, then he reached for a prescription pad.

'I'm going to prescribe a combination of several antiretroviral drugs right away, to be taken for four weeks. Then you will stop the medication for three weeks before taking the test. Do you have a GP?'

'Yes, but . . .'

'Look, it doesn't matter who does what, just follow the plan, all right?'

She nodded.

'Take the medication with food,' he said, writing up the prescription. 'Make sure you stick to the stated times and doses. You might have diarrhoea, nausea or dizziness, but do not stop the treatment, whatever you do. Is that clear? The unpleasant side effects will disappear after a few days. I'm also going to prescribe some blood tests.'

He cast her a look that managed to be both stern and embarrassed.

'A word of warning: this treatment will not protect you from any new contamination. Nor will it protect your partners – partner – do you understand?'

Right. He thought she was a nympho. Then all of a sudden his gaze was gentler.

'Look, there is a good chance you're fine. These are simply precautionary measures. But if, unfortunately, it turns out you have been infected, it's better to follow the treatment for four weeks than to have to take medication all your life.'

He knew – and she also knew – that the treatment was no guarantee she would avoid infection. But she nodded all the same, to show that she had understood.

Replicant. That was what was written above the door. The 'R' was shaped like a submachine gun. Great. She went through the glass door; the jingle of the little bell was replaced by a wailing police siren of the kind you could hear on the streets of Chicago or Rio de Janeiro.

All around her were showcases, displays, locked cabinets, neon lights, reflections, security glass. And all the artefacts born of the human race's eagerness to tear itself to pieces, since time immemorial. Firearms: hunting rifles, pump-action shotguns, handguns, authorised pistols and revolvers made of brown steel, polished and virile. Pellet guns, airsoft guns, BB guns. Ammunition of every kind. Optical instruments: shooting glasses, binoculars, reflector sights, night vision goggles. Knives: daggers, throwing knives, machetes, katanas, tomahawks, axes, ninja stars . . . and also crossbows, slingshots, nunchakus, blowguns, clubs. And most of these things were for sale on the open market. Fascinating.

The tall, bearded fat man was wearing the same baseball cap as the previous time. She could almost picture herself in a small town in the Midwest or at an NRA firing range. The guy was a walking cliché.

'Can I help you?' he asked, his voice as high-pitched as a little boy's.

The smell of sweat still hung in the air around him, like some sort of gas, and Christine wrinkled her nose.

'I think so,' she said.

Ten minutes later, she left the shop with a Mace tear-gas key ring, a rechargeable 500,000-volt stun gun with an integrated LED lamp, and a stainless steel fifty-three-centimetre telescopic Piranha club with a neoprene handle. Her arsenal was stashed in a black sports bag. It felt strange when she stopped for coffee at a bar, with the bag at her feet, then when she took the Métro with it. Her next destination was a hardware store not far from her flat, where she bought a roll of thick adhesive tape and a box-cutter.

When she came out of the store, her mobile was buzzing. It was Gérald.

'She's at home alone.'

She almost burst out laughing when she saw him by the Reynerie Métro station: the clothes he had put on – a sort of shapeless hoodie, huge baggy black trousers and leopard-print Puma trainers – were at least four sizes too big, except for the shoes. He was also wearing a Snapback cap with a flat red visor under his hood, and dark glasses. He looked like a caricature of a rapper in an episode of *South Park*.

'Where did you find those clothes?' she asked, horrified.

'Yo,' he answered.

'They will strip you bare to get their hands on them,' she joked.

'Yo. Jes' try, motherfuckers. You don't look too bad yourself,' he added.

Christine stopped smiling when she realised there was a good chance he'd be noticed, dressed like that. She looked worriedly at the tall rows of buildings beyond the esplanade and the little lake.

'I think those guys over there noticed me,' he said when they started walking. 'They must think I'm a plain-clothes policeman. We'd better watch out.'

She gave him a cautious look, and smiled.

'No plain-clothes policeman would be crazy enough to wear that kind of get-up. Is she still alone?'

He pointed to the building while they slowly climbed the hill in the fog. Christine saw the same frightening figures in the mist as the previous time.

'With her kid, yes,' he replied.

'Go home.'

'What are you going to do?'

'Go home – if you dare to take the Métro dressed like that. If you stay here in those clothes, you'll end up in your boxers.'

Beneath his visor and hood he grimaced like a stubborn little boy.

'No, I'm coming with you.'

Christine stopped short and turned to face him.

'Gérald, listen: do you have any idea what we look like, the pair of us? Like two clowns. It will take them thirty seconds to see through us, and even less to jump us. Have you seen your outfit? We'd be less noticeable if we were wearing suits and ties!'

'What are you going to do?' he asked.

'Don't worry, I have a plan.'

'A plan? What sort of plan are you talking about? Other than parading around in fancy dress . . .'

'I'm grateful for what you've done. But now you're going home.'

'Nope, I'm staying here.' He stopped at the foot of a tree and rolled up the sleeve of the sweatshirt to look at his watch. 'Fifteen minutes. Any more than that and I'm coming to get you.'

Christine's nerves were as tight as piano strings. There was no reason to smile, it was far too dangerous. Still, Gérald's obstinacy and his efforts to be brave made her smile.

'All right. But I need twenty.'

He looked around anxiously.

'I'm not sure I can last that long,' he said, frowning.

She scanned their surroundings, on the lookout for any suspicious behaviour, while the fog thickened.

'I'm not sure either,' she agreed. 'They might think you're a member of a rival gang.' She looked him up and down and smiled. 'But who knows. By the time they figure out which one, I'll be back,' she said jokingly as she walked away.

She was hardly in the light-hearted mood she had affected. She was wearing the same dark sweatshirt as last time, but she was almost certain their little game was already being closely observed. Her hands clutched the tear-gas key ring in one pocket and the stun gun in the other. She arrived without incident at the entrance to the building. The kids from the time before had vanished. The wind was blowing the snow and mist in pale white swirls; the snow was melting. There was no one in the entrance. She left muddy tracks as she hurried towards the lifts. There was a distant drumming in her ears, and she wondered if it was from a stereo somewhere in the building or her own blood – a sound that was growing familiar: the sound of adrenaline.

Once the doors to the lifts had closed behind her, she took out the key ring and the stun gun; the end of it looked like a jaw. She had inserted two batteries, and now she wound the strap around her wrist and opened the safety catch. The shop attendant had advised her to choose gel rather than spray for the tear gas (he had explained that gas could blow back into your face if you were downwind) but she had gone with the spray all the same, because on the one hand it required less precision and, on the other, she intended to use it indoors. She had, however, taken the precaution of wearing a scarf. Now everything was down to timing and luck: she had rehearsed her moves a dozen times or more in front of the mirror before going to meet Gérald, but she was not sure that was enough. She had a stomach ache and her back hurt. When the lift doors opened she took a deep breath.

Corridor. Sounds of television. Graffiti.

Door 19B. Christine tried to breathe calmly. Like last time, music was coming through the door. She rang the bell. *Bang bang*, went her heart. Footsteps. She could tell she was being inspected through the spyhole. *Breathe . . .*

'What the fuck are you doing here?'

Cordélia looked down at her from her full height. This time she was wearing knickers and a T-shirt. Her face still showed the traces of the blows she'd received: bruises going from mustard yellow to black, bloodshot eyes, her nose flattened.

Christine wondered who had done this to her. And whether she had submitted willingly to the blows or not.

'Are you deaf? I asked you what the fuck you're doing.'

Christine pulled back her hood. And saw the surprise in the intern's eyes. She had lined her eyes with black pencil and eyeshadow, put white foundation on her face, then painted her lips black. She looked Goth – or crazy. Or dressed up for Halloween.

'Fuck, I don't know what you're playing at, but—'

Christine raised her arm and aimed the spray right in Cordélia's eyes. 'Fuuuuck!' The girl screamed. Recoiled, staggered. Bent double. She raised her hands to her face. Coughed. Christine pulled the scarf over her nose and mouth, then pushed Cordélia inside the flat with the palm of her hand and closed the door behind her. Cordélia was leaning over, frantically rubbing her eyes. She could not look at Christine. She was wracked by coughing fits. Christine placed the little electrodes of the stun gun right between her shoulder blades, and through the thin cotton (so thin that Christine could feel the outline of her vertebrae underneath) went 500,000 volts: a crackle and the blue light of the electric arc. The young woman's body trembled all over, and her legs gave way. She fell like a puppet whose strings have been cut. Christine moved with her, the gun still pressed between Cordélia's shoulder blades. She prolonged the charge beyond five seconds. Game over. The girl lay on the floor; she hadn't passed out but was disorientated and incapable of getting up: the electric shock had momentarily interrupted the messages her brain sent to her muscles.

Christine slid her bag off her shoulder, put it down at her feet, and opened the zip. *So, what does it feel like to be the victim instead of the torturer? Huh? It's strange, no? I'll bet you didn't like it all that much. Well, let me tell you something: it's nothing compared to what's coming next.*

She looked like a mummy. The thick metallic adhesive tape was rolled around her ankles, her thighs, her torso and her arms. Lying on the floor on her side, knees bent, in a foetal position. Her arms bound in an L position, wrists and hands joined. Only a few patches of her body were visible beneath the tape: her knees, elbows, collarbones, and the upper part of her head. Cordélia's neck, chin and mouth were also imprisoned under thick layers of sticky tape. It stopped just below her nose and she was breathing noisily.

Sitting on the edge of the coffee table, one metre away, Christine was watching her: in her hand, the telescopic club had replaced the stun gun.

'Doesn't hurt too much?' she asked. 'They said this thing doesn't cause any lasting effects or physical injuries. The liars.'

'Gggrrrrmmmhh . . .'

'Shut up.'

The stainless steel tip of the club came close to a bare spot on Cordélia's back, where the superficial burns left by the electric shock were visible; the girl shuddered when Christine touched them.

'That wasn't deliberate,' she said flatly.

'*Ggoo . . . ffff . . . kkkk . . . ssselfff . . .*'

With a sigh, Christine gazed at one of the kneecaps the tape had left bare. A round, vaguely triangular, smooth bone beneath pale, thin skin. She took aim and swung the club. Her move cut through the air with a gentle whoosh. A strange sound, like that of a mug shattering, came next. Cordélia's eyes popped out of her head. Through the tape she screamed, but the sound was nothing more than a stifled whinny. Tears were flowing down her cheeks and she looked at Christine with a terrifying mixture of pain and rage.

Christine gave her time to get her wits about her. Her eyes were like two blocks of ice.

'I'm going to remove the tape. If you cry for help, if you try to scream or raise your voice, I'll smash in your teeth.'

Her tone was so cold, harsh and metallic that she did not recognise her own voice. Another Christine was replacing the one she had known. *But you like her, don't you? Even if a tiny bit of that civilised, self-righteous Christine, full of hypocritical feelings, is still disavowing everything you're doing, you cannot help but think it's kind of cool to be taking justice into your own hands. An eye for an eye. Like in the Old Testament. Admit it: you like this new Christine.*

Clearly, Cordélia had also understood that the situation had changed; she nodded vigorously to show she would comply. Christine leaned down and tore the tape off her mouth. Cordélia winced but didn't make a sound.

'I'll bet you didn't expect this, did you? That Christine-the-ideal-victim, Christine-the-perfect-target, poor poor Christine would change into Christine-the-dangerous-nutter. Do you realise: even my language has changed. I have to say that what you managed to do in just a few days is really remarkable. Remarkable.'

Cordélia did not comment.

'Now the big question,' added Christine quietly, 'is who is behind this?'

Cordélia stared at her.

'That was a question, Cordélia. Didn't you hear the question mark at the end?'

No answer.

'Cordélia . . .'

'Don't ask me. Please.'

'Cordélia, you are not in a position to refuse.'

'You're wasting your time.'

'I don't think so. Time is the one thing I have plenty of.'

Her voice was increasingly calm and frosty. There was panic in the young woman's eyes.

'Please, please, stop. He can do anything. I know he's watching me. You'd better get out of here. You have no idea what you're doing. You have no idea who you're dealing with and how dangerous he is.'

Christine sighed, put the tape back on the girl's mouth and pressed on it several times to make sure it was sticking properly. Cordélia shook her head vigorously, her eyes wide with fear.

Christine stared at her bony shoulder sticking through her T-shirt.

She was weighing things up. Evaluating. She raised the club, trying to control the trembling of her wrist. She gauged the pain, enormous, when the girl's collarbone gave way under the impact, then the resignation in her eyes, before she closed her lids, tears flowing abundantly beneath her lashes.

For a split second Christine wondered if she had passed out. She pulled the tape to one side.

'Are you sure you don't want to tell me?'

The girl's eyes opened suddenly.

'Fuck off.'

Christine stopped to think. She might have changed but she didn't want to be a torturer: could what she had just done be qualified as 'acts of torture' before a tribunal? Without a doubt. The fact remained, she thought, that in the end everyone acts according to their own principles and morality. There are only rules peculiar to each individual, and according to her own criteria, this did not constitute a veritable torture session: it was what might come later . . .

'Go away,' begged Cordélia. 'Please. You don't know him: he'll hurt you. And me too.'

'He already has, I think,' retorted Christine.

She put the tape back in place on Cordélia's lips. But there was a creeping doubt. And a new wave of fear. Who was the man who was terrorising her like this?

There might be a solution . . . But it was despicable.

She reached into her handbag and took out the box-cutter. Saw Cordélia's gaze, eyes gaping, terrified, at the sight of the blade.

'Is Anton asleep?'

Her gaze turned hard and fierce.

'You want me to take care of your baby?' said Christine suddenly. She pulled off the tape.

'If you touch even a single hair on his head, I'll kill you,' spat Cordélia, her voice vibrant with hatred. 'You won't do it . . . you're bluffing, it's all an act. You could never do such a thing, you're incapable.'

'I used to be. But that was *before*, Cordélia . . .'

'You wouldn't dare,' insisted Cordélia, but her voice was trembling slightly.

'Really? Just look: *look what you did to me.*'

Christine got up. Went over to the next room. Pushed on the open door. She felt as if the soles of her feet were made of lead. The baby was there, sleeping peacefully in his pram. A mobile made of planets and a crescent moon hung above him, along with a rattle, within reach of his little fist. The blade began trembling in her hand as she drew nearer. Cordélia was right, of course: she was bluffing. Regarding the box-cutter, at least. She held out her free hand. *Oh, shit.* Her fingers pinched the soft, fine skin, the plump little pink arm. Anton opened his eyes and immediately began to wail. She pinched him again, harder: his screaming intensified.

'Come back!' shouted Cordélia from the living room. 'Please!'

Christine felt nauseous. What was she doing?

'Please, oh please!' screamed Cordélia from the next room. 'I'll talk!'

Christine heard her crying uncontrollably.

*Don't give in. Focus on your anger.*

She went back to the living room. The baby was still crying. Cordélia looked up at her with frantic eyes, and spoke all in a rush:

'I don't know his name. He contacted us, Marcus and me, and offered us money. In the beginning, all we had to do was call the radio, drop off a letter, he told us exactly what to do. And then he wanted us to scare you, to . . .'

Her tears were overflowing.

'. . . to break your dog's leg. I didn't want to go along with it, but it was too late to back out, and there was a lot of money on offer . . . *A lot.* I'm so sorry, I didn't know it would go so far, I swear!'

'Who is Marcus?'

'My boyfriend.'

'Is he the one who raped me? Who killed my dog?'

There was shock in the young woman's eyes.

'What? He was only – he was only supposed to *drug* you!'

She was shaking her head now, filled with dismay.

'This man who contacted you – who is he?'

292

'I don't know! I don't know anything! I don't know his name, I swear!'

'What does he look like?'

Cordélia glanced at something behind Christine.

'The computer . . . there's a photograph in there. You can see him getting in his car. Marcus took it when he wasn't looking, just in case something happened to us, after the first time we met. The file is called . . .'

Christine turned around. The computer was on the coffee table. Open, and switched on. She felt a strange sensation, mingled with dizziness, when she got up. Would she recognise him? Was it someone she knew? Suddenly she was no longer in such a hurry to find out the truth.

'There's an icon on the desktop,' said Cordélia behind her back. 'It says, "X".'

Christine went around the laptop. Leaned towards the screen. She saw the icon. The strange feeling was still there. Her forefinger reached for the trackpad and moved the cursor. A slight tremor. She double-clicked; the file opened. Half a dozen pictures.

Before she had even enlarged the first one, she knew: she had recognised him.

She could no longer feel anything, just a void, sucking away all thought.

*Léo* . . .

# 36

## Dress Circle

Just then, the front door opened.

'Cordie? Are you there?'

Christine turned around and met Cordélia's gaze. *Shit!* She rushed over to the tear-gas key ring and the stun gun.

'Marcus! Help!' shrieked Cordélia.

Paying no attention to the girl writhing on the floor, Christine rushed up to the man who had just come in and sprayed him with the tear gas. But the little man had already put up his hands to shield himself and only part of the cloud reached his face. He coughed violently all the same, furiously blinking then opening his eyes wide. Which gave Christine enough time to zap him with 500,000 volts in the shoulder. She saw him stiffen and begin to tremble. Then he collapsed. Once again she prolonged the electricity for over five seconds, but the batteries were draining fast. She reached for the club and struck both legs several times, before delivering one last blow between them – which didn't really hit the target, because he had curled up into himself.

She grabbed the black bag, stuffed the tear gas and club inside and pulled on the zip.

'You bitch!' moaned Cordélia behind her. 'You're going to pay for this! Marcus will have your hide, you slut!'

Christine slammed the door and took long strides down the corridor towards the lift. It seemed to take forever to go down, but once she went back out into the hall, she tried to breathe calmly and walk more slowly. She went out into the cold, damp mist and was startled when she saw the two hooded figures on either side of Gérald, a bit further along.

She still had the strap of the stun gun around her wrist, in her pocket, and with her fingertips she made sure the safety catch was off. But there must not be much charge left.

'Here she is,' said Gérald when he saw her approaching.

She stiffened, but kept walking towards them; small clouds of vapour formed in front of their mouths as they spoke. But Gérald did not seem worried or nervous.

'Don't hesitate to send me your CVs, guys,' he said. 'I'll see what I can do, all right?'

'That's cool. Thanks, man.'

'Don't mention it. Have a nice day.'

'You too. Hello, mademoiselle.'

She returned their greeting, then she and Gérald began walking quickly towards the Métro station.

'You're conducting job interviews on the street, now?'

'Those boys used to be my students,' he said.

She gave him an astonished look.

'And they recognised you, despite your disguise?'

He gave a short laugh.

'They asked me what I was doing here, and I said I was waiting for a friend. They also asked me if I was on my way to a fancy-dress party.'

He turned to her.

'Well? Did it work? Your plan?'

She winked at him.

'Perfectly.'

There was a glow of curiosity in his eyes.

'And what did you find out?'

'The name of the bastard behind all this.'

Her voice was icy as she said it. She met his questioning gaze. Just then her mobile began to vibrate in her jeans; she pulled it out and looked at the screen. Nothing. Then she understood: it wasn't coming from her *official* telephone, but from the prepaid mobile she had used to reach Léo. She found it in another pocket – and saw she had just received a text message. She opened it and read:

*Meet me at the McDonald's by Compans. Léo.*

She stared at the screen. Her brain was trying to work it out. Where was the trap? Had Cordélia and Marcus already got hold of Léo? But if Cordélia was as afraid of his reaction as she had said she was, why would she call him? It could not be a coincidence, however: her visit, Cordélia's revelations, and now this text message . . . there was something not quite right. If it was a trap, why would Léo choose McDonald's – a public place, where there were lots of students and young people, even families with children, and which must be filling up by now?

'Hey, what's going on?' asked Gérald.

They had reached the esplanade. She turned around.

'I have to go somewhere. I'll explain later . . .'

He looked at her, puzzled. She began jogging towards the Métro station.

'Chris, for God's sake! Wait for me!'

He began running behind her. She spun around.

'No! I have to go on my own. I'll explain later!'

He froze in the middle of the esplanade, puzzled and annoyed. The mist swirled around him. A grotesque, motionless figure, he disappeared from view once she was in the Métro.

Unsmiling, he watched her coming closer, his gaze right on her, all the time it took her to walk across the room with its vaguely modernist décor that resembled a geometry lesson in space. He was wearing a grey woollen coat over a chunky-knit polo-neck jumper. She sat down across from him, never taking her eyes off him.

'Hi, Léo.'

He looked preoccupied. *Because he knew that she knew?* The fine crow's feet at the edges of his eyes creased further.

'I owe you an apology,' he said.

She raised her eyebrows.

'For what I said on the telephone, the other day. It was unfair. And cruel.'

She remained silent.

'But there was a good reason for it.'

He looked around, as if to make sure no one was close enough to hear them, then lowered his voice and she understood he had chosen this spot, so unlike him, because the noise and hubbub guaranteed a certain confidentiality.

'I needed some time and . . . I was afraid someone was wiretapping me.'

'Wiretapping you?'

'Yes.'

She looked at him for a moment, pensively.

'What did you need time for?' She raised her voice to be heard above the ever-increasing noise.

'I had to check on a few things.'

He leaned forward, entering her personal space. Looking right in her eyes.

'Marcus and Corinne Délia, do those names mean anything to you?' he said.

She nodded. Her gaze hardened, went cold.

'I've just seen them,' she replied.

He seemed genuinely surprised.

'When?'

'A few minutes ago.'

'What do you mean?'

'They gave me a name, Léo . . .'

He stared at her intensely, his muscles twitching nervously in his cheeks.

'Really?'

'They gave me your name.'

'Huh?'

'Is it because I dumped you for Gérald? Is it because your pride, your self-esteem couldn't take it, is that it? Or was there something else? Some sort of perverse game you like playing with women, except for your wife?'

Léo's eyes flickered. She could tell he was searching for an answer.

'Marcus was at the hotel the day we saw each other,' she continued. 'I remember his tattoos. Not terribly discreet, I will say that. His size isn't either, for that matter. I bumped into him when I came out of the lift. Why would he have been there? I took every precaution to make sure I wasn't being followed.'

She shot him a defiant look and continued, 'Who, other than you, knew that we were meeting?'

He shook his head.

'For God's sake, Christine: didn't it occur to you that he could have followed you all the same? You're not a pro. Or that your phone might be tapped?'

'I used a new one, with a prepaid card.'

He paused, then said, 'They could have put a bug in your things

297

. . . to find you again if they lost track of you . . . Place Wilson, for God's sake! It's not as if we'd arranged to meet in the woods!'

She looked him up and down, her lips pinched, aware that all the colour had drained from his face.

'Cordélia confessed to everything . . . When I threatened her child, she cracked.'

'When you did what?'

He seemed stunned. Once again, he shook his head.

'You're completely off beam. You don't get it all.'

'What don't I get, Léo? Why are you behaving like this? It's true. So, explain.'

A veil of sadness seemed to shroud his face, which looked suddenly old and withered; an expression she had never seen. It was as if he were suddenly ten years older. He looked her right in the eye.

'It's a long story,' he said.

She no longer knew what to think. She had heard Léo out and then, on her way home, she went back over his explanation, trying to find the flaw.

Léo had told her about a person harassing him, the person who was pulling the strings. Such a strange story . . . Someone harassing Léo, she thought. For years. Someone who was also harassing the people close to him, or rather the women who were close to him. Making their life hell.

Christine thought of Léo's worried face. Should she believe him? For the time being he had refused to give her a name: 'There are a few more things I have to check . . . I can't bring charges without proof. But you know, that detective I told you about, that woman detective, she followed this person, and that's how she traced Cordélia and Marcus.' His voice had sounded heavy, preoccupied.

For a split second, he seemed lost in thought.

'I have €30,000 in an account,' he said abruptly. 'Do you have any money invested anywhere?'

'I have €20,000 in life insurance,' she replied, surprised. 'Why?'

'Take it out. First thing tomorrow. We might need it.'

'To do what?'

'To buy back your freedom, Christine. To get you out of their clutches. To put an end to the story – if it's what I think it is.'

She had the impression that the darkness surrounding her was filled with obstacles. It was raining, and the city was nothing but shadows, reflections, headlights, a glow. Everything was sharp, cutting, this evening. She walked as if she were in a trance, while she took in what Léo had said. He had also talked to her about a young woman he had known who had committed suicide. At the time, he hadn't suspected anything. Particularly, he said, as Célia – that was her name – had suddenly distanced herself from him. Now he thought it must have been connected to his harasser, he was sure of it. Finally, he told her something that would have filled her with joy, before: he was going to get a divorce. His wife had left and taken the children. They'd agreed on an arrangement for custody, and he'd seen his lawyer that very day.

A passing bus briefly interrupted her thoughts. Should she believe him? Cordélia had accused Léo, and Léo was accusing someone else. She turned into her street then suddenly slowed down when she saw the swirling glow illuminating the facades, the wrought-iron balconies, the cornices, the moulding: the profusion of adornments that made her think of wedding cakes lined up in a pastry shop window. Most of the windows and balconies were lit up. And people were rushing to look down, like spectators at the theatre.

Two police cars were blocking the road. It was their coloured lights that were sweeping across the facades. Christine suddenly felt all her senses on alert. Part of the street had been cordoned off: the very bit where her building was located. She removed her hood and went up to a policeman. A cluster of people had gathered by the police tape.

'I live here,' she said, pointing to her building a few metres away.

'Just a moment,' said the policeman.

He turned to a man whom she instantly recognised: it was Beaulieu, the lieutenant who had taken her into custody. Beaulieu came up and stared at her.

'Mademoiselle Steinmeyer,' he said.

His tone was icier than ever. The rain was sprinkling his poodle mop and dripping from the tip of his nose.

'Did you know him?'

A crackle of messages over the radio, cameras flashing, rain sparkling in the spotlights, effervescence, agitation. Christine tried to control her malaise, to breathe calmly. Max . . . He lay sprawled among his cardboard boxes. From where she stood, she could see only his face – and his eyes, wide open, staring unblinking at the sky.

Men in white coats, gloves and blue disposable overshoes were bending over him. They were taking photographs with a big square camera, coming and going between his body and a van with a raised roof.

'Yes. His name was Max.'

'Max . . . ?'

'I don't know his last name. I occasionally stopped to chat with him. He used to be a teacher, before. And then he fell on hard times, the street . . . What happened?'

'Oh,' said Beaulieu, nodding his head in a self-important manner. Then he gave her a stern look.

'His name wasn't Max,' he corrected her.

'What?'

'His name was Jorge Do Nascimento, and he was never a teacher. He'd been living on the street for nearly thirty years, and he's certainly lived like this as long as I've known him. Jorge was pretty well known around Toulouse, believe me. Oh yes. And incidentally, Jorge was a drug addict. Back in the days when I was a uniformed officer, we were already hauling him in for being drunk and disorderly. I saw him take his shoes off, once. If you could have seen his feet, Mademoiselle Steinmeyer – what a mess they were. Do you know why? Multiple drug use,' he replied, to his own question. 'Since they don't have any money, homeless people will swallow anything that comes along. It starts with alcohol and medication, because some of that is reimbursed by Social Security: tranquillisers, drugs prescribed by doctors who aren't too fussy. Then comes the hash, of course. And heroin, too, it's cheaper than coke . . . But let me reassure you, Jorge didn't have Aids: he was just Hepatitis B and C positive. He probably got that way from sharing needles with other junkies. Oh, and he had just recovered from tuberculosis. You might have found him somewhat thin and tired. Apparently he was only forty-seven: he looked fifteen years older. He just suddenly seemed worn out.'

She saw again that weary glow she had noticed in his eyes, the first time: the look of someone who has admitted defeat, seen the absurdity of struggling.

'But one thing's for sure, he did love his books.' He raised his right hand, and she saw that he was holding a plastic evidence bag with a book inside: the Tolstoy she had seen in Max's pocket when he came up to her flat. She shuddered: it was splattered with blood. 'And classical music. I remember you could talk with him for hours about Russian novelists, and baroque music, and opera . . . Some people at the police station told him to shut up; I'd be there writing down titles, names of authors . . . I think I owe a good amount of my cultural knowledge to him,' he concluded with a faint, sad smile.

'Was he ever married?'

Beaulieu shook his head. He wiped his runny nose.

'Not to my knowledge, no.'

'Why did he lie to me?'

He shrugged his shoulders; Christine noticed they were drenched.

'You know, Jorge loved to make up stories, anecdotes, loved to invent fictional lives for himself. A bit like you. Maybe he was trying to fill a void, to embellish a reality that was too prosaic. Perhaps he got it from his penchant for novels, who knows? Through his lies he became a sort of character in a story, an offshoot of Dickens or Dumas.' He winked at her. 'It was thanks to him that I discovered all those authors. So I really liked Jorge.'

Then he shot her a look she could only qualify as suspicious.

'And now, he's dead. Right outside your building. And according to your neighbours, the two of you often stopped to chat. You even had him up to your flat.'

Her neighbour . . . She would gladly strangle that moralising, hypocritical bitch.

'What happened?' she asked again.

'He was stabbed. Last night. Except that no one noticed a thing until the blood stains were found on the pavement.'

*Last night.* The night her dog was killed. And she had been drugged and raped. She felt her entire body turning into a block of ice.

'Were you at home last night, Mademoiselle Steinmeyer?'

'No.'

'Where were you?'

'At the Grand Hôtel de l'Opéra. I spent the night there.'

'Why?'

'That's my business.'

Another suspicious gleam in his eyes.

'Why did you invite this man to your flat?'

She searched for an answer.

'Out of . . . compassion?' he prompted. 'You felt sorry for him because it was cold, it was snowing, and you saw him through your window every morning, is that it? And you decided to give him a hot meal and some human warmth?'

'Yes, that's right.'

He leaned over to her and she could feel his breath on her ear.

'Stop having me on. You're not that kind of person. You're lying; it's plain to see. You've crossed my path twice now, and both times, something rather violent has happened, isn't that right? I don't know what you're up to, or exactly what you're doing, but I'm going to find out. And I'm going to make your life hell until I discover your dirty little secret.'

He sniffed. He was getting a cold. Or else it was the expression of his scorn. She shook her damp hair and pulled up her hood.

'Have you finished?'

'For now.'

The rain had soaked the facade and the light stone had turned dark and shiny. She was trembling so hard with anger and fear that it took her three attempts to type in the door code correctly.

Servaz took out a handkerchief and blew his nose. He was shivering all over from the icy rain trickling down the back of his neck. Who was that woman? He noticed how Beaulieu went red in the face while speaking to her, his eyes glowing with rage – this from a man whose gaze ordinarily expressed only apathy. Earlier, while he had been shadowing Léonard Fontaine, he had seen the same woman meet him at McDonald's, and from where he sat at some distance he had observed their tense conversation. From time to time he had lost them from view, but he had managed all the same to register Fontaine's preoccupied air, as well as the perplexed, worried look on the woman's face when she went back out. Was she the next victim? He suddenly decided to follow her: he knew where Fontaine lived and worked, and now he knew his habits he would have no trouble finding him again, whereas he knew nothing about this woman.

And now here she was again at what looked very much like a crime scene. And incensing a lieutenant from the crime squad, by the looks of it. He made sure there were no public prosecutors around anywhere, then bent down and ducked under the police tape.

He flashed the badge dangling from his belt at the policeman on guard.

'Martin?' said Beaulieu, when he saw him approach. 'What are you doing here? I thought you were on sick leave.'

'Some friends live in this building and they called me. They want to know what's going on. And as I was in the neighbourhood . . .'

Beaulieu stared at him, not fooled for a minute.

'Tell them to watch the local news next time,' he replied, pointing to a camera under a big umbrella.

Servaz also saw onlookers filming the scene with their mobile phones. Fucking voyeurs. The lieutenant took out a pack of cigarettes and offered it to Servaz.

'No, thanks, I've quit.'

'Homeless man,' said Beaulieu. 'Stabbed last night. But as no one paid him any attention, it took a few hours for someone to realise there was blood oozing out of the cardboard. Jorge, does that ring a bell? At one point, he used to hang out by the police station near the Canal and Compans . . .'

Servaz nodded. 'He was sleeping in this street?'

'Recently, yes.'

Servaz sneezed and took out his handkerchief again.

'I saw you talking to a woman when I arrived. You looked very . . . annoyed. Who was it?'

The lieutenant shot him a cautious look.

'Why should you care?'

Servaz gave a falsely casual shrug of the shoulders.

'You know what it's like . . . Work is an addiction: it's hell trying to wean yourself off it.'

Beaulieu stared at him, as if he were about to say, 'No, I don't know, and I don't want to know.'

'She's a nutter,' he said at last. Servaz saw him become thoughtful. 'It's weird. She was involved in another matter recently; I even took her into custody. I can't believe it's just a coincidence.'

'Oh, really?'

'There was a girl who filed a complaint for assault and battery. She was a real mess. She said it was this woman who did it. Apparently, they had been indulging in some sexual experimentation that turned nasty. The victim had been *paid* to take part, and this woman wanted her money back. Or something like that. Two dykes who ended up in a catfight – both equally nuts, if you want my opinion.'

Beaulieu shook his head, disgusted, as if what the world was coming to was beyond all comprehension.

'But that's not all. Before that, the bitch showed up twice at the police station. The first time, she swore she had got a letter in her mailbox from some woman who said she was going to commit suicide, and she wanted us to investigate. It was plain to see she'd written it herself. The second time, it was an outright conspiracy story: some man took a leak on her doormat, broke into her flat, called her up at the radio station where she worked, and again at home. She even alleged she'd been drugged by the same young intern who filed the complaint for assault and battery, and then was taken unconscious back to her house, where she woke up stark naked! Completely out to lunch. And now they find a body outside her building, poor Jorge who she used to talk to more often than not and even invited up to her place once, according to the neighbour. Fuck, can you tell me what sort of woman invites a homeless man to her house and pays to have it off with a nineteen-year-old girl?'

'What's her name?' asked Servaz after a moment.

'Steinmeyer. Christine Steinmeyer.'

*Christine.*

'Did she talk about opera?'

The lieutenant spun around and gave him a sharp look.

'Bloody hell, how did you know that? She said the man who was harassing her had left an opera CD in her flat. You didn't just happen this way, did you?'

'No.'

'You bloody piss me off, Servaz: you could have said so sooner! What exactly do you know about this business? Because I don't know if you are aware of the fact, but I'm the one conducting the investigation!'

'Let me ask her a few questions,' he said. 'After that, I'll put you in the picture. What if she was telling the truth?'

He watched Beaulieu change colour. His mouth gaped.

'If you believe that, then you're as sick or as nuts as she is! You can't just interrogate her like that, it's up to me to do it.'

'Have you got the door code?'

'Servaz, for fuck's sake! What are you playing at?'

'I don't think you're seeing the whole picture. You're way off. Tell me one thing: have I often been mistaken?' He saw the young lieutenant hesitate. 'I'm not on duty, I'm on sick leave. So you're the one who will get the credit. I just want to ask her a few questions, that's all.'

He saw the other man shake his head.

'1945.'

'Seriously?'

'Seriously.'

She switched on the overhead light and listened to the silence. *He had been here.* She felt absolutely certain of it, all of a sudden. During her absence. It took terrific nerve for him to come back to the scene of his crime with Max's body – Jorge's body – downstairs. She held her breath, looked all around for any trace of him, then saw it: a CD. On the coffee table. She walked over.

*The Rape of Lucretia.* Benjamin Britten.

She bet anything it ended in suicide.

She noticed one more thing, next to it. A sheet of paper. A hand-written letter. Her hand shook slightly when she picked it up, and the shaking increased as she read it:

*You see what's in store for you. You had better do the job yourself. Finish it off. And if you try to rebel again, we'll go after your mother.*

Her head was spinning. For a moment, she was tempted to go to the bedroom window and call to the policeman downstairs. Then one detail caught her attention. And she felt weak at the knees. The note was in her own handwriting. Or a perfect imitation of it, in any case, for anyone who wasn't an expert. She wondered if even a graphologist would be able to tell the difference. She was trapped. Yet again. Because she knew what that bastard cop would think: that she'd written it herself, like the other letter. That she was crazy. And dangerous. Oh yes, fucking dangerous.

Yet again, her enemy was several steps ahead of her.

In all likelihood, before all this she would have been tempted to feel sorry for herself, given everything that had happened. But now her eyes were dry. Her thoughts turned to Iggy's body in the bath-room. She had to find him a grave; she couldn't leave him there indefinitely. What would happen if the police found him? She thought about the fact that her enemy had killed her dog, had raped her and killed a man, all in the space of one night: he had moved into a higher gear. There would be no more limits; nothing stopping his fury, now: it was a battle to the death. The thought was staggering. She remembered the woman who had committed suicide. Célia. She felt her rage return: she would be stronger, she was going to fight; she had nothing left to lose. She had to tell Léo what had happened last night, tell him that He had crossed a new line. She had to warn him of the danger. And Gérald, too.

Then the doorbell jangled in the silent flat and she froze.

She swung round to look at the front door. Was he crazy enough, bold enough, careless enough to come and see her with the street full of police? Why not? It would be one hell of an apotheosis . . . For a moment she pictured him pushing her out of the window and into the void, then disappearing.

*No*, said Madeleine's voice. *Stop inventing things; he's much too careful to show up here now. He's trying to wear you down, Chris. He won't take any pointless risks.*

The bell rang a second time. They were insisting.

The cops, she thought. *They've come to arrest me.*

She walked to the door and looked through the spyhole. She was sure she had never seen the man standing on the other side. In his forties. Thick brown hair and a six-day beard. Shadows under his eyes, hollow cheeks, but pleasant enough looking. He didn't look like a murderer. Or a sicko.

Then a police badge flashed in front of the spyhole, blocking her view, and she backed away. Shit . . .

She put on the safety chain and opened the door. He blinked as if he had just woken up, and they looked at each other cautiously through the opening.

'Yes?'

The man blinked again. He was silent for a moment, observing her, gauging her while he took the time to put his badge away. But there was nothing hostile about the way he looked at her. There was even the faint trace of a smile on his lips.

'My name is Martin Servaz,' he said. 'I'm a police commandant. And unlike my colleagues, I believe your story.'

# 37

# Accessories

At one point she had dozed off, curled up on the sofa. It was the effect of the adrenaline wearing off, he thought. How long had it been since she felt safe? She had pulled the woollen blanket up to her chin and, slumped in an armchair, he continued to observe her in silence.

Compared to her, he almost looked on top form. Dark shadows marked her cheeks, her hair was dry, the ends split, and her cheek-bones were visible beneath the skin like fossils in a palaeontologists' dig. She had been through hell and you could tell. And yet how strong she must have been, to have withstood the massive tremor that had devastated her life, sweeping aside entire aspects of it in just a few days.

She had told him about her meeting with Fontaine. Her doubts, and Cordélia's confession. But there was one element she did not have at her disposal: Mila's diary. Why didn't he mention it to her? He poured himself another glass of the excellent Côte-Rôtie she had opened two hours earlier. Why? Well, because he couldn't tell her he wanted to catch Fontaine red-handed and that basically she, Christine, was his . . . his . . . *bait*.

The telephone vibrated. Beaulieu again. He had already sent four text messages. Servaz got up and went into the bedroom.

'Servaz,' he said.

'For God's sake, what are you doing? You said a few questions! And why are you speaking so quietly?'

'Hush, she's sleeping.'

'What?!'

'It's not her. She didn't kill him.'

'Oh, yeah? How do you know?'

307

'Because I have my own little theory about who did.'

He distinctly heard Beaulieu sigh.

'Martin, are you raving mad or what? You show up out of nowhere and you know more than anyone else. And what about the door to door? And the pathologist's conclusions? You haven't even looked at the body, for Christ's sake! Who is it, in your opinion?'

'If I tell you, you won't believe me.'

'Huh, what? I've had my fill of your riddles, Servaz. Out with it.'

'Léonard Fontaine.'

There was a brief, incredulous silence before Beaulieu's voice came back on the line:

'The astronaut?'

'Mm-hmm.'

'You're joking, aren't you? Tell me it's a joke.'

'Not at all.'

'Servaz, I don't know what's going on, but if you're having me on . . .'

'I've never been more serious. Fontaine is mixed up in a business you cannot even begin to imagine. He is clever, and twisted, and he's behind all this. As surely as two and two make four. Do you remember that artist who took her own life last year at the Grand Hôtel Thomas Wilson? She was his mistress. As was Mila Bolsanski, the former astronaut, and she gave me her diary where she describes everything Fontaine made her go through. She accuses him of having beaten and raped her on multiple occasions while they were together at Star City, but the affair was hushed up by the Russians and the European Space Agency. As for Christine Steinmeyer, she met Fontaine at a bar, at his request, this very afternoon, before she ran into you on her way home.'

'How do you know?'

'I was there.'

This time the silence lasted longer.

'Until now, I had no way of cornering the bastard,' he continued. 'But if we manage to prove that it is Fontaine behind Jorge's death, well then that will change everything.'

Beaulieu let out a whistle.

'Bloody hell. Are you sure you're not leading me up the garden path?'

Behind the lieutenant's voice, Servaz heard a little beep informing him of an incoming text message.

'So then all this stuff about prank calls and kidnapped dogs and harassment was actually true?'

'It's all true. This woman is the victim of a very intelligent, very sick madman who has been making her life hell for quite a while already.'

'That's freaky,' said the copper quietly, on the other end of the line.

'It certainly is.'

'What do you think we should do?'

'Corinne Délia,' said Servaz. 'As of tomorrow, don't let her out of your sight. And her boyfriend – his name's Marcus. Above all her boyfriend. He might be the one who killed Jorge. I can't actually see Léonard Fontaine getting his own hands dirty. But if they're in touch, and we manage to corner them, they will help us bring Fontaine down.'

'And you?'

'I'm going to see what else I can get out of this woman.'

'And what do we tell our superiors?'

'Nothing. I'm supposed to be on sick leave, don't forget. And if Fontaine's name got out, they would all try to cover themselves. And we'd be fucked.'

'I was a bit tough on the woman,' said Beaulieu, his tone somewhat contrite.

'Well then, next time you can apologise.'

He hung up. Saw a little red '1' on the envelope symbolising his text messages. He pressed the button. Plop. Margot. He opened the message. Plop.

*I'll stop by tomorrow. 8 a.m. Kisses.*

He smiled. She didn't ask if it was convenient. If he planned to have a lie-in. If he would even be presentable at such a time. Or even if he would be there at all. No. She didn't ask any of that. He didn't really have a choice. But when had his daughter ever left him a choice, in anything? He smiled and typed 'OK', because it was shorter than 'all right', which he preferred, naturally, and he hit send.

She was awake. For a moment, she seemed not to recognise him, and he saw a fleeting spark of terror in her eyes, but it vanished immediately.

'I fell asleep,' she said. 'For long?'

'Not even an hour.'

He pointed to the packets of medication piled on the sofa.

'Are you . . . taking all that?'

She blushed.

'It's temporary,' she replied. 'I needed it . . . to keep going.'

'Mmm.'

He went over to the window, pressed his forehead against the cold glass, and looked out at the night streaked with lights. He could see his own face, so close, superimposed on the image. A worried face. Something was out there, outside. Something evil. Cunning. He must not underestimate it. The victims were not easy prey: they were women who were strong and intelligent. But their torturer was all that, too, and more: a formidable adversary, even for someone like Servaz. This thing manoeuvring in the shadows was just waiting for the next move, for new signals. Like a shark. They must be careful to give off as few signals as possible from now on.

'I know a place,' he said. 'A wonderful place. In the Montagne Noire. Above the lake at Saint-Ferréol. It's magnificent in autumn and in spring. And in winter, too, under a fine layer of snow. In fact, it's beautiful in every season. We could bury him up there, what do you think? It doesn't take much more than an hour to drive there.'

'Will you come with me?' she asked.

'Of course.'

He put Iggy's body in the freezer compartment, which he had emptied out beforehand. *A makeshift morgue . . .*

'The bottom drawer,' he said. 'Don't open it again, all right? Until I come back.'

'All right.'

He checked his watch.

'He won't come tonight,' he said. 'He probably won't come again with the police hanging about.'

She looked at him.

'Are you sure? Once all your colleagues have gone home? And everyone in the building is asleep again? And the street is deserted? How can I be sure?' He saw her hesitate. 'Can't you stay? Just for tonight. The time it will take me to get organised.'

He knew he could not ask for a surveillance team: he was not supposed to be on duty.

'I have someone to see tomorrow morning,' he replied, looking for Beaulieu's number in his contacts. 'First thing.'

'You can use my alarm clock. Please.'

He hesitated, then stopped.

'All right, I'll stay. But I'm taking the bed: I hate sleeping on sofas.' She smiled.


The woman lit a cigarette. The flame from her lighter briefly showed her features. She was parked a hundred metres further down the road, and she had watched the entire scene from her car without anyone noticing. The moment she'd heard the sirens, she had stopped strolling around and gone back to her car on the third floor of the Carmes car park.

Then she came to the street, far enough away to remain unnoticed, but close enough to see the entrance to the building.

The woman calmly switched on the ignition, put the car into gear, pulled out and went to park a bit closer, now that the forensic team and bystanders had left and the street was quiet again. Three o'clock in the morning. The cop had not come back out. She sat there, motionless, smoking one cigarette after the other, blowing the smoke towards the roof, in the dark, thinking that Christine had turned out to be tougher than expected. She would never have believed that bitch could withstand such a cataclysm. And even less, that she would fight back. Cordélia had called her earlier that day. She would have to deal with that, too. Things were getting out of hand. But it was all just a question of adjustments, corrections. The most annoying thing was that Christine had met this cop. She now had a forceful ally; she was no longer cut off and left to her own resources; they could no longer count on her to commit suicide. Shit. Perhaps it had been a mistake to put the cop on Célia Jablonka's and Léonard's trail. But she knew very well why she had done it. Except that now, it no longer seemed like such a good idea. Even if the cop was bound to suspect Léonard. This time, Léo would not get off so easily; she had left plenty of little clues that led straight to him.

Christine would not commit suicide. The woman felt a rush of hatred welling up in her throat.

*Stay calm.*

The time had come to finish her off. In a more . . . *radical* way.

She took one last puff, sending the delicious poison through her lungs; hatred, jealousy and anger were poisons, too, every bit as delicious.

# 38

# Exit the Stage

It was seven o'clock when the alarm went off but Servaz was already in the shower: he didn't want to be late for his meeting with his daughter. If Margot went to the rest home and he wasn't there, she would surely try to find out where he had spent the night.

The solution: get there early.

He looked at himself in the mirror as he came out of the shower. He would have liked to shave, but he had nothing to shave with. He didn't even have a change of clothes. He would change quickly when he got to the centre: his clothes had got wet and now they were dry they looked like cardboard. He combed his damp hair with his fingers and left the bathroom. In the living room, he glanced at the framed photograph on one of the few pieces of furniture. A picture of Christine with a bespectacled man in his thirties.

She was sitting on a stool lifting a mug of coffee to her lips, both elbows on the bar, when he asked:

'Who's this?'

She glanced over her shoulder.

'Gérald. My . . . partner.'

'Is everything going well with him'?

Again, a glance over her shoulder. Hesitant. Then she nodded.

'Well, like every couple, I suppose . . . there are ups and downs. But Gérald is a good man.'

'What does he do for a living?'

'Research . . . Space research.'

One drawer opening, another closing. Gérald. A name on a mental label. And a little light blinking: Space . . . Servaz felt restless.

'I have to go,' he said. 'Don't open the door to anyone but me or Lieutenant Beaulieu. You have my number. You can call me at any time. And here is Beaulieu's, just in case you can't get through to me. And if someone comes to the door with a police badge, tell them to get lost: there are a multitude of fake cards out there.'

She nodded, worried.

'What if we tried to trap him?' she said.

He raised an eyebrow.

'If I leave the flat and someone waits for him inside?'

Servaz shook his head.

'He won't fall for it. He'll know we're here. He's far too clever.'

These last words seemed to make her nervous. With a thrust of her chin she showed she had understood, not looking at him, her jaw clenched. Then she picked up her coffee cup again, eyes down, her back turned.

'I'll drop by again later,' he said. 'We'll come up with a strategy.'

That last word sounded a bit too grand, he thought. And not necessarily reassuring: it meant he hadn't got one yet.

There was fog, that Thursday morning. Dense, damp fog.

He climbed quickly up to his room then came back down just as a red Citroën with a white roof pulled into the car park. He emerged from the lobby and saw Margot give him a luminous smile as she locked her car.

He felt his heart contract on seeing her. But he liked the feeling.

Her long, lanky legs strode across the car park, her slim figure in tight jeans and a chunky jumper. To say she had changed over recent years was a momentous understatement. Three years earlier – when Margot had found herself at the epicentre of an affair that had ended with the suicide of one boy in her class and the imprisonment of another – she had been pierced and tattooed, and had dyed her hair a colour that was unusual, to say the least, and stuck up in unruly tufts. She had been admitted to the most prestigious prep school in the region (he still remembered that magnificent summer's day when he had driven her to Marsac for the first time): a place steeped in ancestral traditions and an almost monastic rigour; but for all that, during that period Margot still papered her walls with posters from horror films, and listened to music like Marilyn Manson. He didn't know what she was into nowadays, but he did know that in hardly longer than it takes for a tadpole to become a frog, his daughter had transformed into a woman.

'Papa,' she said simply as she gave him a kiss (even her voice had changed: the first time he had noticed he had thought it was her mother on the telephone).

And yet her face was the same. She would always look like a little wild animal, which could hardly fail to charm all the young men conquered by her poise and her rebellious side. She was carrying a handbag, from which she took a little gift-wrapped package tied with golden ribbon and a bow. He smiled like a kid.

'What is it?'

'Open it.'

The damp fog enveloped him.

'Come, let's go inside,' he said. 'It's too cold out.'

He took her to the little lounge on the northern side of the building; as he expected, there was no one there.

He tore off the paper. A box set. Mahler, *The Complete Works*. A profile of the master against a background of very Klimtian inspiration: very kitsch. Sixteen CDs. EMI Classics. He had heard about this box set, released in 2010; he seemed to recall that there were none of the interpretations he preferred, no Bernstein or Haitink or Kubelik; but a quick look revealed, to his relief, names such as Kathleen Ferrier, Barbirolli, Christa Ludwig, Bruno Walter, Klemperer and Fischer-Dieskau.

'Do you like it?'

'It's absolutely marvellous. I could not dream of a better gift. Thank you.'

His words sounded exaggerated, but she pretended not to notice. They hugged again.

'You're looking better than last time,' she said.

'I'm feeling better.'

'I'm going away, Papa.'

He looked up.

'Really? Away, where?'

'Québec. I've got a temporary job there.'

Québec? He felt something like an air pocket in his stomach. He could not stand plane travel.

'Why not . . . *here*?'

No sooner had he said it than he realised how naïve his question was.

'In one year at the job centre, I have applied for 140 positions.

315

End result, ten actual replies, all negative, and that's all I got. Last month, I sent four emails to companies in Québec. I got four answers, two of them positive. It's dead here, Papa. There is no future in this country. I'm leaving in four months. On a work-holiday permit.'

He knew his daughter wanted to work in communication. But he had no idea what that meant. Baker, cop, firefighter, engineer, mechanic, even dealer or contract killer: those were concrete trades. But communication? What did that mean?

'For how long?' he asked.

'A year. To begin with.'

A year! He pictured himself crossing the Atlantic for hours on board a commercial airliner, stuck against the window in economy, nothing but ocean as far as he could see, and clouds, and turbulence, and flight attendants looking at him pityingly and condescendingly.

He looked down at the photograph of Mahler again. And thought of the picture of Christine's boyfriend in her living room. Gérald. He'd got a funny feeling when he saw him.

'. . . but if I get a young professional permit, I'll stay on, and then I . . .'

'Stay' . . . the word rang out as if it were tolling the knell of their father–daughter relationship.

That face. A thought suddenly struck him: it was familiar. He was sure he'd seen it somewhere before. He hadn't recognised it at the time because . . . because what? And suddenly, he knew: because in the other photograph, he was pictured in profile and not face on. *The gala evening at the Capitole*: the man in the mirror, wearing glasses, the one who was handing his business card to Célia Jablonka.

Did it mean anything? Of course it did! This Gérald had known Célia, and he knew Christine: he was another link between the two, along with Fontaine. Yes, but there was nothing to show he had crossed paths with Mila. And her journal was all about Fontaine. Still, the detail bugged him. He was a cop: he didn't believe in coincidence.

'You know, in Québec,' his daughter was saying, 'if you make an effort, they start giving you responsibility in no time. You can rise quickly. You—'

His mobile vibrated in his pocket.

'Excuse me.'

She gave him a dark look. It was Beaulieu. He felt a tingling at the back of his neck.

'Yes?'

'We've got a real problem.' Beaulieu's voice was tense. 'I've lost Marcus. This morning he left for the Métro. I followed him. Along the entire line. Except that his car, or someone else's, was waiting for him at the Balma car park. He got away. I just had time to write down the number plate.'

'Fuck!'

'What's going on?' said his daughter. 'Have you started working again? I thought you were on sick leave.'

And what he heard in her voice was more of a reproach than a question. Disappointment that once again he didn't have time for her, just when she was telling him she had made one of the most important decisions of her life.

'It's nothing,' he said. 'Go on.'

But it wasn't nothing. There was a knot in his stomach.

In the bathroom, she let a scorching flow of water from the shower wash away all the tension and pain from spending a night on the sofa. She had bolted the front door. Locked the door to the bathroom. Next to the sink she had her club, her tear-gas key ring and the stun gun.

She relaxed for a moment until she thought she heard something through the noise of the water. She turned off the tap, on the alert, but it must have been a sound from within the building or the pipes. She got back out, dried off with the huge towel hanging from the towel rail, and was about to brush her teeth when the telephone rang. Not her official telephone. The one with a prepaid card.

Léo.

'Christine, are you there? At home? I have to see you.'

'What's going on?'

'I'll explain. Something is going to happen today. Listen carefully: here's what we're going to do.'

She wrote down the place and the time. What was he driving at? She wondered if she should tell the cop, but Léo had told her not to mention it to anyone for the time being. She left the bathroom and went to the living room. Her laptop was open on the bar. She had a moment of doubt: had she opened it this morning? She went back to get the stun gun and the club then walked over to the open-plan kitchen. A new email had arrived. Her pulse sped up.

She climbed up onto the bar stool and saw that it was from Denise. There was a lump in her throat as she opened it:

*I'm sorry: I didn't believe you, I thought you were crazy. I was wrong.*
*I have to see you. It's about Gérald. Don't tell anyone. Here's my address.*
*I'll wait for you all day.*
*Denise*

'Will you come and see me?'

Aeroplanes: turbulence, clouds breaking open against the aircraft, vibrations in his seat and his spine to remind him that there were 11,000 metres of void beneath him. He felt his throat seize up.

'Of course I will, sweetheart.'

He knew his daughter. It was pointless trying to make her change her mind. And anyway, what kind of excuse could he give? The cold? The snow? The endless winters? His fear of flying?

For a moment, they looked at each other in silence, then Margot spoke.

'Take care of yourself, Papa.'

She pressed her remote key ring and the red and white car beeped.

'Will I see you again before you leave?'

'Of course you will.'

He watched her turn around and give him a little wave, and he waved back, then she pulled out onto the narrow, straight road and vanished. He knew that what had just happened was important, but his mind was completely absorbed by other things. He took out his mobile. Dialled Christine's number. It rang, then he heard it go into voicemail.

He parked in a prohibited spot, leapt out and ran to the door of the building through the fog. *1945.* When the lift reached the third floor, he flung the cage door open. Rammed his finger on the doorbell. Once, twice. No answer. He pounded on the door. Called out. Was tempted to break the door down.

He put his ear up against the door. Silence. Only the pounding in his chest. A door opened on the landing behind him.

'Are you looking for Mademoiselle Steinmeyer?'

A stern, shrill voice. He swung round and saw a tiny little grey-haired woman looking daggers at him.

'Yes,' he replied, showing her his card.

'She went out.'

'Did she say where she was going?'

A scornful sniff.

'What Mademoiselle Steinmeyer says or does is of no interest to me whatsoever.'

'I thank you,' he replied, his tone implying just the opposite.

Shit! He did not know which was more infuriating. That Beaulieu had let Marcus get away, or that Christine had gone out without telling him. His mind was racing. Why the hell didn't she answer her phone? It was as if his veins were being injected with regular doses of adrenaline; he no longer felt fatigue, only an ever-increasing anxiety. A feeling of imminent catastrophe. He went back downstairs and out onto the pavement. A warden was slipping a parking ticket under his windscreen wiper. He showed her his warrant card, not saying anything. She gave him roughly the same look as the old biddy upstairs. His daughter leaving for the ends of the earth, Marcus on the loose, Christine vanished into thin air . . . Bloody fucking waste of a morning.

By noon, they still hadn't found her. Or Marcus. And she wasn't answering their calls. There was something wrong. In his mind, alarm signals were going off one after the other.

'What shall we do?' said Beaulieu on the phone. (This was definitely his favourite question.)

'I've got her number. Start an urgent requisition . . . for "preservation of human life". We'll inform the public prosecutor's office after that. One for the network provider and one for Deveryware. Go through Lévêque at Operational Documentation: he knows them; it will be quicker. Tell him the request is from me.'

'Fine,' said Beaulieu.

'Keep me posted.'

Beaulieu hung up. Servaz was nervous. Very nervous. He hoped that Lévêque would understand the urgency of the matter, and allow them to gain precious time: as a criminal analyst, he had a privileged relationship with the three network providers. Deveryware, on the other hand, was a company that specialised in the geolocation of smartphones: they had sold their software to the police. Once the network provider had sent them the coordinates, the company would forward Lévêque a link to a map-based portal, where the analyst could keep constant track of Christine's mobile. Normally this took three or four hours to set up, but it could be done in thirty or forty-five minutes if they put the pressure on. Even so, Servaz was under no illusions: if Christine was in town, it would mean hundreds or even thousands of possible addresses and hiding places. It would be impossible to check them all. It would be impossible even if they could pinpoint the position by triangulating several relays, on the assumption they could put enough pressure on the provider to do that. All they could do was pray that the zone would be out in the sticks. Or would correspond to the address of someone he already knew: Fontaine, Gérald or Cordélia.

He looked at the door. He had come back to the flat. *Fuck it.* He slipped a jemmy into the space between the door and the doorframe and pressed on it with all his strength. There was a cracking sound; he heard the lock yield, then fall with a clang to the floor on the other side, while the door opened out towards him. He rushed in.

'Christine?'

No answer. He went into the living room. And saw it right away: her mobile . . .

His own rang in his pocket. He answered.

'She's at home,' said Beaulieu. 'Or not far from there. They located her.'

He looked at the device.

'No, she's not here. Just the phone.'

He hung up. And suddenly, he knew. Because he'd been here before. The moment when people slip through your fingers. When things don't go as planned. *He'd lost her.* And it was his fault, once again: he shouldn't have left her alone.

The email address and the credit card number on the hotel system had led to an impasse; as had the list of guests who had lost their key. The box in which he'd received the clue had been mass produced: whoever was behind it all knew how to cover his tracks.

Servaz closed his eyes, and took a deep breath.

Cursed himself.

He knew he would not see her alive again.

# 39

# Pit

Trees swept by, like ghosts in the mist, on either side of the road. They emerged from the fog and immediately returned to it, like images from a dream that fade with the awakening.

She thought about the policeman who had slept at her place. *Servaz.* He seemed a decent sort. She wanted to confide in him. But Léo had explained that given the present state of things, her policeman – however well intentioned he might be – had no evidence, and could not prove anything against his enemy; in other words, no judge would ask for an indictment, let alone preventive detention, on the basis of such theoretical evidence. The cop knew this, naturally. It was out of the question for him to let them take the law into their own hands. For Christine, the problem lay elsewhere: from now on it was her, or the enemy . . . There was no alternative: an equation with two unknowns.

She spared a thought for Max/Jorge, whose corpse must be resting at the morgue in Toulouse, and felt a direct injection of anger that was immediately converted into action.

*A yellow house in the mist . . .*

She could see it now, nestled in the fog-shrouded landscape. The GPS was clear. This was the place.

She slowed down, shifted into second gear.

A little house that was neither elegant nor imposing. Just isolated. A garden with a chain-link fence, a kennel, a chalet-style garden shed under a tall scrawny fir tree. Cultivated fields all around, blankets of fog rolling over them. The gate was open. She drove across the gravel and stopped; she reached for the stun gun and the spray, slipped them into the pockets of her sweatshirt, and got out. She instantly felt the damp chill. Through the fog came a faint scent of ploughed earth, cows, and something burning. She left the engine running. The smoke from the exhaust pipe dissolved into the mist. She walked towards the front door, the gravel crunching under her feet.

'Hello, Christine.'

She recognised the voice. She turned around, holding the stun gun.

'Tsk, tsk, you don't intend to use that again, do you? Once was enough, thank you.'

He was sitting cross-legged in the kennel, the top of his head almost touching the sloping roof, his face half in shadow, and the black eye of the barrel of his gun was staring right at her.

'Throw them down, please,' said Marcus.

He crawled out of the kennel, stood up, stretched and made a face.

'You really did me over, I have to say.'

He limped to her across the gravel, and when he was close enough he slapped her. She staggered, took a step back, and lifted one hand to her stinging cheek. She thought what a strange asymmetrical couple they made, he and that beanstalk of a Cordélia.

'That was for my knees,' he said, looking at her calmly, as if he were twice his actual height. He pointed to the house. 'Don't worry, the owners have gone on holiday. I'm the one who opened the shutters.'

He stepped forward and started frisking her.

'It's not what you expected, is it?' He pretended to be surprised as he ran his hands all over her body. 'Don't worry. We'll do things my way, if you don't mind. I don't want to see the cops show up here any more than you do. Where is your phone?'

'On the passenger seat.'

He went round, opened the door, reached for the prepaid mobile, threw it to the ground and stamped on it several times until it was in a carrion-like state, its entrails exposed to the air.

'Good. Let's go. Get behind the wheel.'

They set off down the road. Marcus made a quick phone call: 'I've got her.' For thirty minutes or more, he showed the way: *turn right . . . turn left . . . keep straight . . .* until they eventually drove up a long straight stretch beneath a tunnel of plane trees, whose gnarled branches met above the road like the arches of a cathedral. There was a tall house at the very end. She slowed down over the last hundred metres, and a house emerged from the fog, slowly coming nearer, cube-like with its two floors of tall, identical windows. Cube-like but imposing: thick walls, double chimneys on either side, and small windows at ground level opening onto cellars she imagined must be vast, deep and very dark. This house, unlike the yellow one, had seen centuries go by; it had watched whole generations grow up and die; it had known many secrets, many deaths and births – this was, oddly, what she was thinking as she drove along the open, barren space, which was bordered by a graceful row of poplars that had replaced the plane trees at the end of the tunnel. There were no vehicles in sight, but there was a corrugated metal garage a dozen or so metres further on.

'Here we are.'

The front door opened as they were getting out of the car. The woman who stood on the threshold was tall and slim in the pale swirls of mist; Christine was sure she had never met her before and yet, strangely, her face looked familiar. She glanced at Marcus, who gestured towards the entrance with his gun, his hand curled around the smooth black grip. The woman was smiling.

'Who are you? Where is Denise?'

The woman's smile broadened. She had big shoulders and the complexion of a sportswoman.

'Hello, Christine. We meet at last.'

Strains of music rose in the cold air from inside the house. Christine shuddered.

*Opera . . .*

The corridor. An endless passageway leading to a well-equipped kitchen, vast and modern, unlike the corridor which was full of antique furniture and paintings.

*Opera . . .* The music was coming from another room and spread all through the house. It swelled, receded, swelled again, like sails on a ship. Christine got the impression it was flowing directly through her veins.

Then she was there before her: a dark woman with a handsome face, slightly worn by the years.

'Were you expecting someone else? You must have thought you were so close.'

'Where is Denise?'

'There is no Denise. I'm the one who sent you that email. Is she clean? Did you search her?' Marcus gave an almost imperceptible nod, his way of informing her that this sort of question was unnecessary: he knew his job, for fuck's sake. 'Or rather,' said the woman, turning back to Christine, 'Denise has nothing to do with this. Oh, and while I think of it, she *is* fucking him, your Gérald. She was fucking him long before he started to go cold on you. She put on quite an act for you in that café, didn't she? Oh, come on, don't be too hard on her: who could resist Denise? Not someone like Gérald, in any case. Far too weak, far too lazy, far too *boring*: she'll tire of him, you'll see.'

The woman's tone was light, but Christine sensed something sinister and threatening underneath.

'Who are you?' Her voice was still firm. She was almost surprised.

'My name is Mila Bolsanski.'

The woman cried out, 'Thomas!' and Christine saw something move on her right, a door opening, faint footsteps. A small boy came in. Three or four years old. He gazed at her with sad brown eyes.

'And this is my son, Thomas,' said the woman. 'Say hello, Thomas. *Thomas is Léo's son.*'

'Hello,' said Thomas.

'Go back to your room, darling.'

The boy obeyed and disappeared. He did not seem particularly curious. For a fraction of a second, he made her think of Madeleine at the end, when everything seemed to wash over her without leaving a trace. *Léo's son* . . . Christine noticed that Marcus was again aiming his gun at her, now that the child had left the room. She looked at the woman. Where had she seen her before? She sensed that the answer was imminent.

'Come with me,' said the woman.

She opened the door to the room behind the kitchen and switched on a light. Christine saw an entire wall covered with an immense photograph representing the earth seen from space. There was a white sofa in front of it and a coffee table with some books on it. Christine saw immediately that they were all on the same subject. She thought about Léo. Then, suddenly, it dawned on her. Mila Bolsanski. Of course: the astronaut. She had seen her face on television a few years ago. The second Frenchwoman in space. If her memory served, the mission had been interrupted; something had happened up there. An accident. She even seemed to recall, now, that Léo had been on that same mission. She realised he had never brought up the subject in her presence, and she shivered.

'Do you hear the music?' said Mila. 'Another opera. *Götterdämmerung*. At the end, Brünnhilde, the former Valkyrie, hurls herself into Siegfried's funeral pyre. I've always loved opera. It's incredible how many operas are about suicide. But you've been clinging too dearly to life, Christine, that's your problem.'

Christine looked around the rest of the room. A varnished black piano. Sheet music and, on top, framed photographs. At the back, in front of the picture window, was a very strange fireplace in white marble where a hollowed-out hearth let in glimpses of the fog beyond.

'Opera is the realm of pure emotion. When passion, sorrow, suffering and madness attain such a degree of saturation that words become powerless to express them. Only song can do that. It surpasses the limits of understanding, of logic: it's indescribable.'

The music soared, majestic. Christine thought about the little boy. He must hear it from his room, in spite of the thick walls. His toys – Transformers, a red fire engine, a basketball – were scattered across the carpet.

'Do you know what makes a good libretto? It's simple: the action has to move quickly, and the key moments have to come in succession, all the way to the climax. Which has to be tragic, of course. Musically, the centrepiece is the *aria da capo*, in three parts – the third being a reprise of the first. It must not, however, spoil the dramatic progression; it's all a matter of striking the right balance . . .'

The soprano's voice reached for a high note.

'There, do you hear that?'

'Hear what?' replied Christine, unfazed. 'That ridiculous crooning? It's a bit much, don't you think?'

She saw a moment of doubt in the astronaut's eyes, like a spike on an ECG monitor.

*Yes, my dear, you thought you'd broken me, destroyed me, so you'd be able to enjoy your victory. Not this time. This time, it hasn't gone the way you hoped.*

She saw Mila turn to Marcus.

'Do you have what I asked you for?'

He nodded, put his gloved hand into the pocket of his parka and brought out a little phial. He looked blankly at Christine through his long blond lashes.

Christine saw the water jug. And the glass on the coffee table. She saw Mila bend over, pick up the jug, fill the glass halfway. *Don't show them you're frightened,* thought Christine. Then Mila broke the phial above the glass and mixed it in.

'Here. Drink this,' she said.

'Again? You don't think this is getting a bit repetitive?'

'Drink,' said Marcus, waving his gun at her. 'Hurry up. You have three seconds. One . . . Two . . .'

She hesitated, looked at the glass, lifted it to her lips. It tasted like the vitamin drinks from her childhood, the ones her mother bought at the chemist's. She drank.

'So, Célia: that was you?'

Mila shot her an icy look.

'She thought she had a right to Léo, she was clinging. And Léo seemed prepared to leave his wife for her. It was legitimate defence: Léo is mine, he's the father of my child.'

'But he's married.'

Her gaze turned even darker.

'You call that a marriage? I call it a joke. They're getting divorced, didn't you know?' She shrugged. 'Sooner or later, he'll come back to me. When he finally understands, when I'm all he's got. But that ridiculous Célia stood in our way – and you did, too. So I made her life hell. And when she began to act like a crazy woman, losing weight, losing her looks, losing her sense of humour, getting more and more drab and grim-looking . . . Well, our dear Léo left her. She couldn't take it. You know what happened after that.'

Christine nodded.

'Hmm. So now it's my turn,' she said. 'It's a pity you've done all this for nothing. I dumped Léo last month. He would have told you if you'd asked.'

'You're lying.'

'Why should I lie? In any case, it's a bit late for turning back, isn't it?'

Again Mila looked at her, surprised. No doubt she was expecting Christine to plead with her to spare her life. To start crying.

'And how did you find Marcus?'

'I met Marcus thanks to some friends in Moscow. Very precious friends. Friendships I forged while we were at Star City. Marcus is one of their *subagents*, as it were, in France. He came here three years ago but he learned French in Russia. He and his friends are very good at going through the trash, finding information, sneaking into people's places at night, finding out everything there is to know about them, extracting confessions from them, tinkering with locks and computers . . .'

With her fingertip she caressed the tattoo on the little man's neck.

'Marcus is not very curious. He doesn't ask questions. That is his chief quality. Except questions about his pay.'

Christine noticed that daylight was fading outside. And the fog was lifting. She could see dark leaves beyond the picture window, and a red glow.

'Marcus and Cordélia: a strange couple, don't you think? According to what he told me, they met when she was trying to pick his pockets in the Métro. No doubt she thought the little man was harmless. It wasn't planned, but since Cordélia proved particularly gifted at duplicity and fraud, when I found out that your radio station was looking for an intern, I suggested she apply for the position – with a fake CV, naturally. Your Guillaumot was none the wiser. In all fairness, Cordélia is very good at finding people's weak spots. Did you know that your boss likes a striptease in the office after hours? Men are all the same.'

'I – I don't feel very well.'

It was true. Christine felt as if the entire room was slowly beginning to spin, like a merry-go-round starting up.

'I . . . What was in that phial?' Her eyes flickered. 'You won't get away with this. Léo suspects something. And that cop, he'll trace you.'

There was a smile as thin as a razor blade on Mila's lips.

'I wrote a diary,' she said quietly. 'A fake diary. About what supposedly happened at Star City. About what Léo is supposed to have done to me.'

She smiled.

'I gave it to Servaz. He's reading it at this very moment. And when he's done he will no longer have the slightest doubt about Léo's guilt.'

'Why?'

'Because, when Léo ends up alone, abandoned by everyone, I'll go and see him in prison, I'll reconquer him one day at a time. And he'll realise I'm all he has; he'll realise the strength of my love. And my devotion. Everything I've done for him. He'll open his eyes and he will love me the way he did before . . . at the beginning.'

Christine bit her lower lip. *Christ, this woman was crazy. Certifiable.* She glanced over at Marcus, but he kept his gun trained on her with perfect indifference. He'd been paid. That was enough.

'Let's go,' said Mila, looking at her watch, then at Marcus.

She opened a low wooden door in the thick stone wall behind her. Outside, the fog was nearly all gone; only a few banners of mist curled around the base of the trees. On this side, a concrete pergola led from the house to the edge of the woods, supporting Virginia creeper that had become dry and grey in winter.

'Move,' said Marcus, prodding Christine in the back with the barrel of his gun.

She stiffened. Took three steps. Stopped.

'What are you going to do?'

'Move, I said!'

They reached the forest. The way ahead was scarcely visible. The sun was setting behind the branches and trees that framed it like a cage at the top of the hill, shooting pale rays, red and cold like frozen blood, between the thin black trunks. A little stream shone like a copper sculpture, flowing through a thick spongy carpet of dead leaves.

She felt her heart begin to beat wildly, uncontrollably. The sky was bleeding.

'Move.'

They walked along the stream, climbing the slope with difficulty. Marcus went ahead of her. He knew she wouldn't get far if she tried to escape.

'Shit, my head is spinning,' she said, slowing down.

She skidded and landed on her hands and knees. Brown mud and leaves stuck to her palms. She got up; paused for a moment to regain her balance and wipe her hands. Marcus had stopped to wait, his face rigorously inexpressive. Mila drew level.

'Let's go.'

A gentle rain began to fall. Cold little drops like a spray on her face.

'So this is where it's going to end?' she said. 'In the woods.'

In front of her, Marcus bent down to go under a low hanging branch.

'Hurry up!' he said with his slight accent. 'We have other things to do.'

He came back and they each grabbed her by one arm to make her move more quickly. They went down into a small gully, a place where the trees were not as dense. Almost a clearing. Suddenly, she began to fight back, digging her heels into the slippery ground with all her strength when she saw the dark hole at the end of the hollow, a shovel lying next to it. They dragged her forward.

'No! No!'

She struggled.

They let her go; Marcus aimed his gun at her.

'Lie down in the hole.'

A gnarled old tree twisted like a gymnast by the edge of the pit. A few of its roots had been cleanly severed by the steel edge of the shovel.

She turned around and faced them.

'*No! Wait! Wait!*'

Marcus pushed her. She fell backwards. *She was sinking like a stone. She was drowning.* Fortunately, the earth in the pit was loose, and she landed on a very soft mattress. Christine opened her eyes. She was lying on her back. The smell of freshly turned soil filled her nostrils; the rain was falling harder now on her face, into her eyes and her hair full of dirt.

'Women make better killers than men,' said Mila above her. 'They're more sophisticated and have more imagination, they think things through.'

'You do it,' said Marcus, nodding towards Christine.

From inside the hole, she saw him hand the gun to Mila, holding it by the barrel. And she saw the fierce expression on Mila's face.

'What? What are you talking about? Do your job! It's what I paid you for!'

'*Nyet.* You didn't pay enough for me to risk life in prison,' he said. '*Pazhalsta*: please.'

Mila gave a nasty laugh as she took the weapon by the grip.

'And there was I thinking you had balls . . . So is this what the Russian mafia has come to.'

Calmly, he took out a packet of cigarettes, without bothering to respond, and lit one. Smiled. Christine turned her head slightly. Was she dreaming, or were those really earthworms wriggling where the shovel had severed the forest's tender flesh? She saw them stirring just a few inches from her cheek, beneath a tangle of fine white roots.

Marcus's voice:

'Up to you, now, *Gaspazha*. There are only two bullets. So don't waste them.'

Christine closed her eyes.

Suddenly she felt herself trembling with both fear and despair. She wanted to leap out of the pit and run away as fast as she could. With her eyes closed, she did not see Mila take a step closer to the edge of the grave and point the gun in her direction.

She did not see her trembling slightly.

Taking aim.

Squeezing the trigger.

The report exploded through the woods and reverberated. It made all the birds in the forest fly away. The two bullets hit her right in the thorax, and her body jolted with each impact. A moment later, two red flowers spread across her jumper, soaking the wool. One last tremor. Her body arched and stiffened. A trail of blood from her lips, and it was all over.

Simple.

Clean.

Final.

The barrel of the gun was still smoking. Mila stared at Christine's body. The gun in her hand was trembling violently. She had never killed anyone before. Or in any case, not directly.

Marcus picked up the shovel.

'Welcome to the club,' he said, tossing the first shovelful of earth onto the dead woman's face.

# ACT III

I know that for her deep distress
there is no consolation.
But it is necessary to provide
for the child's future.

*Madame Butterfly*

# 40

## Aria da capo

It was a cold, clear January morning, and Fontaine was swimming naked in the pool while Servaz, through his binoculars, observed his muscular back, his slender legs cleaving through the steaming water. Then he went back to his car, which was as cold as a freezer, put the binoculars in the glove box and slowly pulled away.

Too early. It was still too early to confront Léonard Fontaine, but he knew that sooner or later they would meet. It was inevitable. As soon as he had more cards to play; a better hand.

Where had Christine Steinmeyer gone?

She had given no sign of life for the last ten days. While he was driving, staring ahead of him at the ribbon of motorway and the pale lights of the cars, it seemed to him that there was one word blinking in dazzling neon letters in his mind. *Dead.* Christine Steinmeyer was dead. Buried somewhere. They had all tried to piece together her trail on the morning she left the house never to return, but in vain. No one had seen her since. Not her fiancé, nor her parents, nor her former colleagues from Radio Five. An investigation had been opened for suspicious disappearance. Corinne Délia and Marcus – whose real name was Yegor Nemtsov – had been questioned at length. But they had not let anything slip. Servaz was sorry he couldn't be there for the interviews. But he had heard about them in detail from Vincent and Samira, and also from Beaulieu, who had decided to collaborate and who seemed to be feeling rather guilty.

Like Servaz, Beaulieu was now convinced that Yegor 'Marcus' Nemtsov had something to do with Christine's disappearance. Servaz thought about Mila's diary, still in his possession. About the photographs showing Fontaine together with Célia Jablonka. About what Christine had shared with him. Mila-Célia-Christine:

333

the triangle of three women who had been the astronaut's mistresses. Mila's testimony was devastating. Ever since he had crept into the house and seen the book on Fontaine's night table, Servaz had been convinced that Fontaine was the man he was looking for. And now Christine had disappeared. But no judge would order an investigation with so little to go on. He knew he would have to push Fontaine to make a mistake. But how? The man was cautious, and tough.

Mila watched as Thomas gave her a last wave before running off to join his mates under the huge plane trees in the playground, his satchel on his back. Then she went back to her car. It was Friday. She didn't work on Fridays. She turned the ignition on the four-wheel drive and headed for her usual hypermarket, left the car in the car park, walked over to the rows of shopping trolleys, and slotted a coin into one of them.

Mila pushed her trolley unhurriedly for almost an hour up and down the aisles. Despite the fact it was Friday morning, the store was crowded. She wove in and out, shoved past those who got in her way, was shoved in return, checked her list at regular intervals even though she always bought the same things week after week, and made one exception for a bottle of Clos Vougeot. She would go to the farmers' market the following day to take care of the perishable stuff.

She hunted for the shortest queue and joined it: there were fifteen people ahead of her and by the time she got to the till, roughly just as many behind her.

The check-out assistant greeted her politely and began to scan her purchases. Mila walked through the metal detector to collect them on the other side. There was a sudden strident wailing; the assistant looked up abruptly and studied Mila more attentively.

'Please step back, madame,' she said, 'and go through again.'

Mila sighed and took one step back. And another forward. Again there was the wail of the alarm, deafening, causing everyone in the store to look their way. The check-out assistant gave her a nasty look.

'Step back, madame, step back.' Her voice was increasingly irritated. 'Are you sure you don't have anything in your pocket?'

It wasn't exactly an accusation, but it was a bit more than a question. Mila realised that it was not only the customers in her queue who were staring at her, but also those in the neighbouring lines. Her cheeks went red with shame.

She put one hand in her coat pocket. There *was* something, all the way at the bottom. Her fingers closed around a plastic box, and she pulled it out. She looked at it: a gift card for perfume. For a value of €150.

The check-out assistant was frowning.

'I don't understand,' said Mila.

'Do you want it or not?' she snapped, with a menacing look.

'I don't know what this card is doing in my pocket,' answered Mila curtly, looking daggers at the assistant.

'Okay. Give it to me and go back through the metal detector, please.'

Mila swallowed her fury and put the gift card in the woman's outstretched hand. She took one step backwards, another one forwards, a knot in her belly.

The detector wailed, jangling her nerves. She could hear exclamations in the queue behind her.

'Bloody hell!' shouted the check-out assistant.

She gave Mila a furious look, picked up the telephone and spoke quickly into the receiver, then looked down the aisle that went past the check-outs, drumming impatiently on her counter. In the queue, people were beginning to complain vociferously. Mila could hear them: 'What's going on?' 'Why aren't we moving?' And their blunt replies: 'A shoplifter', 'Unfortunately, this is what France has come to.' She saw a security guard walking briskly up the aisle. A tall black man, dressed in a dark grey suit. He gave her a quick, professional look then leaned down to hear the check-out assistant's explanation. All with the utmost discretion: they wouldn't make waves, they would handle the problem efficiently; they were used to it.

Her legs were shaking, her head was spinning. Dozens of people looking at her.

'Please come with me.'

'Listen, I don't know what—'

'Please follow me, madame. Don't make a fuss. We'll deal with this calmly, all right?'

'What's going on?' said a voice behind them.

A second security guard. White, older, in a too-tight suit. A great

335

hulking brute who clearly didn't look after himself, with a sly expression and cheeks pitted like vines after a hailstorm. He scrutinised Mila, while the other man repeated in a low voice what the check-out assistant had told him. Then he put a large hand on her arm. She shook him off abruptly.

'Get off me!'

'Okay, now, you stop that fuss and you come with us, all right? And whatever you do, don't go asking for trouble, because I'm not in the mood. Understand?'

In the car park, she put her trembling hands on the steering wheel. She was breathless with fury and shame. The store manager had interrogated her in a windowless little room. He had agreed not to file a complaint because she was not in their database, and she had returned the two 'stolen' gift cards. 'Are you calling me a thief?' she'd said. The two security guards were present, and she could feel the three men's gazes weighing on her. The big bastard with the pitted skin took the liberty of staring at her breasts; the manager was scornful and condescending. She wished she could have slapped him. The first security guard didn't care. Fuck, she would like to come back and set the bloody place on fire. Or ask Marcus to put the wind up that arrogant little boss. She switched on the ignition and pulled slowly out of the row where she was parked. A strident horn made her jump out of her seat: lost in thought, she hadn't seen the Prius coming the other way.

On Monday, another incident left her puzzled. Mila had been working for several years for Thales Alenia Space, one of the world leaders in satellites; their futuristic headquarters occupied a vast space in the Mirail neighbourhood to the southwest of Toulouse, not far from the A64 motorway. She was head of communications and media relations. Mila was not universally popular: some co-workers had difficulty putting up with her uncompromising character, disinclined as she was to make concessions or try to be diplomatic. But from that to going and puncturing all four tyres on her car, in the huge car park reserved for 2,500 employees . . .

Her anger had not abated by the time she got home, two hours late (she'd had to call the nanny to ask her to pick Thomas up from school). That evening, to calm down, once she had read Thomas

336

his bedtime story, she put her favourite opera into the CD player: Verdi's *Don Carlos*. Another story of impossible, thwarted love. That was what she liked about opera: it always reflected her own life. *Everyone's life*. Wasn't everyone fighting for the same thing? Money, power, success – all with the same goal in mind, unchanged since childhood: to be loved. She collapsed in the comfortable armchair she'd placed in the spot with the best acoustics. At this hour, however, she could not put her spherical Elipson Planet L loudspeakers on full blast, so she picked up the Bose headphones, then pressed the remote.

She closed her eyes. Tried to breathe calmly. This delicious silence that precedes the opening bars . . . She opened her eyes again when she heard the first notes.

This wasn't *Don Carlos*.

She listened for a few more seconds.

*Lucia di Lammermoor!*

She must have put the CD away in the wrong case. She got up and went over to her CD collection. She hunted for the case for Donizetti's tragic opera, where Lucia succumbs irreversibly to madness. She opened it thinking she would find *Don Carlos* inside. And looked, puzzled, at the CD that was in there: *Tales of Hoffmann*.

There was something wrong. Increasingly uneasy, she opened another case, at random: *L'italiana in Algeri*. And found *La Traviata*. She tried again with Schönberg's *Moses und Aron*: it was *Tannhäuser*. Then *Les Indes galantes*: *Cavalleria Rusticana*. Ten minutes later, dozens of cases were scattered across the floor. Not a single one contained the right CD. And *Don Carlos* was nowhere to be found.

Either she was going mad, or . . .

Someone was playing with her. *Someone had been here*.

She looked all around, as if that person might still be there. Right, she thought. The incident at the hypermarket, the four punctured tyres on the car, and now this. Someone was trying to pay her in kind. In revenge for the death of that whore. Inflicting on her what she herself had inflicted on Christine Steinmeyer – as in an *aria da capo*, where the last part is a reprise of the first.

Thomas. She had left him alone with the night light on. As she did every night. She ran up the stairs four at a time. He was sleeping, his thumb in his mouth and his head deep in his three pillows. The halo of the little bedside lamp left a glow against the half-light in the room, which smelled of baby shampoo. She made sure the shutters were closed properly, went over to her son, stroked his shoulder where his pyjama top had left it bare, and felt the fragile structure of his bone beneath the skin.

Just as she was about to switch off the light, she noticed the open book on the bedspread. Mila had read to Thomas, but it wasn't like her to forget to put the book back on the shelf. She went over to pick it up, and snapped it shut. And took a step backwards.

It wasn't Thomas's picture book, but a book entitled *Opera, Or, the Undoing of Women*. She recognised it: it was one of the many books in her library devoted to opera. But she was almost certain she had never brought it up to Thomas's room.

It wasn't exactly reading material for a young child.

She was about to take it down to the library and give it no further thought, when she froze.

She had read this book several years earlier, but she remembered the contents very well: it described the long procession of fallen, wounded, abandoned, betrayed, scorned, murdered women, not to mention those driven to madness or death: in short, all the women whose misfortunes had always enchanted opera lovers. In operas, women always died. In operas, women were always unhappy. In operas, women always came to a tragic end. Princesses, commoners, mothers, whores: opera was the place for their ineluctable defeat – and Mila began to feel more and more uneasy.

That night, she walked around the house twice to make sure all the doors and windows were properly locked, including the shutters. But she didn't sleep more than a few hours, and she listened to the sound of the winter wind against the window until morning.

She called work the next day to say she had a fever and would stay at home. Then she began to look on the Internet for someone to install an alarm system. She compared products, companies, ratings, and made several phone calls. The system she eventually chose had movement detectors in strategic spots around the house, and would photograph any undesired visitors; a powerful 110-decibel siren, signalling to an electronic surveillance centre in the event of an intrusion; and text message alerts sent at regular intervals to Mila's mobile. If there were the slightest doubt, she could even check remotely whether she had set the alarm. A man came to install the system that afternoon. He was small, with grey hair, and looked as if he ought to be retired, but he seemed to know his stuff and was very reassuring, installing the system in record time. He verified that everything was working with the electronic surveillance centre and Mila's mobile phone, then declared, 'There, now you can sleep soundly,' and drove away in his blue mini-van.

The little man was right: that night she slept like a baby; there were no creaking shutters and the next morning she dropped Thomas off at school and went back to work.

The light bulb at the top of the stairs must have burned out, because when she flipped the switch the following evening, nothing happened. She told Thomas to wait downstairs and she went to the shed to fetch a new one, along with a stepladder. She climbed up, changed the bulb, and the light came back on. Then she read to Thomas (*The Grinch Who Stole Christmas*), tucked him in, and closed the door on her sleeping boy.

She went back to the living room, put *Don Carlos* on the stereo (she had gone to FNAC, which did not have the version with Renato Tebaldi, Carlo Bergonzi and Dietrich Fischer-Dieskau, so she had to make do with Placido Domingo, Montserrat Caballé and Ruggero Raimondi), and listened to the entire opera before going to bed.

She thought about Léo and that cop. When was he going to make a move? She knew the police needed more proof to corner Léo, but she was in no hurry. All in good time. She also had to take care of Cordélia and Marcus: two witnesses who were far too troublesome. And she had to find a way to respond to these attacks. Was Léo behind them? Yes, that was possible. Christine had asked for his help, she knew that: Marcus had followed her to the hotel despite her clumsy attempts to shake him off. Léo must have realised that Christine was dead – and who was responsible. Perhaps he had eventually put two and two together. She considered the possibility, weighed it up. What could he do to stop her? Nothing. Everything pointed to him. Including the journal, which he knew nothing about. Whether he ended up in prison or not, Léo was hers, he belonged to her. He was the father of her child. He would eventually come back to her. Even if he didn't know it yet. She would devote her entire life to it if she had to, but he would come back to her. That was all she wanted. And, in the meantime, if he

339

got a bit too close to her house, she would fix it so the cop would catch him. It would mean yet more evidence, absolutely damning evidence, that he was involved. She felt calm now. Her anxiety had left her. Everything was as it should be. She was in control of the situation.

The opera ended with Act 5, when Charles V's tomb opens up and his ghost comes out of the darkness to drag Don Carlos with him. (*My son, the sorrows of the earth are still with us in this place. The peace your heart is hoping for can only be found with God.*')

She switched off the light and went up to bed.

At around two o'clock in the morning she suddenly woke up. And scarcely had time to run to the toilet, where she was sick as a dog. She pulled the chain. She was just getting her breath back, wheezing hoarsely, her hair clinging to her sweaty brow, when a second wave welled up inside her. The acrid bile again splattered the porcelain bowl. She threw up, cleared her throat, spat, breathed. Twenty minutes later, she was still crouching on the tiled floor, shivering, her eyes closed and her stomach heaving with convulsions, and she thought she ought to call the emergency services.

Léonard Fontaine sat in his Porsche 911 and watched the lights in the house go off again, after they had come on in the middle of the night, five hundred metres from where he sat. His face was lit only by the glow-worm of his cigarette when he inhaled. He started up the engine and slowly left the rough track that led out to the plane trees, then drove on in second gear without switching on his headlights: moon and stars were visible among the gnarled branches, and lit up the road. The wind had banished the clouds, and the temperature was getting warmer with each passing day. When he was sure he was far enough away he put on the lights and accelerated, gently: the sound of his legendary six-cylinder engine could carry far, and was easily recognisable. If Mila thought her alarm system could protect her, she was kidding herself. Most of these new wireless systems were extremely vulnerable: a simple jamming device could get the better of them.

No, the danger lay elsewhere: that cop who was following him around. No doubt he thought that Léo hadn't noticed him. But the little commandant did not realise that the woman he'd run into in his house was the detective he had told Christine about. A competent, proactive professional. Twice a week she came to his house to deliver her report. She had carefully noted the odd postman's number plate. Now Léo was going to have to manoeuvre carefully. If the cop caught him lurking around Mila's house, he'd be risking a lot. After all, the policeman seemed convinced he had something to do with Christine's disappearance.

# 41

## 'Sola, perduta, abbandonata'

The light in the stairway went out again. There must be a short circuit somewhere blowing the bulb. She changed it. The next day, another bulb went: the one on her desk in the music room. Then again in the stairway, two days later. And one of the spotlights in the kitchen a few days after that.

In a rage, she hurled a glass and broke it, then called an electrician who, naturally, could only come in two days' time at the earliest. On the appointed day, he spent a long time checking the switches, the plugs, the fuse box, and the lights themselves. His diagnosis was that everything was normal. She shouted at him and he walked out, slamming the door, refusing to be paid.

She was sick again the following night. She was about to toss out all the food in the fridge when she realised that Thomas had not been sick. She ate the same thing as him in the evening.

Two thirty in the morning: terrible cramps in her belly had her writhing in the sheets. She had put a basin by the side of the bed, just in case, and now she threw up into it. An acrid smell wafted all through the room, but she had neither the strength nor the courage to go and empty the basin. She slept very poorly that night, her stomach growling with hunger. She went to work the next morning, exhausted, and dragged her feet all day long, feeling like death warmed up. Several of her colleagues – out of concern, or just the opposite – pointed out that she did not look at all well. She told them to go to hell.

When she got home that evening, she tested the alarm system, and it immediately shrieked in her ears. She typed in the code. The wailing stopped. She tested it one more time. Again it began to wail. Her mobile rang a moment later.

'Good evening, this is the electronic surveillance centre. Please answer the security question.'

'*What Ever Happened to Baby Jane?*' Her favourite film. 'It's nothing,' she said. 'I was just distracted for a moment.'

'Thank you.'

'Um . . . by the way, you haven't had any other instances of intrusion into the system?'

'What do you mean?'

'No, it's fine, forget it.'

The light bulbs continued to blow. And she went on being sick, in spite of the anti-emetic she took every evening, and the fact that she was ordering dinner online from various restaurants and having it delivered. She finally stopped having an evening meal.

Every time she flipped the switch and the light failed to come on, it was a blow to her morale. She knew what was going on: someone had decided to wreak havoc in her life the way she herself had done in the case of Célia Jablonka and Christine Steinmeyer. But just knowing this didn't help. She had to find a way to retaliate.

Apparently, someone knew how to get into her place in her absence, despite the alarm system.

She needed help. But neither Marcus nor Cordélia was answering their phone. She had left over twenty messages. One Saturday morning she went to La Reynerie. She rang the bell at 19B. The door was opened by a young man she did not recognise.

'Yes?'

'Is Corinne Délia here?'

The man studied her.

'She moved – didn't she tell you?'

'And who are you?'

'The new tenant. And you?'

She walked away.

On 14 February, Servaz woke with a start at four o'clock in the morning. He had had a dream that he was floating weightless around the earth. He was moving from one module to another, awkwardly waving his arms and legs, but a woman who did not look like Mila Bolsanski but who was Mila Bolsanski – he did not know how he knew this, but he did – was pursuing him, saying things like, 'Take me, fuck me; right here, now . . .' over and over, no matter how politely he explained that no thank you, he was married, he didn't want to, no thank you, really – and that men, too, had the right to say no, but she went on chasing after him, relentlessly, through the space station. He woke up just as the voice of his mother, who had died thirty-three years earlier, was saying: 'Martin, what are you doing with that lady?' He knew the source of his dream: he had reread Mila Bolsanski's journal that evening. And there had been music, too: opera.

He stayed sitting up in bed for a long time, feeling a great sadness because of his mother's voice and face. She had been so clear, so *alive*.

*You never recover from childhood.* Who had said that? He got up, went for a shower, then made some instant coffee with the kettle on his desk. Outside, the wind was blowing in the dark. He waited for daylight to appear while he reflected. He'd had a dream. A dream with music in it. An unconscious process had started up during his sleep; it had slowly put the elements in place, elements which until then had not fitted. At seven fifteen, he could wait no longer, and he went down for a real coffee in the common room. A few of the boarders greeted him, others didn't. He drank his coffee, thinking about what he knew: what had been plain to see, right from the beginning, but which he hadn't seen. At seven thirty, he left the centre and drove along the little country roads, through an ever-brighter greyness.

Léonard Fontaine was ploughing through the water in the pool almost noiselessly, in the supple, fluid manner of a competition swimmer.

He was feeling the water glide over his face and back as if along the hull of a sailing boat, when he heard a voice from the edge of the pool.

'Hello.'

Fontaine stopped swimming. His head emerged from the water and he looked up at the man standing by the pool. He was in his forties and did not seem to be in very good shape, physically. There was something pale and rumpled about him, a sort of weariness that rounded his shoulders a little. He recognised him, but asked all the same:

'Who are you? Who let you in?'

'I rang the bell,' lied Servaz. 'As no one answered, I took the liberty of . . . of walking around.'

'You didn't answer my first question.'

Servaz took out his warrant card.

'Commandant Servaz, from the Criminal Investigation Department.'

'Do you have a warrant? Something authorising you to go into people's houses without permission? Just because there is no fence—'

Servaz raised his hand.

'I've got better than that. I think I know who killed Christine Steinmeyer. Because she's dead, of course. As you know. But I have at least one bit of good news: I don't think it was you.'

Fontaine shot him a look which, for a moment, betrayed how distraught and pained he felt. He shook his head sadly, swam over to the steps, then climbed slowly out of the water.

'Follow me.'

As they went through the French windows, Servaz felt his stomach turn over when he thought of his previous visit and the dog, Darkhan. Now the huge beast came down from the mezzanine but did not seem to recognise Servaz. He went up to his master, who stroked him affectionately on the forehead. 'Basket.' Satisfied, the dog went back up to his bed. Wearing an ivory bathrobe which looked soft, thick and comfortable – his initials embroidered on the chest pocket – Fontaine pointed to the sofa and offered Servaz a coffee, then went over to the open-plan kitchen. They didn't say a word until the coffee was poured and their cups were on the table. Fontaine finished drying his hair then sat on a big pouffe on the other side of the coffee table. Servaz saw a huge scar on his left leg; a jagged outline of shrivelled flesh decorating his calf and tibia in a crescent shape over thirty centimetres from his ankle to his knee. The astronaut put the towel down. He studied Servaz. His pride and strength seemed to have deserted him, and all that was left was sadness and dismay.

'So you think Christine is dead?'

'Don't you?'

Fontaine tilted his head. For a split second he seemed about to say something, then merely nodded.

Servaz took the diary out of his pocket and slid it over.

'What's this?'

'Mila Bolsanski's diary.'

He saw Fontaine's almost imperceptible reaction at the mention of her name before he put down his cup and reached for the book.

'She claims to have written it while you were staying at Star City,' explained Servaz. 'Read it.'

Fontaine looked at him, surprised, then cautiously opened the diary. He began reading. Servaz saw him frown right from the start. Five minutes later, he had totally forgotten the policeman's presence and his coffee was getting cold in the cup. He began turning the pages more and more quickly, skimming, lingering on certain passages and skipping others, or turning back to reread.

'This is unbelievable,' he said finally, closing it.

'What is unbelievable?'

'She went to the trouble to write this . . . *thing*. It's a proper novel! Mila missed her vocation.'

'It didn't happen like that?'

Fontaine looked indignant.

'Of course not!'

Servaz saw a mixture of anger and disbelief on the astronaut's features.

'Why don't you tell me your version?'

'It isn't *my* version,' he snapped. 'There is only one version: what really happened. We may live in a society where lies and distortion of the facts have become practically normal, but the truth remains the truth. Shit.'

'I'm listening.'

'It's very simple, for a start: Mila Bolsanski is insane. She always has been. I don't know how she managed to pass the psychological tests. Apparently some people who are mentally unstable can do it. And after all, it took me some time, too, to realise she was crazy.'

He put down his empty cup. Servaz noticed he was left-handed and that there was the clear line of a wedding ring, but no ring on his finger. Instead, there was a tiny circle where the skin had tightened slightly, as if that were the meaning of marriage: a shrinking. Servaz, who had been married for seven years before he got divorced, thought that it wasn't chance that the ring finger was the least useful.

'The investigation they conducted afterwards revealed that during her adolescence she had a spell in a psychiatric hospital following several suicide attempts. The diagnosis was some sort of schizophrenia, I think. It hardly matters. When I met Mila, she was a beautiful young woman – intelligent, ambitious, captivating. A ray of sunlight. It was practically impossible not to fall in love with her. The problem was that Mila wore a mask: all that cheerfulness, all that energy were just play-acting, a facade. Mila adapts her appearance to what the person opposite her wants to see; she's very good at that. I eventually realised when I watched her interacting in society: she subtly changed her attitude depending on who she was dealing with. She seemed to have a calm, assertive personality. But in fact it's exactly the opposite: inside, Mila Bolsanski is empty. She just moulds herself into the shape of others. Becomes a mirror that she holds up to their desires. She immediately understands what the other person is looking for, and gives it to them. I examined the issue after what happened. I read a lot about it.'

Servaz thought about the book on the night table.

'I tried to understand who she was, what she was. She is one of those manipulative people who are like human traps: in the beginning they are pleasant, extrovert, attentive to others, smiling and generous. They often give you little presents, they're full of praise for you, they'll do anything for you, you cannot help but enjoy their company . . . Of course, this doesn't mean that everyone friendly is manipulative: the adage about trusting first impressions is absolute rubbish. Good manipulators always make a positive first impression. So how do you go about unmasking them? Over time, that's the thing. If you belong to their inner circle, if you're close to them, their lies and flaws will show up sooner or later. Except if you've already become too dependent to see the obvious signs, when they do become apparent.'

Servaz's eyes met Fontaine's.

'Mind you, I'm not suggesting Mila is not a brilliant woman: you have to be brilliant to get as far as she has. All through her youth she worked hard to succeed. Mila hates failure. She was always top of the class. At university, when her girlfriends were going to parties, having boyfriends or discovering politics, she stayed at home with a thermos and her notes and worked all night long. In her first year of med school she finished top in her year of five hundred students. She was only seventeen! And she got engaged the same year. That's another aspect of her personality: Mila Bolsanski is terrified by the thought of solitude, she needs someone at her side all the time, someone who admires her, who can reflect a high opinion of her.'

Fontaine broke off. Servaz thought of the big, isolated house: didn't that clash with the picture? No. Because there was Thomas. Little Thomas, the adorable blond child, and for him, his mother shone more brightly in the sky than anyone else. Finally a male of the species she could shape over and over again.

'The only problem,' continued Fontaine, 'was that the champion of exams and academic ranking did not have much time to devote to her fiancé, and he ended up dumping her. Her first failure. Devastating, for this woman who succeeded in everything. She had trouble accepting it, from what I could tell: I conducted a little investigation. And do you know what? The poor man ended up in prison for raping a minor. The details of the case seemed to establish his guilt, but he never stopped claiming he was innocent. Until the day he hanged himself. In prison. Life is not easy in jail for alleged paedophiles . . .'

'What makes you so sure he was innocent?'

'The girl who filed the complaint has a police record as long as the Channel Tunnel: theft, extortion, fraud, false accusations, abuse of vulnerable persons. Her adult life has been nothing but a string of attempts to swindle, extort or rob her fellow man. At the time I'm referring to, she was only sixteen and had no police record, obviously. I don't know how Mila found her, but she must have offered her a handsome amount. Or maybe she didn't have to: that girl was clearly the sort who would sell her own mother for a few hundred francs.'

Servaz thought of Célia Jablonka and Christine Steinmeyer, how they had ended up in Mila Bolsanski's sights. He noted in passing that Fontaine must have contacts in the police in order to have obtained that sort of information.

'Anyway, once she'd punished the fiancé, Mila went on her merry way. Towards success and, so she thought, happiness. She always wanted to be the best. Everywhere. All the time. When she needs to charm, to convince, to establish her influence, Mila puts all her energy into it; afterwards, once she is in control, her heart is no longer in it to the same degree, gradually the mask slips. I watched her change, bit by bit. She couldn't help but criticise me – direct criticism, she constantly brought up the same things, over and over, increasingly insidious allusions. All of them, or almost all, were unfounded, or greatly exaggerated. She was also increasingly jealous of my marriage, my family; she accused me of having other mistresses . . . I know:

I'm no saint. I like women and they feel exactly the same about me. But I've never had more than one mistress at a time, and in my way I have loved all those women: it was never just for sex. I married my wife because I believed she was the one who would make me forget all the others. It turned out she wasn't.'

He paused.

'In short: anyone more fragile than I am psychologically would probably end up feeling guilty for all these flaws, and would have wondered what was wrong with them, instead of wondering, the way I did, fairly early on, what was wrong with Mila. I'm not easily influenced, Commandant. When she realised that her usual little games weren't working on me, she turned almost hysterical. She threatened to call my wife and to reveal everything. When we left for Star City our relationship deteriorated dramatically and I was considering putting an end to it, but I was stuck: I was afraid she would get her revenge by telling Karla everything, that she would destroy my marriage and my family. No matter how I looked at it, I could not see a way out. She had me, and she knew it.'

For a moment the mask of the space hero slipped to reveal a defeated, distraught man – a guilty man, too, as are all men, from birth.

'And then, there in Russia, she was suddenly the enthusiastic Mila again, or so it seemed: Mila the sunbeam. She made amends, and apologised for her previous attitude. She told me that no one in her life had ever mattered as much as I did, and that was why she had lost control: that sort of sweet talk . . . She said she would never again behave the way she had. I had nothing to fear, she would never break up my family or separate me from my children. She swore it. I accepted her apology. Once again she was the joyful, impulsive, funny, irresistible Mila she had been in the beginning. All the clouds seemed to have vanished. And when she's like that, it is very difficult to resist her. I saw her turn back into that wonderful woman who can light up every moment of your day, and I suppose that was all I wanted, basically. I told myself that it had been the stress, the waiting and uncertainty that had made her the way she was when we were in France. I wanted her to forgive me, I felt guilty.'

He rolled his eyes.

'Oh, I know what you're thinking: that sure, I was guilty. I was going to break up with her, but later, gently: in the meantime, I would do everything I could to make her stay in Russia as splendid as possible, so she would be happy at Star City. I was a coward, of course; I was lying to myself, I was simply buying time, I was under her influence again. I should have been more careful. She had told me she was taking the pill. So when she announced her pregnancy and said she intended to keep the child, I realised that she had screwed me over. It drove me crazy. I insulted her, I told her that there was no way on earth I would ever recognise the child, I told her I had never loved her and that she could go to hell, along with her kid. It was over between us and I never wanted to see her again, except when I had to, during training. I grabbed her by the arm and threw her out with her belongings. She immediately went to see her Russian teacher.'

He broke off and shook his head, as if the whole story made no sense.

'I don't know what she did exactly, but by the time she got there, she had bruises and marks all over her face, and her eyebrow was split. She said I hit her. That it wasn't the first time. That I behaved violently on a regular basis, intimidating and insulting her. It caused a hellish row; I thought the mission was truly fucked. And my marriage, too. Fortunately, the mission leader wanted to hush up the matter: we'd gone too far with the preparations. Besides, Star City's reputation might be damaged. They kept us apart and everything went on as before. I understood that if I wanted to go into space I was going to have to keep a low profile until launch day – once we were up there, with the others, she could no longer have any hold over me. That's where I was mistaken,' he added, a sinister tone in his voice.

He took a moment to gather his thoughts before he went on.

'With the same tactics she'd used to soft-soap Sergey at Star City, Mila began to manipulate the astronauts who were already on board the International Space Station, setting us against each other. There were three of us newcomers: the commander Pavel Koroviev, Mila and me. And three already on board: two Americans and one Russian. The International Space Station is like a long tube with compartments, a bit like a submarine, or a giant Lego piece floating in space. The Russian compartments are at the rear: that's where we slept and spent most of our time, Pavel, Mila and me. We didn't know what she was saying behind our backs, but we realised something was wrong from the way the others gave us the cold shoulder. In the beginning we had all our meals together in module 3, Unity, which joins the fore and aft sectors. Then little by little, although we didn't really know why, the tension between us and those already on board increased, and there was more and more friction. We didn't know that Mila was behind it. She spent a lot of time with the others, she must have been saying things about us, but I know Mila: she would have been clever enough to do it subtly so that the others would not realise a thing, would just view us as two stupid wankers. I was able to get hold of the minutes of the investigation the Russians conducted after the incidents, and the testimonies of the other residents: apparently, those three idiots didn't realise a thing; they thought they were worming something out of her. She claimed she had only reluctantly confessed to them that Pavel and I were humiliating and harassing her on a daily basis, that we were trying to cut her off from them, and that we spent most of our time denigrating her, ridiculing her and even fondling her: that sort of rubbish.'

He gave a nervous laugh.

'Pavel Koroviev is the bravest, most upstanding man I know, a pillar of integrity. I've never known a man who was more respectful of women. He never got over her accusations.'

Fontaine paused, then continued.

'We had another discussion about the child up there, Mila and me. She told me it was too late for an abortion, and I repeated that I would never recognise it. She begged me. She was completely crazy. That was the night she made it look as if I'd raped her and went over to the other side with her torn clothing and her face covered with bruises. The medical exams showed that she . . . that she even had internal lesions, for fuck's sake! I don't know how she did that to herself. But even when I began to suspect she wasn't quite right, no way did I imagine she could be so unhinged as to inflict that on herself. She must have done it while Pavel and I were asleep. After that, the others made such a fuss that they sent up a rescue mission to bring the three of us back down.'

He leapt up from his seat and went to fetch a glass of water. Then he returned and shot Servaz a hard look, with something more than anger on the surface: *hatred*. The glass in his hand was shaking.

'They put us in isolation for weeks, and finally the committee of inquiry cleared us, Pavel and me, but we knew that after this, whether we had been victims or not, our careers in space were over, fucked.

351

Particularly mine. After all, Mila was my girlfriend and everyone knew it, and they held me responsible for what happened. Since then, I've been representing the Space Agency at cocktail parties; I'm window dressing – I'm an actor, basically. And I put together my own company. But I miss space. Fuck it, I do. I even went through a sort of depression in the beginning. It's fairly common with former astronauts: space blues. Some of them sink into mysticism, others cut themselves off from the world, others drown their sorrows in alcohol. It's hard to accept that you will never go back up there, Commandant. So when, on top of everything, it ends like that . . .'

Servaz nodded, pensive.

'When you got here,' said Fontaine, 'you said you knew who killed Christine. Were you thinking of Mila?'

'Yes,' he said.

'How did you find out?'

Servaz recalled the words in Mila's journal, where she said she used to listen to opera up in the space station. She must not have realised; you can't think of everything.

'Because of opera,' he said.

Fontaine looked baffled.

'Last night, I had a dream about opera. And when I woke up, I remembered reading in her diary that Mila liked listening to opera.'

'And . . . that's it? What do you intend to do?'

'Corner her. However long it takes. I need to carry out a search in and around the house, but for the time being, I don't have enough evidence to convince a judge.'

Fontaine shot him a sceptical look.

'I know what you're thinking,' said Servaz. 'But believe me, once I've got my teeth into something, I'm no more likely to let go than your dog is. And your *girlfriend* may not know it yet, but I already have my teeth in her calf. The only thing is, I'm going to need a little help from you, Monsieur Fontaine. You're going to have to give me something, anything, that will enable me to go and see the judge.'

Fontaine's gaze was riveted on Servaz, piercing and wary at the same time, as if he were trying to read his brain.

'What makes you think I have what you're looking for?'

Servaz stood up. He shrugged.

'You are a very resourceful man, Monsieur Fontaine. And if there's one role that does not suit a man like you, it is that of victim. Think about it.'

February was rainy, windy and dreary. Long driving downpours from morning to night. The skies were always grey, unchanging, the roads awash with water, and Mila felt the sadness and despair seep deep into her flesh.

The previous week she had had four cameras installed under the roof to film all around the house. Movement detectors would set them off at the slightest suspicious activity. But the only images recorded were those of her car leaving and coming back. Yet she went on being sick. Night after night. And changing light bulbs that burnt out, inexplicably.

That morning she had weighed herself: she had lost eight kilos in five weeks. She had little appetite. And the lack of sleep was beginning to tell on her. Even playing with Thomas no longer filled her with joy. Sadness clung to her like a spider's web pearled with rain. She looked at herself in the mirror and saw a ghost: blackish-brown shadows under her eyes, a feverish gaze, her face bony and gaunt, her skin translucent – she looked like Mimi in the final act of *La Bohème*. She had developed a rash around her elbows and wrists. She bit her nails until her fingers bled. At work, she had screwed up on several cases and forgotten to answer important emails. She'd had a proper telling-off from her boss. And she'd overheard some of her colleagues sniggering vindictively.

That evening, when she came home after picking Thomas up from the nanny's, all she had was a hot, sweet tea as she watched him eat with relish.

'What's the matter, Mummy?' he asked.

'What do you mean?'

'You look sad.'

She ruffled his hair and forced herself to smile, holding back her tears.

'No, not at all, sweetie.'

She read to him, waited until he fell asleep, switched off the night light and went to bed, exhausted – but not before checking the alarm system, even if she was ever more convinced that it was serving no purpose. She took half a sleeping tablet, and quickly fell asleep.

★

Something struck her forehead. Something cold. That was what woke her up. *Plop.* A drop of water.

She reached out to find the switch for the lamp, and turned it on. She raised a hand to her forehead. It was wet. Mila looked up and saw a damp spot on the ceiling. She wiped her face with the sheet. The damp spot had already spread over fifty centimetres at least, and at the centre a new drop was forming, like a huge teardrop about to fall.

*The upstairs bath . . .*

There was a bathroom on the floor above that was never used, with an old claw-foot bath. Mila had had a new, modern one installed when she bought the house. The pipes upstairs were old, like the bath itself.

*Her self-defence gun . . .*

She opened the drawer in the night table and took it out. It only shot rubber bullets, but it made her feel safer. She sat on the edge of the bed, took a deep breath. Her brain was fuzzy (*bloody sleeping tablets*) and she still hovered between fear and fury. She grabbed her dressing gown from the chair and slipped it on over her nightie, then went up the corridor, past Thomas's room, to the stairs.

The rain was still streaming down the windows. She found the light switch. Turned it on. Nothing. *Shit!* Her mind let anger triumph. But there was enough light coming through the skylight for her to climb the steps two by two, with her self-defence gun aimed at the top of the stairs. When she reached the landing, she went down the corridor towards the bathroom at the very end. She had started insulation work and long swathes of glass wool hung from the walls like a gigantic furry animal. She pushed the half-open door in the gloom, and it yielded with a sharp creaking noise.

She flicked the switch. *Light . . .* She stepped forward.

And felt the cold water lapping against her toes. The bathroom floor was awash in a good inch of water. She looked over at the bath. It was shrouded in a net of dusty spider's webs that stretched to the corners of the room, and in them all sorts of dead insects were trapped. The old bath was full, overflowing on every side. Mila walked up to it, splashing through the water; she parted one of the clingy spider's webs and leaned forward to turn off the old copper tap, which turned round and round in her hand, squeaking: someone had opened it all the way.

She turned around. Her heart skipped a beat, and she had the sudden sensation that her reason was failing her. Whoever had turned on the water had also written on the wall, in enormous red letters:

*You're going to die, you filthy whore.*

The red paint (if it was paint) was dripping onto the white tiles, which were covered with a thick layer of dust. Elsewhere on the walls, in thick marker, someone had written:

*Whore – Nutter – Crackpot – Sicko – Cow – Crazy – Bitch – Retard – Slag – Tart – Slut – Headcase – Loony – Liar – Monster – Prostitute*

The same words repeated dozens of times.

She felt as if she had just been slapped. Her temples were buzzing. Her entire body flushed with heat. Fuck! She rushed down the stairs and into her bedroom. She opened the cupboard, pulled out a suitcase and filled it at random with clothes and underwear. She rushed into the bathroom. Stuffed her sponge bag with anything she could find. Then she ran to wake Thomas: 'Wake up, sweetie. We're going away.' The boy's eyelids fluttered: 'What?' It was three o'clock in the morning according to the big pink and yellow alarm clock that stood on the night table stupidly smiling.

The boy sat up and rubbed his eyelids.

'We have to leave. Right now.'

Thomas turned over to go back to sleep; she shook him by the shoulder and he sat up again.

'What? Mummy!'

'I'm sorry, my love, but we have to leave right away. *Get dressed. Quick!*'

She could see in his eyes that he was beginning to be frightened. Her tone of voice had upset him. She was sorry she had lost her cool. Thomas was looking worriedly at the door now.

'Is there someone in the house, Mummy, is that it?'

Mila stared at her son and frowned.

'Of course not! Why do you say that?'

'Because sometimes I hear strange sounds at night.'

It came in waves, the feeling of horror. Fear washed over her, and her mind took off like a mad train about to derail. So then, it was true: fucking useless alarm system! She was alone in this huge house with her son, at the mercy of a raving mad psychopath. All you had to do was look at what he had written in the bathroom. She pushed back the duvet.

355

'Come on! Quick! Get up!'

'Mummy, what is it? What is it, Mummy?'

The boy was terrified. She forced herself to calm down, and to smile.

'Nothing. It's just that they said it might flood because of the rain. We can't stay here, do you understand?'

'Tonight, Mummy? Tonight?'

'Hush . . . There's nothing to be afraid of: we'll be gone long before that, my angel. But we mustn't waste any time.'

'Mummy, I'm scared.'

She took the boy in her arms and held him close.

'I'm here. You see, there's nothing to be afraid of. We'll just go and stay at the hotel while we wait for it to be over, all right? And then we'll come back.'

She dressed him hurriedly, put on his socks and shoes, then took him downstairs to the living room where she switched on the TV. At this time of night the children's channels were not broadcasting. She put on a DVD. His favourite: that should work.

'I'll go and get the car.'

But he was already absorbed in what was on the screen – or about to fall back to sleep – curled up on the sofa. In the corridor, she reached for her raincoat, then she unlocked the front door and tried the light switch. *Well well, this one was working, at least.* It was pouring buckets; the countryside was black all around; the corrugated metal garage was a dozen metres away. She never locked it. She would run to the garage through the dark – not exactly a cheering prospect. But she had no choice.

She took a deep breath, and rushed out.

She was instantly drenched, rain pouring down her face, seeping up through her shoes, trickling into her ears and down the back of her collar. When she reached the metal sliding door, she tugged on it, and it gave a rusty groan. Her hand fumbled in her pocket for the keys, and found them. She sat behind the wheel and turned on the headlights, which transformed the rain into myriad sparks. She started the ignition and drove a few metres. The downpour hammered on the roof of the car. She got out, leaving the motor running, was heading towards the front door when the engine shuddered and died behind her. She was seized with panic. She rushed back and sat at the wheel, turned the key. *Nothing!* She tried again. Still no luck.

*Damn, damn, damn!* No matter how she tried, the engine would not start. They were stuck there. *Thomas!* That psychopath might still be in the house. She slammed the car door hard and ran back into the house, leaving a wet trail in her wake. Her son had dropped off again with his thumb in his mouth. The vibrant glow from the television was reflected on his closed lids.

*The phone.*

She had to get help this time. Up until now, she had always tried to keep the police away from the house, and the woods behind it in particular. Now she hurried over and picked up the receiver. No dialling tone! *He'd cut the line* . . . Her mobile! Ordinarily she left it on the countertop in the kitchen. Or on the dining table. But it wasn't there.

By the time she had searched all the rooms she'd been into during the day, she was convinced that *he* had taken it.

*He was here. He had always been here.*

She shivered. Not a simple shiver. But a long shudder through her entire body, like a flow of ice through her bones, her neck, her heart. The self-defence gun: where had she left it? She found it on the bed in her room, and grabbed it. Desperate, she entertained the prospect of opening the trapdoor to the loft, pulling down the ladder and climbing up. But what if he was up there? It would be too easy for him to overcome her as she emerged through the trapdoor, and she was terrified at the very idea of leaving him alone with Thomas. She went back down to the ground floor.

Fear was snapping at her heels. And yet she had been to outer space, she had survived every ordeal, she had always been strong.

*Pull yourself together! Fight back!*

But she was so tired. As she had been for so long. She hadn't eaten anything in such a long time. She woke up at night to throw up. She hardly slept, and when she did it was so badly. *Thomas! Do it for him!* Her maternal instinct gained the upper hand. No way would he touch a hair on her son's head. She would protect him the way a lioness protects her cubs.

Downstairs on the ground floor everything was silent except for the rain engulfing the house. A terrible silence. Thomas was asleep on the sofa. She went to fetch his winter parka, his scarf and an umbrella.

She figured that the nearest farm, the Grouards, was a kilometre away. Ten minutes' walk when she was on her own. It would take twenty with Thomas half asleep. In the night. In the rain.

She woke him gently.

'Come on, sweetie.'

For a moment, he seemed disoriented. Again he rubbed his sleep-heavy eyelids.

'The flood?' he asked.

'Yes. Let's go.'

She tried to make her voice sound reassuring. Docile, he let her put on his parka and scarf. She decided against the umbrella. She would carry him on her back. She pulled the hood up over his head. Opened the front door wide.

'Climb on my back.'

He obeyed. When he was snuggled tight against her, his arms around her neck, she straightened up and went down the front steps, across the empty, gloomy space around the house, and headed for the dark road.

'Mummy, why aren't we taking the car?'

'It won't start, sweetie.'

'Where are we going, Mummy?'

'To the Grouard farm.'

'Mummy, let's go back. I'm frightened, Mummy. *Please.*'

'Hush. Don't worry: in ten minutes, we'll be nice and warm. And safe.'

'*Mummy . . .*'

She could tell he was beginning to sob uncontrollably against her back. She could hear the rain pattering against his hood, against her ear; she felt it, cold and unfriendly, on her scalp.

'*I'm frightened.*'

She looked down and saw the tunnel of trees straight ahead. Silence all around. The countryside was completely black. She marched down the centre of the straight road. Every step shook her body with the weight of her son trembling on her shoulders. She was trembling, too. With cold, with fear. Huge knotty branches were entwined above their heads. She could feel the tears on her cheeks, their salt on her lips. Above all, she did not want to start crying in front of him. He was quiet, but she was aware of how he was shaking, uncontrollably.

She realised her eyes were closing as she walked. She shook her head to rouse herself. Head down, she saw the toes of her trainers moving forward, step by step. Mechanically. Except that something had changed. The surface of the road: it was lit up. Every piece of gravel, every bump, every hole, every crack had its own hard dark shadow, and the tarmac was shining with a yellow glow like a sheet of metal under a lamp . . .

'MUMMY!'

Thomas had almost screamed. She looked up. And blinked. She was dazzled by a pair of headlights. A car, facing them, less than three hundred metres away. Immobile. Its headlights lit up the tunnel of trees as if someone had switched on a projector inside a cathedral. She felt as if her brain was beginning to melt. Then the headlights were switched off. Darkest night. She couldn't hear anything other than the wind. Her pounding heart, tunnelling through her chest. She tried to think. What could she do? Panic was taking over. Then the headlights came back on, blinding them, and she heard the sound of an engine starting up.

'Mummy, Mummy!'

Thomas on her shoulders, wailing. She felt her mind give way, like a dyke yielding to pressure. She crouched down and set her son on the ground. She turned back to face the house. Took him by the hand.

'Run!' she cried. 'RUN!'

She heard the car shift gear behind them.

# 42

## Finale

'Questo è il fin di chi fa mal' (*Don Giovanni*)

Fontaine met Servaz in a bar on the place des Carmes the next morning, 24 February. He had requested the appointment. When he saw the cop coming, Fontaine moved his beer to one side and reached into his jacket pocket.

'Hey,' he said.

He pushed the prints across the damp table.

'Is this what I asked you for?' said Servaz.

'The "little something",' Fontaine confirmed.

Servaz leaned closer. He recognised her right away: Mila. Going into the building where Cordélia lived in La Reynerie. And coming back out. Annoyed. Photographs taken with a telephoto lens.

'How did you get this?'

Fontaine simply smiled.

'Did you take them?'

Another smile. 'Do you know where they are now?' Fontaine asked.

Servaz was studying him.

'Cordélia and Marcus? Vanished without a trace. If you ask me, they've already left the area.'

'Perhaps they're in Russia by now,' suggested Fontaine.

He thought of the €20,000 he had given Marcus, and the phone call he'd made to Moscow, to his friends who had other friends. He never thought he would make such a call. He had deposited the money in an account in Luxembourg, and gave his contact the flight number and arrival time. Marcus's body would never be found. And Cordélia must be on board another plane by now.

'I'll ask you again: did you take these pictures?'

360

'Does it matter?' said Fontaine. 'It doesn't, does it? What does matter is that you have what you wanted: evidence connecting Mila to this Marcus person and to Corinne Délia – both of whom have fled and whom the police strongly suspect of being involved in the disappearance, and possibly murder of Christine Steinmeyer. That should be enough for you to get your warrant.'

'We'll have to have a chat, one of these days, Léo,' said Servaz, getting to his feet, the photographs in his hand.

'I thought we already had,' he replied. 'But it will be with pleasure, Commandant. We'll talk about whatever you want. About space, for example. An interesting subject.'

Servaz smiled in turn; he really was beginning to like this guy, more and more. Who was the imbecile who said that first impressions were always right?

She opened the door and glanced outside. There was no one in sight. A dreary day was beginning on the grey plain. She went back inside, in her dressing gown, features drawn and her hair a mess. Mila remembered a time – not so long ago – when she used to call the shots. She felt as if a century had gone by since then. Everything had changed. How could she have lost her touch in so little time? When had the pendulum begun to swing the other way?

The night before, once they'd made it back to the house, they had locked themselves in and she had collected everything that might serve as a weapon: knives from the rack, a hammer, a poker from the fireplace, the self-defence gun, a large two-pronged carving fork . . . Thomas had been terrified at the sight of it all. He'd opened his big, frightened eyes wide and stared at her. She'd had to give him a mild tranquilliser, then hug him and reassure him until eventually he fell asleep on the sofa in the living room. She had fortified her courage with two gin and tonics and stayed up until dawn began to lighten the windows. By morning she felt too tired to concentrate, unable to put any sort of strategy together. These last few days and hours had severely tested her nerves. Thomas was still asleep. She drank a second coffee. When he woke up, they would hurry to the Grouard farm to ask for help. Then she heard the paper boy's scooter, and she rushed outside.

'Have you got a phone?' she asked. 'Mine's not working, and the car isn't either.' She pointed to the open garage. 'We're stuck here!'

'That sounds like really bad luck,' said the young man, handing her his mobile.

'Can you wait five minutes? I just want to call a breakdown vehicle . . .'

When she came back out, the young man asked her, 'Are you the one who forgot to put the cap back on the fuel tank?'

'No.'

'Then someone probably put something nasty in your petrol. Either sugar or sand. You really have to be sick to think it's funny doing stuff like that.'

The breakdown mechanic confirmed the diagnosis: the engine was dead. A wave of despair came over her as she watched him go away again. Thomas was still sleeping. Distraught, dishevelled, in her dressing gown, she wandered through the house, and the echo of her slippers shuffling along the floor was a pitiful accompaniment to her aimlessness. She was exhausted, at the end of her tether. Thomas would not go to school today: she would let him sleep. She wanted to call work to say she wouldn't be in either, when she remembered she had no phone. Fuck! She swore, furious with herself. She should have ordered a taxi at the same time as the mechanic. She switched on the computer, but the verdict was instant: cannot connect. Obviously. The bloody connection was linked to the telephone line. She stared at the ceiling.

Someone wanted to mess with her life and, by the looks of it, they were succeeding.

She thought for a moment.

The postman! He would be here soon.

That morning, she waited hours for him to arrive, increasingly nervous as time went by, pulling her dressing gown closer because of the chill in her bones. What if there was no post? What if he didn't come today? She no longer had the strength to go to the Grouard farm. What would they think if they saw her in this state? Maybe she'd go tomorrow. When she got her strength back. *It was so much easier to let oneself go, to throw in the towel, to put it off till tomorrow . . .*

'Aren't I going to school today, Mummy?'

'No, darling. It's a holiday today. Go up to your room and play.'

He didn't have to be told twice. She stared out of the window at the road. At last she saw the yellow scooter. She rushed out of the front door and explained the situation once again; the first call she made was to Isabelle, her colleague at work.

'Mila, what is going on?' said Isabelle anxiously.

'I'll explain.'

'Mila, this is the fourth time this month! And there have been those two incidents.'

She knew what Isabelle was referring to. There had been two major incidents when she'd shown up for a meeting with important foreign partners looking absolutely terrible, and had not prepared her presentation properly.

'You'd better come in,' insisted Isabelle. 'They won't let you off this time, believe me. Shit, you're already in the management's bad books . . .'

Mila muttered some excuse and hung up. She was too tired to argue. Then she called a taxi. The first thing to do would be to rent a car and get a new phone. Escape this isolation.

'Here,' said the postman, handing her some letters and taking back his mobile – with a disapproving look at her appearance.

She watched him walk away in the darkening light. A mass of clouds was arriving from the west; gloomy, spreading across the entire horizon. The sky was turning black, and there was thunder. Crows were whirling in flight, tense with the approaching storm. She noticed there was one envelope among the letters that had neither stamp nor return address. It was like the one she'd put in a mailbox on Christmas Eve. Mila opened it, her hand trembling. Photographs. She had a shock when she saw them: *someone had photographed the turned earth at the foot of an old, twisted tree.* Three prints, all identical: three pictures of the grave.

In a sudden panic, she hurried up the hill through the woods. The wind was rising, and the first drops of rain fell as she ran down into the hollow. The carpet of leaves hiding the pit was intact: nothing had been touched.

A car horn sounded, back at the house.

*The taxi: she'd forgotten it!*

She hurried down the hill again, while the rain fell harder. Another impatient beep of the horn. She ran around the house and emerged in the downpour, breathless. The driver stared at her clothes and her appearance, stunned: her streaming dressing gown, her Crocs covered in mud, her wet, tangled hair, her wild eyes. She saw him frown and look at his watch.

'I'm sorry,' she said, 'I'd forgotten you! As you can see, I'm not ready. Go on home.'

'Bloody hell, who's going to pay for the trip then? You look like you've got some serious problems,' he said, staring critically at her and pointing at his temple with his forefinger.

'What did you say? Get the fuck out of here!' she roared. 'Right now!'

'Fucking nutter,' he grumbled, getting back in the taxi.

He made a sharp turn that sent a spray of mud and water in her direction.

'Bitch!' he cried out of the window, to be sure to have the last word, and it made her think of all those words still smeared on the bathroom walls.

She glanced at the rest of the letters. Bills, junk mail, special offers. Then her gaze lingered on an envelope from the Social Assistance to Children Division for the Haute-Garonne. She tore it open with foreboding, and took out a letter, typed and folded in two.

*Madame,*

*You have been brought to our attention by Valérie Dévignes, the head of the school at Névac, and Pierre Chabrillac, a teacher there, on the suspicion of physical and psychological mistreatment of your three-year-old son, Thomas. Several times Thomas has come to school with bruises on his elbows, knees and face* [pictures accompanied this description of events]. *Mlle Dévignes and M. Chabrillac also told the authorities of Thomas's frequent absences of late, and said that he seemed uninterested in what was going on in class, that his behaviour was erratic and that he often seemed sad. He has been interviewed by a psychologist, and admitted to being afraid of you.*

*Consequently, a multidisciplinary team has been appointed by the Social Assistance to Children Division in order to establish the facts of the matter. They will interview you in the near future. But given the gravity of the suspected situation, a request for placement has already been submitted to the prosecutor of the Republic, and the matter has been referred to the family judge. Should Thomas be entrusted to our services by the judge, you will be able to give your opinion regarding the choice*

*and conditions of placement. Thomas himself will also be consulted. These*
*opinions will be considered but may not be adhered to.*
*Yours faithfully . . .*

For a moment, Mila stood there paralysed. Her eyes looked over the letter a second time, unbelieving, while the paper quivered in her hands. There were several photographs attached, where she could indeed see bruises on Thomas. She tried to laugh at it, but her laugh turned into a sob. Ridiculous! Thomas was an intrepid little boy, a daredevil, who was constantly falling down or banging into things. She had often sent him to school with bumps and bruises – but to imagine that someone might think . . .

At another time in her life she would have reacted instantly and called her lawyer – and that imbecile of a head teacher. She would have shown her claws and lashed out where it hurt, would have unleashed the full fury of her indignation; she would have made them cower. How dare they imagine she could ever lay a finger on her son! But now she was so weak, so emaciated. So distraught. Tomorrow. It could wait another day . . . or two. The time it took for her to regain her strength. She was so weary. She put the letters down on the kitchen table, poured another gin and tonic, went to fetch the box of tranquillisers from the medicine cabinet and took three in a row.

Servaz looked at the notes he had taken as he made one phone call after another.

*Mila Hélène Bolsanski, born 21 April 1977 in Paris. Only daughter of Konstantin Arkadyevich Bolsanski and Marie-Hélène Jauffrey-Bertin (deceased 21 August 1982 in a car accident). Foster families and boarding school – where her marks improved rapidly under the influence of a form tutor: M. Willm. Went on to become the top student in the class. Medical doctor, specialised in aeronautical medicine, doctor of science, second Frenchwoman in space, in 2008 took part in a Soyuz mission to the International Space Station.*

*Two stays in a psychiatric hospital in 1989, at the age of twelve, after two suicide attempts (diagnosis: depression, severe personality disorder). Subsequent ongoing psychiatric and therapeutic treatment which she herself interrupted as soon as she was of age, contrary to better judgment of uncles and aunts. Brilliant student, engaged to Régis Escande on 21 April 1995 on her eighteenth birthday, also against family's better judgment. Engagement broken off six months later. Note: Escande committed suicide in prison two years later after conviction for rape of a minor.*

*Selected as astronaut for the National Centre for Space Studies in 2003 before joining the group of astronauts from the European Space Agency in 2005: it would seem neither the NCSS nor the ESA got wind of existing psychiatric file, and she passed all the psychological tests.*

*Left for Star City with Léonard Fontaine on 20 November 2007.*

It wasn't much to go on, but it corroborated what Fontaine himself had said. For no precise reason, Servaz had a sudden vivid memory of Mila's house. He saw again the long corridor leading to the kitchen, as dark as a tunnel in a mine, and the haughty figure of the woman walking ahead of him. Had he had a shiver of anticipation at the time? A premonition? No, nothing at all.

He looked at the mobile on the desk. What was Beaulieu up to? He should have got through to the prosecutor's office ages ago. Why was it taking so long? Servaz looked at the pack of cigarettes. He took one out and stuck it between his lips without lighting it. His mobile vibrated.

'Servaz here.'

'It's Beaulieu.'

'Well?'

'That bloody judge is the type who wants to protect herself from every angle, and her career with it: the former astronaut, the second Frenchwoman in space, celebrities, you can imagine… I had to push her a bit. We exchanged a few niceties, but it's done, we've got it. I suppose you'd like to join us, this time?'

'Since you've asked.'

He crushed the cigarette in his palm into a thousand tiny flakes of tobacco.

Her child. *They were going to take her child.* Give him to strangers, a substitute family. He was so fragile, so dependent on her. What would become of him? Her Thomas, her treasure. They had no right! No one must touch him! His father had rejected him, she was his only family. *Thomas, my darling, my love, I won't let them.* She was on to her second or third gin and tonic; she had stopped counting. The proportion of gin increased a bit each time. Her pills were muddling her brain. She had to get hold of herself. *Tomorrow, tomorrow she would feel better, she would fight, for her child, for both of them.* She was so weary, so tired.

Tomorrow.

She went stealthily up the stairs and walked barefoot to Thomas's bedroom. She peered through the half-open door. Thomas was sitting on his bed, playing with his console. He looked focused but smiling, relaxed. She felt tears flowing down her cheeks, as if they were washing her face – salt tears in her mouth when she went back down to the kitchen. For a long and terrifying minute, she stared at one of the knives on the table, and her bare wrist emerging from her dressing gown. A memory like a flash: when she was twelve, her wrists bandaged, being taken away by an ambulance.

The storm was wild. A livid glow of lightning beyond the rain-lashed windows. The doorbell rang. She shivered. Was that him, coming to claim his victory? She walked down the long corridor.

'Mademoiselle Bolsanski? Police,' called a voice through the door. 'Open up!'

Police . . . the word went through her like a sword. She opened the door slowly, and the sound of rain instantly surrounded her; someone thrust a police badge under her nose. There were several of them. Wearing raincoats, or streaming windbreakers. Orange armbands on their sleeves. A little man with curly hair like a poodle was staring at her from the top step; he had a runny nose. He held himself very straight, blinked at her through the downpour, put his hand into his parka.

'We have a search warrant from the judge. If you don't mind, I will show it to you inside,' he said, peering at the drenching rain.

She swept her gaze over the others – three men and a woman – and suddenly she paused to look at the man who was standing apart, his arms limp at his side. She recognised him. He was the one to whom she had sent the key to room 117 and the photograph of the International Space Station. The one who had been on the front page of the newspaper, several times. The one to whom she had given her diary. He was standing there, motionless, in the rain. Bare-headed. And he was staring at her, in silence. They held each other's gaze for a few endless seconds. And in that moment she understood that she had lost.

What happened next, she perceived only in fragments, flashes, disordered impressions. Words on a printed sheet of paper: *officer from the Criminal Investigation Department . . . acting by virtue of the warrant granted hereafter . . . have come to search the domicile of* Mila Bolsanski (her name filled in, in pen) *. . . to be allowed in by the same . . . decline to inform him* [sic] *of our identity . . .* A stamp. A signature. Her head was spinning. They spread out through the house. Their gloved hands lifted cushions, opened boxes, CD cases, drawers, cupboards, rubbish bins, doors . . .

'Mummy, who are these people?' said Thomas, rushing over to her.

'It's nothing, my treasure. They're policemen,' she answered, pressing him to her belly.

'What are they looking for?'

'I asked them to come, they're here to help us,' she lied.

She looked at the man who had visited her one evening in January, the one who had read her diary, the one she thought she had managed to manipulate: he was not taking part in the search. He merely watched, and from time to time he gave Thomas a sad look.

'Why don't you tell them?' she said to him. 'What you know, what I showed you.'

'Because your journal is a fake,' he said.

She faltered. A wave of despair. She was aware of her thoughts tumbling over each other, overlapping. She squeezed Thomas, pressed him up against her, took his face in her hands and kissed his pale forehead. She plunged her gaze into her son's beautiful eyes, her beautiful blond son.

'I love you; don't ever forget that, my treasure.'

'Mummy, everything will be fine,' he said as if he had suddenly become the head of the family, conscious that it was up to him to protect her now.

'Yes, everything will be fine,' she echoed, her eyes moist.

Gently, she pushed him away. For fear of falling and dragging him down with her. He looked worriedly at her. He was so grown-up for his age; he had the intelligence and maturity of a child of seven or eight.

A young woman with an astonishingly ugly face chose that moment to burst in through the door that led to the woods.

'Come and see!' she cried. 'I think I've found something!'

They followed her, and one of the cops ordered Mila to put something on and go with them. Another cop stayed behind with Thomas. The rain was splattering on their hoods, and the damp earth and leaves stuck to the soles of their shoes. They headed up the hill, following the young female cop, through all that rain and mud, a liquid world without beginning or end. Mila felt as if she were regressing, returning to the moisture and peace of amniotic liquid. Peace, at last. She knew where they were going. They had found her.

The young woman was kneeling next to an old, gnarled tree, as twisted as a demented contortionist. The freshly turned rectangle of earth was apparent, darker among the roots, beneath the carpet of leaves she had partially swept aside with her gloved hands. She looked up at Mila from beneath her hood. Everyone was staring at her. And she could read the same thing in all those converging gazes: *guilty, guilty, guilty*.

'What is this?' asked the poodle.

She didn't answer.

'Call the CSI team,' said the man whose name was Servaz, staring at her with a neutral expression. 'And get hold of the prosecutor.'

Thunder was booming like a sheet of metal in the hands of a sound effects engineer. Before they even gave a first thrust of the shovel, the technicians in white overalls had taken samples of soil and leaves, which they sealed up in their test tubes. They took pictures with a flash, using measuring tapes to establish the dimensions of the pit. Because of the dusk, they had switched on projectors, and cables ran like snakes through the mud. Now they were all staring at the pit in the harsh white light. *Empty.* The men from forensics looked furious as they snapped off their blue latex gloves.

'Thanks, guys. May I remind you that 1 April is not for another month and a half,' said one of them. The cops all looked at each other and turned to Servaz.

'Bloody hell,' said Beaulieu, walking away.

'An empty grave,' he said, sitting at the wheel of his car.

Everyone had left except Beaulieu and Servaz.

'It wasn't dug for nothing,' said Servaz, staring at the house through the streaming windscreen.

'No. And it really does look remarkably like a fucking grave, a hole like that in the middle of the forest. So why is it empty?'

Servaz shrugged.

'No idea.'

'I'm sure she could tell us,' said Beaulieu, nodding towards the house.

'She won't talk.'

'So, what do we do?'

'We wait.'

'Wait for what?'

'The results from the samples. All we need is a bit of DNA.'

She tries to sleep, but can't. They've already been gone a long time. The storm has not released its hold on the house. She tries to sleep but she can't. How could she, with that empty tomb out there in the woods? What does it mean? She has been trying to make sense of it, but her thoughts are so muddled, so confused. She killed that bitch herself, she saw her body jerk under the impact of the bullets, then stiffen. She saw the blood. And Marcus, tossing the first shovelfuls of earth over the corpse. She had let him finish the job while she went back down to the house.

Did he move the body? But why would he do that? Was he afraid that one day they would trace it back to her, and through her, to him? He's not here any more, to answer. Where did he get to? Where are they, the pair of them, Cordélia and Marcus?

She listens to the silence. She is cold, shivering, trembling. Silence all through the house – and then suddenly she hears it.

It is coming from downstairs. There can be no doubt, she isn't dreaming: opera. She recognises it from the very first bars: the third act of *Madame Butterfly*. The scene where Cio-Cio San takes her own life. An icy chill comes over her. The music is coming from the ground floor; it's the duet between Pinkerton and Sharpless.

> Sharpless:
> *Come, speak to that kind lady*
> *and bring her in here.*

*Even if Butterfly should see her,*
*no matter . . . On the contrary,*
*better if she should realise*
*the truth through seeing her.*
*Come, Suzuki, come . . .*
Pinkerton:
*But the coldness of death is in here.*

She sits up in bed, and the voice penetrates the darkness of the house, relentlessly. *Thomas . . . it will wake him up.* She looks at the red numbers on the alarm clock: they move from 3:05 to 3:06. Another crack of thunder shakes the windows. Now her eyes are wide open in the gloom.

*Yes, all in an instant*
*I see how I have sinned*
*and realise I shall never*
*find respite from this torture.*

This music . . . it is enough to make her cry.

*Farewell, flowery refuge, of happiness and love.*

She pushes back the duvet, climbs out of bed and puts on her dressing gown. Her mind is blank, her body drained of strength. Like a sleep-walker she goes to the door and out into the corridor. She flips the light switch but nothing happens. Of course.

The door to Thomas's bedroom is closed.

It takes three steps to reach the landing at the top of the stairs. There is a faint light down there, dim and far away. A lamp must be lit, somewhere. She tries the light switch in the stairway, but as she expected, nothing happens. So she goes down, counting her steps, with the faint light there is. Her heart is almost embracing the rhythm of the music, as if she were backstage in a theatre where she was about to go onstage.

Hundreds of gazes staring at her in the darkness. Attentive. Hoping she will triumph, dreading her failure.

At the bottom of the steps, louder and clearer now, the voice of the mezzosoprano Lucia Danieli playing the role of Suzuki:

*She'll cry so bitterly!*

She peers into the darkness, seeks her bearings: the light is coming from the little corridor leading to the bathroom on the other side of the kitchen. On her way, she picks up one of the knives from the rack. *Dear Lord, this music!* It is so beautiful! So sad! At last comes the voice of Maria Callas as Butterfly:

*Suzuki, Suzuki! Where are you?*

She walks through the kitchen and down the corridor. The light is getting brighter. There is a door open on the left. She was right: the light is coming from the bathroom.

*He's here, he's here . . . where's he hidden?*

She pushes open the door with her fingertips, with the knife in her other hand. There is a smell of wax – heady, heavy – and the light of dozens of candles dancing on the ceiling and the walls, like a fire. It is also dancing on the face of the dead woman who is not dead, and on her skull, which she has shaved, where a fine down is beginning to grow again. It is dancing in her steady gaze, calm and resolute, outlined in heavy black mascara, and for a split second, Mila thinks she has gone mad. It is Madame Butterfly who is there, Cio-Cio San. In a dark kimono, her face painted white, her eyes reduced to two slits, her mouth as thin as the stroke of a blade.

But the hallucination fades and now it is worse: a ghost. A revenant. A blurred phantom through the thick steam rising in the room. The phantom is wearing a man's clothing. And pointing a gun at her.

'Good evening,' says Christine, while Callas goes on singing:

*This woman! What does she want at my house?*

Her mind is blank. She thinks of Thomas: how can he sleep with this music?

'Put the knife down,' says Christine. 'Take your clothes off and get in the bath.'

She could refuse, resist, but what is the point: everything – the music, her weakness, the immense weariness of these recent days, this final act echoing throughout the house – everything compels her to obey. She no longer has a will of her own; she doesn't feel like fighting any more. She is simply tired. And the weapon the phantom is brandishing leaves her no choice, in any case. She drops the knife, which clatters on the floor, then her clothes, one by one, at her feet. The steam from the hot water filling the bath rises in the room, swirls around her. Mila's skin instantly begins to gleam with sweat.

'Please,' says Christine calmly.

For a long while she doesn't move; then she puts one leg over the edge of the bath. She notices there is a barber's razor open on the edge of the bath, its long blade gleaming in the dancing candlelight. She puts her leg in the hot water, and then her entire body. She sits down in the bath. For a moment she feels good, relieved, as if the surrendering of control has set her free.

'My son!' she exclaims, suddenly.

'Don't worry. He's asleep. And we'll take care of him.'

'We?'

Outside the room, Butterfly is singing:

> *They want to take everything away from me!*
> *My son!*
> *Oh, unhappy mother!*
> *To be obliged to give up my son!*

'His father and I,' says Christine. 'Léo will look after his son; he has promised to recognise him and bring him up. Thomas will have both your names. He will go to the best schools and enjoy the best education, Mila. Léo will never reveal the truth to Thomas about what happened. What his mother did. He will tell him that his mother had an accident. He has sworn to do that. But on one condition . . .'

'What condition?' murmurs Mila.

The phantom gazes down at the open razor on the edge of the bath. Mila shudders.

'I saw you die,' she tells the phantom. 'I shot you.'

'With blanks,' answers Christine.

'And the blood?'

'Simple cinema tricks, hidden underneath my jumper: little pouches of fake blood that explode on cue. All I had to do was convulse at the moment of impact, and bite my tongue until it bled.'

'But . . . Marcus?'

'As soon as you left, he helped me out of the ditch.' She smiled. 'The drug you were supposed to have given me was just vitamins.'

'Why?'

'Because Marcus sells himself to the highest bidder, Mila: you ought to know that. And Léo and I raided our accounts. It wasn't very hard to convince Marcus, I must say. Even if I did have to sacrifice my life insurance policy. When I got the email from Denise that morning, I knew right away it was a trap. Léo had already called to tell me something was going to happen: he'd heard from Marcus, who knew because of you. Marcus organised everything. It was that, or prison, for him.'

'Where is he?'

'Who? Léo? I told him to keep an eye on that cop.'

'And Marcus?'

'I'm afraid he might be pushing up daisies in his beloved Russian soil. We bought him a ticket to Moscow, but I rather fear someone might have been waiting for him there. You know, he did drug me after all, and rape me, and slit my dog's throat, for fuck's sake . . . But he was only following your orders, wasn't he?'

Silence. Mila glances at the open razor on the edge of the bath. She could try to grab it and strike the phantom. But she knows the phantom will be quicker. She thinks about Léo and her son, the two of them, together, finally reunited. The music, alternating decrescendo and crescendo . . . the entire room is waiting for her to speak. To breathe. The entire audience in a trance, petrified with emotion and ecstasy.

And now there it is, soaring, the famous final aria they've all been waiting for: 'Con onor muore.' *He dies with honour who cannot live with honour.*

Yes. Why not?

'So the nausea, the punctured tyres, the hypermarket – that was you?'

She is so weary . . .

'Yes.'

'How did you do it?'

So tired of all this.

'Do what?'

'All those nights I was sick, but couldn't sleep. I threw out the food, I bought new medication at the chemist's; I was eating the same thing as Thomas, and he wasn't sick.'

The phantom points the gun barrel towards the other side of the bath. Mila follows the movement with her gaze. At first she doesn't understand. Then, suddenly, it dawns on her. The bath salts. She took a bath every evening. After she put Thomas to bed. But she didn't bathe Thomas: he only took showers.

Suddenly, the phantom picks up a remote control, presses a button and the music stops.

'I've been watching you for weeks. It's crazy all the stuff you can buy nowadays – a micro-camera in the kitchen, another one in your bedroom, a third in the bathroom . . . I probably know more about your habits and your obsessions than you do yourself, Mila. And the alarm system you had installed: it's laughable.'

From one of the many pockets in her trousers she takes out a black rectangular box.

'A jammer,' she explains. 'One hundred euros on the Internet. There's a bright future for burglars.'

'Because of you, they want to take my son away,' spits Mila in a final outburst.

The phantom simply looks at her.

'That is why you must let Léo raise his son. But that's enough chit-chat.'

She points to the razor, waving her gun, and Mila does not notice the increasingly obvious trembling of the barrel. Or the tears on Christine's cheeks.

'Tonight you are going to kill yourself. And I will make sure that Léo looks after Thomas. That he brings him up . . . that he recognises him. *You have my word.*'

She wipes the tears and sweat from her face with the back of her gloved hand. Her eyes are glowing amid the dark mascara.

'If you refuse, you'll go to prison, and Thomas will be given to one foster family after another. And do you know what will become of him? Do you have any idea? *Is that what you want for him?* It's your decision, Mila, and your decision alone. Now.'

'Can you put the music back on, please? I'd like to hear the end.'

Christine reaches for the remote. The music starts up where it had stopped: *Final act.* The voices mingling, coming one after another, responding.

375

'Mila?'

'So tired . . .'

'You can free yourself from all this, Mila.'

Maria Callas is singing:

> *You? You? You?*
> *Little idol of my heart.*
> *My love, my love,*
> *Flower of the lily and the rose.*
> *Never know that, for you,*
> *For your innocent eyes . . .*

There is a long moment of silence while the two women listen to the music. Then, suddenly, Mila reaches for the razor. Christine watches her. Without saying a word.

> *Look well, well*
> *On your mother's face,*
> *That you may keep a faint memory of it,*
> *Look well!*
> *Little love, farewell!*
> *Farewell, my little love!*

'Rest now, Mila.'

'He loved me.'

'I know, he told me,' Christine lies.

Mila smiles. Her gaze lost in the distance, she slits the skin on her forearm, the muscle, the radial artery, from elbow to wrist, in one precise, slow gesture. Left arm. The razor in the other hand. Right arm. More clumsily. The blood pours out: two geysers . . . It splatters the porcelain and the bathwater, instantly red.

With each throb of her beating heart, a new spurt of blood. Then suddenly the beating slows. She can feel the chill rising all at once, through her torso. It is as if she were freezing, at great speed, like a pond in winter. The music soars, peaks. Mila sheds a final tear, on hearing Pinkerton's last cry:

> *Butterfly! Butterfly! Butterfly!*

Christine spent the next five minutes covering up her traces and preparing to leave. She found Mila's mobile in one of her pockets and placed it in her fingers, already cold, before dialling 17. When at last there was an answer, she murmured softly, '*Please . . . come quickly . . . I'm dying . . . and my son is alone . . .*'

'What? What? Say that again, madame? Madame?'

She said it again and left the phone in Mila's dead fingers on the edge of the bath. Suddenly she spun round to the door and started: Thomas was there, his eyes wide open. *He was staring at her.* She blinked and the vision disappeared. *It was just a shadow in the corridor.* She left the bathroom, went upstairs, her plastic overshoes around her wet trainers. She peered through the door: he was asleep, with his thumb in his mouth. She felt a sudden wave of nausea, hurried back down to the ground floor of the big silent house, and ran to the front door. She breathed in huge lungfuls of the damp fresh air. Then rushed to her car, leaving the front door wide open, and only removed her slippers and gloves once she was behind the wheel.

She started up slowly, drove through the tunnel of trees and turned at the crossroads. It had stopped raining. The moon was visible through a tear in the clouds. She pulled over in the windy night. Switched off the engine, the headlamps, and jumped out. Just in time to let the bile rise up and leave all her dinner in the ditch by the front wheel.

She took a long jagged breath, trying to slow the pounding of her heart. She sat behind the wheel and didn't move, waiting. The storm was receding. The lightning was nothing more than a pale phosphorescence in the night, and the thunder a distant rumbling. Thirteen minutes went by before she heard the familiar sound of the siren and saw a van from the gendarmerie speed past her. The headlights whizzed along the tunnel of trees, blinking between each trunk. She picked up her binoculars and saw the van just as it was parking outside the house. She saw them get out of the vehicle and disappear inside. There were three of them. She put the binoculars away and looked at herself in the vanity mirror. In the glow from the ceiling light her gaze was empty: her dark pupils had engulfed her irises. She did not recognise herself.

She closed the door quietly and drove off into the night.

# EPILOGUE

The miracle of life, once again. She was at the end of the fifth month and her belly had a nice round shape. She knew that the baby's brain and spinal cord were completely formed now, and that as long as he lived he would not acquire even one additional neuron. 'I'm sorry, Léo Junior; you'll just have to get used to the idea, my love. I hope you'll at least know how to put them to good use. I'm counting on you.' She had got into the habit of calling him Léo when she talked to him, even though they had not yet managed to agree on a name. His father was keen on Mathis, or Louis. He didn't know it yet, but she had decided once and for all that it would be Léo.

She turned her head to the open French windows.

Day had dawned less than an hour ago but it was already hot. She was hungry. Voraciously hungry, to be honest: she had a constant desire to eat. A full breakfast: cereal, coffee, fruit juice, boiled eggs, soldiers, jam, butter. Her mouth was watering. She smiled. She felt terrific: all the nausea and fatigue of the early months had vanished. She was on fine form.

He moved and opened his eyes.

'You're already awake?'

He looked at her. Then, almost immediately, as he did every morning, he looked down at her belly.

'Hi, Mathis,' he said, putting his hand on their child.

'Léo.'

'Hi, Louis.'

'Léo.'

'He's not moving.'

'It's normal, he sleeps a lot.'

He looked at her. Differently.

379

'Then in that case, he won't notice if . . .' and as she didn't react: 'You're magnificent, you know, pregnancy really—'

'Hush.'

They kissed and caressed for a moment while the summer light grew brighter and the temperature rose.

'Thomas won't be awake yet, and Karla won't bring the children until nine o'clock,' he whispered. 'We have plenty of time to—'

'Hush!'

She laughed. It was only six o'clock in the morning. She leaned over to the night table for the box of condoms in the drawer. Tried to forget what they meant. Marcus hadn't lied to her that night: he had left one last souvenir before departing this world. In her own blood: she was HIV-positive. The treatment hadn't helped. They were doomed to have safe sex forever. When Léo had told her he wanted to have a child with her, she had hesitated for a long time. They had made enquiries, and she had found out that the risk of transmitting the virus from mother to child was extremely low, less than one per cent, if the mother underwent an antiretroviral treatment starting with the second trimester of pregnancy. And since Léo was not infected, they had resorted to the time-honoured method known as 'self-in-semination'. Grimacing, she recalled the little ritual they had repeated until the god of fertility deigned to reward their efforts. Fortunately, they were lucky with the third attempt.

They made love in front of the open French windows: anyone walking on the path that led by the house could have seen them, but they didn't care. Christine let him do as he liked, her fingers in his hair. He put a pillow under her and it was very gentle, very slow, like the endlessly lingering summer. She wondered whether Léo Junior could feel what was happening, this fusion of desire and dread, their hopes and fears, his parents' love. Yes, love, because they loved each other more than they ever had. All those months she'd had to keep out of sight, months when he had hidden her from everyone, including his own children, the risks they had taken together. The secret they shared and Thomas's presence had strengthened their relationship beyond anything they could have imagined. And besides, she had changed. She had to acknowledge that she had become *someone else* in the course of all her ordeals. And she was aware, even though sometimes it weighed on her, that it was this new Christine that Léo was in love with.

He propped himself on his elbow and looked at her.

'Do you want to marry me?'

'Huh?'

'You heard me.'

'You've only just got divorced and you already want to get married again?'

He laughed.

'I know what you're thinking.' He stopped smiling, and his serious expression was almost comical. 'Ordinarily, men are faithful in the beginning, and unfaithful later on. I'm doing things backwards.'

'Which means?'

'That you can pretty much count on my being faithful.'

'*Pretty much?*'

'Let's say the odds are ninety-eight per cent – does that suit you?'

'And what if it's the remaining two per cent that win?'

'I promise I won't ever lie to you, or ever hide anything from you.'

'That's a good start, but I'm not sure it's enough. I hope you're aware that it's a rather unusual marriage proposal?'

'If it's usual you wanted, you should have found an accountant. You don't have to say yes,' he added. 'Not right away.'

'That's what I think, too.'

'So it's no?'

'It's yes. But only because I'm not obliged to.'

He woke up that morning listening to music. Mahler, of course, just like every morning. *Das Klagende Lied*. The first lied was called *Waldmärchen*, 'Forest Legend', and Servaz smiled, thinking that he knew a good one, as far as legends went. It also talked about the forest. The music soared. This was his daughter's gift, his daughter who now lived on the other side of the ocean, among the caribous, grey squirrels and Chantecler chickens.

He heard a police siren, then the buzzing of a moped, and looking around him, for a moment he was completely disoriented until he recognised his room. Not the room under the eaves. *His* room. *His* flat. He sat up in *his* bed, stretched, and remembered he also had a job and an office waiting for him. He showered, got dressed, drank a black coffee and fifteen minutes later he was on his way to the police station.

He stepped off the escalator in the Métro and crossed the esplanade outside the tall brick facade. Police employees were locking their bikes to the fence, going up the steps and disappearing through the revolving door. A bit further along the canal, the prostitutes had gone home to sleep, and council employees were clearing away the condoms scattered here and there in the bushes, not to mention the syringes. The dealers were counting their profits, and their scouts were waking up in their council estates. This was his city's musical score, his everyday opera: the choir of cars and buses, the *arioso* of rush hour, the tempo of money too easily obtained, the leitmotiv of crime. He felt extraordinarily well. He knew this music by heart. It was his city, his music. He knew every note.

The file was waiting on his desk.

He read it quickly, then went down to borrow a company car. He left Toulouse to the northwest, drove for less than an hour along little back roads. The designer house was still there, in the dip of the valley, with its swimming pool, white fences and stables.

He parked on the grass next to the Porsche 911 and got out. She came out onto the terrace, a ball in her hand, wearing jeans, a hooded sweatshirt and tennis shoes. Servaz looked at her. She had cut her hair very short, an urchin cut, and was not wearing any make-up; this, along with her narrow hips and her height, gave her an androgynous, tomboyish look, despite her obvious pregnancy. She was radiant. As sure of herself, of her charms and of her power as any woman can be.

'Coffee?' asked Christine.

He smiled and came forward, and they went into the house one after the other. Léo and Thomas were playing in the pool. Servaz saw them through the picture window. The boy's clear laughter reached them along with the sound of his father splashing him.

'I have what you asked for,' he said.

She had her back to him, facing the coffee maker. He saw her square her shoulders. She hesitated for a second then turned around.

'You were right,' he added, sliding the folder across the counter.

He remembered that day in April when she had reappeared out of the blue. She was the one who called him. 'I'm back,' she said, simply. They met at the café in town. He asked where she had been all that time. She told him she had run away, that she needed to get away from everything, to be alone; that she had travelled a great deal. Of course, he was no fool. But it didn't matter any more. Suicide. The file was closed.

'I wonder . . . if we could compare the voice of the person who called that night with Mila Bolsanski's, whether it would be the same,' he said, nevertheless, staring at her thoughtfully.

She did not seem the least bit ruffled.

'Do you think it might be murder?' she asked.

He shook his head.

'The pathologist was categorical: she did indeed cut her own wrists. But that does not exclude the possibility that someone who hasn't come forward found her like that and called the police, pretending to be her. Because of the child, that is. Without that call, God knows what would have happened to him. It was a woman, obviously . . .'

He looked at her for a moment. But she had learned to hide her emotions.

He slid the folder a few inches closer.

'There was an autopsy before your sister was cremated,' he said. 'You were right: she was pregnant. No one ever tried to find out who the father was: even if it had something to do with her suicide, it was not a criminal investigation. And besides, DNA tests back then were very rare. The foetus was cremated with the mother.'

'Do we know who requested the cremation?'

'Yes.'

He took a sheet of paper from the folder.

'This was in the file.'

An authorisation for cremation. She read:

*Taking into consideration the request of the individual who is organising the funeral . . . In view of the decision of the prosecutor of the Republic to the county court of Toulouse . . . Hereby authorise to proceed with the cremation of the deceased.*

She reread the two names on the paper: her father's, and that of the doctor she had attacked when she was twelve, the family doctor.

'Thank you.'

He slid another piece of paper over to her.

'That's not all. There's something else,' he said. 'Regarding what happened at Mila Bolsanski's. Here. Read it, then destroy it. It's not a copy.'

'What is it?'

'Read it.'

She leaned closer and he saw her stiffen. Then she looked up at him, astonishment in her eyes.

383

'Why?'

'Because I don't know what this means, and in any case, the investigation is closed.'

She stared at him.

'Thank you,' she said again.

He shrugged and turned around to get ready to go; the paper she was holding was an excerpt from the police report: it stated that they had found *two* samples of DNA in the ditch that was dug behind Mila Bolsanksi's house: the first belonged to Marcus, and the second to Christine Steinmeyer.

He was about to go out, then he turned around.

'And your dog,' he said, 'what did you do with it?'

She smiled.

'Léo and I buried him where you suggested. You were right: it's a very beautiful place.'


He was driving along the bypass; traffic jams were reported ahead, even if it was still flowing where he was, when, all of a sudden, he pulled over onto the hard shoulder, unable to breathe. He did not hear the furious blaring of horns behind him. Or see the angry faces. He was staring at the road and a little wall through the windscreen, his mouth open, his heart pounding fit to burst.

*Two DNA samples . . .*

Could it be? He stared into space, and she was looking at him, smiling at him. He stared into space and he saw *her*.

It was as if, all of a sudden, he was rewinding the film. Was it possible? Good God, yes, it was!

He had never prayed in his life.

But now he prayed.

He prayed as he pressed his foot to the floor and headed off again full speed along the bypass. He prayed among the concert of insults and horns blowing that accompanied his sudden exhilaration, as he zigzagged in and out of the cars towards insane hope.


He left the car in the courtyard of the police station and ran flat out to the forensic science lab, which was off to one side. He burst in through the doors as if his life depended on it, bumping into an indignant employee, then headed towards the biology unit.

She was there, Catherine Larchet, the scientist who headed the unit. She was the one whom, a few months earlier, he had asked to analyse the DNA from Marianne's heart. She had got it for him in record time – twelve hours – because she knew how much it meant to him. She had watched as he went to pieces, knocking over a desk, screaming with pain, when she told him the terrible truth.

'Martin?' she said now, when she saw him rush towards her like a rugby player hurtling towards touchdown.

'The DNA,' he began, breathless.

She immediately understood which DNA he was referring to, and she was on her guard: she knew his story, she had heard about his depression, and his stay at the centre.

'Martin . . .'

He shook his head.

'Don't worry, I'm fine. The DNA,' he said again. 'Where did you get it from?'

'What?'

'Which DNA did you use for your analysis?'

She frowned.

'Are you questioning my competence?'

He waved his hands, then bowed very low, as if in a Japanese greeting.

'Catherine, you are the most competent person I know! I just want to know: you did a parental test, right? Ascending/descending?'

'Yes. You wanted me to compare it to her son Hugo's DNA. It was definitely Marianne's blood, Martin: there could not be the slightest doubt. Mitochondrial DNA is transmitted intact from mother to child; all human beings inherit their mitochondrial DNA exclusively from their mother.'

Servaz recalled the insulated box – Marianne's heart bathing in congealed blood, the diabolical gift from Hirtmann to his favourite cop . . .

'The blood, you said?'

'Yes, the blood. Obviously, the blood. Blood, along with sperm, contains the most DNA. Moreover, need I remind you, you were in a great hurry – you wanted the results as quickly as possible. So we took a sample of intracardiac blood with a syringe. It was the best way to do it quickly, and there was no reason to do it any other way.'

He felt as if his own heart was about to go flying.

'And you didn't look any further?'

Once again, she blushed, and gave him a questioning glance.

'Why should we? The result was positive.'

'And do you still have the heart?'

'Of course – it's evidence for an ongoing investigation. It's stored at the Forensics Institute. Martin, listen, you should—'

The Forensics Institute was part of the University Hospital Centre at Rangueil, to the south of Toulouse. He looked at her.

'Could you do a new test?' he said. 'This time with cells from the heart itself?'

She stared at him.

'Are you serious?' He could see she was thinking. 'You don't honestly believe that . . . Oh, for Christ's sake! If it's true, it would be a first. If it's true, it will be all over the forensic journals!'

She hurried to her desk and picked up the telephone, looking at him.

'I'll call them right away.'


In the dim light of the dress circle, Denise was smiling. Down below her, the soprano Natalie Dessay was singing her farewell to the opera stage. The same stage where she had begun twenty-five years earlier: the Théâtre du Capitole in Toulouse.

Denise put her hand on her belly. The fifth month. The month for travelling. Tomorrow they would fly off to Thailand. A honeymoon, in a way, even though they were not married. Denise looked at Gérald, sitting next to her. She had got him, in the end. All to herself. She observed him, serious and absorbed, his glasses reflecting the lights from the stage. He would be a good father and a good husband – oh yes, of that there could be no doubt. But it wasn't exactly what she had dreamed of. For a start, in bed he was a bit . . . *dull.* Not like 'little' Yannis, the new intern. Dark as an Eastern prince, with long eyelashes, a body to die for, white teeth and a pirate's smile. But she was carrying Gérald's child. And she loved him. Yes, of course she loved him: she hadn't done all this for nothing. Except that she could see the way young Yannis looked at her . . . and how he managed to be alone with her as often as possible, and showered her with compliments so bold they made her blush. And she was not someone who blushed easily. She tried to concentrate on the opera, but she just couldn't. She could not stop thinking about Yannis – his body, his jeans, his tanned, tattooed arms. Yes, she was going to be a mother,

386

she was expecting Gérald's child: she had got what she wanted, hadn't she?

As for all the rest, wait and see. *When the time came . . .* They were off to Thailand the next day, for an entire month: she was already eager to get back.

Cordélia handed her ticket and passport to the flight attendant, who ushered her through priority boarding, and smiled when she saw Anton sleeping on his mother's back in his padded sling. She walked up the closed air bridge, dragging her little red wheeled suitcase behind her, ignored the steward when he greeted them with a broad smile, then headed towards her seat in the middle of the cabin. She felt nervous.

As she did every time she took a plane. Which had only happened three times in the nineteen years of her life. In less than fifteen minutes she would have left Moscow behind her. The people who had greeted them when they disembarked – and who had made Marcus disappear – had let her choose her next destination. They had paid for the tickets for her and her child. They even paid for her brand-new luggage. They got her all the documents she needed. There was only one condition: she had to go far, far away. She knew that Anton's father was dead. And even if he had prepared her for that possibility, and had told her over and over that men like him did not live long, the prospect of being a single mother at the age of twenty in an unfamiliar country, without a job and only €15,000 to get started, was not an appealing one.

But she was tough, and she hadn't given up yet. During her stay in Moscow she'd got rid of her piercings and had spent one quarter of the €20,000 hidden in her suitcase to have some of the more visible tattoos removed by laser – just the black ones, the ones in colour were virtually indelible. She'd bought some clothes that were simple but classy (including the grey suit she was wearing today). She had adopted the hairstyle and make-up typical of business-class passengers and luxury-hotel guests who referred to glossy magazines when it came to taste. Of course she would have preferred to be travelling business, in the event that some well-heeled sucker might be sitting next to her: she wouldn't find her sugar daddy in economy. Before departure she had picked up some documentation at the embassy of the country she was heading to, and she was already starting to study it. Lists of companies that provided nannies, cleaning women and babysitters to a wealthy clientele. In her luggage she had a CV and references, all fake of course. Not that she had any intention of doing housework or looking after any snotty little brats other than her own for long. But it could be a gateway to a brighter future. All she needed was a sucker or two . . . She pressed her head back against the seat and closed her eyes when she felt the thrust of the jets vibrate through her. Life had not been kind to her, so why should she be kind to others?

Guy Steinmeyer was smiling as he got out of his sporty, ecologically friendly Fisker Karma that had set him back more than one hundred thousand euros. Today he had gone for a walk through the streets of Toulouse and three people recognised him and asked him for an autograph. They had called him 'Monsieur Dorian'. Of course. If they had called him Steinmeyer he didn't know whether he would have recognised his own name. He had been Guy Dorian for so long. Wouldn't he always be known, under that name, as one of the pioneers of French television and radio?

He unlocked the American-style mailbox on a post ten metres from their lovely home. He took out the letters. And his eye was immediately drawn to a brown envelope with his name on it, with neither stamp nor address. He unfolded the sheet inside. Letters cut out of the newspaper, and glued together to form the words.

*You are going to commit suicide. You don't know it yet, but you're going to do it.*

The letter was unsigned.

She came in person to give him the results. He wasn't in his office. Catherine Larchet, head of the biological unit at the forensics lab, looked everywhere for him and eventually found him in Espérandieu's office, leaning over his assistant's shoulder and staring at a screen. She gave a quick knock. He turned around, and before she had even said a word, he understood.

It wasn't hers. It wasn't her.

Servaz opened his mouth: he'd been right.

'You were right,' she confirmed. 'It was her blood, but it was another woman's heart. There was even a tiny hole, where he had injected Marianne's blood.'

Servaz stood there for a long time, not moving, dumbfounded. He didn't know what to do, what to say, how to react. Something was expanding in his chest, and it wasn't joy, or even relief, but it might be hope. An infinitesimal but real hope.

*Hirtmann, that bloody fucking bastard.*

He rushed past her, straight to the lift, out through the lobby and into the warm, buttery summer light. He needed to be alone. He began walking along the canal under the dusty trees. Instinctively, his hand reached for the pack of cigarettes in his pocket, and took it out. He placed one cigarette between his lips and this time he lit it.

The poison went slowly, deliciously, down into his lungs. Hope – as he was well aware – was just as lethal a poison.

He thought about the man who had sent him that gift, the former prosecutor from Geneva, the erstwhile inmate at the asylum Institut Wargnier. He won't show his face but he's out there, somewhere, maybe thousands of miles away, maybe not far at all, but one thing is certain, Martin: *he never stops thinking about you.* He is wearing a perfect disguise, he does not know what pity is, but he does know love, in his way. And he *loves you.* Otherwise, he would have put her real heart there instead. This gift, this offering, is an invitation.

He walked on, oblivious of everything around him; sun and shadow slipped over his face, his mouth was dry, his mind was ablaze.

He's like an unwanted older brother, a sort of Cain. He does horrible things, and he's got Marianne . . . Because she's alive. You know she is alive. One day, one morning, you will get up and in your mailbox there will be another sign: he won't leave you alone. She is waiting for you, because you are all she has. Seven billion human beings, and only one who can save her.

A bicycle bell roused him from his reverie. He gave a start, spun around and looked, full of emotion, at the dazzling light coming through the leaves, and he almost knocked over the cyclist, who swerved just in time. He could feel waves of warmth, and hear the rumbling of the boulevard. His face contorted in a silent laugh. His eyes were shining. The miracle of life, once again.

Marianne . . .

# Acknowledgements
# and Principal Sources

All my thanks to Messrs. Christophe Guillaumot, Yves Le Hir, José Mariet and Pascal Pasamonti, from the Toulouse Regional Criminal Investigation Department; and to André Adobes, sparring partner; they have all given generously of their time. None of them should be held responsible for my mistakes or my opinions.

While doing research to give a certain authenticity to this fiction, I found the following books to be an enormous help: *Femmes sous emprise et Le Harcèlement moral, la violence perverse au quotidien* by Marie-France Hirigoyen; *Les manipulateurs sont parmi nous* by Isabelle Nazare-Aga; *La Perversité à l'oeuvre; Le harcèlement moral dans l'entreprise et le couple* by Jean-Paul Guedj; *Une Française dans l'espace* by Claudie André-Deshays and Yolaine de La Bigne; *Carnet de bord d'un cosmonaute* by Jean-Pierre Haigneré and Simon Allix; *L'Exploration spatiale* by Arlène Ammar-Israël and Jean-Louis Fellous; *Almost Heaven, the Story of Women in Space* by Bettyan Holtzmann Kevles; *À leur corps defendant: Les femmes à l'épreuve du nouvel ordre moral* by Christine Détrez and Anne Simon; *Toulouse hier, aujourd'hui, demain* by Fernand Cousteaux and Michel Valdiguié; *L'Opéra ou la Défaite des femmes* by Catherine Clément; *Tout l'opéra, de Monteverdi à nos jours* by Gustave Kobbé; *Cinq grands opéras* by Henry Barraud; *Dictionnaire amoureux de l'opéra* by Alain Duault; *Russian Criminal Tattoo Encyclopaedia*.

Caroline Sers helped me improve the text, as did Gwenaëlle Le Goff.

My warmest thanks for their remarkable work to the team at Éditions XO and Pocket, starting with Bernard, Caroline and Édith, my first readers.

Any errors are my own. My characters are pure invention.

Regarding Servaz's musical taste, once again I am grateful to Jean-Pierre Schamber for having guided me along the thorny path he takes more frequently than I do; and here I must add the contribution of the eminent Georges Haessig regarding those marvellous fragments of piano-roll recordings that Mahler himself performed.